THE LAST COLONY

John Scalzi's debut novel, *Old Man's War*, was a finalist for the Hugo Award for Best Novel. In 2006 he won the John W. Campbell Award for Best New Writer. His weblog, *The Whatever*, is one of the longest-running and most widely read journals on the Internet. He lives in Ohio with his wife and daughter.

Also by John Scalzi

THE
LAST
COLONY

John Scalzi

TOR

First published 2007 by Tor
an imprint of Tom Doherty Associates, LLC, New York

First published in Great Britain in paperback 2008 by Tor
an imprint of Pan Macmillan Ltd
Pan Macmillan, 20 New Wharf Road, London N1 9RR
Basingstoke and Oxford
Associated companies throughout the world
www.panmacmillan.com

ISBN 978-0-330-45712-5

Copyright © John Scalzi 2007

The right of John Scalzi to be identified as the
author of this work has been asserted by him in accordance
with the Copyright, Designs and Patents Act 1988.

All rights reserved. No part of this publication may be
reproduced, stored in or introduced into a retrieval system, or
transmitted, in any form, or by any means (electronic, mechanical,
photocopying, recording or otherwise) without the prior written
permission of the publisher. Any person who does any unauthorized
act in relation to this publication may be liable to criminal
prosecution and civil claims for damages.

3 5 7 9 8 6 4 2

A CIP catalogue record for this book is available from
the British Library.

Printed and bound in the UK by
CPI Mackays, Chatham ME5 8TD

This book is sold subject to the condition that it shall not,
by way of trade or otherwise, be lent, re-sold, hired out,
or otherwise circulated without the publisher's prior consent
in any form of binding or cover other than that in which
it is published and without a similar condition including this
condition being imposed on the subsequent purchaser.

Visit **www.panmacmillan.com** to read more about all our books
and to buy them. You will also find features, author interviews and
news of any author events, and you can sign up for e-newsletters
so that you're always first to hear about our new releases.

To Patrick and Teresa Nielsen Hayden,
friends and editors.
To Heather and Bob, brother and sister.
To Athena, daughter.
To Kristine, everything.

THE LAST COLONY

ONE Let me tell you of the worlds I've left behind.

Earth you know; everyone knows it. It's the birthplace of humanity, although at this point not many consider it our "home" planet—Phoenix has had that job since the Colonial Union was created and became the guiding force for expanding and protecting our race in the universe. But you never forget where you come from.

Being from Earth in this universe is like being a small-town kid who gets on the bus, goes to the big city and spends his entire afternoon gawking at all the tall buildings. Then he gets mugged for the crime of marveling at this strange new world, which has such things in it, because the things in it don't have much time or sympathy for the new kid in town, and they're happy to kill him for what he's got in his suitcase. The small-town kid learns this fast, because he can't go home again.

I spent seventy-five years on Earth, living mostly in the same small Ohio town and sharing most of that life with the same woman. She died and stayed behind. I lived and I left.

The next world is metaphorical. The Colonial Defense Forces took me off Earth and kept the parts of me they wanted: my consciousness, and some small part of my DNA. From the latter they built me a new body, which was young and quick and strong and beautiful and only partially human. They stuffed my consciousness inside of it, and gave me not nearly enough time to glory in my second youth. Then they took this beautiful body that was now me and spent the next several years actively trying to get it killed by throwing me at every hostile alien race they could.

There were a lot of those. The universe is vast, but the number of worlds suitable for human life is surprisingly small, and as it happens space is filled with numerous other intelligent species who want the same worlds we do. Very few of these species, it seems, are into the concept of sharing; we're certainly not. We all fight, and the worlds we can inhabit swap back and forth between us until one or another gets a grip on it so tight we can't be pried off. Over a couple of centuries, we humans have managed this trick on several dozen worlds, and failed this trick on dozens more. None of this has made us very many friends.

I spent six years in this world. I fought and I nearly died, more than once. I had friends, most of whom died but some of whom I saved. I met a woman who was achingly like the one I shared my life with on Earth, but who was nevertheless entirely her own person. I defended the Colonial Union, and in doing so I believed I was keeping humanity alive in the universe.

At the end of it the Colonial Defense Forces took the part of me that had always been me and stuffed it into a third and final body. This body was young, but not nearly as quick and strong. It was, after all, only human. But this body would not be asked to fight and die. I missed being as strong as a cartoon superhero. I didn't miss every alien creature I met trying very hard to kill me. It was a fair trade.

The next world is likely unknown to you. Stand again on Earth, our old home, where billions still live and dream of the stars. Look up in the sky, at the constellation Lynx, hard by Ursa Major. There's a star there, yellow like our sun, with six major planets. The third one, appropriately enough, is a counterfeit of Earth: 96 percent of its circumference, but with a slightly larger iron core, so it has 101 percent of its mass (you don't notice that 1 percent much). Two moons: one two-thirds the size of Earth's moon, but closer than Luna, so in the sky it takes up the same amount of real estate. The second moon, a captured asteroid, is much smaller and closer in. It's in an unstable orbit; eventually it will tumble and fall into the planet below. Best estimate is this will happen in about a quarter of a million years. The natives are not terribly concerned at the moment.

This world was found by humans nearly seventy-five years ago; the Ealan had a colony there but the Colonial Defense Forces corrected that. Then the Ealan, shall we say, checked the math on that equation and it was another couple of years before it was all sorted out. When it was, the Colonial Union opened the world to colonists from Earth, mostly from India. They arrived in waves; the first one after the planet was secured from the Ealan, and the second shortly after the Subcontinental War on Earth, when the Occupation-backed probationary government offered the most notable supporters of the Chowdhury regime the choice of colonization or imprisonment. Most went into exile, taking their families with them. These people didn't so much dream of the stars as had them forced upon them.

Given the people who live on the planet, you would

think it would have a name that reflects their heritage. You would be wrong. The planet is called Huckleberry, named no doubt by some Twain-loving apparatchik of the Colonial Union. Huckleberry's large moon is Sawyer; the small one is Becky. Its three major continents are Samuel, Langhorne and Clemens; from Clemens there is a long, curling string of volcanic islands known as the Livy Archipelago, set in the Calaveras Ocean. Most of the prominent features were dubbed in various aspects Twainania before the first settlers arrived; they seem to have accepted this with good grace.

Stand on this planet with me now. Look up in the sky, in the direction of the constellation Lotus. In it there is a star, yellow like the one this planet circles, around which I was born, two other lives ago. From here it is so far away as to be invisible to the eye, which is often how I feel about the life I lived there.

My name is John Perry. I am eighty-eight years old. I have lived on this planet for nearly eight years now. It is my home, which I share with my wife and my adopted daughter. Welcome to Huckleberry. In this story, it's the next world I leave behind. But not the final one.

The story of how I left Huckleberry begins—as do all worthy stories—with a goat.

Savitri Guntupalli, my assistant, didn't even look up from her book as I came back from lunch. "There's a goat in your office," she said.

"Hmmmm," I said. "I thought we'd sprayed for those."

This got an upward glance, which counted as a victory as these things go. "It brought the Chengelpet brothers with it," she said.

"Crap," I said. The last pair of brothers who fought as much as the Chengelpet brothers were named Cain and

Abel, and at least one of them finally took some direct action. "I thought I told you not to let those two in my office when I wasn't around."

"You said no such thing," Savitri said.

"Let's make it a standing order," I said.

"And even if you had," Savitri continued, setting down her book, "this assumes that either Chengelpet would listen to me, which neither would. Aftab stomped through first with the goat and Nissim followed right after. Neither of them so much as looked in my direction."

"I don't want to have to deal with the Chengelpets," I said. "I just ate."

Savitri reached over to the side of the desk, grabbed her wastebasket and placed it on top of her desk. "By all means, vomit first," she said.

I had met Savitri several years before while I was touring the colonies as a representative of the Colonial Defense Forces, talking it up to the various colonies I was sent to. At the stop in the village of New Goa in the Huckleberry colony, Savitri stood up and called me a tool of the imperial and totalitarian regime of the Colonial Union. I liked her immediately. When I mustered out of the CDF, I decided to settle in New Goa. I was offered the position of village ombudsman, which I took, and was surprised on the first day of work to find Savitri there, telling me that she was going to be my assistant whether I liked it or not.

"Remind me again why you took this job," I said to Savitri, over the wastebasket.

"Sheer perversity," Savitri said. "Are you going to vomit or not?"

"I think I'll keep it in," I said. She grabbed the wastebasket and set it in its former position, and then picked up her book to resume reading.

I had an idea. "Hey, Savitri," I said. "Want my job?"

"Sure," she said, opening her book. "I'll start right after you finish with the Chengelpets."

"Thanks," I said.

Savitri grunted. She had returned to her literary adventures. I steeled myself and walked through the door of my office.

The goat in the middle of the floor was cute. The Chengelpets, sitting in the chairs in front of my desk, were less so.

"Aftab," I said, nodding to the older brother. "Nissim," I said, nodding to the younger. "And friend," I said, nodding to the goat. I took a seat. "What can I do for you this afternoon?"

"You can give me permission to shoot my brother, Ombudsman Perry," Nissim said.

"I'm not sure that's in my job description," I said. "And anyway, it seems a little drastic. Why don't you tell me what's going on."

Nissim pointed to his brother. "This bastard has stolen my seed," he said.

"Pardon?" I said.

"My seed," Nissim said. "Ask him. He cannot deny it."

I blinked and turned toward Aftab. "Stealing your brother's seed, then, is it, Aftab?"

"You must forgive my brother," Aftab said. "He is prone to hysteria, as you know. What he means to say is that one of his goats wandered from his pasture into mine and impregnated this nanny here, and now he claims that I have stolen his goat's sperm."

"It wasn't just any goat," Nissim said. "It was Prabhat, my prizewinner. I stud him out for a very good price, and Aftab didn't want to pay the price. So he stole my seed."

"It's Prabhat's seed, you idiot," Aftab said. "And it's not my fault you take such poor care of your fence that your goat was able to get onto my land."

"Oh, that's rich," Nissim said. "Ombudsman Perry, I'll have you know that fence wire was cut. Prabhat was tempted onto his land."

"You're delusional," Aftab said. "And even if it were true, which it is not, so what? You have your precious Prabhat back."

"But now you have this pregnant goat," Nissim said. "A pregnancy that you did not pay for, and which I did not give permission for. It's theft, pure and simple. And more than that, you're trying to ruin me."

"What are you talking about?" Aftab said.

"You're trying to breed a new stud," Nissim said, and pointed at the goat, which was nibbling the back of Aftab's chair. "Don't deny it. This is your best nanny. By breeding it with Prabhat you'll have a buck you can stud out. You're trying to undercut my business. Ask him, Ombudsman Perry. Ask him what his goat is carrying."

I looked back to Aftab. "What is your goat carrying, Aftab?"

"By sheer coincidence, one of the fetuses is male," Aftab said.

"I want it aborted," Nissim said.

"It's not your goat," Aftab said.

"Then I'll take the kid when it's born," Nissim said. "As payment for the seed you stole."

"This again," Aftab said, and looked over to me. "You see what I am dealing with, Ombudsman Perry. He lets his goats run rampant across the countryside, impregnating at will, and then he demands payment for his own shoddy animal husbandry."

Nissim bellowed in outrage and began yelling and gesticulating wildly at his brother; Aftab followed suit. The goat came around the desk and eyed me curiously. I reached into my desk and fed the goat a candy I found there. "You and I don't actually need to be here for this," I said to the goat. The goat didn't respond, but I could tell she agreed with me.

As originally planned, the village ombudsman's job was supposed to be simple: Whenever the New Goa villagers had a problem with the local or district government, they would come to me, and I could help them run through the red tape and get things done. It was, in fact, just the sort of job you give a war hero who is otherwise useless to the daily life of a largely rural colony; he's got just enough notoriety with the higher-ups that when he shows up on the doorstep, they have to pay attention to him.

The thing was that after a couple of months of this, the New Goa villagers started coming to me with their other problems. "Oh, we don't want to bother with the officials," I was told by one of the villagers, after I questioned why I was suddenly the go-to guy for everything from farm equipment advice to frontline marriage counseling. "It's easier and quicker to come to you." Rohit Kulkarni, New Goa's administrator, was delighted with this state of affairs, since I was now handling the problems that used to come to him first. It gave him more time to fish and play dominoes at the tea shop.

Most of the time this new and expanded definition of my ombudsman's duties was perfectly fine. It was nice to help people, and it was also nice that people listened to my advice. On the other hand any public servant is likely to tell you that just a few annoying people in their community will take up the vast majority of their time. In New Goa, those roles were occupied by the Chengelpet brothers.

No one knew why they hated each other so much. I thought it might be something with their parents, but Bhajan and Niral were lovely people who were just as mystified about it as anyone. Some people just don't get along with some other people, and unfortunately, these two people who did not get along happened to be brothers.

It wouldn't have been so bad if in fact they hadn't built farms right next to each other and thus were in each other's faces and business most of the time. At one point early in my tenure I suggested to Aftab, whom I regarded as the slightly more rational Chengelpet, that he might consider checking out a new plot of land that had just been cleared out on the other side of the village, because living away from Nissim might solve the majority of his problems with him. "Oh, he'd like that," Aftab said, in a perfectly reasonable tone of voice. After that I abandoned any hope of rational discourse on the matter and accepted that my karma required me to suffer through the occasional visit from the Outraged Chengelpet Brothers.

"All right," I said, quieting the brothers down from their fratriphobic rantings. "Here's what I think. I don't think it really matters how our lady friend the goat got knocked up, so let's not focus on that. But you both agree that it was Nissim's buck that did the deed."

Both the Chengelpets nodded; the goat stayed modestly quiet. "Fine. Then the two of you are in business together," I said. "Aftab, you can keep the kid after it's born and stud it out if you like. But the first six times you do, Nissim gets the full stud fee, and after that half of your stud fee goes to your brother."

"He'll just stud it out for free the first six times," Nissim said.

"Then let's make the stud fee after those first six times the average of those first six," I said. "So if he tries to screw you he'll end up screwing himself, too. And this is a small village, Nissim. People here won't stud with Aftab if they think the only reason he's hiring out his goat is to mess with your livelihood. There's a fine line between value and being a bad neighbor."

"And what if I don't want to be in business with him?" Aftab said.

"Then you can sell the kid to Nissim," I said. Nissim opened his mouth to protest. "Yes, sell," I said, before he could complain. "Take the kid to Murali and get an appraisal. That'll be the price. Murali doesn't like either of you very much so you'll get a fair estimate. Okay?"

The Chengelpets thought it over, which is to say they racked their brains to see if there was any way either one of them was more unhappy with this state of affairs than the other. Eventually they both seemed to come to the conclusion that they were equally displeased, which in this situation was the optimal result. They both nodded their assent.

"Good," I said. "Now get out of here before there's a mess on my rug."

"My goat wouldn't do that," Aftab said.

"It's not the goat I'm worried about," I said, shooing them out. They left; Savitri appeared in the door.

"You're in my seat," she said, nodding to my chair.

"Screw you," I said, propping up my feet on the desk. "If you're not going to handle the annoying cases, you're not ready for the big chair."

"In that case I will return to my humble role as your assistant and let you know that while you were entertaining the Chengelpets, the constable called," Savitri said.

"What about?" I asked.

"Didn't say," Savitri said. "Hung up. You know the constable. Very abrupt."

"Tough but fair, that's the motto," I said. "If it was really important there'd be a message, so I'll worry about that later. In the meantime I'll catch up with my paperwork."

"You don't have paperwork," Savitri said. "You give it all to me."

"Is it done?" I asked.

"As far as you know, yes," Savitri said.

"Then I think I'll relax and bask in my superior management skills," I said.

"I'm glad you didn't use the wastebasket to vomit earlier," Savitri said. "Because now there's a place for mine to go." She retreated back to her desk before I could think up a good retort.

We'd been like this since after the first month we'd worked together. It took her that first month to get used to the fact that even though I was former military I wasn't actually a colonialist tool, or at the very least if I was, I was one with common sense and a reasonable sense of humor. Having established I wasn't there to spread my hegemony over her village, she relaxed enough to start mocking me. It's been our relationship for seven years, and it's a good one.

With all the paperwork done and all the problems of the village solved, I did what anyone in my position would do: I took a nap. Welcome to the rough and tumble world of colonial village ombudsmanning. It's possible it's done differently elsewhere, but if it is, I don't want to know.

I woke up in time to see Savitiri closing up the office for the day. I waved good-bye to her and after a few more minutes of immobility hauled my own ass out of the chair and through the door, on the way home. Along the way I happened to see the constable coming toward me on the other side of the road. I crossed the road, walked up to the constable and kissed my local law enforcement official full on the lips.

"You know I don't like it when you do that," Jane said, after I was done.

"You don't like it when I kiss you?" I asked.

"Not when I'm on the job," Jane said. "It erodes my authority."

I smiled at the thought of some malfeasant thinking Jane, a former Special Forces soldier, was soft because she kissed her husband. The ass-kicking that would ensue would be terrible in its magnitude. However, I didn't say that. "Sorry," I said. "I'll try not to erode your authority anymore."

"Thank you," Jane said. "I was coming to see you, anyway, since you didn't return my call."

"I was incredibly busy today," I said.

"Savitri briefed me on just how busy you were when I called back," Jane said.

"Oops," I said.

"Oops," Jane agreed. We started walking in the direction of our home. "What I was going to tell you is that you could expect Gopal Boparai to come by tomorrow to find out what his community service would be. He was drunk and disorderly again. He was yelling at a cow."

"Bad karma," I said.

"The cow thought so, too," Jane said. "It butted him in the chest and sent him through a shop window."

"Is Go okay?" I asked.

"Scratches," Jane said. "The pane popped out. Plastic. Didn't break."

"This is the third time this year," I said. "He should be up in front of the actual magistrate, not me."

"That's what I told him, too," Jane said. "But he'd be up for a mandatory forty days in the district gaol and Shashi is due in a couple of weeks. She needs him around more than he needs gaol."

"All right," I said. "I'll figure out something for him."

"How was your day?" Jane asked. "Besides the nap, I mean."

"I had a Chengelpet day," I said. "This time with a goat."

Jane and I chatted about our day on our walk home,

like we do every day on our walk home, to the small farm we keep just outside the village proper. As we turned onto our road we ran into our daughter Zoë, walking Babar the mutt, who was typically deliriously happy to see us.

"He knew you were coming," Zoë said, slightly out of breath. "Took off halfway down the road. Had to run to keep up."

"Nice to know we were missed," I said. Jane petted Babar, who wagged up a storm. I gave Zoë a peck on the cheek.

"You two have a visitor," Zoë said. "He showed up at the house about an hour ago. In a floater."

No one in town had a floater; they were ostentatious and impractical for a farming community. I glanced over to Jane, who shrugged, as if to say, *I'm not expecting anyone*. "Who did he say he was?" I asked.

"He didn't," Zoë said. "All he said was that he was an old friend of yours, John. I told him I could call you and he said he was happy to wait."

"Well, what does he look like, at least?" I asked.

"Young," Zoë said. "Kinda cute."

"I don't think I know any cute guys," I said. "That's more your department, teenage daughter."

Zoë crossed her eyes and gave a mock sneer. "Thanks, ninety-year-old dad. If you had let me finish speaking, you would have heard the clue that tells me you might actually know him. Which is that he's also *green*."

This got another shared glance between me and Jane. CDF members had green skin, a result of modified chlorophyll that gave them extra energy for combat. Both Jane and I had had green skin once; I was back to my original hue and Jane was allowed to choose a more standard skin tone when she changed bodies.

"He didn't say what he wanted?" Jane asked Zoë.

"Nope," Zoë said. "And I didn't ask. I just figured I'd come find you and give you advance warning. I left him on the front porch."

"Probably sneaking around the house by now," I said.

"Doubtful," Zoë said. "I left Hickory and Dickory to watch him."

I grinned. "That should keep him in one place," I said.

"My thought exactly," Zoë said.

"You are wise beyond your years, teenage daughter," I said.

"Makes up for you, ninety-year-old dad," she said. She jogged back to the house, Babar padding behind.

"Such attitude," I said to Jane. "She gets it from your side."

"She's adopted," Jane said. "And I'm not the smart-ass in the family."

"These are details," I said, and took her hand. "Come on. I want to see just how scared shitless our guest is."

We found our guest on the porch swing, watched intently and silently by our two Obin. I recognized him immediately.

"General Rybicki," I said. "This is a surprise."

"Hello, Major," Rybicki said, referring to my former rank. He pointed to the Obin. "You've made some interesting friends since the last time I saw you."

"Hickory and Dickory," I said. "They're my daughter's companions. Perfectly nice, unless they think you're a threat to her."

"And then what happens?" Rybicki asked.

"It varies," I said. "But it's usually quick."

"Wonderful," Rybicki said. I excused the Obin; they went off to find Zoë.

"Thank you," Rybicki said. "Obin make me nervous."

"That's the point," Jane said.

"I realize that," Rybicki said. "If you don't mind me asking, why does your daughter have Obin bodyguards?"

"They're not bodyguards, they're companions," Jane said. "Zoë is our adopted daughter. Her biological father is Charles Boutin." This got a raised eyebrow from Rybicki; he was of sufficiently advanced rank to know about Boutin. "The Obin revere Boutin, but he's dead. They have a desire to know his daughter, so they sent these two to be with her."

"And this doesn't bother her," Rybicki said.

"She grew up with Obin as nannies and protectors," Jane said. "She's comfortable with them."

"And it doesn't bother *you*," Rybicki said.

"They watch and protect Zoë," I said. "They help out around here. And their presence with us is a part of the treaty the Colonial Union has with the Obin. Having them here seems like a small price to pay for having them on our side."

"That's true enough," Rybicki said, and stood up. "Listen, Major. I have a proposition for you." He nodded to Jane. "For both of you, actually."

"What is it?" I asked.

Rybicki motioned with his head toward the house, in the direction Hickory and Dickory just went. "I'd rather not talk about it where those two might hear, if it's all the same. Is there some place we can talk privately?"

I glanced over at Jane. She smiled thinly. "I know a place," she said.

"We're stopping here?" General Rybicki asked as we pulled up short, halfway across the field.

"You asked if we had someplace where we could talk privately," I said. "You've now got at least five acres of grain between us and the next set of ears, human or Obin. Welcome to privacy, colonial style."

"What kind of grain is this?" General Rybicki asked, pulling at a stalk.

"It's sorghum," Jane said, standing next to me. Babar sat next to Jane and scratched his ear.

"It sounds familiar," Rybicki said, "but I don't think I've ever actually seen it before."

"It's a staple crop here," I said. "It's a good crop because it's heat and drought tolerant, and it can get pretty hot around here in our summer months. People here use it for a bread called *bhakri* and for other things."

"Bhakri," Rybicki said, and motioned toward town. "These folks are mostly from India, then."

"Some of them," I said. "Most of them were born here. This particular village is sixty years old. Most of the active colonization here on Huckleberry is on the Clemens continent now. They opened it up around the same time we arrived."

"So there's no tension about the Subcontinental War," Rybicki said. "With you being American and them being Indian."

"It doesn't come up," I said. "People here are like immigrants everywhere. They think of themselves as Huckleberries first and Indians second. In another generation none of it will matter. And Jane's not American, anyway. If we're seen as anything, we're seen as former soldiers. We were a curiosity when we arrived, but now we're just John and Jane, with the farm down the road."

Rybicki looked at the field again. "I'm surprised you farm at all," he said. "The two of you have real jobs."

"Farming is a real job," Jane said. "Most of our neighbors do it. It's good for us to do it too so we can understand them and what they need from us."

"I meant no offense," Rybicki said.

"None taken," I said, interjecting myself back into the conversation. I motioned to the field. "We've got about forty acres here. It's not a lot—and not enough to take money away from the other farmers—but it's enough to make the point that the concerns of New Goa are our concerns, too. We've worked hard to become New Goans and Huckleberries ourselves."

General Rybicki nodded and looked at his sorghum stalk. As Zoë had noted, he was green, good-looking and young. Or at least gave the appearance of youth, thanks to the CDF body he still had. He'd look twenty-three years old for as long as he had it, even though his real age was some number over one hundred by now. He looked younger than me, and I was his junior by fifteen years or more. But then, when I left the service, I traded my CDF body for a new, unmodified body based on my original DNA. I looked at least thirty by now. I could live with that.

At the time I had left the CDF, Rybicki had been my superior officer, but he and I went back before that. I met him on my first day of combat, back when he was a lieutenant colonel and I had been a private. He'd offhandedly called me *son*, as a reference to my youth. I was seventy-five at the time.

This was one of the problems with the Colonial Defense Forces: all that body engineering they do really messes with your age sense. I was in my nineties; Jane, born an adult as part of the CDF Special Forces, was sixteen or so. It can hurt your head if you think about it.

"It's time you tell us why you're here, General," Jane said. Seven years of living with naturally occuring humans had not blunted her Special Forces-bred way of ramming through social courtesies and getting right to the point.

Rybicki grinned wryly, and tossed his sorghum to the ground. "All right," he said. "After you left the service,

Perry, I got a promotion and a transfer. I'm with the Department of Colonization now; the folks who have the
job of seeding and supporting new colonies."

"You're still CDF," I said. "It's the green skin that
gives you away. I thought the Colonial Union kept its
civilian and military wings separate."

"I'm the liaison," Rybicki said. "I get to keep things
coordinated between the both of them. This is about as
fun as you might think it is."

"You have my sympathy," I said.

"Thank you, Major," Rybicki said. It'd been years
since anyone referred to me by my rank. "I do appreciate
it. The reason I'm here is because I was wondering if
you—the two of you—would do a job for me."

"What kind of job?" Jane asked.

Rybicki looked over to Jane. "Lead a new colony," he
said.

Jane glanced over to me. I could tell she didn't like
this idea already. "Isn't that what the Department of Colonization is for?" I asked. "It should be filled with all
sorts of people whose job it is to lead colonies."

"Not this time," Rybicki said. "This colony is different."

"How?" Jane said.

"The Colonial Union gets colonists from Earth," Rybicki said. "But over the last few years the colonies—the
established colonies, like Phoenix and Elysium and
Kyoto—have been pushing the CU to let their people
form new colonies. Folks from those places have made
the attempt before with wildcat colonies, but you know
how those go."

I nodded. Wildcat colonies were illegal and unauthorized. The CU turned a blind eye to wildcatters; the rationale was that the people who were in them would
otherwise be causing trouble at home, so it was just as
well to let them go. But a wildcat colony was well and

truly on its own; unless one of your colonists was the kid of someone high up in the government, the CDF wouldn't be coming when you called for help. The survival statistics for wildcat colonies were impressively grim. Most didn't last six months. Other colonizing species generally did them in. It wasn't a forgiving universe.

Rybicki caught my acknowledgment and went on. "The CU would prefer the colonies keep to their own knitting, but it's become a political issue and the CU can't brush it off anymore. So the DoC suggested that we open up one planet for second-generation colonists. You can guess what happened then."

"The colonies started clawing each other's eyes out to be the one whose people got to colonize," I said.

"Give the man a cigar," Rybicki said. "So the DoC tried to play Solomon by saying that each of the agitants could contribute a limited number of colonists to the first wave colony. So now we have a seed colony of about twenty-five hundred people, with two hundred and fifty from ten different colonies. But now we don't have anyone to lead them. None of the colonies want the other colonies' people in charge."

"There are more than ten colonies," I said. "You could recruit your colony leaders from one of those."

"Theoretically that would work," Rybicki said. "In the real universe, however, the other colonies are pissed off that they didn't get *their* people on the colony roster. We've promised that if this colony works out we'll entertain the idea of opening other worlds. But for now it's a mess and no one else is inclined to play along."

"Who was the idiot who suggested this plan in the first place?" Jane asked.

"As it happens, that idiot was me," Rybicki said.

"Well done," Jane said. I reflected on the fact it was a good thing she wasn't still in the military.

"Thank you, Constable Sagan," General Rybicki said. "I appreciate the candor. Clearly there were aspects of this plan I didn't expect. But then, that's why I'm here."

"The flaw with this plan of yours—aside from the fact that neither Jane nor I have the slightest idea how to run a seed colony—is that we're colonists now, too," I said. "We've been here for nearly eight years."

"But you said it yourself: you're former soldiers," Rybicki said. "Former soldiers are a category all their own. You're not really from Huckleberry. You're from Earth, and she's former Special Forces, which means she's not from anywhere. No offense," he said to Jane.

"That still leaves the problem of neither of us having any experience running a seed colony," I said. "When I was doing my public relations tour of the colonies way back when, I went to a seed colony on Orton. Those people never stopped working. You don't just throw people into that situation without training."

"You *have* training," Rybicki said. "Both of you were officers. Christ, Perry, you were a major. You commanded a regiment of three thousand soldiers across a battle group. That's larger than a seed colony."

"A colony isn't a military regiment," I said.

"No it's not," Rybicki agreed. "But the same skills are required. And since you've been discharged, both of you have worked in colony administration. You're an ombudsman—you know how a colony government works and how to get things done. Your wife is the constable here and is responsible for maintaining order. Between the two of you, you have pretty much all the skills you'll need. I didn't just pull your names out of a hat, Major. These are the reasons I thought of you. You're about eighty-five percent ready to go as it is, and we'll get you the rest of the way there before the colonists head for Roanoke. That's the name we've chosen for the colony," he added.

"We have a life here," Jane said. "We have jobs and responsibilities, and we have a daughter who has her own life here as well. You're casually asking us to uproot ourselves to solve your little political crisis."

"Well, I apologize about the casual part," Rybicki said. "Normally you would have gotten this request by Colonial diplomatic courier, along with a full load of documents. But as it happened, I was on Huckleberry for entirely different reasons and thought I would kill two birds with one stone. I honestly didn't expect I'd be pitching you this idea standing in the middle of a field of sorghum."

"All right," Jane said.

"And as for it being a little political crisis, you're wrong about that," Rybicki said. "It's a medium-sized political crisis, on its way to becoming a large one. This has become more than just another human colony. The local planetary governments and press have built this up as the biggest colonization event since humans first left Earth. It's not—trust me on that—but that fact doesn't really matter at this point. It's become a media circus and a political headache, and it's put the DoC on the defensive. This colony is getting away from us because so many others have a vested interest in it. We need to get on top of it again."

"So it's all about politics," I said.

"No," Rybicki said. "You misunderstand me. The DoC doesn't need to get back on top of this because we're counting political coup. We need to get back on top of this because *this is a human colony*. You both know what it's like out there. Colonies live or die—*colonists* live or die—based on how well we prepare and defend them.

The DoC's job is to get the colonists as prepared as we can get them before they colonize. The CDF's job is to keep them safe until they get a foothold. If either side of that equation breaks down, that colony is screwed.

"Right now, the department's side of the equation isn't working because we haven't provided the leadership, and everyone else is trying to keep anyone else from filling the vacuum. We're running out of time to make it work. Roanoke is going to happen. The question is whether we manage to do it right. If we don't—if Roanoke dies—there's going to be hell to pay. So it's better that we do it right."

"If this is such a political hot potato, I don't see why throwing us into the mix is going to help things," I said. "There's no guarantee anyone will be happy with us."

"Like I said, I didn't just pull your names out of a hat," Rybicki said. "Over at the department we ran a slate of potential candidates that would work for us and would work for the CDF. We figured if the two of us could sign off on someone, we could make the colony governments accept them. You two were on the list."

"Where on the list?" Jane asked.

"About halfway down," Rybicki said. "Sorry. The other candidates didn't work out."

"Well, it's an honor just to be nominated," I said.

Rybicki grinned. "I never did like your sarcasm, Perry," he said. "I understand I'm dropping a lot on you at once. I don't expect you to give me an answer now. I have all the documents here," he tapped his temple, signifying he'd stored the information in his BrainPal, "so if you have a PDA I can send them to, you can take a look at them at your leisure. As long as your leisure is no longer than a standard week."

"You're asking us to walk away from everything here," Jane said again.

"Yes," Rybicki said. "I am. And I'm appealing to your sense of duty, too, since I know you have one. The Colonial Union needs smart, capable and experienced people to help us get this colony going. You two fit the bill. And what I'm asking of you is more important than what you're doing here. Your jobs here can be handled by others. You'll leave and someone else will come in and take your place. Maybe they won't be as good, but they'll be good enough. What I'm asking of you two for this colony isn't something that just anyone else could do."

"You said we were in the middle of your list," I said.

"It was a short list," Rybicki said to me. "And there's a steep drop-off after you two." He turned back to Jane. "Look, Sagan, I can see this is a tough sell for you. I'll make you a deal. This is going to be a seed colony. That means that the first wave gets in and spends two or three years preparing the place for the next wave. After the second wave comes in, things will probably be settled enough that if you want, you and Perry and your daughter can come back here. The DoC can make sure your house and jobs will be waiting for you. Hell, we'll even send someone to get in your crop."

"Don't patronize me, General," Jane said.

"I'm not," Rybicki said. "The offer is genuine, Sagan. Your life here, every part of it, will be waiting for you. You won't lose any of it. But I need the two of you *now*. The DoC will make it worth your while. You'll get this life back. And you'll be making sure Roanoke colony survives. Think about it. Just decide soon."

I woke up and Jane wasn't beside me; I found her standing in the road in front of our house, staring up at the stars.

"You're going to get hit, standing in the road like

that," I said, coming up behind her, and placing my hands on her shoulders.

"There's nothing to get hit by," Jane said, taking my left hand in hers. "There's hardly anything to get hit by during the day. Look at them." She pointed to the stars with her right hand, and began tracing out constellations. "Look. The crane. The lotus. The pearl."

"I have a hard time with the Huckleberry constellations," I said. "I keep looking for the ones I was born with. I look up and some part of me still expects to see the Big Dipper or Orion."

"I never looked at stars before we came here," Jane said. "I mean, I saw them, but they didn't mean anything to me. They were just stars. Then we came here and I spent all that time learning these constellations."

"I remember," I said. And I did remember; Vikram Banerje, who had been an astronomer back on Earth, had been a frequent visitor to our house in our first years in New Goa, patiently tracing out the patterns in the sky for Jane. He died not too long after he finally taught her all the Huckleberry constellations.

"I didn't see them at first," Jane said.

"The constellations?" I asked.

Jane nodded. "Vikram would point them out to me, and I'd just see a clump of stars," she said. "He'd show me a map and I'd see how the stars were supposed to connect together, and then I'd look up at the sky and just see . . . stars. And it was like that for a long time. And then one night, I remember walking home from work and looking up and saying to myself 'there's the crane,' and seeing it. Seeing the crane. Seeing the constellations. That's when I knew this place was my home. That's when I knew I had come here to stay. That this place was *my* place."

I slid my arms down Jane's body and held her around the waist.

"But this place isn't your place, is it?" Jane asked.

"My place is where you are," I said.

"You know what I mean," Jane said.

"I know what you mean," I said. "I like it here, Jane. I like the people. I like our life."

"But," Jane said.

I shrugged.

Jane felt it. "That's what I thought," she said.

"I'm not unhappy," I said.

"I didn't say you were," Jane said. "And I know you're not unhappy with me or Zoë. If General Rybicki hadn't shown up, I don't think you would have noticed that you're ready to move on."

I nodded and kissed the back of her head. She was right about that.

"I talked to Zoë about it," Jane said.

"What did she have to say about it?" I asked.

"She's like you," Jane said. "She likes it here, but this isn't her home. She likes the idea of going to a colony that's just starting out."

"It appeals to her sense of adventure," I said.

"Maybe," Jane said. "There's not a lot of adventure here. That's one thing I like about it."

"That's funny coming from a Special Forces soldier," I said.

"I say it because I *am* Special Forces," Jane said. "I had nine years of nonstop adventure. I was born into it and if it wasn't for you and Zoë I would have died in it, and not had anything else. Adventure is overrated."

"But you're thinking of having some more anyway," I said.

"Because you are," Jane said.

"We haven't decided anything," I said. "We could say no. This is your place."

" 'My place is where you are,' " Jane said, echoing me.

"This *is* my place. But maybe somewhere else could be, too. I've only had this one place. Maybe I'm just frightened of leaving it."

"I don't think you're frightened by much," I said.

"I'm frightened by different things than you are," Jane said. "You don't notice because sometimes you're not too observant."

"Thanks," I said. We stood there in the road, entwined.

"We can always come back," Jane said, eventually.

"Yes," I said. "If you want."

"We'll see," Jane said. She leaned back to kiss my cheek, untangled herself from my grasp and began to walk down the road. I turned back toward the house.

"Stay with me," Jane said.

"All right," I said. "I'm sorry. I thought you wanted to be by yourself."

"No," Jane said. "Walk with me. Let me show you my constellations. We have time enough for that."

TWO The *Junipero Serra* skipped and suddenly a green and blue world hovered large outside the window of the *Serra*'s observation theater. In the seats, a couple hundred invited guests, reporters and Department of Colonization officials oohed and aahed as if they'd never seen a planet from the outside before.

"Ladies and gentlemen," said Karin Bell, Secretary of Colonization, "the new colony world of Roanoke." The room burst into applause, which faded into the hiss of reporters quickly whispering notes into recorders. In doing so most of them missed the sudden appearance in the middle distance of the *Bloomington* and the *Fairbanks*, the two CDF cruisers that were accompanying this little press junket in the stars. Their presence suggested to me that Roanoke might not be as entirely domesticated as the Colonial Union would like to suggest; it wouldn't do to have the Secretary of Colonization—not to mention the aforementioned reporters and invited guests—blown out of the sky by some alien raider.

I noted the appearance of the cruisers to Jane with a

flick of my eyes; she glanced and nodded almost imperceptibly. Neither of us said anything. We were hoping to get through this entire press thing without having to say anything. We had discovered that neither of us were particularly good with the press.

"Let me give you just a little background on Roanoke," Bell said. "Roanoke has an equatorial diameter of just under thirteen thousand kilometers, which means it's larger than either Earth or Phoenix, but not as large as Zhong Guo, which retains the title the CU's largest colonized planet." This prompted a halfhearted cheer from a couple of Zhong Guo reporters, followed by a laugh. "Its size and composition means the gravity is ten percent heavier here than on Phoenix; most of you will feel like you've put on a kilo or two when you go down. The atmosphere is the usual nitrogen-oxygen mix, but it's unusually heavy on the oxygen: close to thirty percent. You'll feel that, too."

"Who did we take the planet from?" asked one of the reporters.

"I'm not there yet," Bell said, and there was a little grumbling. Bell was apparently known for giving dry press conferences off notes, and she was in fine form here.

The image of Roanoke's globe disappeared, replaced with a delta, in which a small river joined in with a much larger one. "This is where the colony will settle," Bell said. "The smaller river here we've named the Albemarle; the larger one here is the Raleigh. Raleigh drains this entire continent, like the Amazon does back on Earth or the Anasazi does on Phoenix. A couple hundred kilometers to the west"—the image scrolled—"and we're at the Virginian Ocean. Plenty of room to grow."

"Why isn't the colony at the shore?" someone asked.

"Because it doesn't have to be," Bell said. "This isn't the sixteenth century. Our ships are crossing stars, not oceans. We can put colonies in places where it makes sense for them to be. This place"—Bell rewound to the original location—"is far enough inland to be insulated from the cyclones that hit at the mouth of the Raleigh, and has other favorable geological and meteorological advantages as well. Also, the life on this planet has incompatible chemistry to ours. The colonists can't eat anything from here. Fishing is out. It makes more sense to put the colony on an alluvial plain, where it has space to grow its own food, than it does on a coast."

"Can we talk about who we took the planet from yet?" asked the first reporter.

"I'm not there yet," Bell repeated.

"But we know all this stuff already," said someone else. "It's in our press packs. And our viewers are going to want to know who we took the planet from."

"We didn't take the planet from anyone," Bell said, clearly annoyed at being knocked off her pace. "We were given the planet."

"By whom?" asked the first reporter.

"By the Obin," Bell said. This caused a stir. "And I'll be happy to talk about that more, later. But first—" The image of the river delta vanished, replaced by some furry tree-like objects that weren't quite plants, not quite animals, but were the dominant life form on Roanoke. Most of the reporters ignored her, whispering into their recorders about the Obin connection.

"The Obin called it Garsinhir," General Rybicki had said to me and Jane a few days earlier, as we took his personal shuttle from our transport to Phoenix Station for our formal briefing, and to be introduced to some of the colonists who would act as our deputies. "It means *seventeenth planet*. It was the seventeenth planet they colonized. They're not a very imaginative species."

"It's not like the Obin to give up a planet," Jane said.

"They didn't," Rybicki said. "We traded. We gave them a small planet we took from the Gelta about a year back. They didn't have much use for Garsinhir anyway. It's a class-six planet. The chemistry of the life there is similar enough to the Obin's that the Obin were always dying off from native viruses. We humans, on the other hand, are incompatible with the local life chemistry. So we won't be affected by the local viruses and bacteria and whatnot. The Gelta planet the Obin are taking isn't as nice but they can tolerate it better. It's a fair trade. Now, have you two had a chance to look at the colonist files?"

"We did," I said.

"Any thoughts?" Rybicki said.

"Yes," Jane said. "The selection process is insane."

Rybicki smiled at Jane. "One day you're going to be diplomatic and I'm not going to know what to do," he said.

Jane reached for her PDA and pulled up the information on the selection process. "The colonists from Elysium were selected from a lottery," she said.

"A lottery they could join after proving they were physically capable of the rigors of colonization," Rybicki said.

"Kyoto's colonists are all members of a religious order that avoids technology," Jane said. "How are they even going to get on the colony ships?"

"They're Colonial Mennonites," Rybicki said. "They're not whackjobs, and they're not extremists. They just strive for simplicity. That's not a bad thing to have on a new colony."

"The colonists from Umbria were selected through a *game show*," Jane said.

"The ones that didn't win got the take-home game," I said.

Rybicki ignored me. "Yes," he said, to Jane. "A game show that required the contestants to compete in several tests of endurance and intelligence, both of which will also come in handy when you get to Roanoke. Sagan, every colony was given a list of physical and mental criteria that every potential Roanoke colonist had to fulfill. Other than that we left the selection process up to the colony. Some of them, like Erie and Zhong Guo, did fairly standard selection processes. Some of them didn't."

"And this doesn't cause you any concern," Jane said.

"Not as long as the colonists passed our own set of requirements, no," Rybicki said. "They presented their potential colonists; we checked them against our own standards."

"They all passed?" I asked.

Rybicki snorted. "Hardly. The Albion colony leader chose colonists from her enemies list, and the colonist positions on Rus went to the highest bidder. We ended up supervising the selection process on both those colonies. But the end result is that you have what I think is an excellent class of colonists." He turned to Jane. "They're a damn sight better than colonists you're going to get from Earth, I'll tell you that much. We don't screen *them* nearly as rigorously. Our philosophy there is that if you can walk onto a colony transport, you're in. Our standards are a little higher for this colony. So relax. You've got good colonists."

Jane settled back, not entirely convinced. I didn't blame her; I wasn't entirely convinced myself. The three of us fell silent as the shuttle negotiated the terms of docking at the gate.

"Where's your daughter?" Rybicki said, as the shuttle settled in.

"She's back at New Goa," Jane said. "Supervising our packing."

"And having a good-bye party with her friends that it's best we not think too much about," I said.

"Teenagers," Rybicki said. He stood up. "Now, Perry, Sagan. Remember what I said about this colony process having become a media circus?"

"Yes," I said.

"Good," he said. "Then prepare to meet the clowns." And then he led us off the shuttle to the gate, where apparently the entire news media of the Colonial Union had camped out to meet us.

"Holy God," I said, stopping in the tunnel.

"It's too late to panic, Perry," Rybicki said, reaching back and taking my arm. "They already know everything about you. Might as well come out and get it over with."

"So," Jann Kranjic said, sidling up to me not more than five minutes after we had landed on Roanoke. "What's it like to be one of the first humans to set foot on a new world?"

"I've done it before," I said, toeing the turf under my boot. I didn't look at him. Over the last few days I'd come to loathe his smooth vocal delivery and telegenic good looks.

"Sure," Jann said. "But this time you don't have anyone trying to shoot that foot off."

Now I glanced over to him and saw that annoying smirk of his, which was somehow regarded as a winning smile on his home world of Umbria. Out of the corner of my eye I saw Beata Novik, his camerawoman, do her slow perambulation. She was letting that camera cap of hers record everything, the better to be edited down later.

"It's still early in the day, Jann. There's still time for someone to get shot," I said. His smile faltered slightly. "Now, why don't you and Beata go bother someone else."

Kranjic sighed and broke character. "Look, Perry," he

said. "You know that when I go into edit with this there's no way you're not going to look like a jerk. You should just lighten the tone a little, hey? Give me something I can work with. We really want to work the war hero thing, but you're not giving me much. Come on. You know how this goes. You did advertising back on Earth, for God's sake."

I waved him off, irritably. Kranjic looked over to my right at Jane, but didn't try to get a comment out of her. At some point when I wasn't looking, he had crossed some sort of line with her and I suspect she ended up scaring the hell out of him. I wondered if there was any video of the moment. "Come on, Beata," he said. "We need some more footage of Trujillo, anyway." They wandered off in the direction of the landing craft, looking for one of the more quotable future colony leaders.

Kranjic made me grumpy. This whole trip was making me grumpy. This was ostensibly a research trip for me and Jane and selected colonists, to recon our colony site and to learn more about the planet. What it really was was a press junket with all of us as the stars. It was a waste of time to drag us all to this world just for a photo opportunity, and then drag us all back home. Kranjic was just the most annoying example of the sort of thinking that valued appearance over substance.

I turned to Jane. "I'm not going to miss him when we start this colony."

"You didn't read the colonist profiles close enough," Jane said. "Both he and Beata are part of the Umbrian colonist contingent. He's coming with us. He and Beata got married to do it because the Umbrians weren't letting singles colonize."

"Because married couples are more prepared for colonial life?" I ventured.

"More like couples competing made for better entertainment on that game show of theirs," Jane said.

"He competed on the show?" I asked.

"He was the emcee," Jane said. "But rules are rules. It's entirely a marriage of convenience. Kranjic hasn't ever had a relationship that's lasted more than a year, and Beata is a lesbian in any event."

"I'm terrified you know all this," I said.

"I was an intelligence officer," Jane said. "This is easy for me."

"Anything else I need to know about him?" I asked.

"His plan is to document the first year of the Roanoke colony," Jane said. "He's already signed for a weekly show. He's also got a book deal."

"Lovely," I said. "Well, at least now we know how he weaseled his way onto the shuttle." The first shuttle down to Roanoke was meant to be only the dozen colonist representatives and a few Department of Colonization staffers; there was a near riot when the reporters on the *Serra* figured out that none of them was invited on the shuttle with the colonists. Kranjic broke the deadlock by offering to put the footage Beata shot into the pool. The rest of the reporters would come down in later shuttles, to do their establishing shots and then to cut to Kranjic's material. For his sake it was just as well he was going to become a Roanoke colonist; after this some of his more resentful colleagues would be likely to walk him to an air lock.

"Don't worry about it," Jane said. "And besides, he was right. This *is* the first new planet you've been on where someone wasn't trying to kill you. Enjoy it. Come on." She started walking across the vast expanse of native grasses we had landed on, toward a line of what looked like—but weren't exactly—trees. For that matter, the native grasses weren't exactly grasses, either.

Whatever they were precisely, not-grasses and not-trees both, they were a lush and impossible green. The extra-rich atmosphere lay moist and heavy on us. It was late winter in this hemisphere, but where we were on the planet, latitude and prevailing wind patterns conspired to make the temperature pleasantly warm. I was worried what midsummer was going to be like; I expected I was going to be perspiring a lot.

I caught up with Jane, who had stopped to study a tree thing. It didn't have leaves, it had fur. The fur seemed to be moving; I leaned in closer and saw a colony of tiny creatures bustling about in it.

"Tree fleas," I said. "Nice."

Jane smiled, which was rare enough to note. "I think it's interesting," she said, petting a bough of the tree. One of the tree fleas jumped from the fur to her hand; she looked at it with interest before blowing it off her with a gust of breath.

"Think you could be happy here?" I asked.

"I think I could be *busy* here," Jane said. "General Rybicki can say what he wants about the selection process for this colony. I've read the colonist files. I'm not convinced most of these colonists aren't going to be a danger to themselves and others." She nodded in the direction of the shuttle, where we last saw Kranjic. "Look at Kranjic. He doesn't want to colonize. He wants to write about other people colonizing. He's under the impression that once we get here he's going to have all the time in the world to do his show and write his book. He's going to get to the edge of starvation before he figures it out."

"Maybe he's an outlier," I said.

"You're an optimist," Jane said, and looked back at the fur tree, and the crawly things in it. "I like that about you. But I don't think we should operate from an optimistic point of view."

"Fair enough," I said. "But you have to admit you were wrong about the Mennonites."

"I'm *provisionally* wrong about the Mennonites," Jane

said, looking back to me. "But, yes. They're much stronger candidates than I expected."

"You just never knew any Mennonites," I said.

"I never knew any religious people at all before I got to Huckleberry," Jane said. "And Hinduism didn't do much for me. Although I can appreciate Shiva."

"I'll bet," I said. "That's a little different than being a Mennonite, though."

Jane looked up over my shoulder. "Speak of the devil," she said. I turned and saw a tall, pale figure coming toward us. Simple clothes and a wide hat. It was Hiram Yoder, who had been chosen by the Colonial Mennonites to accompany us on the trip.

I smiled at his form. Unlike Jane, I *did* know Mennonites—the part of Ohio I had lived in had a lot of them, as well as Amish, Brethren and other variations of Anabaptists. Like all sorts of folks, individual Mennonites had the usual range of personalities, but as a class they seemed to be good and honest people. When I needed work done on my house I'd always picked Mennonite contractors because they would do the job right the first time, and if something didn't turn out right, they didn't argue with you about it; they'd just fix it. That's a philosophy worth getting behind.

Yoder raised his hand in welcome. "I thought I'd join you," he said. "I figure if the leaders of the colony are looking so intently at something, I might want to know what it is."

"It's just a tree," I said. "Or, well, whatever it is we end up calling this thing."

Yoder looked up at it. "Appears to be a tree to me," he said. "With fur. We might call it a fur tree."

"Just my thinking," I said. "Not to be confused with a *fir* tree, of course."

"Of course," Yoder said. "That would be silly."

"What do you think of your new world?" I asked.

"I think it could be a good one," Yoder said. "Although much will depend on the people in it."

"I agree," I said. "Which brings me to a question I'd meant to ask you. Some of the Mennonites I knew in Ohio kept to themselves—would separate themselves from the world. I need to know if your group will do the same."

Yoder smiled. "No, Mr. Perry," he said. "Mennonites vary in how we practice our faith, from church to church. We are Colonial Mennonites. We choose to live and dress simply. We don't shun technology when it's required, but we don't use it when it's not. And we choose to live *in* the world, as the salt and the light. We hope to be good neighbors to you and the other colonists, Mr. Perry."

"I'm glad to hear that," I said. "Looks like our colony is off to a promising start."

"That could change," Jane said, and nodded off toward the distance again. Kranjic and Beata were heading our way. Kranjic was moving animatedly; Beata was moving at a distinctly more sluggish pace. Chasing after colonists all day was clearly not her idea of fun.

"There you are," Kranjic said to Yoder. "I have comments from every other colonist here—well, except for her." He waved in the direction of Jane. "And now I just need something from you to put into the pool stock."

"I've told you before, Mr. Kranjic, that I would prefer not to be photographed or interviewed," Yoder said, pleasantly.

"This is a religious thing, isn't it," Kranjic said.

"Not really," Yoder said. "I'd just prefer to be let alone."

"The folks back on Kyoto are going to be disappointed if they don't see their hometown . . ." Kranjic stopped, and stared behind all three of us. "What the hell are those?"

We turned, slowly, to see two deer-sized creatures about five meters into the fur trees, eyeing us placidly.

"Jane?" I asked.

"I have no idea," Jane said. "There's not a whole lot on the local fauna in our reports."

"Beata," Kranjic said. "Go get closer so we can get a better shot."

"The hell I will," Beata said. "I'm not going to get eaten so *you* can get a better shot."

"Oh, come on," Kranjic said. "If they were going to eat us they would have done it by now. Look." He started to inch closer to the things.

"Should we let him do that?" I asked Jane.

Jane shrugged. "We haven't technically started the colony yet."

"Good point," I said.

Kranjic had snuck up to within a couple meters of the pair when the larger of the two decided it had had enough, bellowed impressively, and took a quick step forward. Kranjic shrieked and took off like a shot, nearly stumbling as he sprinted back toward the shuttle.

I turned to Beata. "Tell me you got that," I said.

"You know I did," she said.

The two creatures in the trees, their work done, sauntered casually away.

"Wow," Savitri said. "It's not every day that you get to see a major colonial news figure wet himself in fear."

"This is true," I said. "Although to be entirely honest I'm pretty sure I could have gone my entire life without having seen that and still died happy."

"Then it's just a bonus," Savitri said.

We were sitting in my office on the day before my final departure from Huckleberry. Savitri was sitting in the chair behind my desk; I was sitting in one of the chairs in front of it.

"How do you like the view from the chair?" I asked.

"The view is fine. The chair is kind of lumpy," Savitri said. "Like someone's lazy ass had deformed it beyond all recognition."

"You can always get a new chair," I said.

"Oh, I'm sure Administrator Kulkarni would be delighted with that expense," Savitri said. "He's never gotten over the idea of me as a troublemaker."

"You *are* a troublemaker," I said. "It's part of the job description of being an ombudsman."

"Ombudsmen are supposed to resolve trouble," Savitri noted.

"Well, fine," I said. "If you want to get snippy about it, Miss Literal Pants."

"What a lovely name," Savitri said, and swung back and forth in her chair. "And anyway, I'm only an assistant troublemaker."

"Not anymore," I said. "I've already recommended to Kulkarni that you be made village ombudsman, and he's agreed."

Savitri stopped swinging around. "You actually got him to agree?"

"Not at first," I admitted. "But I was persuasive. And I convinced him that at least this way you'd be required to help people rather than bother them."

"Rohit Kulkarni," Savitri said. "Such a fine man."

"He does have his moments," I allowed. "But he did give his approval, finally. So just say yes, and the job is yours. And so is the chair."

"I definitely don't want the chair," Savitri said.

"Fine," I said. "Then you'll have nothing to remember me by."

"I don't want the job, either," Savitri said.

"What?" I said.

"I said, I don't want the job," Savitri said. "When I found out that you were leaving, I went looking for another job. And I found one."

"What is it?" I asked.

"It's another assistant job," Savitri said.

"But you could be ombudsman," I said.

"Oh, yes, be ombudsman in *New Goa*," Savitri said, and then noticed my look; after all, that had been my job. "No offense. You took your job after you'd seen the universe. I've been in the same village all my life. I'm thirty years old. It's time to leave."

"You've found a job in Missouri City," I said, naming the district capital.

"No," Savitri said.

"I'm confused," I said.

"This is not news," Savitri said, and then continued on before I could retort. "My new job is off-planet. On a new colony called Roanoke. Maybe you've heard of it."

"Okay, now I'm *really* confused," I said.

"Seems that a two-person team is leading the colony," Savitri said. "I asked one of them for a job. She said yes."

"You're Jane's assistant?" I asked.

"Actually, I'm assistant to the colony leader," Savitri said. "Since there are two of you, I'm your assistant, too. I still won't get you tea."

"Huckleberry's not one of the colonies that was allowed to send colonists," I said.

"No," Savitri said. "But as the colony leaders, you are allowed to hire whomever you like for your support staff. Jane already knows and trusts me and knows that you and I work together well. It made sense."

"When did she hire you?" I asked.

"The day you gave notice here," Savitri said. "She

came in while you were out to lunch. We talked about it and she offered me the job."

"And neither of you bothered to tell me about this," I said.

"She was going to," Savitri said. "But I asked her not to."

"Why not?" I asked.

"Because then you and I wouldn't have had *this* wonderful, wonderful conversation," Savitri said, and then spun around in my chair, laughing.

"Get out of my chair," I said.

I was standing in the bare living room of my packed-up and stored-away home, getting misty, when Hickory and Dickory approached me.

"We would like to talk to you, Major Perry," Hickory said to me.

"Yes, all right," I said, surprised. In the seven years that Hickory and Dickory had been with us we had conversed a number of times. But they had never once initiated a conversation; at most, they would wait silently to be acknowledged.

"We will use our implants," Hickory said.

"Fine," I said. Both Hickory and Dickory fingered collars that rested at the base of their long necks, and pressed a button on the right side of the collar.

The Obin were a created species; the Consu, a race so far advanced of ours that it was almost unfathomable, had found the Obin's ancestors and used their technology to force intelligence on the poor bastards. The Obin indeed became intelligent; what they didn't become was *aware*. Whatever process that allowed for consciousness—the sense of self—was entirely missing from the Obin. Individual Obin had no ego or personality; it was only as a group that the Obin were aware that they were lacking a thing all other intelligent species had. Whether the Consu accidentally or intentionally made the Obin nonconscious was a matter of debate, but given my own encounters with the Consu over the years, I suspect they were simply curious, and the Obin were just another experiment to them.

The Obin desired consciousness enough that they were willing to risk a war with the Colonial Union to get it. The war was a demand of Charles Boutin, a scientist who was the first to record and store a human consciousness outside the supporting structure of the brain. Boutin was killed by Special Forces before he could give the Obin consciousness on an individual level, but his work was close enough to completion that the Colonial Union was able to strike a deal with the Obin to finish the work. The Obin went from foe to friend overnight, and the Colonial Union came through on Boutin's work, creating a consciousness implant based on the CDF's existing BrainPal technology. It was consciousness as an accessory.

Humans—the few who know the story, anyway—naturally regard Boutin as a traitor, a man whose plan to topple the Colonial Union would have caused the slaughter of billions of humans. The Obin equally and naturally regard him as one of their great racial heroes, a Prometheus figure who gave them not fire but awareness. If you ever needed an argument that heroism is relative, there it is.

My own feelings on the matter were more complicated. Yes, he was a traitor to his species and deserved to die. He's also the biological father to Zoë, who I think is as wonderful a human as I've met. It's hard to say that you're glad the father of your beautiful and terribly clever adopted daughter is dead, even when you know it's better that he is.

Given how the Obin feel about Boutin, it's not in the

least surprising they would feel possessive about Zoë; one of their primary treaty demands was, essentially, visitation rights. What eventually got agreed to was a situation where two Obin would live with Zoë and her adopted family. Zoë named them Hickory and Dickory when they arrived. Hickory and Dickory were allowed to use their consciousness implants to record some of their time with Zoë. Those recordings were shared among all the Obin with consciousness implants; in effect, they *all* shared time with Zoë.

Jane and I allowed this under very limited conditions while Zoë was too young to really understand what was going on. After Zoë was old enough to grasp the concept it was her decision. Zoë allowed it. She likes the idea of her life being shared with an entire species, although like any teenager she has extended periods of wanting to be left alone. Hickory and Dickory turn their implants off when that happens; no point wasting perfectly good consciousness on time not spent with Zoë. Their wanting to be conscious talking to me alone was something new.

There was a slight lag between the moment Hickory and Dickory activated their collars, which stored the hardware that housed their consciousness, and the moment the collar communicated with the neural overlay in their brains. It was like watching sleepwalkers wake up. It was also a little creepy. Although not as creepy as what came next: Hickory smiling at me.

"We will be deeply sad to leave this place," Hickory said. "Please understand we have lived our entire conscious life here. We feel it strongly within us, as do all Obin. We thank you for allowing us to share your lives."

"You're welcome," I said. This seemed a trivial thing for the two Obin to want to discuss with me. "You sound as if you were leaving us. I thought you were to be coming with us."

"We are," Hickory said. "Dickory and I are aware of the burden we carry both to attend to your daughter and to share our experiences with all other Obin. It can be overwhelming. We cannot keep our implants engaged for long, you know. The emotional strain is so great. The implants are not perfect, and our brains have difficulties. We get . . . overstimulated."

"I didn't know that," I said.

"We would not wish to burden you with it," Hickory said. "And it was not important for you to know. We managed it so that you would not need to know. But recently, both Dickory and I have found that when we turn on our implants, we are immediately overwhelmed with emotion for Zoë, and for you and Lieutenant Sagan."

"It's a stressful time for all of us," I said.

Another Obin smile, even more ghastly than the first. "My apologies," Hickory said. "I have been unclear. Our emotion is not formless anxiety over leaving this place or this planet, or excitement or nervousness about traveling to a new world. It is a very specific thing. It is *concern*."

"I think we all have concerns," I began, but then stopped when I saw a new expression on Hickory's face, one I had never noticed before. Hickory looked *impatient*. Or possibly it was frustrated with me. "I'm sorry, Hickory. Please continue."

Hickory stood there for a minute, as if debating something with itself, then abruptly turned from me to confer with Dickory. I spent the time reflecting that suddenly the names that a small child puckishly gave these two creatures several years ago no longer seemed to fit in the slightest.

"Forgive me, Major," Hickory said, finally, returning its attention to me. "I regret I may be blunt here. We may be unable to fully express our concern. You may be ignorant of certain facts and it may not be our place to provide them to you. Let me ask you: What do you think is the status of this part of space? The portion in which we the Obin and you the Colonial Union reside among other species."

"We're at war," I said. "We have our colonies and we try to keep them safe. Other species have their colonies and try to keep them safe, too. We all fight over planets that fit our species' needs. We all fight each other."

"Aah," Hickory said. "We all fight each other. No alliances? No treaties?"

"Obviously there are a few," I said. "We have one with the Obin. Other races may have treaties and allies with a few other species. But generally, yes. We all fight. Why?"

Hickory's smile passed from ghastly into rictus territory. "We will tell you what we can," Hickory said. "We can tell you about things already spoken of. We know that your Secretary of Colonization has claimed that the colony you are calling Roanoke was given to you by the Obin. The planet we call Garsinhir. We know that it is claimed we have taken a planet from you in return."

"That's right," I said.

"There is no such agreement," Hickory said. "Garsinhir remains Obin territory."

"That can't be right," I said. "I've been to Roanoke. I've walked the ground where the colony will be. I think you may be mistaken."

"We are not mistaken," Hickory said.

"You must be," I said. "Please don't take this the wrong way, but you two are companions and bodyguards to a teenage human. It's possible whoever your contacts are at your level don't have the best information."

A flicker of something crossed over Hickory's face; I suspect it was *amusement*. "Be assured, Major, that the Obin do not send mere *companions* to guard and care for Boutin's child or her family. And be assured that Garsinhir remains in Obin hands."

I thought about this. "You're saying that the Colonial Union is lying about Roanoke," I said.

"It's possible your Secretary of Colonization may be misinformed," Hickory said. "We cannot say. But whatever the cause of the error, there is an error of fact."

"Maybe the Obin are allowing us to colonize your world," I said. "I understand that your body chemistry makes Obin susceptible to native infections. Having an ally there is better than leaving the world unoccupied."

"Perhaps," Hickory said. Its voice was noncommittal in a very studied way.

"The colony ship leaves Phoenix Station in two weeks," I said. "Another week beyond that and we'll be landing in Roanoke. Even if what you say is true, there's not anything I can *do* about it now."

"I must apologize again," Hickory said. "I did not mean to suggest there was anything you could or should do. I would only wish for you to *know*. And to know at least some of the nature of our concern."

"Is there more than that?" I asked.

"We have said what we can," Hickory said. "Except for this. We are at your service, Major. Yours, Lieutenant Sagan's and especially and always Zoë's. Her father gave us the gift of ourselves. He asked a high price, which we willingly would have paid." I shuddered slightly at this, remembering what the price had been. "He died before that price, that debt could be repaid. We owe that debt now to his daughter, and the new debt accrued in her sharing her life with us. We owe it to her. And we owe it to her family."

"Thank you, Hickory," I said. "I know we are grateful that you and Dickory have served us so well."

Hickory's smile returned. "I regret to say you misunderstand me again, Major. Certainly I and Dickory are at your service and always shall be. But when I say we are at your service, I mean the Obin."

"The Obin," I said. "As in, *all* of you."

"Yes," said Hickory. "All of us. Until the last of us, if necessary."

"Oh," I said. "I'm sorry, Hickory. I'm not quite sure what to say to that."

"Say that you'll remember it," Hickory said. "When the time comes."

"I will," I said.

"We would ask you to keep this conversation in confidence," Hickory said. "For now."

"All right," I said.

"Thank you, Major," Hickory said. It looked back at Dickory and then back at me. "I fear we have made ourselves overly emotional. We will turn off our implants now, with your permission."

"Please," I said. The two Obin reached up to their necks to switch off their personalities. I watched as the animation slid from their faces, replaced with blank intelligence.

"We rest now," Hickory said, and it and its partner left, leaving me in an empty room.

THREE Here's one way to colonize: You take two hundred or three hundred people, allow them to pack what supplies they see fit, drop them off on the planet of their choice, say "see you," and then come back a year later—after they've all died of malnutrition brought on by ignorance and lack of supplies, or have been wiped out by another species who wants the place for themselves—to pick up the bones.

This isn't a very successful way to colonize. In our all-too-short ramp-up period, both Jane and I read enough reports on the demise of wildcat colonies that were designed in just this fashion to be convinced of this salient fact.

On the other hand you don't want to drop a hundred thousand people onto a new colony world either, complete with all the comforts of civilization. The Colonial Union has the means to do something like this, if it wanted to. But it doesn't want to. No matter how close a planet's gravitational field, circumference, land mass, atmosphere or life chemistry is to Earth's, or to any other planets humans have as yet colonized, it isn't Earth, and there's no practical way of knowing what sort of nasty surprise a planet has in store for humans there. Earth itself has a funny way of devising new diseases and ailments to kill off unwary humans, and there we're a native species. We're foreign bodies when we land on new worlds, and we know what any life system does to a foreign body in its midst: it tries to kill it as quickly as possible.

Here's an interesting bit of trivia I learned about failed colonies: Not counting wildcat colonies, the number one cause of abandoned human colonies is not territorial disputes with other species; it's native bugs killing off the settlers. Other intelligent species we can fight off; that's a battle we understand. Battling an entire ecosystem that's trying to kill you is an altogether trickier proposition.

Landing a hundred thousand colonists on a planet just to watch them all die of a fast-moving native infection you can't cure in time is just a waste of perfectly good colonists.

Which is not to *underestimate* territorial disputes. A human colony is *exponentially* more likely to be attacked in the first two or three years of its lifespan than it is at any other point in time. The colony is focused on creating itself and is vulnerable to attack. The Colonial Defense Forces' presence at a new colony, while not insignificant, is still a fraction of what it will be once a space station is built above the colony a decade or two later. And the simple fact that someone has colonized a planet makes it rather more attractive to everyone else, because those colonists have done all the hard work of colonization for you. Now all you have to do is scrape them off the planet and take it for your own.

Landing a hundred thousand colonists on a planet just to have them scraped off it is *also* a waste of perfectly good colonists. And despite the Colonial Union essentially farming Third World countries on Earth for colonists, if you start losing a hundred thousand colonists every time a new colony fails, eventually you run short of colonists.

Fortunately there is a happy medium between these two scenarios. It involves taking twenty-five hundred or so colonists, landing them on a new world in the early spring, providing them sustainable and durable technology to address their immediate needs, and giving them the task of both becoming self-sufficient on the new world, and of preparing the world, two or three years down the line, for roughly ten thousand more new colonists. Those second wave colonists will have another five years or so to help prepare for fifty thousand new colonists, and so on.

There are five formal and initial waves of colonists, by which time the colony ideally has a population of a million or so, spread out over numerous small towns and one or two largish cities. After the fifth wave becomes established and the colony's infrastructure is established, everything switches to a rolling colonization process. When the population reaches ten million or thereabouts, immigration stops, the colony gets limited self-rule within the CU federal system, and humanity has another bulwark against racial extinction at the hands of a callous universe. That is, if those initial twenty-five hundred survive a hostile ecosystem, attacks from other races, humanity's own organizational shortcomings and simple, ever-present damn bad luck.

Twenty-five hundred colonists are numerous enough to start the process of making a world a human world. They are few enough that if they die, the CU can shed a tear and move on. And, indeed, the tear-shedding part of that is strictly optional. It's an interesting thing, to be both critical and expendable to humanity's effort to populate the stars. On the whole, I thought, I might have been smarter to stay on Huckleberry.

"All right, I give up," I said, pointing to the massive container that was being maneuvered into the cargo hold of the *Ferdinand Magellan*. "Tell me what that is."

Aldo Ferro, the cargo foreman, checked the manifest on his PDA. "That contains all the mixin's for your colony's sewage treatment plant," he said, and pointed at a row of containers. "And those are your sewer pipes, septic tanks and waste transports."

"No outhouses for Roanoke," I said. "We're going to poo in style."

"It's not a matter of style," Ferro said. "You're going to a class-six planet, complete with a noncompatible ecological system. You're going to need all the fertilizer you can get. That sewage treatment system will take all your biological waste, from crap to carcasses, and make sterile compost for your fields. It's probably the single most important thing you have on this manifest. Try not to break it."

I smiled. "You seem to know a lot about sewage," I said.

"Yeah, right," Ferro said. "More like I know about packing a new colony. I've been working in this cargo hold for twenty-five years, and we've been transporting new colonies all that time. Give me a manifest and I can tell you what sort of planet the colony's going to, what its seasons are, how heavy its gravity is and whether that colony is going to make it through its first year. You want to know how I knew your colony had a noncompatible ecosystem? Besides the sewage plant, I mean. That's standard on any colony."

"Sure," I said.

Ferro tapped something on the PDA screen and handed the screen to me, with a list of containers. "Okay, first off," Ferro said. "Food stores. Every colony ships with a three-month supply of dry goods and basic foodstuffs for every member of the colony, and another month supply of dry rations, to allow the colony time to start hunting and producing its own food. But you have a six-month supply of foodstuffs and two months of dry rations per colonist. That's the sort of load out you see for a non-compatible ecosystem, because you can't eat off the land right away. In fact, it's actually *more* than usual for an NCE; usually there's a four-month supply of dry goods and six weeks of rations."

"Why would they give us more food than usual?" I asked. I actually knew the answer to this—I was supposed to be running the colony, after all—but I wanted to see if Ferro was as good as he thought he was.

Ferro smiled. "Your clue is right in front of you, Mr. Perry. You're also shipping with a double load of soil conditioners and fertilizers. That tells me the soil there is no good, as is, for growing human food. That extra food buys you time if some idiot doesn't condition a field properly."

"That's right," I said.

"Yup," Ferro agreed. "Final thing: You've got more than the usual load out in your medical supplies for poison treatment, which is typical for NCEs. You've also got a hell of a lot of veterinary detoxifiers, too. Which reminds me." Ferro took back the PDA and pulled up a new list of containers. "Double load of feed for your livestock."

"You are a master of manifests, Ferro," I said. "You ever think of colonizing?"

"Hell, no," Ferro said. "I've seen enough of these new colonies go out to know that some of them don't make it.

I'm happy to load you up and load you out and then wave good-bye and come home to Phoenix to my wife and cat. No offense, Mr. Perry."

"None taken," I said, and nodded to his manifest. "So, you said you can tell from a manifest whether a colony is going to make it. How about us?"

"You're loaded for bear," Ferro said. "You're going to be fine. But some of your stuff is a little weird. There's stock on your manifest I haven't seen shipped before. You've got containers full of obsolete equipment." Ferro handed back the manifest to me. "Look, you have everything you need for a blacksmith's shop. In 1850. I didn't even think this stuff existed outside a period recreation fair."

I looked at the manifest. "Some of our colonists are Mennonites," I said. "They prefer not to use modern technology if they can avoid it. They think it's a distraction."

"How many of your colonists are whatever it is you just said?" Ferro asked.

"About two hundred, two hundred and fifty," I said, handing back the PDA.

"Huh," Ferro said. "Well, then, it seems you're pretty much prepared for everything, up to and including time travel back to the Wild West. If the colony fails, you can't blame it on the inventory."

"So it'll be all my fault," I said.

"Probably," Ferro said.

"I think the one thing we can all say is that we don't want to see this colony *fail*," said Manfred Trujillo. "I don't think we're in danger of that. But I do worry about some of the decisions that have been made. I think they make things more difficult."

Around the conference table was a round of nods. At my right, I saw Savitri take notes, marking which heads were nodding. On the other end of the table, Jane sat impassively, but I knew she was counting heads, too. She was in intelligence. This is what she does.

We were coming to the close of the inaugural official meeting of the Roanoke Council, which consisted of me and Jane as the colony heads, and the ten representatives of the colonists themselves, one for each world, who would act as our deputies. Theoretically, at least. Here in the real word, the jockeying for power had already begun.

Manfred Trujillo was primary among them. Trujillo had started the push to allow colony worlds to seed a new colony several years earlier, from his perch as Erie's representative to the CU legislature. He had been miffed when the Department of Colonization took his idea but neglected to install him as leader; he'd been even more miffed when the colony leaders turned out to be us, whom he did not know, and who did not seem to be especially impressed with him. But he was smart enough to mask his frustration in general terms, and spent most of the meeting trying to undermine Jane and me in the most complimentary way possible.

"For example, this council," said Trujillo, and looked up and down the table. "Each of us is charged with representing the interests of our fellow colonists. I don't doubt each of us will do that job admirably. But this council is an advisory council to the colony heads—advisory only. I wonder if that allows us to best represent the needs of the colony."

We're not even out of the dock and he's already talking revolution, I thought. Back in the days when I still had a BrainPal, I could shoot that entire thought over to Jane; as it was she caught my glance to her, which told her well enough what I was thinking.

"New colonies are administered under Department of Colonization regulations," Jane said. "The regulations require colony leaders to wield sole administrative and executive power. Things will be chaotic enough when we arrive that mustering a quorum for every decision is not ideal."

"I'm not suggesting that you two not do your jobs," Trujillo said. "Merely that our input should be more than symbolic. Many of us have been involved with this colony since the days it was only on the drawing board. We have a wealth of experience."

"Whereas we only have a couple months of involvement," I prompted.

"You are a recent and valuable addition to the process," Trujillo said. Smooth. "I would hope you would see the advantages to our being part of the decision-making process."

"It seems to me that the Colonization regulations are there for a reason," I said. "The DoC has overseen the colonization of dozens of worlds. They might know how to do it."

"Those colonists came from disadvantaged nations back on Earth," Trujillo said. "They do not have many of the advantages that we have."

I sensed Savitri tense up next to me; the arrogance of the old-line colonies, which had been founded by Western countries before the CU took over colonization, had always appalled her.

"What advantages are those?" Jane said. "John and I just spent seven years living among 'those colonists' and their descendants. Savitri here is one of them. I'm not sensing any notable *advantages* among those at this table to them."

"I may have phrased that poorly," Trujillo said, beginning what I suspected was another concilitory knife-twisting.

"You may have," I said, cutting him off. "However, I'm afraid the point is academic. DoC regulations don't give us much flexibility on the administration of first-wave colonies, nor do they make allowances for the previous national affiliation of its colonists. We are obliged to treat all colonists equally, no matter where they come from. I think that's a wise policy, don't you?"

Trujillo paused for a beat, clearly annoyed at the turn of rhetorical events. "Yes, of course."

"I'm glad to hear it. So for the moment, we'll continue to follow regulations. Now," I said before Trujillo could ramp himself up again, "anyone else?"

"Some of my people are complaining about their berth assignments," said Paulo Gutierrez, Khartoum's representative.

"Is there something wrong?" I asked.

"They're unhappy that they're not closer to other colonists from Khartoum," he said.

"The entire ship is only a few hundred meters long," I said. "And berth information is readily accessible through PDAs. They shouldn't have any problems locating each other."

"I understand that," Gutierrez said. "I just think the expectation would be that we would be berthed together in our groups."

"That's why we didn't do it that way," I said. "You know, once we set foot on Roanoke, none of us will be from Khartoum, or from Erie, or from Kyoto." I nodded toward Hiram Yoder, who nodded back. "We're all going to be from Roanoke. Might as well get a head start on that. There's only twenty-five hundred of us. That's a little small for ten separate tribes."

"That's a nice sentiment," said Marie Black, from Rus. "But I don't think our settlers are going to very quickly forget where they came from."

"I don't expect them to," I said. "I don't want them to forget where they came from. I would hope that they would focus on where they are. Or will be, soon enough."

"Colonists are represented here by their worlds," Trujillo said.

"It makes sense to do it that way," Jane said. "For now, at least. Once we're on Roanoke, we may revisit this." That tidbit sat in the air for a few seconds.

Marta Piro, from Zhong Guo, raised her hand. "There's a rumor that two Obin are coming with us to Roanoke," she said.

"It's not a rumor," I said. "It's true. Hickory and Dickory are members of my household."

"Hickory and Dickory?" asked Lee Chen, from Franklin.

"Our daughter Zoë named them when she was younger," I said.

"If you don't mind me asking, how is it two Obin are members of your household?" Piro asked.

"Our daughter keeps them as pets," Jane said. This got an uneasy laugh. That wasn't so bad. After an hour of being not-so-subtly hammered on by Trujillo, it wouldn't hurt to be seen as the sort of people who could keep terrifying aliens as domestic companions.

"You need to push that son of a bitch Trujillo out of a shuttle bay," Savitri said after the room had cleared.

"Relax," I said. "Some people are just no good at not being in charge."

"Gutierrez, Black and Trujillo have made their own political party," Jane said. "And of course, Trujillo's gone running to Kranjic to spill the details of this meeting. They've gotten very cozy."

"But it doesn't cause us any problems," I said.

"No," Jane said. "None of the rest of the representatives seems to have much truck with Trujillo, and the individual colonists are still boarding; he's had no time to get known to any of them who aren't from Erie. Even if he had, there's no way the DoC would replace us. Secretary Bell hates Trujillo and has since they were representatives. Taking his idea and installing us as colony leaders is just another way she has of sticking it to him."

"General Rybicki warned us things have gotten political," I said.

"General Rybicki has a way of not quite telling us everything we need to know," Jane said.

"You may be right," I said. "But on this point he was right on the nose. Anyway, for now let's not worry about it too much. We've got enough to do and after the *Magellan* leaves Phoenix Station we're going to get even busier. Speaking of which, I promised Zoë I would take her down to Phoenix today. Either of you want to come? It's me, Zoë and the Obin twins."

"I'll pass," Savitri said. "I'm still getting used to Hickory and Dickory."

"You've known them for nearly eight years," I said.

"Yes," Savitri said. "Nearly eight years, for five minutes at a time. I need to work up to extended visits."

"Fine," I said, and turned to Jane. "What about you?"

"I'm supposed to meet with General Szilard," she said, referring to the commander of Special Forces. "He wants to catch up."

"All right," I said. "You're missing out."

"What are you doing down there?" Jane asked.

"We're going to visit Zoë's parents," I said. "The other ones."

I stood at the gravestone that bore the name of Zoë's father and mother, and of Zoë herself. Zoë's dates, based on the belief she had died in a colony attack, were obviously incorrect; less obviously, so were her father's. Her mother's dates were accurate. Zoë had crouched down to get close to the names; Hickory and Dickory had connected their consciousnesses just long enough to have a ten-second ecstasy at the idea of being at the death marker of Boutin, then disconnected and stood at a distance, impassive.

"I remember the last time I was here," Zoë said. The small bouquet of flowers she brought lay propped up on the gravestone. "It was the day Jane asked me if I wanted to come live with you and her."

"Yes," I said. "You found out you were going to live with me before I found out I was going to live with either of you."

"I thought you and Jane were in love," Zoë said. "That you planned to live together."

"We were," I said. "We did. But it was complicated."

"Everything about our little family is complicated," Zoë said. "You're eighty-eight years old. Jane is a year older than I am. I'm the daughter of a traitor."

"You're also the only girl in the universe with her own Obin escort," I said.

"Speaking of complicated," Zoë said. "By day, typical kid. By night, adored by an entire alien race."

"There are worse setups," I said.

"I suppose," Zoë said. "You'd think being the object of worship for a whole alien race would get me out of homework now and then. Don't think I haven't noticed that it doesn't."

"We didn't want it to go to your head," I said.

"Thanks," she said. She pointed to the gravestone. "Even *this* is complicated. I'm alive, and it's my father's clone who is buried here, not my father. The only real person here is my mother. My *real* mother. It's all very complicated."

"I'm sorry," I said.

Zoë shrugged. "I'm used to it by now. Most of the time it's not a bad thing. And it gives you perspective, doesn't it? I'd be at school, listening to Anjali or Chadna complain about how complicated their lives were, and I'd be thinking to myself, girl, you have no idea what complicated is."

"Good to hear you've handled it well," I said.

"I try," Zoë said. "I have to admit it wasn't a very good day when the two of you told me the truth about Dad."

"It wasn't much of a fun day for us, either," I said. "But we thought you deserved to know the truth."

"I know," Zoë said, and stood up. "But you know. I woke up one morning thinking my real dad was just a scientist and went to bed knowing he could have wiped out the entire human race. It messes with you."

"Your father was a good man to you," I said. "Whatever else he was and whatever else he did, he got that thing right."

Zoë walked over to me and gave me a hug. "Thank you for bringing me here. You're a nice man, ninety-year-old dad," she said.

"You're a great kid, teenage daughter," I said. "You ready to go?"

"In a second," she said, and walked back over to the gravestone, knelt quickly and kissed it. Then she stood up and suddenly looked like an embarrassed teen. "I did that the last time I was here," she said. "I wanted to see if it made me feel the same."

"Did it?" I asked.

"Yeah," she said, still embarrassed. "Come on. Let's go." We walked toward the gates of the cemetery; I took out my PDA and signaled for a taxi to come pick us up.

"How do you like the *Magellan*?" I asked, as we walked.

"It's interesting," Zoë said. "It's been a long time since I've been on a spaceship. I forgot what it was like. And this one's so *big*."

"It has to fit twenty-five hundred colonists and all of their stuff," I said.

"I get that," Zoë said. "I'm just saying it's large. It's starting to fill up, though. The colonists are there now. I've met some of them. The ones my age, I mean."

"Meet any you like?" I asked.

"A couple," Zoë said. "There's one girl who seems to want to get to know me. Gretchen Trujillo."

"Trujillo, you say," I said.

Zoë nodded. "Why? You know her?"

"I think I may know her father," I said.

"It's a small world," Zoë said.

"And it's about to get a lot smaller," I said.

"Good point," Zoë said, and looked around. "I wonder if I'll ever make it back here."

"You're going to a new colony," I said. "Not the afterlife."

Zoë smiled at this. "You weren't paying attention to the gravestone," she said. "I've been to the afterlife. Coming back from that's not a problem. It's life you don't get over."

"Jane's taking a nap," Savitri said, as Zoë and I returned to our stateroom. "She said she wasn't feeling well."

I raised my eyebrows at this; Jane was the healthiest person I knew, even after she had been transferred into a standard human body. "Yes, I know," Savitri said, catching the eyebrow. "I thought it was odd, too. She said she'd be fine, but not to disturb her for at least a few hours."

"All right," I said. "Thanks. Zoë and I were going to go to the rec deck anyway. You want to come along?"

"Jane asked me to work on some things before I got her up," Savitri said. "Some other time."

"You work harder for Jane than you ever did for me," I said.

"It's the power of inspiring leadership," Savitri said.

"Nice," I said.

Savitri made shooing motions. "I'll ping your PDA when Jane is up," Savitri said. "Now, go. You're distracting me."

The *Magellan*'s recreation deck was arrayed like a small park, and was packed with colonists and their families, sampling the diversions the *Magellan* would offer them on our week-long journey to skip distance, thence to Roanoke. As we arrived, Zoë spied a trio of teenage girls and waved; one waved back and beckoned her over. I wondered if it was Gretchen Trujillo. Zoë left me with a quick backward glance good-bye. I wandered around the deck, watching my fellow colonists. Soon enough most of them would recognize me as the colony leader. For now, however, I was safely and happily anonymous.

At first glance the colonists seemed to be moving freely among each other, but after a minute or two I noticed some clumping, with groups of colonists standing apart. English was the common language of all the colonies, but each world also had its secondary languages, largely based on the stock of its original colonists. I heard snatches of these languages as I walked: Spanish, Chinese, Portuguese, Russian, German.

"You hear them, too," someone said behind me. I turned and saw Trujillo. "All the different languages," he said, and smiled. "Residue from our old worlds, I guess you would say. I doubt people will stop speaking them when we get to Roanoke."

"This your subtle way of suggesting that the colonists

won't be in a rush to trade in their own nationalities to become newly minted Roanokers?" I said.

"It's just an observation. And I'm sure in time we all will become . . . *Roanokers,*" Trujillo said, pronouncing that last word as if it were something spiky that he'd been required to swallow. "It will just take some time. Possibly more time than you now suspect. We are doing something different here, after all. Not just creating a new colony from the old-line colony worlds, but mixing ten different cultures into one colony. To be entirely honest about it, I have my reservations. I think the Department of Colonization should have taken my original suggestion and let just one of the colonies field settlers."

"That's bureaucracy for you," I said. "Always messing up perfect plans."

"Yes, well," Trujillo said, and waved his hand slightly, to encompass the polyglot settlers, and possibly me. "We both know this is as much about my feud with Secretary Bell as anything else. She was against Roanoke from the start, but there was too much momentum from the colonies for her to stop this from happening. But there was nothing stopping her from making it as impractical as possible to manage. Including offering the colony leadership to a pair of well-meaning neophytes who have no idea where the landmines are in this situation, and who will make convenient scapegoats if the colony fails."

"You're saying we're patsies," I said.

"I'm saying that you and your wife are intelligent, competent and politically expendable," Trujillo said. "When the colony fails, the blame will fall on you, not on Bell."

"Even though she chose us," I said.

"Did she?" Trujillo said. "I heard you were suggested by General Rybicki. He's well enough insulated from political fallout because he's CDF, and they're not re-quired to care about politics. No, when the shit hits, Perry, it's going to roll downhill, right onto you and your wife."

"You're sure the colony will fail," I said. "And yet, here you are."

"I'm sure the colony *could* fail," Trujillo said. "And I'm sure there are those—Secretary Bell among them—who would be happy to see it fail, as payback against their political enemies and to cover up their own incom-petence. They certainly designed it to fail. What can keep it from failing are people with the will and *experi-ence* to help it survive."

"Someone like you, for example," I said.

Trujillo took a step closer to me. "Perry, I understand it's *easy* to think that this is all just about my ego. Really, I do. But I want you to consider something else for a moment. There are twenty-five hundred people on this ship who are here because six years ago I stood up in the CU representa-tive chamber and demanded our colonization rights. I am responsible for their being here, and because I was power-less to stop Bell and her cronies from jury-rigging this colony to self-destruct, I'm responsible for putting these people in danger. This morning, I wasn't suggesting you let us help with colony administration just because I need to run things. I was suggesting it because given what the DoC has given you to work with, you're going to need all the help you can get, and those of us in that room with you this morning have been living with this for years. If we don't help you, the alternative is failure, straight and sure."

"I appreciate the confidence in our leadership skills," I said.

"You're not hearing what I'm saying," Trujillo said. "Damn it, Perry, I want you to succeed. I want this *colony* to succeed. The very last thing I want to do is un-dermine the leadership of you and your wife. If I did that, I'd be jeopardizing the lives of everyone in the colony. I'm not your enemy. I want to help you fight the people who are."

"You're saying the Department of Colonization would put twenty-five hundred people at risk to get back at you," I said.

"No," Trujillio said. "Not to get back at me. But to counter a threat to its colonial practices? To help the CU keep the colonies in their place? Twenty-five hundred colonists are not too many for a thing like that. If you know anything about colonization, you know twenty-five hundred colonists is the standard size for a seed colony. We lose seed colonies from time to time; we expect to lose a few. We're *used* to it. It's not *twenty-five hundred* people, it's just *one* seed colony.

"But this is where it gets interesting. One seed colony lost is well within expectations for DoC colonization protocols. But the colonists come from ten different CU worlds, all of which are colonizing for the first time. Each of those worlds will feel the failure of the colony. It's a blow to the national psyche. And then the DoC can turn around and say, this is why we don't let you colonize. To protect you. They'll spoon-feed that argument to the colonies, all the colonies will swallow it down, and we'll be back to the status quo."

"It's an interesting theory," I said.

"Perry, you were in the Colonial Defense Forces for years," Trujillo said. "You know the end results of CU policies. Can you honestly tell me, with all your experience, that the scenario I've outlined for you is completely outside the realm of possibility?"

I kept quiet. Trujillo smiled grimly. "Food for thought, Perry," he said. "Something for you to consider the next time you and your wife are slamming the door on the rest of us at one of our advisory meetings. I trust you'll do what you think is best for the colony." He glanced over my shoulder, looking at something beyond it. "I think our daughters have met," he said.

I turned around to see Zoë talking animatedly with one of the girls I had seen earlier; she was the one who had beckoned Zoë over. "It appears they have," I said.

"They seem to get along," Trujillo said. "Our Roanoke colony starts there, I think. Maybe we can follow their example."

"I'm not sure I can swallow the idea of a selfless Manfred Trujillo," Jane said. She had propped herself up in bed. Babar lolled at the end of the bed, his tail thumping contentedly.

"That's two of us," I said. I was sitting in the chair next to the bed. "The problem is I can't entirely discount what he's saying, either."

"Why not?" Jane said. She began to reach for the pitcher of water she had at the bedside table, but was awkwardly positioned. I took the pitcher and the glass next to it and started pouring.

"You remember what Hickory said about Roanoke planet," I said, handing her the glass.

"Thanks," she said, and downed the entire glass in about five seconds.

"Wow," I said. "You sure you're feeling better?"

"I'm fine," she said. "I'm just thirsty." She handed the glass back to me; I poured her more water. She sipped this one more moderately. "Roanoke planet," she said, prompting me.

"Hickory said that Roanoke planet was still under the control of the Obin," I said. "If the Department of Colonization really thinks this colony is going to fail, that might actually make sense."

"Why trade for a planet you know your colonists aren't going to keep," Jane said.

"Exactly," I said. "And there's another thing. I was in the cargo hold today, going over the manifest with the cargo chief, and he mentioned that we were packing a whole lot of obsolete equipment."

"That's probably to do with the Mennonites," Jane said, and sipped her water again.

"That's what I said, too," I said. "But after I talked to Trujillo I went through the manifest again. The cargo chief was right. There's more obsolete equipment there than we can chalk up to the Mennonites."

"We're underequipped," Jane said.

"That's the thing," I said. "We're not underequipped. We have a whole bunch of obsolete equipment, but it's not in place of more modern equipment, it's there in *addition* to it."

Jane considered this. "What do you think it means?" she asked.

"I don't know that it means anything," I said. "Supply error happens all the time. I remember one time when I was in the CDF we were shipped dress socks instead of medical supplies. Maybe this is that kind of screwup, a couple degrees of magnitude larger."

"We should ask General Rybicki about it," Jane said.

"He's off the station," I said. "He left this morning for Coral, of all places. His office says he's overseeing the diagnostics of a new planetary defense grid. He won't be back for a week standard. I asked his office to look into the colony's inventory for me. But it's not a high priority for them—it's not an obvious problem for the well-being of the colony. They have other things to worry about before we ship out. But maybe we're missing something."

"If we're missing something, we don't have a lot of time to find it," Jane said.

"I know," I said. "As much as I'd like to peg Trujillo as just another self-aggrandizing prick, we have to work on the theory that he might actually have the interests of the colony at heart. It's galling, all things considered."

"There's the possibility he's a self-aggrandizing prick *and* he has the interests of the colony at heart," Jane said.

"You always look on the bright side," I said.

"Have Savitri go through the manifest with an eye toward what we might be missing," Jane said. "I had her do a lot of research on recent seed colonies. If there's something missing, she'll find it."

"You're giving her a lot of work," I said.

Jane shrugged. "You always underutilized Savitri," Jane said. "That's why I hired her. She was capable of a lot more than you gave her. Although it's not entirely your fault. The worst you had to deal with were those idiot Chengelpet brothers."

"You're just saying that because you never had to deal with them," I said. "You should have tried it, one time."

"If I had dealt with them, one time would be all I needed," Jane said.

"How was your thing today with General Szilard?" I asked, changing the subject before my competence could be questioned further.

"It was fine," Jane said. "He was saying some of the things Trujillo was saying to you today, actually."

"That the DoC wants the colony to fail?" I asked.

"No," Jane said. "That there's a lot of political maneuvering going on that you and I don't know much about."

"Like what?" I asked.

"He didn't get into specifics," Jane said. "He said that was because he was confident in our ability to handle things. He asked me if I wanted my old Special Forces body back, just in case."

"That General Szilard," I said. "A first-class kidder."

"He wasn't entirely joking," Jane said, and then raised a placating hand when I gave her my best confused look. "He doesn't have my old body on hand. That's not what I mean. He just means he'd prefer not to have me go to this colony with an unmodified human body."

"That's a cheerful thought," I said. I noticed Jane had begun to sweat. I felt her forehead. "I think you actually have a fever. That's new."

"Unmodified body," Jane said. "Had to happen sometime."

"I'll get you some more water," I said.

"No," Jane said. "I'm not thirsty. I feel like I'm starving, though."

"I'll see if I can get you something from the galley," I said. "What do you want?"

"What have they got?" Jane said.

"Pretty much everything," I said.

"Good," Jane said. "I'll have one of everything."

I reached for my PDA to contact the galley. "It's a good thing the *Magellan* is carrying a double load of food," I said.

"The way I feel right now, it won't be carrying it for long," Jane said.

"All right," I said. "But I think the old saying is that you should starve a fever."

"In this case," Jane said. "The old saying is dead wrong."

FOUR "It's like a New Year's Eve party," Zoë said, looking around the recreation deck from our perch on a small dais, at the mass of colonists celebrating around us. After a week of travel by the *Magellan,* we were less than five minutes from the skip to Roanoke.

"It's *exactly* like a New Year's Eve party," I said. "When we skip, the colony's clock officially starts. It'll be second one of minute one of day one of year one, Roanoke time. Get ready for days that are twenty-five hours, eight minutes long, and years that are three hundred and five days long."

"I'll have birthdays more often," Zoë said.

"Yes," I said. "And your birthdays will last longer."

Beside me and Zoë, Savitri and Jane were discussing something Savitri had queried in her PDA. I thought of ribbing them about catching up on work, now of all times, but then I thought better of it. The two of them had quickly become the organizational nexus of the colonial leadership, which was not at all surprising. If they felt something needed to be dealt with right that moment, it probably did.

Jane and Savitri were the brains of the outfit; I was the public relations guy. Over the course of the week I spent several hours with each colonist group, answering their questions about Roanoke, myself and Jane, and anything else they wanted to know about. Each group had its quirks and curiosities. The colonists from Erie seemed a bit distant (possibly reflecting the opinion of Trujillo, who sat in the back of the group while I talked) but warmed up when I played the idiot and trotted out the fractured Spanish I learned in high school, which led to a discussion of the "new Spanish" words that had been coined on Erie for native plants and animals.

The Mennonites from Kyoto, on the other hand, started off genially by presenting me with a fruit cobbler. That pleasantry out of the way, they then grilled me mercilessly on every aspect of colonial management, much to the amusement of Hiram Yoder. "We live a simple life, but we're not simple," he told me afterward. The colonists from Khartoum were still upset about not being berthed according to planetary origin. The ones from Franklin wanted to know how much support we would have from the Colonial Union and whether they could travel back to Franklin for visits. Albion's colonists wondered what plans were in place if Roanoke were attacked. The ones from Phoenix wanted to know if I thought they would have enough time after a busy day of colonizing to start a softball league.

Questions and problems large and small, immense and trivial, critical and frivolous—all of them got pitched to me, and it was my job to gamely field them and try to help people to come away, if not satisfied with the answers, then at least satisfied that their concerns were taken seriously. In this, my recent experience as an ombudsman turned out to be invaluable. Not just because I had experience in finding answers and solving problems, but because I had several years practice in listening to people and reassuring them something would get done. By the end of our week on the *Magellan* I had colonists coming up to me to help them settle bar bets and petty annoyances; it seemed like old times.

The question-and-answer sessions and fielding issues of the individual colonists were useful for me as well—I needed to get a sense of who all these people were and how well they would mesh with each other. I didn't subscribe to Trujillo's theory of a polyglot colony as a bureaucratic sabotage tactic, but I wasn't pollyanna about harmony, either. The day the *Magellan* got under way we had at least one incident of some teenage boys from one world trying to pick a fight with some others. Gretchen Trujillo and Zoë actually mocked the boys into submission, proving that one should never underestimate the power of teenage girl scorn, but when Zoë recounted the event over dinner, both Jane and I took note of it. Teenagers can be idiotic and stupid, but teenagers also model their behavior from the signals they get from adults.

The next day we announced a dodgeball tournament for the teenagers, on the theory that dodgeball was universally played in one form or another across all the colonies. We hinted to the colony representatives that it would be nice if they could get their kids to show up. Enough did—the *Magellan* didn't have *that* much for them to do, even after just one day—that we could field ten teams of eight, which we created through random selection, casually thwarting any attempt to team up by colony. Then we created a schedule of games that would culminate with the championship match just before the skip to Roanoke. Thus we kept the teenagers occupied and, coincidentally, mixing with the kids from the other colonies.

By the end of the first day of play, the adults were watching the games; there wasn't much for *them* to do, either. By the end of the second day, I saw adults from one colony chatting up adults from other colonies about which teams had the best chance of going all the way. We were making progress.

By the end of the third day, Jane had to break up a betting ring. Okay, so maybe it wasn't *all* progress. What are you going to do.

Neither Jane nor I were under the illusion that we could create universal harmony through dodgeball, of course. That's a little much to rest on the shoulders of a game played with a bouncy red ball. Trujillo's sabotage scenario wouldn't be sent out of the game with a snappy *pong* sound. But universal harmony could wait. We would settle for people meeting and getting used to each other. Our little dodgeball tournament did that well enough.

After the dodgeball final and the award ceremony—the underdog Dragons managed a dramatic victory over the previously undefeated Slime Molds, whom I had adored for their name alone—most of the colonists stayed on the recreation deck, waiting for the few moments until the skip. The multiple announcement monitors on the deck were all broadcasting the forward view of the *Magellan*, which was a blank black now but would be filled with the image of Roanoke as soon as the skip happened. The colonists were excited and happy; when Zoë had said it was like a New Year's Eve party, she hit it right on the nose.

"How much time?" Zoë asked me.

I checked my PDA. "Whoops," I said. "A minute twenty seconds to go."

"Let me see that," Zoë said, and grabbed my PDA. Then she grabbed the microphone that I had used when I was congratulating the Dragons on their victory. "Hey!" she said, her voice amplified across the rec deck. "We've got a minute left until we skip!"

A cheer went up from the colonists, and Zoë took it on herself to count off the time in five-second intervals. Gretchen Trujillo and a pair of boys ran up to the stage and clambered up to take their places next to Zoë; one of the boys put his arm around Zoë's waist.

"Hey," I said to Jane, and pointed over to Zoë. "Do you see that?"

Jane looked over. "That must be Enzo," she said.

"Enzo?" I said. "There's an Enzo?"

"Relax, ninety-year-old dad," Jane said, and then rather uncharacteristically hooked her arm around my waist. She usually saved displays of affection for our private time. But she'd also been friskier since getting over her fever.

"You know I don't like it when you do that," I said. "It erodes my authority."

"Cram it," Jane said. I grinned.

Zoë got to the ten-second mark; she and her friends counted down each second, joined by the colonists. When everyone got to zero, there was a sudden hush as eyes and heads turned to the monitor screens. The blank blackness held for what seemed an eternity, and then it was there, a world, large and green and new.

The deck erupted in cheers. People began to hug and kiss, and for lack of a more appropriate song, belted out "Auld Lang Syne."

I turned to my wife and kissed her. "Happy new world," I said.

"Happy new world to you, too," she said. She kissed me again, and then we were both nearly knocked over by Zoë jumping between us and trying to kiss us both.

After a couple of minutes I untangled myself from Zoë and Jane, and saw Savitri staring intently at the closest monitor.

"The planet's not going anywhere," I said to her. "You can relax now."

It took a second before Savitri seemed to hear me. "What?" she said. She looked annoyed.

"I said," I began, but then she was looking at the monitor again, distracted. I came up closer to her.

"What is it?" I asked.

Savitri looked back at me and then suddenly came in close, as if to kiss me. She didn't; instead she put her lips to my ear. "That's not Roanoke," she said, quietly but urgently.

I backed up from her a step and for the first time gave the planet in the monitor my full attention. The planet was green and lush, like Roanoke. Through the clouds I could see the outline of the landmasses below. I tried recalling a map of Roanoke in my head but was drawing a blank. I had focused mostly on the river delta where the colony would live, not on the maps of the continents.

I came back over to Savitri, so our heads were close. "You're sure," I said.

"Yes," Savitri said.

"*Really* sure," I said.

"Yes," Savitri said.

"What planet is it?" I asked.

"I don't know," Savitri said. "That's just it. I don't think *anyone* knows."

"How—" Zoë barged over and demanded a hug from Savitri. Savitri gave her one but her eyes never left me.

"Zoë," I said, "can I have my PDA back?"

"Sure," Zoë said, and gave me a quick peck on the cheek as she handed it over. As I took it the message prompt began to flash. It was from Kevin Zane, captain of the *Magellan*.

"It's not in the registry," Zane said. "We've done a quick read for size and mass to match it. The closest match is

Omagh, and that is definitely not Omagh. There is no CU satellite in orbit. We haven't done an entire orbit yet, but so far there's no sign of any intelligent life, ours or anyone else's."

"There's no other way to tell what planet this is?" Jane asked. I had pulled her away from the celebration as discreetly as I could, and left Savitri to explain our absence to the rest of the colonists.

"We're mapping stars now," Zane said. "We'll start with the relative positions of the stars and see if it matches any of the skies we know. If that doesn't work we'll start doing spectral analysis. If we can find a couple of stars we know, we can triangulate our position. But that's likely to take some time. Right now, we're lost."

"At the risk of sounding like an idiot," I said, "can't you put this thing in reverse?"

"Normally we could," Zane said. "You have to know where you're going before you make a skip, so you could use that information to plot a trip back. But we programmed in the information for Roanoke. We should be there. But we're not."

"Someone got into your navigation systems," Jane said.

"More than that," said Brion Justi, the *Magellan*'s executive officer. "After we skipped, engineering was locked out of the primary engines. We can monitor the engines but we can't feed them commands, either here on the bridge or in the engine rooms. We can skip in close to a planet, but to skip out we need to get a distance away from the planet's gravity well. We're stuck."

"We're drifting?" I asked. I was not an expert on these things, but I knew that a spaceship didn't necessarily skip into perfectly stable orbits.

"We have maneuvering engines," Justi said. "We're not going to fall into the planet. But our maneuvering engines aren't going to get us to skip distance anytime soon. Even if we knew where we were, at the moment we don't have a way to get home."

"I don't think we want to make that public knowledge just yet," Zane said. "Right now the bridge crew knows about the planet and the engines; the engineering crew knows just about the engines. I informed you as soon as I confirmed both issues. But at the moment, I think that's the extent of it."

"Almost," I said. "Our assistant knows."

"You told your *assistant*?" Justi asked.

"She told us," Jane said sharply. "Before *you* did."

"Savitri isn't going to tell anyone," I said. "It's bottled up for now. But this isn't something we're going to be able to keep from people."

"I understand that," Zane said. "But we need time to get our engines back and to find out where we are. If we tell people before then, there's going to be a panic."

"That is if you can get yourself back online at all," Jane said. "And you're ignoring the larger issue, which is that this ship has been sabotaged."

"We're not ignoring it," Zane said. "When we get back control of the engines we should have a better idea of who did this."

"Did you not run diagnostics on your computers before we left?" Jane asked.

"Of course we did," Zane said testily. "We followed all standard procedures. This is what we're trying to tell you. Everything checked out. Everything *still* checks out. I had my tech officer run a full system diagnostic. The diagnostics tell us everything is fine. As far as the computers are concerned, we are at Roanoke, and we have full control of the engines."

I thought about this. "Your navigation and engine systems aren't right," I said. "What about your other systems?"

"So far, so good," Zane said. "But if whoever did this

can take away our navigation and engines and fool our computers into thinking there's no problem, they could take away *any* of the systems."

"Shut down the system," Jane said. "Emergency systems are decentralized. They should keep functioning until you reboot."

"That's not going to be very useful in not causing a panic," Justi said. "And there's no promise that we'd have control again after we reboot. Our computers think everything's fine now; they'll just revert to their current status."

"But if we don't reboot we run the risk of whoever's screwing with your engines and navigations messing with life support or gravity," I said.

"I have a feeling that if whoever did this wanted to play with life support or gravity, we'd be dead already," Zane said. "You want my opinion, there it is. I'm going to keep systems as is while we try to root out whatever it is that's locking us out of navigation and engines. I'm captain of this ship. It's my call to make. I'm asking you two to give me time to fix this before you inform your colonists."

I looked at Jane. She shrugged. "It will take us at least a day to prepare supply containers for transport down to the planet surface. Another couple of days before the majority of the colonists are ready to go. There's no reason we can't go through the motions of getting the containers ready."

"That means putting your cargo hold people to work," I said to Zane.

"As far as they know, we're where we're supposed to be," Zane said.

"Start your cargo prep tomorrow morning, then," I said. "We'll give you until the first containers are ready to make the trip to the planet. If you haven't figured out the problem then, we're talking to the colonists anyway. All right?"

"Fair enough," Zane said. One of Zane's officers came up to speak to him; he shifted his attention away. I turned my attention to Jane.

"Tell me what you're thinking," I said quietly.

"I'm thinking about what Trujillo said to you," Jane said, also keeping her voice down.

"When he said that the Department of Colonization was sabotaging the colony, I don't think he was suggesting they'd do it like this," I said.

"They would if they wanted to make the point that colonization is a dangerous business, and if someone was worried that it might actually succeed when they wanted it to fail," Jane said. "This way they have a lost colony right out of the box."

"Lost colony," I said, and then my hand went to my eyes. "Jesus Christ."

"What?" Jane said.

"Roanoke," I said. "There was a Roanoke colony on Earth. First English settlement in America."

"So?" Jane said.

"It disappeared," I said. "Its governor went back to England to ask for help and supplies, but when he returned all of the settlers were gone. The famous lost colony of Roanoke."

"Seems a bit obvious," Jane said.

"Yeah," I said. "If they really planned to lose us, I don't think they'd tip their hand like that."

"Nevertheless, we are Roanoke colony, and we are lost," Jane said.

"Irony is a bitch," I said.

"Perry, Sagan," Zane said. "Come here."

"What is it?" I asked.

"We've found someone out there," he said. "Encoded tightbeam. He's asking for the two of you."

"That's good news," I said.

Zane grunted noncommittally and pressed a button to put our caller on the intercom.

"This is John Perry," I said. "Jane Sagan and I are here."

"Hello, Major Perry," the voice said. "And hello Lieutenant Sagan! Wow, an honor to talk to you both. I'm Lieutenant Stross, Special Forces. I've been assigned to tell you what you're supposed to do next."

"You know what's happened here?" I asked.

"Let's see," Stross said. "You skipped to what you thought was Roanoke colony, only to find yourselves orbiting an entirely different planet, and now you think you're completely lost. And your Captain Zane there has found out he can't use his engines. That sound about right?"

"Yes," I said.

"Excellent," Stross said. "Well, there's good news and there's bad news. The good news is that you're not lost. We know exactly where you are. The bad news is you're not going anywhere anytime soon. I've got all the details for you when we meet, you two and Captain Zane and me. How about in fifteen minutes?"

"What do you mean, meet?" Zane said. "We're not picking up any ships in the area. We have no way of verifying who you say you are."

"Lieutenant Sagan can vouch for me," Stross said. "As for where I am, clip in a feed from your external camera fourteen and turn on a light."

Zane looked exasperated and confused, and then nodded over to one of his bridge officers. Zane's overhead monitor blinked to life, showing a portion of the starboard hull. It was dark until a floodlight clicked on and scooped out a cone of light.

"I'm not seeing anything but hull," Zane said.

Something flickered, and suddenly there was a turtle-like object in the camera, floating a foot or so off the hull.

"What the hell is that?" Zane said.

The turtle waved.

"Son of a bitch," Jane said.

"You know what that thing is?" Zane said.

Jane nodded. "That's a Gameran," she said, turning to Zane. "That's Lieutenant Stross. He's telling the truth about who he is. And I think we have just entered a world of shit."

"Wow, air," said Lieutenant Stross, waving his hand back and forth in the expanse of the shuttle bay. "I don't get to feel this much." Stross was floating lazily in the air he was grooving on, thanks to Zane having cut the gravity in the bay to accommodate Stross, who lived primarily in microgravity situations.

Jane explained it to me and Zane, as we took the elevator to the shuttle bay. Gamerans were humans—or at least, their DNA originated from human stock and had other things added in—radically sculpted and designed to live and thrive in airless space. To that end they had shelled bodies to protect them from vacuum and cosmic rays, symbiotic genetically altered algae stored in a special organ to provide them with oxygen, photosynthetic stripes to harness solar energy and hands on the ends of all their limbs. And, they were Special Forces soldiers. All those rumors in the general CDF infantry about wildly mutant Special Forces turned out to be more than rumors. I thought of my friend Harry Wilson, who I met when I first joined the CDF; he lived for this sort of stuff. I'd have to tell him the next time I saw him. If I ever saw him again.

Despite being a Special Forces soldier, Stross acted deeply informal, from his vocal mannerisms (*vocal* being a figurative term; vocal cords would be useless in space, so he didn't have any—his "voice" was generated in the BrainPal computer in his head and transmitted to our PDAs) to his apparent tendency to get distracted. There was a word for what he was.

Spacey.

Zane didn't waste any time on courtesy. "I want to know how the hell you got control of my ship," he said, to Stross.

"Blue pill," Stross said, still waving his hand about. "It's code that creates a virtual machine on your hardware. Your software runs on top of it, and never even knows it's not running on the hardware. That's why it can't tell anything's wrong."

"Get it off my computers," Zane said. "And then get off my boat."

Stross held open three of his hands, the other one still cutting air. "Do I look like a computer programmer to you?" he asked. "I don't know how to code it, I just know how to operate it. And my orders come from someone who outranks you. Sorry, Captain."

"How did you get here?" I asked. "I know you're adapted to space. But I'm pretty sure you don't have a Skip Drive in there."

"I hitched a ride with you," Stross said. "I've been sitting on the hull for the last ten days, waiting for you to skip." He tapped his shell. "Embedded nano-camo," he said. "Reasonably new trick. If I don't want you to notice me, you won't."

"You were on the hull for ten days?" I asked.

"It's not that bad," Stross said. "I kept busy by studying for my doctorate. Comparative literature. Keeps me busy. Distance learning, obviously."

"That's nice for you," Jane said. "But I'd prefer to focus on *our* situation." Her voice snapped out, cold, a counterpoint to Zane's hot fury.

"All right," Stross said. "I've just zapped the relevant files and orders to your PDAs, so you can peruse them at your leisure. But here's the deal: The planet you thought was Roanoke was a decoy. The planet you're over now is the *real* Roanoke colony. This is where you'll colonize."

"But we don't know anything about this planet," I said.

"It's all in the files," Stross said. "It's mostly a better planet for you than the other one. The life chemistry is right in line with our food needs. Well, *your* food needs. Not mine. You can start grazing right away."

"You said the other planet was a decoy," Jane said. "A decoy for what?"

"That's complicated," Stross said.

"Try me," Jane said.

"All right," Stross said. "For starters, do you know what the Conclave is?"

FIVE Jane looked like she'd been slapped.

"What? What is it? What is the Conclave?" I asked. I looked over to Zane, who opened his hands apologetically. He didn't know, either.

"They got it off the ground," Jane said, after a pause.

"Oh, yeah," Stross said.

"What is the Conclave?" I repeated.

"It's an organization of races," Jane said, still looking over at Stross. "The idea was to band together to control this part of space and to keep other races from colonizing." She turned to me. "The last I heard about it was just before you and I went to Huckleberry."

"You knew about this and you didn't tell me," I said.

"Orders," Jane said; it came out snappishly. "It was part of the deal I had. I got to leave the Special Forces on my terms, provided I forgot everything I'd ever heard about the Conclave. I couldn't have told you even if I had wanted to. And anyway, there was nothing to tell. Everything was still in the preliminary stages and from what I knew, it wasn't going anywhere. And I learned about it through Charles Boutin. He wasn't the most credible observer of interstellar politics."

Jane seemed genuinely angry; whether at me or the situation I couldn't tell. I decided not to push it and turned toward Stross. "But now the Conclave thing is a growing concern."

"It is," Stross said. "For over two years now. The first thing it did was warn every species who wasn't part of the Conclave not to colonize anymore."

"Or what?" Zane asked.

"Or the Conclave would wipe out their new colonies," Stross said. "That's the reason for the switcheroo here. We led the Conclave to believe we were forming a colony and settling it on one world. But in fact we sent the colony to another world entirely. One that isn't in the records or on the charts or that anyone knows about, other than a few very highly placed people. And me, because I'm here to tell you this. And now you. The Conclave was all set to attack Roanoke colony before you could even get your people on the ground. Now they can't attack you because they can't find you. It makes the Conclave look foolish and weak. And that makes *us* look better. That's the thinking as I understand it."

Now it was my turn to get angry. "So the Colonial Union is playing hide-and-seek with this Conclave," I said. "That's just *jolly.*"

"*Jolly*'s a word," Stross said. "I don't think it'll be so jolly if they find you, though."

"And how long is that going to take?" I asked. "If this is as much of a blow to the Conclave as you say, they're going to come looking for us."

"You're right about that," Stross said. "And when they

find you, they're going to wipe you out. So now it's our job to make you hard to find. And I think this is the part you're really not going to like."

"Point number one," I said, to the representatives of Roanoke colony. "No contact whatsoever between Roanoke colony and the rest of the Colonial Union."

The table erupted into chaos.

Jane and I sat on either end, waiting for the fracas to calm. It took a few minutes.

"That's insane," said Marie Black.

"I agree entirely," I said. "But every time there's a contact between Roanoke and any other colony world, it leaves a trail back to us. Spaceships have crews that number in the hundreds. It's not realistic that none of those would talk to friends or spouses. And you all already know that people will be looking for us. Your former governments and your families and the press will all be looking for someone who can give them a clue to where we are. If anyone can point a finger back to us, this Conclave will find us."

"What about the *Magellan*?" asked Lee Chen. "It's going back."

"Actually, no, it's not," I said. This news received a low gasp. I remembered the absolute fury in Captain Zane's face when Stross told him this bit of information. Zane threatened to disobey the order; Stross reminded him he had no control over the ship's engines, and that if he and the crew didn't head to the surface with the rest of the colonists, they'd discover they had no control over life support, either. It was a fairly ugly moment.

It got worse when Stross told Zane the plan was to get rid of the *Magellan* by driving it right into the sun.

"The crew of the *Magellan* have families back in the

CU," said Hiram Yoder. "Spouses. Children."

"They do," I said. "That will give you an idea how serious this is."

"Can we afford them?" asked Manfred Trujillo. "I'm not saying we refuse them. But the colony stores were meant for twenty-five hundred colonists. Now we're adding, what, another two hundred?"

"Two hundred and six," said Jane. "It's not a problem. We shipped with half again as much food stores as are usual for a colony this size, and this world has plant and animal life we can eat. Hopefully."

"How long will this isolation continue?" asked Black.

"Indefinitely," I said. Another grumble. "Our survival depends on isolation. It's just that simple. But in some ways that makes things easier. Seed colonies have to prepare for the next wave of colonists two or three years down the line. We don't have to worry about that now. We can focus on what our needs are. That'll make a difference."

There was glum agreement to this. For the moment that was the best I could hope for.

"Point two," I said, and tensed up for the backlash. "No use of technology that can give away the existence of our colony from space."

This time they didn't calm down after a few minutes.

"That's utterly ridiculous," said Paulo Gutierrez, eventually. "*Anything* that has a wireless connection is potentially detectable. All you have to do is sweep with a broad-spectrum signal. It'll try to connect with anything and tell you what it finds."

"I understand that," I said.

"Our entire technology is wireless," Gutierrez said. He held up his PDA. "Look at this. Not a single goddamned wired input. You couldn't connect a wire to it if you tried. All our automated equipment in the cargo hold is wireless."

"Forget the equipment," said Lee Chen. "All of my colonists are carrying an implanted locator."

"So are mine," said Marta Piro. "And they don't have an off switch."

"You're going to have to dig them out, then," Jane said.

"That's a surgical procedure," Piro said.

"Where the hell did you put them?" Jane said.

"Our colonists' shoulders," Piro said. Chen nodded at this; his colonists had theirs in the shoulder as well. "It's not a major surgery, but it's still cutting into them."

"The alternative is exposing every other colonist to the risk of being found and killed," Jane said, clipping off her words. "I guess your people are just going to have to suffer." Piro started to open her mouth to respond, but then seemed to think better of it.

"Even if we dig out the locators, there's still every other piece of equipment we have," Gutierrez said, bringing the conversation back around to him. "It's all wireless. Farm equipment. Medical equipment. All of it. What you're telling us is that we can't use *any* of the equipment we need to survive."

"Not all the equipment in the cargo hold supports a wireless connection," Hiram Yoder said. "None of the equipment we brought with us does. It's all dumb equipment. It all needs a person behind the controls. We make it work just fine."

"You have the equipment," Gutierrez said. "We don't. The rest of us don't."

"We'll share everything we can," Yoder said.

"It's not a matter of sharing," Gutierrez spat. He took a second to calm himself. "I'm sure you would try to help us," he said to Hiram. "But you brought enough equipment for *you*. There's ten times as many of the rest of us."

"We have the equipment," Jane said. Everyone at the

table looked down toward her. "I've sent you all a copy of the ship manifest. You'll see that in addition to all the modern equipment we have, we were also provided with a full complement of tools and implements that were, until today, obsolete. This tells us two things. It tells us that the Colonial Union fully intended for us to be on our own. It also tells us that they don't intend for us to *die*."

"That's one spin on the subject," Trujillo said. "Another is that they knew they were going to abandon us to this Conclave and rather than give us anything we could use to defend ourselves, told us to keep quiet and keep our heads down, and maybe the Conclave won't *hear* us." There were murmurs of agreement around the table.

"Now's not the time for that discussion," I said. "Whatever the CU's rationale, the fact is we're here and we're not going anyplace else. When we're on the planet and have the colony sorted, then we can have a discussion on what the CU's strategy means. But for now, we need to focus on what we need to do to *survive*. Now, Hiram," I said, handing him my PDA. "Among all of us, you are the one who has the best idea of the capability of this equipment for our needs. Is this workable?"

Hiram took the PDA and scrolled through the manifest for several minutes.

"It's hard to say," he said finally. "I would need to see it in front of me. And I would need to see the people who would operate it. And there are so many other factors. But I think we could make it work." He looked up and down the table. "I tell all of you now that whatever I can do to help you, I will. I can't speak for all of my brethren on the matter, but I can tell you that in my experience each of them is ready to answer the call. We can do this. We can make it work."

"There's another option," Trujillo said. All eyes went to him. "We *don't* hide. We use all the equipment we have—all the resources we have—for our survival. When and *if* this Conclave comes calling, we tell it we're a wildcat colony. No affiliation with the CU. Its war is with the Colonial Union, not a wildcat colony."

"We'd be disobeying orders," said Marie Black.

"The disconnect works both ways," Trujillo said. "If we need to be isolated, the CU can't check up on us. And even if we are disobeying orders, so what? Are we in the CDF? Are they going to shoot us? Are they going to *fire* us? And beyond that, do we here at this table honestly feel these orders are legitimate? The Colonial Union has abandoned us. What's more, they always *planned* to abandon us. They've broken faith with us. I say we do the same. I say we go wildcat."

"I don't think you know what you're saying when you say we should go wildcat," Jane said to Trujillo. "The last wildcat colony I was at had all its colonists slaughtered for food. We found the bodies of children in a stack, waiting to be butchered. Don't kid yourself. Going wildcat is a death sentence." Jane's statement hung in the air for several seconds, daring anyone to refute it.

"There are risks," Trujillo finally said, taking up the challenge. "But we're *alone*. We are a wildcat colony in everything but name. And we don't know that this Conclave of yours is as horrible as the Colonial Union has made it out to be. The CU has been deceiving us all this time. It has no credibility. We can't trust it to have our interests at heart."

"So you want proof the Conclave means us harm," Jane said.

"It'd be nice," Trujillo said.

Jane turned to me. "Show them," she said.

"Show us what?" asked Trujillo.

"This," I said. From my PDA—which I would soon no longer be able to use—I turned on the large wall monitor and fed it a video file. It showed a creature on a hill or bluff. Beyond the creature was what looked like a small town. It was bathed entirely in blinding light.

"The village you see is a colony," I said. "It was established by the Whaid, not long after the Conclave told the nonaffiliated races to stop colonizing. The Conclave jumped the gun, because it couldn't enforce its decree at the time. So some of the nonaffiliated races colonized anyway. But now the Conclave is catching up."

"Where is that light coming from?" asked Lee Chen.

"It's coming from the Conclave ships in orbit," Jane said. "It's a terror tactic. It disorients the enemy."

"There's got to be a lot of ships up there," Chen said.

"Yes," Jane said.

The beams of light illuminating the Whaidian colony suddenly snapped off.

"Here it comes," I said.

The killing beams were hardly detectable at first; they were tuned for destruction, not for show, and nearly all their energy went into their targets, not out to the camera. There was only a waver in the air from the sudden heat, visible even at the distance the camera sat.

Then, within a fraction of a second, the entire colony ignited and exploded. Superheated air blew the fragments and the dust of the colony's buildings, structures, vehicles and inhabitants up into the sky in a whirling display that illuminated the power of the beams themselves. The flickering fragments of matter mimicked and mirrored the flames that were now themselves reaching up toward the heavens.

A shock wave of heat and dust expanded out from the charred remains of the colony. The beams flickered off again. The light show in the sky disappeared, leaving behind smoke and flames. Outside the periphery of the destruction, an occasional solitary eruption of flame would appear.

"What is that?" asked Yoder.

"Some of the colonists were outside the colony when it was destroyed, we think," I said. "So they're cleaning them up."

"Christ," Gutierrez said. "With the colony destroyed those people would probably be dead anyway."

"They were making a point," Jane said.

I turned off the video. The room was dead silent.

Trujillo pointed at my PDA. "How did we get that?" he asked.

"The video?" I asked. He nodded. "Apparently, this was hand-delivered to the CU State Department, and to every non-Conclave-affiliated government, by messengers from the Conclave itself."

"Why would they do that?" Trujillo said. "Why would they show themselves committing an . . . *atrocity* like this?"

"So there's no doubt they mean what they say," I said. "What this says to me is that no matter what we think of the Colonial Union at the moment, we can't afford to work on the assumption that the Conclave will act reasonably toward us. The CU has thumbed its nose at these guys, and they're not going to be able to ignore that. They're going to come looking for us. We don't want to give them an opportunity to find us." This was met with more silence.

"Now what?" asked Marta Piro.

"I think you need to have a vote," I said.

Trujillo looked up, a slight look of incredulity on his face. "I beg your pardon," he said. "I almost thought I heard *you* say *we* should have a vote."

"The plan on the table right now is the one we've just put in front of you," I said. "The one that was given to Jane and me. In light of everything, I think it's the best plan we've got for now. But it's not going to work if all of you don't agree. You are going to have to go back to your colonists to explain this. You are going to have to sell this to them. If this colony is going to work, everyone has to be on board with this. And that starts with all of you."

I stood up; Jane followed. "This is a discussion you need to have without us," I said. "We'll be waiting outside." We left.

"Is there something wrong?" I asked Jane, as we exited.

"Is that a serious question?" Jane snapped. "We're stranded outside of known space waiting for the Conclave to find us and burn us into the ground, and you're asking me if there's something *wrong*."

"I'm asking if there's something wrong with *you*," I said. "You were jumping down everyone's throat in there. We're in a bad situation but you and I need to stay focused. And diplomatic, if at all possible."

"You're the diplomatic one," Jane said.

"Fine," I said. "But you're not helping me."

Jane appeared to be counting to ten in her head. And then again. "I'm sorry," she said. "You're right. I'm sorry."

"Tell me what's going on," I said.

"Not now," Jane said. "Later. When we're by ourselves."

"We *are* by ourselves," I said.

"Turn around," Jane said. I turned. Savitri was there. I turned back to Jane, but she had walked away for a moment.

"Everything okay?" Savitri asked, watching Jane walk off.

"If I knew I would tell you," I said. I waited for a snappy comeback from Savitri. It didn't come, which in itself told me about Savitri's frame of mind. "Has anyone noticed our planet problem?" I asked her.

"I don't think so," Savitri said. "Most people are like you—sorry—and they don't actually know what the planet looks like. Now, your absence has been noted. Yours and all the colony reps' as well. But no one seems to think there's anything sinister about it. You people are supposed to meet and talk about the colony, after all. I do know Kranjic is looking for you, but I think he's just looking for a quote from you about the celebration and the skip."

"Okay," I said.

"Anytime you want to tell me what else is going on, that would be fine, too," Savitri said. I started to give a rote, flip response and froze when I saw the look in her eye. "Soon, Savitri," I said. "I promise. We just have a couple things to work out."

"All right, boss," Savitri said. She relaxed just a little.

"Do me a favor," I said. "Track down Hickory or Dickory for me. I need to talk to them about something."

"You think they know something about this?" Savitri asked.

"I know they know something about this," I said. "I just need to find out how much they know. Tell them to meet me in my quarters later."

"Will do," Savitri said. "I'll find Zoë. They're always within a thirty-meter radius of her. I think it's beginning to annoy her, too. Seems they make her new boyfriend nervous."

"This would be that Enzo kid," I said.

"That's the one," Savitri said. "Nice boy."

"When we land I think I'll have Hickory and Dickory take him for a nice long walk," I said.

"I think it's interesting that in the middle of a crisis you can still think of ways to hamstring a boy sweet on your daughter," Savitri said. "In a twisted way it's almost admirable."

I grinned. Savitri grinned back, which was my hope and intent. "One has to have priorities," I said. Savitri rolled her eyes and left.

A few minutes later Jane reappeared, carrying two cups. She handed one to me. "Tea," she said. "Peace offering."

"Thanks," I said, taking it.

Jane motioned toward the door, where the colony reps were. "Any news?"

"Nothing," I said. "I haven't even been listening in."

"Do you have any plan for what you're going to do if they decide our plan is full of crap?" Jane asked.

"I'm glad you asked," I said. "I haven't the slightest idea what to do then."

"Thinking ahead, I see," Jane said, and sipped her tea.

"Don't sass me," I said. "That's Savitri's job."

"Look. Here comes Kranjic," Jane said, motioning down the hall, where the reporter had appeared, Beata as ever in tow. "If you want, I could just take him out for you."

"But that would leave Beata a widow," I said.

"I don't think she would mind," Jane said.

"We'll let him live for now," I said.

"Perry, Sagan," Kranjic said. "Look, I know I'm not your favorite person, but do you think you might give me a line or two about the skip? I promise I'll make you look nice."

The door to the conference room opened, and Trujillo looked out.

"Hold on, Jann," I said to Kranjic. "I'll have something for you in a minute." Jane and I went back into the conference room; I heard Kranjic give an audible sigh before we closed the door.

I turned to the colonist reps. "Well?" I asked.

"There wasn't much to discuss," Trujillo said. "We've decided that for now, at least, we should do as the Colonial Union suggested."

"Okay, good," I said. "Thank you."

"What we want to know from you now is what we should tell our people," Trujillo said.

"Tell them the truth," Jane said. "All of it."

"You were just saying how the CU has been deceiving us," I said to Trujillo. "Let's not go down the same road."

"You want us to tell them everything," Trujillo said.

"Everything," I said. "Hold that thought." I opened the door and called Kranjic. He and Beata entered the room. "Start with him," I said, gesturing to Kranjic.

They all looked at him.

"So," Kranjic said. "What's up?"

"The *Magellan*'s crew will be the last people down," I said to Jane. I had just come back from a logistics meeting with Zane and Stross; Jane and Savitri had been busy reprioritizing the colony's equipment based on our new situation. But for the moment, it was just me, Jane and Babar, who as a dog was happily resistant to the stress around him. "After they're down, Stross will set the *Magellan* to drive itself into the sun. No muss, no fuss, no sign of us."

"What's going to happen to Stross?" Jane said. She wasn't looking at me; she sat at the stateroom table, tapping it gently.

"He said he was going to 'hang out,'" I said. Jane looked up at me quizzically. I shrugged. "He's adapted to live in space," I said. "That's what he's going to do. He said his doctorate research would keep him busy until someone came to get him."

"He thinks someone is coming to get him," Jane said. "That's optimism for you."

"It's nice someone has optimism," I said. "Although

Stross didn't really seem to be the pessimist type."

"Yeah," Jane said. Her tapping changed rhythm. "What about the Obin?"

"Oh, well," I said, remembering my earlier conversation with Hickory and Dickory. "*That*. Seems the two of them know all about the Conclave, but were forbidden from sharing the information because *we* didn't know anything about them. Basically, not unlike some spouses of mine I could name."

"I'm not going to apologize for that," Jane said. "It was part of the deal I made to be with you and Zoë. It seemed fair at the time."

"I'm not asking you to apologize," I said, as gently as I could. "I'm just frustrated. From what I read in the files Stross gave us this Conclave has hundreds of races in it. It's the single largest organization in the history of the universe as far as I can see. It's been coming together for decades, since back when I was on Earth. And I learned about its existence only now. I don't know how that's possible."

"You weren't meant to know," Jane said.

"This is something that spans all of our known space," I said. "You can't hide something like this."

"Of course you can," Jane said, and her tapping suddenly stopped. "The Colonial Union does it all the time. Think about how colonies communicate. They can't talk to each other directly; there's too much space between them. They have to compile their communication and send it in spaceships from one colony to another. The Colonial Union controls all ship travel in human space. All information bottlenecks into the Colonial Union. When you control communication, you can hide anything you want."

"I don't think that's really true," I said. "Sooner or later, everything leaks. Back on Earth—" Jane suddenly snorted. "What?" I asked.

"You," Jane said. " 'Back on Earth.' If any place in human space can be described as profoundly ignorant, it's Earth." She motioned her hand, encompassing the room. "How much of *any* of this did you know about, back on Earth? Think back. You and every other CDF recruit signed up completely ignorant of how things are out here. You didn't even know how they were going to make it possible for you to *fight*. The Colonial Union keeps Earth *isolated*, John. No communication with the rest of the human worlds. No information either way. The Colonial Union doesn't just hide the rest of the universe from Earth. It hides Earth from the rest of the universe."

"It's humanity's home," I said. "Of course the CU wants to keep its profile low."

"For fuck's sake," Jane said, genuinely irritated. "You can't possibly be so stupid as to believe that. The CU doesn't hide Earth because it has *sentimental value*. The CU hides Earth because it's a *resource*. It's a factory that spits out an endless supply of colonists and soldiers, none of whom has the smallest idea what's out *here*. Because it's not in the Colonial Union's interest to have them know. So they don't. *You* didn't. You were just as ignorant as the rest of them. So don't tell me you can't hide these things. The surprising thing isn't that the Colonial Union hid the Conclave from you. The surprising thing is that it's telling you about it at *all*."

Jane resumed her tapping for a moment and then slapped her hand down on the table, hard. "Fuck!" she said, and put her head in her hands and sat there, clearly furious.

"I really want to know what's going on with you right now," I said.

"It's not you," she said. "I'm not angry with you."

"That's good to hear," I said. "Although since you just called me ignorant and stupid, you can understand why I wonder if you're telling me the truth about that."

Jane reached out a hand to me. "Come here," she said. I walked over to the table. She put my hand on it.

"I want you to do something for me," she said. "I want you to hit the table as hard as you can."

"Why?" I asked.

"Please," Jane said. "Just do it."

The table was standard carbon fiber with a veneer of printed wood: cheap, durable and not easily breakable. I made my hand into a fist and brought it down hard on the table. It made a muffled thump, and my forearm ached a bit from the impact. The table rattled a bit but was otherwise fine. From the bed, Babar looked over to see what idiocy I was up to.

"Ow," I said.

"I'm about as strong as you," Jane said, tonelessly.

"I suppose," I said. I stepped away from the table, rubbing my arm. "You're in better shape than me, though. You might be a bit stronger."

"Yeah," Jane said, and from her sitting position hammered her hand down on the table. The table broke with a report like a rifle shot. Half the tabletop sheared off and spun across the room, putting a divot in the door. Babar whined and backed himself up on the bed.

I gaped at my wife, who stared impassively at what remained of the table.

"That son of a bitch Szilard," she said, invoking the name of the head of the Special Forces. "He knew what they had planned for us. Stross is one of his people. So he had to know. He knew what we would be up against. And he decided to give me a Special Forces body, whether I wanted one or not."

"How?" I asked.

"We had lunch," Jane said. "He must have put them in my food." Colonial Defense Forces bodies were upgradable—to an extent—and the upgrades were often accomplished with injections or infusions of nanobots that would repair and improve tissues. The CDF didn't use nanobots to repair normal human bodies, but there was no technical bar to doing it—or using the nanobots to make body changes. "It had to have been a tiny amount. Just enough to get them in me, where more could grow."

A light clicked on my head. "You had a fever."

Jane nodded, still not looking at me. "The fever. And I was hungry and dehydrated the entire time."

"When did you notice this?" I asked.

"Yesterday," Jane said. "I kept bending and breaking things. I gave Zoë a hug and I had to stop because she complained I was hurting her. I tapped Savitri on the shoulder and she wanted to know why I hit her. I felt clumsy all day. And then I saw *Stross*," Jane almost spat the name, "and I realized what it was. I wasn't clumsy, I was *changed*. Changed back to what I was. I didn't tell you, because I didn't think it mattered. But since then it's been in my head. I can't get it out of there. I'm changed."

Jane looked up at me, finally. Her eyes were wet. "I don't *want* this," she said, fiercely. "I left it when I chose a life with Zoë and with you. It was my choice to leave it, and it *hurt* to leave it. To leave everyone I knew behind." She tapped the side of her head to signify the BrainPal she no longer carried. "To leave their *voices* behind after having them with me. To be alone like that for the first time. It hurt to learn the limits of these bodies, to learn all the things I couldn't do anymore. But I *chose* it. Accepted it. Tried to see the beauty of it. And for the first time in my life I knew my life was more than what was directly in front of me. I learned to see the constellations, not just the stars. My life is your life and Zoë's life. All of our lives. All of it. It made it worth everything I left."

I went to Jane and held her. "It's all right," I said.

"No, it's not," Jane said. She gave a small, bitter laugh. "I know what Szilard was thinking, you know. He thought he was helping me—helping *us*—by making me more than human. He just doesn't know what I know. When you make someone more than human, you make them less than human, too. I've spent all this time learning to be human. And he takes it away without a second thought."

"You're still you," I said. "That doesn't change."

"I hope you're right," Jane said. "I hope that it's enough."

SIX   "This planet smells like an armpit," Savitri said.

"Nice," I said. I was still putting on my boots when Savitri had walked up. I finally yanked them on and stood.

"Tell me I'm wrong," Savitri said. Babar roused himself and walked over to Savitri, who gave him a pat.

"It's not that you're wrong," I said. "I just thought you might have a little more awe at being on an entirely new world."

"I live in a tent and pee in a bucket," Savitri said. "And then I have to carry the bucket across the entire camp to a processing tank so we can extract the urea for fertilizer. Maybe I'd have more awe for the planet if I didn't spend a fair portion of my day hauling my own waste across it."

"Try not to pee so much," I said.

"Oh, thanks," Savitri said. "You've just sliced through the Gordian knot with *that* solution. No wonder you're in charge."

"The bucket thing is only temporary, anyway," I said.

"That's what you told me two weeks ago," Savitri said.

"Well, I apologize, Savitri," I said. "I should have realized that two weeks is more than enough time for an entire colony to go from founding to baroque indolence."

"Not having to pee in a bucket is not indolence," Savitri said. "It's one of the hallmarks of civilization, along with having solid walls. And taking baths, which everyone in this colony has taken too few of recently, I'll tell you that."

"Now you know why the planet smells like an armpit," I said.

"It smelled like an armpit to start," Savitri said. "We're just adding to the funk."

I stood there and inhaled greatly through my nostrils, making a show of enjoying the air. Rather unfortunately for me, however, Savitri was right; Roanoke did, in fact, smell all too much like an armpit, so it was all that I could do not to gag after filling my lungs. That being said, I was enjoying the sour look on Savitri's face too much to admit to swooning from the smell.

"Aah," I said, exhaling. I managed not to cough.

"I hope you choke," Savitri said.

"Speaking of which," I said, and ducked back into the tent to retrieve my own nightpail, "I've got some business of my own to take care of. Walk with me to dump this?"

"I'd prefer not to," Savitri said.

"I'm sorry," I said. "I made that sound like a question. Come on." Savitri sighed and walked with me down the avenue of our little village of Croatoan, toward the waste digester, Babar tagging along at our heels, except when he broke off to say hello to kids. Babar was the only dog in the colony who was not a herding dog; he had the time to make friends. This made him both popular and chunky.

"Manfred Trujillo told me that our little village is based on a Roman legion camp," Savitri said, as we walked.

"It's true," I said. "It was his idea, actually." And a good one. The village was rectangular, with three avenues running the length of the camp parallel to each other and a fourth avenue (Dare Avenue) bisecting them. In the center was a communal mess hall (in which our carefully monitored food supply was doled out in shifts), a small square where the kids and teens tried to keep themselves occupied, and the administrative tent that doubled as home for me, Jane and Zoë.

On either side of Dare Avenue were rows of tents, each housing up to ten people, usually a pair of families plus any additional singles or couples we could stick in. Sure, it was inconvenient, but it was also crowded. Savitri had been bunked in a tent with three families of three, all of whom had infant and toddler-aged children; part of the reason for her sour disposition was that she was running on about three hours of sleep a night. Since the days on Roanoke were twenty-six hours, six minutes long, this wasn't a good thing.

Savitri pointed to the edge of the village. "I guess the Roman legions didn't use storage containers as a perimeter barrier," she said.

"Probably not," I said. "But that was their loss." Using the storage containers as a perimeter had been Jane's idea. In the Roman days, the legionnaires' camp would be encircled by a ditch and a palisade, to keep out the Huns and the wolves. We didn't have any Huns, or their equivalent (yet), but there had been some reports of large animals wandering out in the grass, and we also didn't want kids or teens (or certain incautious adults, who had already made their presence known) wandering off into the vegetation a klick away from the village. The storage containers were ideal for this purpose; they were tall and sturdy and there were lots of them—enough to circle the encampment twice, with appropriate spacing between the two layers to allow our angry, marooned cargo hold crew to unload inventory when needed.

Savitri and I made it to the western border of Croatoan, beyond which lay a small and fast stream. For that reason this edge of the village held its only plumbing so far. In the northwest corner a pipe carried in water to a filtration cistern, which churned out potable water for drinking and cooking; it also fed into two shower stalls at which a one-minute time limit for individuals (and three minutes for families) was strictly enforced by everyone else waiting in line. At the southwest corner was a septic digester—a small one, not the one Chief Ferro pointed out to me—into which every colonist dumped their nightpails. During the day they availed themselves of the portable toilets that surrounded the digester. There was almost always a line at these, too.

I walked over to the digester and poured the contents down a chute, holding my breath as I did so; the digester did not smell of roses. The digester took our waste and processed it into sterile fertilizer that was being collected and stored, and also into clean water, most of which was dumped into the stream. There was some discussion about whether to reroute the processed water back into the camp's supply; the general feeling was that clean or not, the colonists were under enough stress without having to drink or bathe in their own processed pee. It was a fair point. A small amount of the water, however, was held back to rinse and clean the nightpails. It's life in the big city.

Savitri jerked her thumb down the west wall as I walked back to her. "Planning to shower anytime soon?" she asked. "I mean, no offense, but for you smelling like an armpit would be a step up."

"How long are you planning to be like this?" I asked.

"Until the very day I get indoor plumbing," Savitri said. "Which, in itself, would imply I had an indoor in which to put it."

"It's the Roanoke dream," I said.

"Which isn't going to be able to *start* until we get all these colonists out of this tent city and into their home-steads," Savitri said.

"You're not the first person to mention this to me," I said. I was about to say more but was interrupted as Zoë crossed our path. "There you are," she said, and then thrust her hand at me, which was filled with something. "Look. I found a pet," she said.

I looked at the something in her hand. It stared back. It looked a little like a rat that got caught in a taffy puller. Its most distinguishing characteristics were its four oval eyes, two on either side of its head, and the fact that it, like every other vertebrate creature we'd seen on Roanoke so far, had opposable thumbs on its three-fingered hands. It was using them to balance on Zoë's hand.

"Isn't he cute?" Zoë asked. The thing appeared to belch, which Zoë took as a sign to feed it a cracker she had stored in a pocket. It grabbed it with one hand and started chomping away.

"If you say so," I said. "Where did you find it?"

"There's a bunch of them outside the mess hall," Zoë said, showing it to Babar. He sniffed at the thing; it hissed back. "They've been watching us as we eat." This rang a bell with me; suddenly I was aware I had been seeing them too over the last week. "I think they were hungry," Zoë continued. "Gretchen and I went out to feed them, but they all ran away. Except for this guy. He came right up and took a cracker from me. I think I'll keep him."

"I'd prefer you didn't," I said. "You don't know where it's been."

"Sure I do," Zoë said. "He's been around the mess hall."

"You're missing my point," I said.

"I got your point, ninety-year-old dad," Zoë said. "But come on. If it were going to inject me with poison and try to eat me, it probably would have done it by now." The thing in her hand finished its cracker and burped again, and then suddenly leapt out of Zoë's hand and scurried off in the direction of the storage container barricade. "Hey!" Zoë cried.

"Loyal like a puppy, that thing is," I said.

"When he comes back, I'm going to tell him all the horrible things you've said," Zoë said. "And then I'm going to let him poo on your head."

I tapped the nightpail. "No, no," I said. "That's what this is for."

Zoë curled her lip at the sight of the nightpail; she was not a big fan. "Yuck. Thanks for the image."

"Don't mention it," I said. Out of the blue, it struck me that Zoë was missing a couple of shadows. "Where are Hickory and Dickory?" I asked.

"Mom asked them to come with her to look at something," Zoë said. "Which is actually why I came looking for you. She wanted you to come look at something. She's on the other side of the barricade. By the north entrance."

"All right," I said. "Where will you be?"

"I'll be in the square, of course," Zoë said. "Where else *is* there to be?"

"Sorry, honey," I said. "I know you and your friends are bored."

"No kidding," Zoë said. "We all knew colonization was supposed to be difficult, but no one told us it was going to be *boring*."

"If you're looking for something to do, we could start up a school," I said.

"We're bored, so you suggest *school*?" Zoë said. "Who *are* you? Also, not likely, since you've confiscated all our PDAs. It's going to be hard to teach us anything when we don't have lessons."

"The Mennonites have books," I said. "Old-fashioned ones. With pages and everything."

"I know," Zoë said. "They're the only ones not going completely insane with boredom, too. God, I miss my PDA."

"The irony must be crushing," I said.

"I'm going to leave you now," Zoë said. "Before I throw a rock at you." Despite the threat, she gave me and Savitri a quick hug before she left. Babar walked off with her; she was more fun.

"I know how she feels," Savitri said, as we resumed walking.

"You want to throw a rock at me, too?" I said.

"Sometimes," Savitri said. "Not right now. No, about missing her PDA. I miss mine, too. Look at this." Savitri reached into her back pants pocket and pulled out a spiral notebook, a small stack of which had been made a gift to her by Hiram Yoder and the Mennonites. "This is what I'm reduced to."

"Savage," I said.

"Joke all you want," Savitri said, and she put the notebook back. "Going from a PDA to a notepad is *hard*."

I didn't argue with this. Instead, we walked out the north gate of the village, where we found Jane with Hickory and Dickory, and two members of the *Magellan*'s security complement whom she had deputized. "Come look at this," she said, and walked over to one of the storage containers on the perimeter.

"What am I looking for?" I asked.

"These," Jane said, and pointed at the container, near the top, about three meters up.

I squinted. "Those are scratches," I said.

"Yes. We've found them on other containers, too. And there's more," Jane said, and walked over to two other containers. "Something's been digging here," she said. "It looks like something's been trying to dig under these containers."

"Good luck with that," I said. The containers were more than two meters in width.

"We found one hole on the other side of the perimeter that was nearly a meter in length," Jane said. "Something's trying to get in at night. It can't jump over the containers, so it's trying to go under instead. And it's not just one. We've got lots of vegetation tramped down around here, and lots of different-sized paw prints on the containers. Whatever they are, they're in a pack."

"Are these the big animals folks have seen in the brush?" I asked.

Jane shrugged. "No one's seen any of them close up, and nothing comes around here during the day. Normally, we'd post infrared cameras up at the top of the containers, but we can't here." Jane didn't have to explain why; the sentry cameras, like almost every other piece of technology we owned, communicated wirelessly, and wireless was a security risk. "And whatever they are, they're avoiding being seen by the night sentry. But the night sentry isn't using nightscopes, either."

"Whatever they are, you think they're dangerous," I said.

Jane nodded. "I don't see herbivores being this dedicated to getting inside. Whatever's out here sees us and smells us and wants to get in to see what we're like. We need to find out what they are and how many of them there are."

"If they're predators, their numbers are limited," I said. "Too many predators will deplete the stock of prey."

"Yes," Jane said. "But that still doesn't tell us how many there are or what sort of threat they are. All we know is that they're out here at night, and they're big enough to almost be able to jump the containers, and smart enough to try tunneling under. We can't let people begin to homestead until we know what sort of threat they represent."

"Our people are armed," I said. Among the supplies was a store of ancient, simple rifles and non-nanobotic ammunition.

"Our people have firearms," Jane said. "But most of them haven't the slightest idea how to use them. They're going to end up shooting themselves before they shoot anything else. And it's not only humans at risk. I'm more concerned about our livestock. We can't really afford to lose many of them to predators. Not this early."

I looked out toward the brush. Between me and the tree line, one of the Mennonite men was instructing a group of other colonists on the finer points of driving an old-fashioned tractor. Farther out a couple of colonists were collecting soil so we could check its compatibility with our crops. "That's not going to be a very popular position," I said to Jane. "People are already complaining about being cooped up in town."

"It won't take that long to find them," Jane said. "Hickory and Dickory and I are going to take the watch tonight, up on top of the containers. Their eyesight drops down into the infrared range, so they might see them coming."

"And you?" I asked. Jane shrugged. After her revelation back on the *Magellan* about being reengineered, she'd kept mostly quiet about the full range of her abilities. But it wasn't a stretch to assume her visual range had expanded like the rest of her abilities. "What are you going to do when you spot them?" I asked.

"Tonight, nothing," Jane said. "I want to get an idea of

what they are and how many there are. We can decide what we're going to do then. But until then we should make sure everyone is inside the perimeter an hour before sunset and that anyone outside the perimeter during the day has an armed guard." She nodded to her human deputies. "These two have weapons training, and there are several others in the *Magellan* crew who have as well. That's a start."

"And no homesteading until we get a grip on these things," I said.

"Right," Jane said.

"It'll make for a fun Council meeting," I said.

"I'll break it to them," Jane said.

"No," I said. "I should do it. You already have the reputation as the scary one. I don't want you always being the one who bears the bad news."

"It doesn't bother me," Jane said.

"I know," I said. "It doesn't mean you should always do it, though."

"Fine," Jane said. "You can tell them that I expect we'll know quickly enough whether these things represent a threat. That should help."

"We can hope," I said.

"Don't we have any information on these creatures?" Manfred Trujillo asked. He and Captain Zane walked beside me now as I headed toward the village's information center.

"No," I said. "We don't even know what they look like yet. Jane's going to find out tonight. So far the only creatures we know anything about are those rat-things at the mess hall."

"The fuglies," Zane said.

"The what?" I asked.

"The fuglies," Zane said. "That's what the teenagers are calling them. Because they're fucking ugly."

"Nice name," I said. "Point is, I don't think we can claim to have a full understanding of our biosphere from the fuglies alone."

"I know you see value in being cautious," Trujillo said. "But people are getting restless. We've brought people to a place they know nothing about, told them they can't ever talk to their families and friends again, and then given them nothing to do for two entire weeks. We're in limbo. We need to get people going on the next phase of their lives, or they're going to keep dwelling on the fact that their lives as they knew them have been entirely taken away."

"I know," I said. "But you know as well as I do we've got *nothing* on this world. You two have seen the same files I have. Whoever did the so-called survey of this planet apparently didn't bother to spend more than ten minutes on it. We've got the basic biochemistry of the planet and that's pretty much it. We've got almost no information on flora and fauna, or even if it breaks down *into* flora and fauna. We don't know if the soil will grow our crops. We don't know what native life we can eat or use. All information the Department of Colonization usually provides a new colony, we don't have. We have to find all this stuff out on our own *before* we start, and unfortunately in that we've got a pretty big handicap."

We arrived at the information center, which was a grand name for the cargo container we'd modified for the purpose. "After you," I said, holding the first set of doors for Trujillo and Zane. Once we were all in, I sealed the door behind me, allowing the nanobotic mesh to completely envelop the outer door, turning it a featureless black, before opening the interior door. The nanobotic mesh had been programmed to absorb and cloak electromagnetic waves of all sorts. It covered the walls, floor and ceiling of the container. It was unsettling if you thought about it; it was like being in the exact center of nothing.

The man who had designed the mesh waited inside the center's interior door. "Administrator Perry," Jerry Bennett said. "Captain Zane. Mr. Trujillo. Nice to see you back in my little black box."

"How is the mesh holding up?" I asked.

"Good," Bennett said, and pointed at the ceiling. "No waves get in, no waves get out. Schrödinger would be jealous. I need more cells, though. The mesh sucks power like you wouldn't believe. Not to mention all the rest of this equipment." Bennett motioned to the rest of the technology in the center. Because of the mesh, it was the only place on Roanoke where there was technology that you wouldn't find past the middle of the twentieth century on Earth, save power technology that did not run on fossil fuels.

"I'll see what I can do," I said. "You're a miracle worker, Bennett."

"Nah," he said. "I'm just your average geek. I've got those soil reports you wanted." He handed over a PDA, and I fondled it for a moment before looking at the screen. "The good news is the soil samples I've seen so far look good for our crops in a general sense. There's nothing in the soil that will kill them or stunt their growth, at least chemically. Each of the samples was crawling with little critters, too."

"Is that a bad thing?" Trujillo asked.

"Got me," Bennett said. "What I know about soil management I read as I was processing these samples. My wife did a little gardening back on Phoenix and seemed to be of the opinion that having a bunch of bugs was good because they aerated the soil. Who knows, maybe she's right."

"She's right," I said. "Having a healthy amount of bio-mass is usually a good thing." Trujillo looked at me skeptically. "Hey, I farmed," I said. "But we also don't know how these creatures will react to our plants. We're introducing new species into a biosphere."

"You're officially beyond anything I know about the subject, so I'll move on," Bennett said. "You asked if there was any way for me to adapt the technology we have to switch off the wireless components. Do you want the long or short answer?"

"Let's start with the short answer," I said.

"Not really," Bennett said.

"Okay," I said. "Now I need the long answer."

Bennett reached over and grabbed a PDA that he had earlier pried apart, lifted the top off it and handed it to me. "This PDA is a fairly standard piece of Colonial Union technology. Here you see all the components; the processor, the monitor, the data storage, the wireless transmitter that lets it talk to other PDAs and computers. Not a single one of them is physically connected to any of the other parts. Every part of this PDA connects wire-lessly to every other part."

"Why do they do it that way?" I asked, turning the PDA over in my hands.

"Because it's cheap," Bennett said. "You can make tiny data transmitters for next to nothing. It costs less than using physical materials. They don't cost much either, but in aggregate there's a real cost differential. So nearly every manufacturer goes that way. It's design by accountant. The only physical connections in the PDA are from the power cell to the individual components, and again that's because it's cheaper to do it that way."

"Can you use those connections to send data?" Zane said.

"I don't see how," Bennett said. "I mean, sending data

over a physical connection is no problem. But getting into each of these components and flashing their command core to do it that way is beyond my talents. Aside from the programming skills, there's the fact each manufacturer locks out access to the command core. It's proprietary data. And even if I could do all that, there's no guarantee it would work. Among everything else, you'd be routing everything through the power cell. I'm not sure how you get that to work."

"So even if we turn off all the wireless transmitters, every one of these is still leaking wireless signals," I said.

"Yeah," Bennett said. "Across very short distances—no more than a few centimeters—but, yeah. If you're really looking for this sort of thing, you could detect it."

"There's a certain point at which this all becomes futile," Trujillo said. "If someone's listening for radio signals this weak, there's a pretty good chance they're scanning the planet optically as well. They're just going to *see* us."

"Hiding ourselves from sight is a difficult fix," I said to Trujillo. "This is an easy fix. Let's work on the easy fixes." I turned to Bennett, and handed back his PDA. "Let me ask you something else," I said. "Could you *make* wired PDAs? Ones without wireless parts or transmitters?"

"I'm sure I could find a design for one," Bennett said. "There are public domain blueprints. But I'm not exactly set up for manufacturing. I could go through everything we have and cobble up something. Wireless parts are the rule but there are some things that are still wired up. But we're never going to get to a place where everyone's walking around with a computer, much less being able to replace the onboard computers on most of the equipment we have. Honestly, outside this black box, we're not getting out of the early twentieth century any time soon."

All of us digested that for a moment. "Can we at least expand *this*?" Zane finally asked, motioning around him.

"I think we should," Bennett said. "In particular I think we need to build a black box medical bay, because Dr. Tsao keeps distracting me when I'm trying to get work done."

"She's hogging your equipment," I said.

"No, she's just really cute," Bennett said. "And that's going to get me in trouble with the wife. But also, I've only got a couple of her diagnostic machines in here, and if we ever have a real medical problem, we're going to want more available."

I nodded. We'd already had one broken arm, from a teenager climbing up on the barrier and then slipping off. He was lucky not to have broken his neck. "Do we have enough mesh?" I asked.

"This is pretty much our entire stock," Bennett said. "But I can program it to make some more of itself. I'd need some more raw material."

"I'll have Ferro get on that," Zane said, referring to the cargo chief. "We'll see what we have in inventory."

"Every time I see him, he seems really pissed," Bennett said.

"Maybe it's because he's supposed to be at home and not here," Zane snapped. "Maybe he doesn't much like being kidnapped by the Colonial Union." Two weeks had not served to make the captain any more mellow about the destruction of his ship or the stranding of his crew.

"Sorry," Bennett said.

"I'm ready to go," Zane said.

"Two quick things," Bennett said to me. "I'm almost done printing most of the data files you were given when we came here, so you can have those in hard copy. I can't print the video and audio files, but I'll run them through a processor to get you transcripts."

"Okay, good," I said. "What was the second thing?"

"I went around the camp with a monitor like you asked and looked for wireless signals," Bennett said. Trujillo raised an eyebrow at this. "The monitor is solid state," Bennett said to him. "Doesn't send, only receives. Anyway, I think you should know there are three wireless devices still out there. And they're still transmitting."

"I haven't the slightest idea what you're talking about," Jann Kranjic said.

For not the first time, I restrained the urge to punch Kranjic in the temple. "Do we really need to do this the hard way, Jann?" I said. "I'd like to pretend we're not twelve years old and that we're not having an 'am to, am not' sort of conversation."

"I turned over my PDA just like everyone else did," Kranjic said, and then motioned back to Beata, who was lying on her cot, a washcloth over her eyes. Beata was apparently prone to migranes. "And Beata turned in her PDA and her camera cap. You have everything we have."

I glanced over at Beata. "Well, Beata?" I said.

Beata raised the edge of her washcloth and looked over, wincing. Then she sighed and reapplied her washcloth. "Check his underwear," she said.

"Excuse me?" I said.

"Beata," Kranjic said.

"His underwear," Beata said. "At least one pair has a pouch in the elastic that hides a small recorder. He's got a pin of the Umbrian flag that's an audio/video input. He's probably got it on right now."

"You bitch," Kranjic said, subconsciously covering his pin. "You're fired."

"That's funny," Beata said, pressing the washcloth

against her eyes. "We're a thousand light-years from any-where, we have no chance of ever getting back to Um-bria, you spend your days reciting overblown notes into your underwear for a book you'll never write, and I'm *fired*. Get a grip, Jann."

Kranjic stood to make a dramatic exit. "Jann," I said, and held out my hand. Jann snatched off his pin and pressed it into my palm.

"Want my underwear now?" he sneered.

"Keep the underwear," I said. "Just give me the recorder."

"Years from now, people are going to want to know the story of this colony," Kranjic said, as he fumbled with his underwear from inside his trousers. "They're going to want to know the story, and when they go looking for it, they're not going to find anything. And they're not going to find anything because its leaders spent their time cen-soring the only member of the press in the entire colony."

"Beata's a member of the press," I said.

"She's a *camerawoman*," Kranjic said, slapping over the recorder. "It's not the same thing."

"I'm not censoring you," I said. "I just can't allow you to jeopardize the colony. I'm going to take this recorder and have Jerry Bennett print you out a transcript of the notes, in very tiny type, because I don't want to waste paper. So you'll have these notes. And if you go find Savitri you can tell her I asked her to give you one of her notepads. *One*, Jann. She needs the rest for our work. Then if you need any more you can see what the Men-nonites have to say about it."

"You want me to write out my notes," Kranjic said. "In longhand."

"It worked for Samuel Pepys," I said.

"You're assuming Jann knows how to write," Beata mumbled from her cot.

"Bitch," Kranjic said, and left the tent.

"It's a stormy marriage," Beata said laconically.

"Apparently," I said. "You want a divorce?"

"Depends," Beata said, raising her washcloth again. "Think your assistant would be up for a date?"

"In the entire time I've known her I haven't known her to date anyone," I said.

"So that's a 'no,' " Beata said.

"It's a 'hell if I know,' " I said.

"Hmmmm," Beata said, dropping the cloth back down. "Tempting. But I'll stay married for now. It irritates Jann. After all the irritation he's provided me over the years, it's nice to return the favor."

"Stormy marriage," I said.

"Apparently," Beata said.

"We must refuse," Hickory said to me. It and Dickory and I were in the Black Box. I figured that when I told the two Obin that they needed to give up their wireless consciousness implants, they should be allowed to be conscious to hear it.

"You've never refused an order of mine before," I said.

"None of your orders has ever violated our treaty," Hickory said. "Our treaty with the Colonial Union allows the two of us to be with Zoë. It also allows us to record those experiences and share them with other Obin. Ordering us to surrender our consciousness interferes with this. It violates our treaty."

"You could choose to surrender your implants," I said. "That would solve the problem."

"We would not choose to," Hickory said. "It would be an abdication of our responsibility to the other Obin."

"I could tell Zoë to tell you to give them up," I said. "I can't imagine you'd ignore her order."

Hickory and Dickory leaned in together for a moment, then leaned out again. "That would be distressful," Hickory said. I reflected that it was the first time I had ever heard that word provide such apocalyptic gravity.

"You understand I have no desire to do this," I said. "But our orders from the Colonial Union are clear. We can't let anything provide easy evidence we're on this world. The Conclave will exterminate us. All of us, including you two and Zoë."

"We have considered the possibility," Hickory said. "We believe the risk to be negligible."

"Remind me to show you a little video I have," I said.

"We have seen it," Hickory said. "It was provided to our government as well as yours."

"How can you see that and *not* see that the Conclave represents a threat to us?" I asked.

"We viewed the video carefully," Hickory said. "We believe the risk to be negligible."

"It's not your decision to make," I said.

"It is," Hickory said. "By our treaty."

"I am the legal authority on this planet," I said.

"You are," Hickory said. "But you may not abrogate a treaty for your convenience."

"Not getting an entire colony slaughtered is not a *convenience*," I said.

"Removing all wireless devices to avoid detection is a convenience," Hickory said.

"Why don't you ever talk?" I said to Dickory.

"I have yet to disagree with Hickory," Dickory said.

I stewed.

"We have a problem," I said. "I can't force you to surrender your implants, but I can't let you run around with them, either. Answer me this: Is it a violation of your treaty for me to require you to stay *here*, in this room, so long as I have Zoë visit you on a regular basis?"

Hickory thought about it. "No," it said. "It is not what we prefer."

"It's not what I prefer, either," I said. "But I don't think I have a choice."

Hickory and Dickory conferred again for several minutes. "This room is covered in wave-masking material," Hickory said. "Give us some. We can use it to cover our devices and ourselves."

"We don't have any more right now," I said. "We need to make more. It might take some time."

"As long as you agree to this solution we will accommodate the production time," Hickory said. "During that time we will not use our implants outside this room, but you will ask Zoë to visit us here."

"Fine," I said. "Thank you."

"You are welcome," Hickory said. "Maybe this will be for the best. Since we have been here, we have noticed she has not had as much time for us."

"She's being a teenager," I said. "New friends. New planet. New boyfriend."

"Yes. Enzo," Hickory said. "We feel deeply ambivalent about him."

"Join the club," I said.

"We can remove him," Hickory said.

"Really, no," I said.

"Perhaps later," Hickory said.

"Rather than killing off Zoë's potential suitors, I'd prefer the two of you focus on helping Jane find whatever it is that's out there pawing on our perimeter," I said. "It's probably less emotionally satisfying, but in the grand scheme of things, it's going to be more useful."

Jane plopped the thing down on the floor of the Council meeting. It looked vaguely like a large coyote, if coyotes had four eyes and paws with opposable thumbs. "Dickory found this one inside one of the excavations. There were two others with it but they ran off. Dickory killed this one as it was trying to get away."

"He shot it?" asked Marta Piro.

"He killed it with a knife," Jane said. This caused some uneasy muttering; most of the Council and colonists were still deeply uncomfortable with the Obin.

"Do you think this is one of the predators you were concerned about?" Manfred Trujillo asked.

"It might be," Jane said.

"Might be," Trujillo said.

"The paws are the right shape for the marks we've seen," Jane said. "But it seems small to me."

"But small or not, something like this could have made the marks," Trujillo said.

"It's possible," Jane said.

"Have you seen any larger ones?" asked Lee Chen.

"No," Jane said, and looked over to me. "I've been out on the night watch on the last three days and last night was the first time we've seen anything approach the barrier at all."

"Hiram, you've been out past the barrier almost every day," Trujillo said. "Have you seen anything like this?"

"I've seen some animals," Hiram said. "But they've been plant eaters, as far as I could see. I haven't seen anything that looks like this thing. But then I've not been out past the barrier at night, either, and Administrator Sagan here thinks these are active during the night."

"But she hasn't seen any more of them," Marie Black said. "We're holding off settling because of phantoms."

"The scratches and holes were real enough," I said.

"I'm not arguing that," Black said. "But maybe they were isolated incidents. Perhaps a pack of these animals was just passing through several days ago and was curious about the barrier. Once they couldn't get through, they moved on."

"It's possible," Jane said again. From her tone I could tell she didn't think much of Black's theory.

"How much longer are we going to hold off on settling because of this?" Paulo Gutierrez asked. "I've got people who are going insane waiting for us to stop farting around. The last few days people have started getting in each other's faces about idiotic things. And we're running against time now, aren't we? It's spring here now, and we've got to start planting crops and readying grazing fields for the livestock. We've already eaten through two weeks of food. If we don't start colonizing, we're going to be in deep shit."

"We haven't been farting around," I said. "We've been dropped onto a planet about which we know nothing. We had to take the time to make sure it wasn't going to flat-out kill us."

"We're not dead yet," Trujillo said, interjecting himself. "So that's a good sign. Paolo, step back for a minute. Perry is absolutely right. We couldn't have just wandered out into this planet and started setting up farms. But Paolo's right, too, Perry. We're at a point where we can't stay stuck behind a barricade. Sagan's had three days to find more evidence of these creatures, and we've killed one of them. We need to be cautious, yes. And we need to keep studying Roanoke. But we need to get colonizing, too."

The entire Council was staring at me, waiting to hear what I would say. I glanced over at Jane, who gave one of her nearly imperceptible shrugs. She wasn't entirely convinced that there wasn't a real threat out there, but aside from the one dead creature, she had nothing definitive. And Trujillo was right; it was time to get colonizing.

"Agreed," I said.

"You let Trujillo take that meeting away from you," Jane said, as we got ready for bed. She kept her voice low; Zoë was already asleep. Hickory and Dickory were standing impassively on the other side of our screen in the administrative tent. They were wearing full body suits made from the first bolt of the newly produced nanobotic mesh. The suits locked in the wireless signals; they also turned the Obin into walking shadows. They might have been asleep as well; it was hard to tell.

"I suppose I did," I said. "Trujillo's a professional politician. He'll do that sometimes. Especially when he's right. We do need to move on getting people out of the village."

"I want to make sure each wave of homesteaders has some weapons training," Jane said.

"I think that's a fine idea," I said. "You're not likely to convince the Mennonites, however."

"I have concerns about that," Jane said.

"You're just going to have to be concerned, then," I said.

"They're our knowledge base," Jane said. "They're the ones who know how to operate all the nonautomated machinery and make things without pressing buttons. I don't want them getting eaten."

"If you want to keep an extra close watch on the Mennonites, I don't have a problem with that," I said. "But if you think you're going to get them to stop being who they are, you're in for a surprise. And it's because of who they are that they're in a position to save our collective bacon."

"I don't understand religion," Jane said.

"It makes more sense from the inside," I said. "Anyway, you don't have to understand it. You just have to respect it."

"I respect it," Jane said. "I also respect the fact this planet still has ways to kill us we haven't figured out yet. I wonder if other people respect that."

"There's one way to find out," I said.

"You and I haven't talked about whether we plan to do any farming ourselves," Jane said.

"I don't think it would be a smart use of our time," I said. "We're colony administrators now, and we don't have automated equipment here we can use. We'll be busy enough. After Croatoan empties out a bit we'll build a nice little house. If you want to grow things, we can have a garden. We *should* have a garden anyway, for our own fruits and vegetables. We can put Zoë in charge of it. Give her something to do."

"I want to grow flowers, too," Jane said. "Roses."

"Really," I said. "You've never really been into pretty things before."

"It's not that," Jane said. "This planet smells like an armpit."

SEVEN Roanoke revolves around its sun every 323 days. We decided to give the Roanoke year eleven months, seven with twenty-nine days and four with thirty. We named a month for each of the colony worlds our settlers came from, plus one for the *Magellan*. We dated the first day of the year to the day we arrived above Roanoke, and named the first month Magellan. The *Magellan* crew was touched, which was good, but by the time we named the months, it was already Magellan twenty-ninth. Their month was already almost over. They weren't entirely pleased about that.

Shortly after our decision to start allowing the colonists to homestead, Hiram Yoder approached me for a private meeting. It was clear, he said, that the majority of the colonists were not qualified to farm; they had all trained on modern farming equipment and were having difficulties with the more labor-intensive farm equipment the Mennonites were familiar with. Our stores of fast-growing, genetically modified seed would allow us to begin harvesting crops within two months—but only if we knew what we were doing. We didn't, and we were looking a potential famine in the face.

Yoder suggested we allow the Mennonites to cultivate crops for the entire colony, thus ensuring that the colony wouldn't turn into an interstellar Donner party three months down the line; the Mennonites would apprentice the other colonists so they could receive on-the-job training. I readily agreed to this. By the second week of Albion, the Mennonites had taken our soil studies and used them to plant fields of wheat, maize and any other number of vegetables; they woke honeybees from their slumber to begin doing their pollination dance, pastured the livestock and were teaching the colonists of nine other worlds (and one ship) the advantages of intensive and companion planting, carbon and calorie farming and the secrets of maximizing yields in the smallest amount of space. I began to relax a little; Savitri, who had been making jokes about "long pig," found something new to snark about.

In Umbria, the fuglies discovered that fast-growing potatoes were good eatin', and we lost several acres in the space of three days. We had our first agricultural pest. We also completed the medical bay, with all its equipment in its own black box. Dr. Tsao was delighted when within hours she was using her surgery 'bot to reattach a finger a colonist had inadvertently sliced off with a bandsaw during a barn raising.

In the first weekend of Zhong Guo, I presided over Roanoke's first wedding, between Katherine Chao, formerly of Franklin, and Kevin Jones, formerly of Rus. There was much rejoicing. Two weeks later I presided over Roanoke's first divorce, fortunately not of Chao and Jones. Beata had finally gotten her fill of antagonizing Jann Kranjic and let him off the hook. There was much rejoicing.

By Erie tenth, we had finished our first major crop

harvests. I declared a national holiday and day of thanks-giving. The colonists celebrated by building the Men-nonites a meeting house, for which they only occasionally needed to ask for advice from the Mennonites themselves. The second set of crops was into the ground less than a week later.

In Khartoum, Patrick Kazumi went with his friends to play by the stream behind Croatoan's western wall. While running along the stream, he slipped, hit his head on a rock and drowned. He was eight years old. Most of the colony attended his funeral. On the last day of Khar-toum, Anna Kazumi, Patrick's mother, stole a heavy coat from a friend, placed rocks in her pockets and waded into the stream to follow her son. She succeeded.

In Kyoto, it rained heavily four days out of every five, spoiling crops and interfering with the colony's second harvest of the year. Zoë and Enzo had a some-what dramatic breakup, as often happens when first loves finally get on each other's nerves. Hickory and Dickory, overstimulated from Zoë's relationship angst, began openly discussing how to solve the Enzo prob-lem. Zoë finally told the two to stop it; they were creep-ing her out.

In Elysium, the yotes, the coyote-like predators we'd discovered on our barrier, made their way back toward the colony, and attempted to work their way through the colony's herd of sheep, a ready source of food. Colonists began working their way through the predators in return. Savitri relented after three months and went on a date with Beata. The next day Savitri described the evening as an "interesting failure" and refused to discuss it further.

With Roanoke autumn in full swing, the last of the temporary housing tents folded for good, replaced with simple, snug houses in Croatoan and on the homesteads outside its walls. Half of the colonists still lived in

Croatoan, learning trades from the Mennonites; the other half carved out their homesteads and waited for the new year to plant their own fields and yield their own crops.

Savitri's birthday—as measured on Huckleberry, translated to Roanoke dates—occurred on the twenty-third of Elysium; I gave her the gift of an indoor toilet for her tiny cottage, connected to a small and easily drained septic tank. Savitri actually teared up.

On the thirteenth of Rus, Henri Arlien battered his wife Therese on the belief that she was having an affair with a former tentmate. Therese responded by battering her husband with a heavy pan, breaking his jaw and knocking out three of his teeth. Both Henri and Therese visited Dr. Tsao; Henri then visited the hastily assembled jail, formerly a livestock hold. Therese asked for a divorce and then moved in with the former tentmate. She hadn't been having an affair before, she said, but now it sounded like a damn fine idea indeed.

The tentmate was a fellow by the name of Joseph Loong. On the twentieth of Phoenix, Loong went missing.

"First things first," I said to Jane, after Therese Arlien came in to report Loong's disappearance. "Where has Henri Arlien been recently?"

"He's on work furlough during the day," Jane said. "The only time he's allowed to be by himself is when he has to pee. At night he's back in his stall at the jail."

"That stall's not exactly escape-proof," I said. In its former life it had held a horse.

"No," Jane said. "But the livestock hold is. One door, one lock, and it's on the outside. He doesn't get anywhere overnight."

"He could get a friend to visit Loong," I said.

"I don't think Arlien has friends," Jane said. "Chad and Ari took statements from their neighbors. Pretty much all of them said Henri had got what he deserved when Therese hit him with that pan. I'll have Chad check around, but I don't think we'll get much there."

"What do you think, then?" I asked.

"Loong's homestead borders the woods," Jane said. "Therese said the two of them had gone for walks out there. The fanties are migrating through the area, and Loong wanted to get a closer look." The fanties were the lumbering animals some of the folks saw at the edge of the woods not long after we landed; apparently they migrated, looking for food. We had caught the tail end of their stay when we arrived; now it was the early part. I thought they looked about as much like elephants as I did, but the name had stuck whether I liked it or not.

"So Loong goes out to look at the fanties and gets lost," I said.

"Or gets trampled," Jane said. "The fanties are large animals."

"Well, then, let's get a search party together," I said. "If Loong just got lost, if he has any sense, he'll stay put and wait for us to find him."

"If he had any sense he wouldn't be chasing after fanties in the first place," Jane said.

"You'd be no fun on a safari," I said.

"Experience teaches me not to go out of my way to chase alien creatures," Jane said. "Because they often chase back. I'll have a search party together in an hour. You should come along."

The search party began its search just before noon. It was a hundred and fifty volunteers strong; Henri Arlien may not have been popular but both Therese and Loong had a number of friends. Therese came to join the party but I sent her home with two of her friends. I didn't want to run the risk of her coming across Joe's body. Jane blocked off search areas for small groups and required each group to stay in voice contact with one another. Savitri and Beata, who had become friends despite their interesting failure of a date, searched with me, Savitri keeping a tight grip on an old-style compass she had traded for with a Mennonite sometime before. Jane, some measure down the woods, was accompanied by Zoë and Hickory and Dickory. I wasn't entirely thrilled with Zoë being part of the search squad, but between Jane and the Obin she was probably safer in the woods than back home in Croatoan.

Three hours into the search, Hickory bounded up, shadowy in his nanomesh suit. "Lieutenant Sagan wishes to see you," it said.

"All right," I said, and motioned for Savitri and Beata to come along.

"No," Hickory said. "You only."

"What is it?" I asked.

"I cannot say," Hickory said. "Please, Major. You must come now."

"We're stuck in the creepy woods, then," Savitri said, to me.

"You can head in if you want," I said. "But tell the parties on either side so they can tighten up." And with that I jogged after Hickory, who kept an aggressive pace.

Several minutes later we arrived where Jane was. She was standing with Marta Piro and two other colonists, all three of whom had blank, numb expressions on their faces. Behind them was the massive carcass of a fantie, wild with tiny flying bugs, and a rather smaller carcass farther beyond that. Jane spied me and said something to

Piro and the other two; they glanced over to me, nodded at whatever it was Jane was saying and then headed back toward the colony.

"Where's Zoë?" I asked.

"I had Dickory take her back," Jane said. "I didn't want her to see this. Marta and her team found something."

I motioned to the smaller carcass. "Joseph Loong, it looks like," I said.

"Not just that," Jane said. "Come here."

We walked over to Loong's corpse. It was a bloody mess. "Tell me what you see," Jane said.

I leaned down and got a good look, willing myself into a neutral frame of mind. "He's been eaten at," I said.

"That's what I told Marta and the others," Jane said. "And that's what I want them to believe for right now. *You* need to look closer."

I frowned and looked at the corpse again, trying to see what it was I was clearly missing. Suddenly it snapped into place.

I went cold. "Holy God," I said, and backed away from Loong.

Jane looked at me intently. "You see it, too," she said. "He wasn't eaten. He was *butchered*."

The Council crowded uncomfortably into the medical bay, along with Dr. Tsao. "This isn't going to be pleasant," I warned them, and pulled the sheet back on what was left of Joe Loong. Only Lee Chen and Marta Piro looked like they were likely to vomit, which was a better percentage than I expected.

"Christ. Something ate him," Paulo Gutierrez said.

"No," Hiram Yoder said. He moved closer to Loong.

"Look," he said, pointing. "The tissues are cut, not torn. Here, here and here." He glanced over at Jane. "This is why you needed to show us this," he said. Jane nodded.

"Why?" Guiterrez said. "I don't understand. What are you showing us?"

"This man's been butchered," Yoder said. "Whoever did this to him used some sort of cutting tool to take off his flesh. A knife or an ax, possibly."

"How can you tell this?" Gutierrez said to Yoder.

"I've butchered enough animals to know what it looks like," Yoder said, and glanced up at Jane and me. "And I believe our administrators have seen enough of the violence of war to know what sort of violence this was."

"But you can't be sure," Marie Black said.

Jane glanced over to Dr. Tsao and nodded. "There are striations on the bone that are consistent with a cutting implement," Dr. Tsao said. "They're precisely positioned. They don't look like what you'd see if a bone was gnawed on by an animal. Some*one* did this, not some*thing*."

"So you're saying there's a murderer in the colony," Manfred Trujillo said.

"Murderer?" Gutierrez said. "The hell with that. We've got a goddamn *cannibal* walking around."

"No," Jane said.

"Excuse me?" Gutierrez said. "You said it yourself, this man's been sliced up like he was livestock. One of us had to have done it."

Jane glanced over at me. "Okay," I said. "I'm going to have to do this formally. As the Colonial Union administrator of the colony of Roanoke, I hereby declare that everyone in this room is bound by the State Secrecy Act."

"I concur," Jane said.

"This means that nothing said or done here now can

be shared outside this room to anyone, under penalty of treason," I said.

"The hell you say," Trujillo said.

"The hell I do say," I said. "No joke. You talk about any of this before Jane and I are ready for you to talk about it, and you'll be in deep shit."

"Define *deep shit*," Gutierrez said.

"I shoot you," Jane said. Gutierrez smiled uncertainly, waiting for Jane to indicate she was kidding. He kept waiting.

"All right," Trujillo said. "We understand. No talking."

"Thank you," I said. "We brought you over here for two reasons. The first was to show you him"—I pointed to Loong, whom Dr. Tsao had hidden again under the sheet—"and the second was to show you this." I reached over to the lab table, pulled an object from underneath a towel and handed it to Trujillo.

He examined it. "It looks like the head of a spear," he said.

"That's what it is," I said. "We found it by the fantie carcass near where we found Loong. We suspect it was thrown at the fantie and it managed to pull it out and break it, or perhaps broke it and then pulled it out."

Trujillo, who was in the act of handing the spearhead over to Lee Chen, stopped and took another look at it. "You're not seriously suggesting what I think you're suggesting," he said.

"It wasn't just Loong who was butchered," Jane said. "The fantie was butchered, too. There were footprints around Loong, because of Marta and her search party and me and John. There were tracks around the fantie as well. They weren't ours."

"The fantie was brought down by some yotes," Marie Black said. "The yotes move in packs. It could happen."

"You're not listening," Jane said. "The fantie was *butchered*. Whoever butchered the fantie almost certainly butchered Loong. And whoever butchered the fantie wasn't human."

"You're saying there's some sort of aboriginal intelligent species here on Roanoke," Trujillo said.

"Yes," I said.

"How intelligent?" Trujillo asked.

"Intelligent enough to make that," I said, noting the spear. "It's a simple spear, but it's still a spear. And they're intelligent enough to make knives for butchering."

"We've been here almost a Roanoke year," Lee Chen said. "If these things exist, why haven't we seen them before?"

"I think we have," Jane said. "I think whatever these things are, were the ones who tried to get into Croatoan not long after we arrived. When they couldn't climb their way over the barrier they tried digging under."

"I thought the yotes did that," Chen said.

"We killed a yote in one of the holes," Jane said. "It doesn't mean the yote dug the hole."

"The holes happened right around the time we first saw the fanties," I said. "Now the fanties are back. Maybe these things follow the herd. No fanties, no Roanoke cavemen." I pointed to Loong. "I think these things were hunting a fantie. They killed it and were butchering it up when Loong wandered onto what they were doing. Maybe they killed him out of fear, and butchered him afterward."

"They saw him as prey," Gutierrez said.

"We don't know that," I said.

"Come on," Gutierrez said, waving toward Loong. "The sons of bitches turned him into fucking *steaks*."

"Yes," I said. "But we don't know if he was *hunted*. I'd rather we don't jump to any conclusions. And I'd rather *we* didn't start panicking about what these things are or what their intentions are toward us. As far as we know they have no intentions. This could have been a random encounter."

"You're not suggesting we pretend that Joe *wasn't* killed and eaten," said Marta Piro. "That's already impossible. Jun and Evan know, because they were with me when we found him. Jane's told us to keep quiet, and we have so far. But this isn't something you can keep quiet forever."

"We don't need to keep that part quiet," Jane said. "You can tell your people that part when you leave here. You need to keep quiet about the creatures that did this."

"I'm not going to pretend to my people that this was just some sort of random animal attack," Gutierrez said.

"No one's saying you should," I said. "Tell your people the truth: that there are predators following the fantie herd, they're dangerous and that until further notice no one goes for walks in the forest, or goes anywhere alone outside of Croatoan if they can help it. You don't have to tell them anything more than that for now."

"Why not?" Gutierrez said. "These things represent a real danger to us. They've already killed one of us. *Eaten* one of us. We need to get our people prepared."

"The reason why not is that people act irrationally if they think they're being hunted by something with a brain," Jane said. "Just like you're acting now."

Gutierrez glared at Jane. "I don't appreciate the suggestion that I'm acting irrationally," he said.

"Then don't act irrationally," Jane said, "because there will be consequences. Remember that you're under the State Secrecy Act, Gutierrez." Gutierrez subsided, clearly not satisfied.

"Look," I said. "If these things *are* intelligent, then among other things I think we have some responsibilities to them, primarily *not* wiping them out over what might have been a misunderstanding. And if they are intelligent, then maybe we can find a way to let them know they'd be best off avoiding *us*." I motioned for the spearhead; Trujillo handed it over. "They're using *these*, for Christ's sake"—waving the spear—"even with the dumb guns we have to use here, we could probably wipe them out a hundred times over. But I'd like to try *not* doing that if we can manage it."

"Let me try to put it a different way," Trujillo said. "You're asking us to withhold critical information from our people. I—and I think Paulo here as well—worry that holding back that information makes our people less safe, because our people don't know the full scope of what they're dealing with. Look where we are *now*. We're all stuffed into a cargo container wrapped in cloaking fabric to keep us hidden, and that's because our government withheld critical information from us. The Colonial government played *us* for fools, and that's why we live like we do now. No offense," he said to Hiram Yoder.

"None taken," Yoder said.

"My point is, our government screwed *us* with secrets," Trujillo said. "Why would we want to do the same to *our* people?"

"I don't want to keep this a secret forever," I said. "But right now we lack information on whether these people are a genuine threat, and I'd like to be able to get it without people going a little crazy out of fear of Roanoke Neanderthals wandering in the brush."

"You're assuming people will go a little crazy," Trujillo said.

"I'd be happy to be proven wrong," I said. "But for now let's err on the side of caution."

"Inasmuch as we don't have a choice in the matter, let's err indeed," Trujillo said.

"Christ," Jane said. I noted an unusual tone in her voice: exasperation. "Trujillo, Gutierrez, use your goddamn heads. *We didn't have to tell you any of this.* Marta didn't know what she was looking at when she found Loong; the only one of you who saw it for himself was Yoder, and only because he saw it here. If we hadn't told you everything right now, you'd never have known. I could have cleaned this all up and not one of you would be the wiser. But we didn't want that; we knew we had to tell all of you. We've trusted you enough to share something we didn't have to share. Trust us that we need time before you tell the colonists. It's not too much to ask."

"Everything I'm telling you is protected by the State Secrecy Act," I said.

"We have a state?" Jerry Bennett asked.

"Jerry," I said.

"Sorry," Jerry said. "What's up?"

I told Jerry about the creatures and an update about the Council meeting the night before. "That's pretty wild," Jerry said. "What do you want me to do?"

"Go through the files we were given about this planet," I said. "Tell me if you see anything there that gives any indication that the Colonial Union knew anything about these guys. I mean *anything*."

"There's nothing on them directly," Bennett said. "I know that much. I read the files as I was printing them out for you."

"I'm not looking for direct references. I mean anything in the files that suggests these guys were here," I said.

"You think the CU edited out the fact this planet has

an intelligent species on it?" Bennett asked. "Why would they do that?"

"I don't know," I said. "It wouldn't make any sense. But sending us to a whole different planet than the one we were supposed to be on and then cutting us off entirely doesn't make any sense either, does it?"

"Brother, you have a point there," Bennett said, and thought for a moment. "How deep do you want me to go?" he asked.

"As deep as you can," I said. "Why?"

Bennett grabbed a PDA from his bench and pulled up a file. "The Colonial Union uses a standard file format for all its documents," he said. "Text, images, audio, they all get poured into the same sort of file. One of the things you can do with the file format is get it to track editing changes. You write a draft of something, you send it to the boss, she makes changes, and the document comes back to you and you can see where and how your boss made the changes. It tracks however many changes get made—stores the deleted material in metadata. You don't see it unless you turn on version tracking."

"So any edits that were made would still be in the document," I said.

"They might be," Bennett said. "It's a CU rule that final documents are supposed to have this sort of metadata stripped out. But it's one thing to mandate it, and another thing to get people to remember to do it."

"Do it, then," I said. "I want everything looked at. Sorry about becoming a pain in your ass."

"Nah," Bennett said. "Batch commands make life easy. After that it's a matter of the right search parameters. This is what I do."

"I owe you one, Jerry," I said.

"Yeah?" Bennett said. "If you mean it you'll get me an assistant. Being the tech guy for an entire colony is a lot of work. And I spend my entire day in a box. It'd be nice to have some company."

"I'll get on it," I said. "You get on this."

"On it," Bennett said, and waved me out of the Box.

Jane and Hiram Yoder were walking up as I came outside. "We have a problem," Jane said. "A big one."

"What?" I said.

Jane nodded to Hiram. "Paulo Gutierrez and four other men came past my farm today," Hiram said. "Carrying rifles and heading toward the woods. I asked him what he was doing and he said that he and his friends were going on a hunting trip. I asked them what he was hunting for and he said that I should know full well what they were planning to hunt. He asked me if I wanted to come along. I told him that my religion forbade the taking of intelligent life, and I asked him to reconsider what he was doing, because he was going against your wishes, and planning to murder another creature. He laughed and walked off toward the tree line. They're out in the woods now, Administrator Perry. I think they mean to kill as many of the creatures as they can find."

Yoder walked us to where he saw the men enter the woods and told us he'd wait for us there. Jane and I went in and started looking for the trail of men.

"Here," Jane said, pointing to boot marks on the forest floor. Paulo and his boys were making no attempt to keep themselves hidden, or if they were, they were very bad at it. "Idiots," Jane said, and took off after them, unthinkingly moving at her new and improved high speed. I ran off after her, neither as fast nor as quietly.

I caught up with her about a klick later. "Don't do that again," I said. "I'm about to heave my lungs out."

"Quiet," Jane said. I shut up. Jane's hearing had no doubt improved with her speed. I tried to suck oxygen into my lungs as quietly as I could. She began walking west when we heard a shot, followed by three more. Jane began running again, in the direction of the shots. I followed as quickly as I could.

Another klick later I entered a clearing. Jane was kneeling over a body that had blood pooling underneath it; another man sat nearby, propped up by the woody stump of a bush. I ran over to Jane and the body, whose front was spattered with blood. She barely glanced up. "Dead already," she said. "Shot between the rib and the sternum. Right through the heart, straight out the back. Probably dead before he hit the ground."

I looked at the man's face. It took me a minute to recognize him: Marco Flores, one of Gutierrez's colonists from Khartoum. I left Flores to Jane and went over to the other man, who was staring blankly ahead. It was another Khartoum colonist, Galen DeLeon.

"Galen," I said, crouching down to get at his eye level. The salutation didn't register. I snapped my fingers a couple of times to get his attention. "Galen," I said again. "Tell me what happened."

"I shot Marco," DeLeon said, in a bland, conversational voice. He was looking past me, at nothing in particular. "I didn't mean to. They just came out of nowhere, and I shot one, and Marco got in the way. I shot him. He went down." DeLeon put his hands on his forehead and started grasping at his hair. "I didn't mean to," he said. "All of a sudden they were just there."

"Galen," I said. "You came out here with Paulo Gutierrez and a couple other men. Where did they go?"

DeLeon waved indistinctly in a westerly direction. "They ran off. Paulo and Juan and Deit went after them. I stayed. To see if I could help Marco. To see . . ." He trailed off again. I stood up.

"I didn't mean to shoot him," DeLeon said, still in that bland tone. "They were just there. And they moved so fast. You should have seen them. If you saw them, you know why I had to shoot. If you saw what they looked like."

"What do they look like?" I asked.

DeLeon smiled tragically and for the first time looked at me. "Like werewolves." He closed his eyes and put his head back in his hands.

I went back over to Jane. "DeLeon's in shock," I said. "One of us should take him back."

"What did he say happened?" Jane asked.

"Said the things came out of nowhere and ran that way," I said, pointing west. "Gutierrez and the rest of them went chasing after them." It hit me. "They're running into an ambush," I said.

"Come on," Jane said, and pointed to Flores's rifle. "Take that," she said, and ran. I took Flores's rifle, checked the load and once again started after my wife.

There was another rifle shot, followed by the sound of men yelling. I put on a burst of speed and came up a rise to find Jane in a broken grove of Roanoke trees, kneeling on the back of one of the men, who was yelling in pain. Paulo Gutierrez was pointing his rifle at Jane and ordering her off the man. Jane wasn't budging. A third man stood to the side, looking like he was about to wet his pants.

I leveled my rifle at Gutierrez. "Drop your rifle, Paulo," I said. "Drop it or I'm going to drop you."

"Tell your wife to get off Deit," Gutierrez said.

"No," I said. "Now drop your weapon."

"She's breaking his goddamn arm!" Gutierrez said.

"If she wanted to break his arm, it'd be broken by now," I said. "And if she wanted to kill every one of you, you'd already be dead. Paulo, I'm not going to tell you again. Drop your rifle."

Paulo dropped his rifle. I glanced over at the third man, who would be Juan. He dropped his, too. "Down," I said to the both of them. "Knees and palms on the ground." They went down.

"Jane," I said.

"This one took a shot at me," Jane said.

"I didn't know it was you!" Deit said.

"Shut up," Jane said. He shut up.

I walked over to Juan and Gutierrez's rifles and picked them up. "Paulo, where are your other men?" I asked.

"They're behind us somewhere," Gutierrez said. "These things popped out of nowhere and started running this way, and we came after them. Marco and Galen probably went off in another direction."

"Marco is dead," I said.

"Those fuckers got him," Deit said.

"No," I said. "Galen shot him. Just like you almost shot her."

"Holy Christ," Gutierrez said. "Marco."

"This is *exactly* why I wanted to keep this quiet," I said to Gutierrez. "To keep some idiot from doing this. You dumbfucks haven't got the first clue what you're doing, and now one of you is dead, one of you killed him, and the rest of you are running into an ambush."

"Oh God," Gutierrez said. He tried to sit up from his four-on-the-floor position but lost his balance, and collapsed in a pile of grief.

"We're going to walk out of here now, all of us," I said, walking over to Gutierrez. "We're going to go back the way we came in, and along the way we're going to pick up Galen and Marco. Paulo, I'm sorry—" I caught movement out of the corner of my eye; it was Jane, telling me to cut it off. She was listening for something. I looked over at her. *What is it?* I mouthed.

Jane looked down at Deit. "What direction did those things you were chasing run off in?"

Deit pointed west. "That way. We were chasing them, and then they disappeared, and then you came running up."

"What do you mean they disappeared?" Jane said.

"One minute we saw them and the next we didn't," Deit said. "Those fuckers are fast."

Jane got off Deit. "Get up. Now," she said. She looked over to me. "They weren't running into an ambush. This *is* the ambush."

Then I heard what Jane had been hearing: a soft mass of clicks, coming from the trees. Coming from directly above us.

"Oh, shit," I said.

"What the hell is that?" Gutierrez said, and looked up as the spear came down, exposing his neck to its tip, which slid into that soft space at the top of the sternum and drove itself into his viscera. I rolled, avoiding a spear of my own, and looked up as I did.

It was raining werewolves.

Two fell near me and Gutierrez, who was still alive, trying to pull out the spear. One grabbed the spear near the end and drove it down farther into Gutierrez's chest and shook it violently. Gutierrez spat up blood and died. The second slashed at me with claws as I rolled, ripping my jacket but missing flesh. I had kept my rifle and drew it up with one hand; the thing grabbed the barrel with both of its paws or claws or hands and prepared to pull it out of my grip. It didn't seem to know that a projectile could come out of the end; I educated it on the subject. The creature brutalizing Gutierrez uttered a sharp click of what I hoped was terror and sprinted east, getting a running start at a tree, which it scaled and then hurled itself from, landing on another tree. It disappeared into the foliage.

I looked around. They were gone. They were *all* gone.

Something moved; I trained the rifle on it. It was Jane. She was pulling a knife out of one of the werewolves. Another werewolf lay nearby. I looked for Juan and Deit and found them on the ground, lifeless.

"Okay?" Jane said to me. I nodded. Jane stood, holding her side; blood slipped between her fingers.

"You're hurt," I said.

"I'm fine," she said. "It looks worse than it is."

In the distance there was a very human scream.

"DeLeon," Jane said, and started running, still holding her side. I gave chase.

Most of DeLeon was missing. Some of him was left behind. Wherever the rest of him was, it was still alive and screaming. A blood trail went from where he had sat to one of the trees. There was another scream.

"They're taking him north," I said. "Come on."

"No," Jane said, and pointed. In the east, there was movement in the trees. "They're using DeLeon as bait to lead us away. Most of them are headed east. Back toward the colony."

"We can't leave DeLeon," I said. "He's still alive."

"I'll get him," Jane said. "You get back. Be careful. Watch the trees and the ground." She was off.

Fifteen minutes later I breached the border of the woods and came back to colony ground to find four werewolves in a semicircle and Hiram Yoder standing silently at their focus. I dropped to the ground.

The werewolves didn't notice me; they were entirely intent on Yoder, who continued to stand stock-still. Two of the werewolves had spears trained on him, ready to run him through if he moved. He didn't. All four of them clicked and hissed, the hisses falling in and out of my sonic range; this was why Jane heard them before the rest of us did.

One of the werewolves came forward to Yoder, hissing and clicking at him, stocky and muscular where Yoder was tall and trim. It had a simple stone knife in one hand. It reached out a claw and poked Yoder hard in the chest; Yoder took it and stood there, silently. The thing grabbed his right arm and began to sniff it and examine it; Yoder offered no resistance. Yoder was a Mennonite, a pacifist.

The werewolf suddenly struck Yoder hard on the arm, perhaps testing him. Yoder staggered a bit from the blow but stood his ground. The werewolf let out a rapid series of chirps and then the others did, too; I suspected they were laughing.

The werewolf raked his claws across Yoder's face, shredding the man's right cheek with an audible scraping sound. Blood poured down Yoder's face; he involuntarily clutched it with his hand. The werewolf cooed and stared at Yoder, its four eyes unblinking, waiting to see what he would do.

Yoder dropped his hand from his ruined face and looked directly at the werewolf. He slowly turned his head to offer his other cheek.

The werewolf stepped away from Yoder and back toward its own, chirping. The two who had spears trained on Yoder let them drop slightly. I breathed a sigh of relief and looked down for a second, registering my own cold sweat. Yoder had kept himself alive by not offering resistance; the creatures, whatever else they were, were smart enough to see that he was not a threat.

I raised my head again to see one of the werewolves staring directly at me.

It let out a trilling cry. The werewolf closest to Yoder

glanced over at me, snarled and drove his stone knife into Yoder. Yoder stiffened. I raised my rifle and shot the werewolf in the head. It fell; the other werewolves bolted back into the woods.

I ran over to Yoder, who had collapsed on the ground, and was pawing gingerly at the stone knife. "Don't touch it," I said. If the knife had nicked any major blood vessels, pulling it out could cause him to bleed out.

"It hurts," Yoder said. He looked up at me and smiled, gritting his teeth. "Well, it almost worked."

"It did work," I said. "I'm sorry, Hiram. This wouldn't have happened if it wasn't for me."

"Not your fault," Hiram said. "I saw you drop and hide. Saw you give me a chance. You did the right thing." He reached out toward the corpse of the werewolf, touching the sprawled leg. "Wish you didn't have to shoot it," he said.

"I'm sorry," I said again. Hiram didn't have anything more to say.

"Hiram Yoder. Paulo Gutierrez. Juan Escobedo. Marco Flores. Deiter Gruber. Galen DeLeon," Manfred Trujillo said. "Six dead."

"Yes," I said. I sat at my kitchen table. Zoë was at Trujillo's, spending the night with Gretchen. Hickory and Dickory were with her. Jane was in the medical bay; on top of the gash in her side she had scraped herself up pretty badly chasing DeLeon. Babar was resting his head in my lap. I was patting it absentmindedly.

"One body," Trujillo said. I looked up at that. "A hundred of us went into those woods, where you told us to go. We found blood, but not a single one of their bodies. Those things took them with them."

"What about Galen?" I said. Jane had told me that she'd

found parts of him, leaving a trail as she went along. She stopped following after he stopped screaming, and when her own injuries kept her from going farther.

"We found a few things," Trujillo said. "Not enough to consider a body."

"Great," I said. "Just great."

"How do you feel?" Trujillo asked.

"Jesus, Man," I said. "How do you think I feel? We lost six people today. We lost godda—we lost Hiram Yoder. We would all be dead if it wasn't for him. He *saved* this colony, him and the Mennonites. Now he's dead, and it's my fault."

"It was Paulo who put that posse together," Trujillo said. "He went against your orders and he got five others killed. And put you and Jane in danger. If someone's going to shoulder the blame, it should be him."

"I'm not looking to blame Paulo," I said.

"I know you're not," Trujillo said. "That's why I'm saying it. Paulo was a friend of mine, as good a friend as I have here. But he did something foolish, and he got those men killed. He should have listened to you."

"Yes. Well," I said. "I thought making these creatures a state secret would *keep* something like this from happening. That's why I did it."

"Secrets have a way of getting out," Trujillo said. "You know that. Or should."

"I should have let everyone know about these things," I said.

"Maybe," Trujillo said. "You had to make a call here and you made it. It wasn't the one I would have thought you would make, I have to say. It wasn't like you. If you don't mind me saying so, you're not that good with secrets. People here aren't used to you having them, either."

I grunted assent and patted my dog. Trujillo shifted

uncomfortably in his chair for a few minutes. "What are you going to do now?" he asked.

"Fuck if I know," I said. "Right now what I'd really like to do is put a fist through my wall."

"I'd advise against that," Trujillo said. "I know you don't like taking my advice on general principle. Nevertheless, there it is."

I smiled at that one. I nodded toward the door. "How are people?"

"They're scared as hell," Trujillo said. "One man died yesterday, six more died today, five of *them* disappeared, and people are worried they'll be next. I suspect most people will be sleeping inside the village for the next couple of nights. I'm afraid the cat is out of the bag about these creatures being intelligent, by the way. Gutierrez told a whole lot of people while he was trying to recruit for his posse."

"I'm surprised another group hasn't gone out looking for the werewolves," I said.

"You're calling them werewolves?" Trujillo said.

"You saw the one that killed Hiram," I said. "Tell me that's not what it looks like."

"Do me a favor and don't share that name," Trujillo said. "People are scared enough."

"Fine," I said.

"And yes, there was another group who wanted to go out and try to get revenge. A bunch of idiot kids. Your daughter's boyfriend Enzo was one of them."

"Ex-boyfriend," I said. "Did you talk them out of doing something stupid?"

"I pointed out that five grown men went out hunting for them and not a single one of them came home," Trujillo said. "That seemed to calm them down a bit."

"Good," I said.

"You need to make an appearance tonight, down at the community hall," Trujillo said. "People will be there. They need to see you."

"I'm not in any shape to see people," I said.

"You don't have a choice," Trujillo said. "You're the colony leader. People are in mourning, John. You and your wife are the only ones that came out of this alive, and she's in the medical bay. If you spend the entire night hiding in here, it says to everyone out there that no one gets away from these things alive. And you kept a secret from them. You need to start making up for that."

"I didn't know you were a psychologist, Man," I said.

"I'm not," he said. "I'm a politician. And so are you, whether you want to admit to it or not. This is the job of a colony leader."

"I tell you truly, Man," I said. "If you asked for the job of colony leader, I would give it to you. Right now, I would. I know you think you *should* have been colony leader. So. The job is yours. Want it?"

Trujillo paused to consider his words. "You're right," he said. "I thought I should have been the colony leader. Occasionally I still do. And someday, I think I probably will be. But right now, it's *not* my job. It's yours. My job is to be your loyal opposition. And what your loyal opposition thinks is this: Your people are scared, John. You're their leader. Do some goddamn leading. Sir."

"That's the first time you've ever called me *sir*," I said, after a long minute.

Trujillo grinned. "I was saving it for a special moment," he said.

"Well, then," I said. "Well done. Well done, indeed."

Trujillo stood up. "I'll see you around this evening, then," he said.

"You will," I said. "I'll try to be reassuring. Thanks, Man." He waved off the thanks and left as someone else came walking up to my porch. It was Jerry Bennett.

I waved him in. "What do you have for me?" I asked.

"On the creatures, nothing," Bennett said. "I did all sorts of search parameters and came out with squat. There's not a lot to go on. They didn't do a whole lot of exploring on this planet."

"Tell me something I don't know," I said.

"All right," Bennett said. "You know that video file of the Conclave blasting that colony?"

"Yes," I said. "What does that have to do with this planet?"

"It doesn't," Bennett said. "I told you, I checked all the data files for edits under a batch command. It scooped up that file with all the rest of them."

"What about the file?" I asked.

"Well, it turns out the video file you have is only part of another video file. The metadata features time codes for the original video file. The time codes say your video is just the tail end of that other video. There's more video there."

"How much more?" I asked.

"A *lot* more," Bennett said.

"Can you get it back?" I asked.

Bennett smiled. "Already done," he said.

Six hours and a few dozen strained conversations with colonists later, I let myself into the Black Box. The PDA Bennett had loaded the video file into was on his desk, as promised. I picked it up; the video was already queued up and paused at the start. Its first image was of two creatures on a hill, overlooking a river. I recognized the hill and one of the creatures from the video I'd already seen. The other one I hadn't seen before. I squinted to get a better look, then cursed myself for being stupid and magnified the image. The other creature resolved itself.

It was a Whaid.

"Hello," I said to the creature. "What are you doing, talking to the guy who wiped out your colony?"

I started the video to find out.

EIGHT

The two stood near the edge of a bluff overlooking a river, watching the sunset over the far prairie.

"You have beautiful sunsets here," General Tarsem Gau said to Chan orenThen.

"Thank you," orenThen said. "It's the volcanoes."

Gau looked over at orenThen, amused. The rolling plain was interrupted only by the river, its bluffs and the small colony that lay where the bluffs descended toward the water.

"Not *here*," orenThen said, sensing Gau's unspoken observation. He pointed west, where the sun had just sunk below the horizon. "Half a planet that way. Lots of tectonic activity. There's a ring of volcanoes around the entire western ocean. One of them went up just as autumn ended. There's still dust in the atmosphere."

"Must have made for a hard winter," Gau said.

OrenThen made a motion that suggested otherwise. "Big enough eruption for nice sunsets. Not big enough for climate change. We have mild winters. It's one of the reasons we settled here. Hot summers, but good for growing. Rich soil. Excellent water supply."

"And no volcanoes," Gau said.

"No volcanoes," orenThen agreed. "No quakes, either, because we're right in the middle of a tectonic plate. Incredible thunderstorms, however. And last summer, tornadoes with hail the size of your head. We lost crops with that. But no place is entirely perfect. On balance this is a good place to start a colony, and to build a new world for my people."

"I agree," Gau said. "And from what I can tell, you've done a marvelous job leading this colony."

OrenThen bowed his head slightly. "Thank you, General. Coming from you, that's high praise indeed."

The two returned their attention to the sunset, watching as the early dusk deepened around them.

"Chan," Gau said. "You know I can't let you keep this colony."

"Aah," orenThen said, and smiled, still looking into the sunset. "So much for this being a social call."

"You know it's not," Gau said.

"I know," orenThen said. "Your knocking my communications satellite out of the sky was my first clue." OrenThen pointed down the slope of the bluff, where a platoon of Gau's soldiers stood, warily eyed by orenThen's own escort of farmers. "They were my second."

"They're for show," Gau said. "I needed to be able to talk to you without the distraction of being shot at."

"And blasting my satellite?" orenThen said. "That's not for show, I suspect."

"It was necessary, for your sake," Gau said.

"I doubt that," orenThen said.

"If I left you your satellite, you or someone in your colony would have sent a skip drone, letting your government know you were under attack," Gau said. "But that's not why I'm here."

"You just told me that I can't keep this colony," oren-Then said.

"You can't," Gau said. "But that's not the same thing as being under attack."

"The distinction escapes me, General," orenThen said. "Particularly with a very expensive satellite blown to bits by your guns, and your soldiers on my soil."

"How long have we known each other, Chan?" Gau said. "We've known each other a long time, as friends and adversaries. You've seen how I do things, up close. Have you ever known me to say one thing and mean another?"

OrenThen was quiet for a moment. "No," he said, finally. "You can be an arrogant ass, Tarsem. But you've always said what you meant to say."

"Then trust me once more," Gau said. "More than anything, I want this to end peacefully. It's why *I* am here, and not anyone else. Because what you and I do here matters, beyond the planet and this colony. I can't let your colony remain here. You know that. But that doesn't mean you or any of your people have to suffer for it."

There was another moment of silence from oren-Then. "I have to admit I was surprised that it was you on that ship," he eventually said to Gau. "We knew there was the risk that the Conclave would come for us. You didn't spend all that time wrestling all those races into line and declaring an end to colonization just to let us slip through the cracks. We planned for this possibility. But I assumed it would be some ship with a junior officer at the helm. Instead we get the leader of the Conclave."

"We are friends," Gau said. "You deserve the courtesy."

"You are kind to say so, General," orenThen said. "But, friend or not, it's overkill."

Gau smiled. "Well, possibly. Or, perhaps it's more accurate to say it *would* be overkill. But your colony is more important than you think, Chan."

"I don't see how," orenThen said. "I like it. There are good people here. But we're a seed colony. There are hardly two thousand of us. We're at subsistence level. All we do is grow food for ourselves and prepare for the next wave of settlers. And all they will do is prepare for the wave of settlers after them. There's nothing important about that."

"Now it's you who is being disingenuous," Gau said. "You know very well that it's not what your colony grows or makes that makes it important. It's the simple fact it exists, in violation of the Conclave Agreement. There are to be no new colonies that are not administered through the Conclave. The fact your people ignored the agreement is an explicit challenge to the legitimacy of the Conclave."

"We didn't *ignore* it," orenThen said, irritation creeping into his voice. "It simply doesn't apply to us. We didn't sign the Conclave Agreement, General. We didn't, nor did a couple hundred other races. We're free to colonize as we will. And that's what we did. You have no right to question that, General. We are a sovereign people."

"You're going formal on me," Gau said. "I remember that being a sure sign that I've pissed you off."

"Don't assume too much familiarity, General," orenThen said. "We have been friends, yes. Perhaps we still are. But you shouldn't doubt where my loyalties lie. Don't think that just because you've ensnared the majority of races into your Conclave that you have some great moral authority. Before the Conclave, if you were to attack my colony, it would be a land grab, pure and simple. Now that you have your precious Conclave, it's still a land grab, pure and simple."

"I remember when you thought the Conclave was a good idea," Gau said. "I remember you arguing for it to the other Whaid diplomats. I remember you convincing them, and them convincing your ataFuey to have the Whaid join the Conclave."

"The ataFuey was assassinated," orenThen said. "You know that. His son was of an entirely different mind."

"Yes he was," Gau said. "Oddly convenient for him that his father was assassinated when he was."

"I can't speak to that," orenThen said. "And after the new ataFuey took the throne it was not my place to go against his will."

"The ataFuey's son was a fool, and you know that," Gau said.

"That may be," orenThen said. "But as I said, you should not doubt where my loyalties lie."

"I don't doubt where they lie," Gau said. "I never have. They lie with the Whaidi people. That's why you fought for the Conclave. If the Whaid had joined the Conclave, you could have colonized this planet, with more than four hundred other races backing your right to be here."

"We *do* have a right to be here," orenThen said. "And we do have the planet."

"You're going to lose it," Gau said.

"And we never would have had this planet under the Conclave," orenThen said, plowing through Gau's words. "Because it would be Conclave territory, not Whaidi. We would merely be sharecroppers, sharing the planet with other Conclave races. That's still part of the Conclave mind-set, isn't it? Multiple races on single worlds? Build a planetary identity that's not based on species but on allegiance to the Conclave, to create a lasting peace. Or so you believe."

"You used to think that was a good idea, too," Gau said.

"Life surprises," orenThen said. "Things change."

"Indeed they do," Gau said. "You remember what set me on the path to the Conclave."

"The Battle of Amin, or so you like to say," orenThen said. "When you took back the planet from the Kies."

"Entirely unnecessarily," Gau said. "They're water dwellers. There was no rational reason we couldn't have shared the planet. But *we* wouldn't. *They* wouldn't. And both of us lost more than we could have won. Before that battle, I was as xenophobic as your damned ataFuey, and as much as you're pretending to be now. After it, I was ashamed how we poisoned that planet when we took it back. *Ashamed*, Chan. And I knew that it would never end. Unless *I* made it end. Unless *I* made things change."

"And here you are with your great Conclave, your so-called hope for peace in this part of space," orenThen said, mockingly. "And what you're doing with it is trying to pry me and my colony off this planet. You *haven't* made it end, General. You haven't made things change."

"No, I haven't," Gau admitted. "Not yet. But I'm getting closer."

"I'm still waiting to hear how any of this makes my colony so important," orenThen said.

"The Conclave Agreement says that those races who are members of the Conclave may not hold new worlds for themselves; they colonize the worlds they discover but other Conclave members will colonize, too," Gau said. "The agreement also says that when the Conclave finds a planet colonized by a non-Conclave species after the Agreement, it takes that planet for the Conclave. No one gets to colonize unless it's through the Conclave. We warned non-Conclave species about this."

"I remember," orenThen said. "I was chosen to lead this colony not long after you said this."

"And yet you colonized," Gau said.

"The Conclave was not a sure thing, General," orenThen said. "Despite your sense of destiny, you still could have failed."

"Fair enough," Gau said. "But I didn't fail. Now the Conclave exists, and now we have to enforce the Agreement. Several dozen colonies were founded after the Agreement was created. Including this one."

"Now I see," orenThen said. "We're the first in a series of conquests for the glory of the Conclave."

"No," Gau said. "Not conquests. I keep telling you this. I'm hoping for something else entirely."

"And what would that be?" orenThen asked.

"For you to leave on your own," Gau said.

OrenThen stared at Gau. "Old friend, you have entirely lost your mind," he said.

"Listen, Chan," Gau said, urgently. "There is a reason it starts here. I *know* you. I know where your loyalties lie— with your people, not with your ataFuey and his policy of racial suicide. The Conclave will *not* allow the Whaid to colonize. It's as simple as that. You will be held to the planets you had before the Agreement. No more. And from those few planets, you will see the rest of space fill up without you. You will be *isolated*—no trade and no travel to any other worlds. You will be contained, my friend. And contained, you will wither and die. You know the Conclave can do this. You know *I* can do this."

OrenThen said nothing. Gau continued. "I can't make the ataFuey change his mind. But you can help me show others that the Conclave would rather work through peace. Give up your colony. Convince your colonists to leave. You can return to your home world. I promise safe passage."

"You know that's an empty offer," orenThen said. "If we abandon this colony we'll be branded as traitors. All of us."

"Then join the Conclave, Chan," Gau said. "Not the Whaid. *You*. You and your colonists. The Conclave's first colony world is about to open to emigrants. Your colonists can be among them. You can still be the first to a new world. You can still be colonists."

"And you would get the public relations coup of not massacring a colony's worth of people," orenThen said.

"Yes," Gau said. "Of course. That's part of it. It will be easier to convince other colonies to leave their worlds if they can see that I spared you on this one. Avoiding bloodshed here can help us avoid bloodshed other places. You'll save more lives than those of your colonists."

"That's part of it, you said," orenThen said. "What's the other part?"

"I don't want you to die," Gau said.

"You mean you don't want to kill me," orenThen said.

"That's right," Gau said.

"But you *will*," orenThen pressed. "Me and every one of my colonists."

"Yes," Gau said.

OrenThen snorted. "Sometimes I really wish you didn't always mean what you say."

"I can't help it," Gau said.

"You never could," orenThen said. "It's part of what passes for your charm."

Gau said nothing, and looked toward the stars, which were beginning to show in the darkening sky. OrenThen followed his gaze. "Looking for your ship?"

"Found it," Gau said, and pointed upward. "The *Gentle Star*. You remember it."

"I do," orenThen said. "It was small and old back when I first met you. I'm surprised you still command from it."

"One of the nice things about running the universe is that you're allowed your affectations," Gau said.

OrenThen motioned back toward Gau's platoon. "If memory serves, you've got about enough space on the *Gentle* for a small company of soldiers. I don't doubt that's enough to do the job here. But if you're determined to make a statement, it seems underwhelming."

"First it's overkill, and now it's underwhelming," Gau said.

"*Your* being here is overkill," orenThen said. "It's your soldiers we're talking about now."

"I was hoping not to use any of them," Gau said. "And that you would listen to reason. That being the case, there wouldn't be a need to bring any more."

"And if I don't listen to 'reason'?" orenThen said. "You could take this colony with a company, General. But we can make you pay for it. Some of my people were soldiers. All of them are tough. Some of your soldiers would be buried with us."

"I know," Gau said. "But it was never my plan to use my soldiers. If you won't listen to reason—or the pleadings of an old friend—I have another plan in mind."

"Which is?" orenThen asked.

"I'll show you," Gau said, and looked back toward his platoon. One of the soldiers came forward; Gau nodded to him. The soldier saluted and began speaking into a communications device. Gau returned his attention to oren-Then.

"Since you once lobbied your own government to join the Conclave—and failed, through no fault of your own—I'm sure you can appreciate it when I tell you that it's nothing short of miraculous that the Conclave exists at all," Gau said. "There are four hundred and twelve races within the Conclave, each of them with their own plans and agendas, all of which had to be taken into consideration as the Conclave came into being. Even now the Conclave is a fragile thing. There are factions and alliances. Some races joined the Conclave thinking they could bide their time before taking it over. Others joined thinking the Conclave would be a free ride to colonization, with nothing else expected from them. I've had to make them *all* understand that the Conclave means security for all of them, and expects responsibility from all of them. And those races who didn't join the Conclave have to learn that what the Conclave does—all of its members do."

"So you're here in the name of all the Conclave races," orenThen said.

"That's not what I mean," Gau said.

"You've lost me again, General," orenThen said.

"Look," Gau said, and pointed toward his ship again. "You can see the *Gentle*?"

"Yes," orenThen said.

"Tell me what else you see," Gau said.

"I see stars," orenThen said. "What else am I supposed to be seeing?"

"Keep watching," Gau said.

A moment later a point of light appeared in the sky, near the *Gentle*. Then another, and another.

"More ships," orenThen said.

"Yes," Gau said.

"How many?" orenThen asked.

"Keep watching," Gau said.

The ships winked in, singly, then in pairs and triplets, then in constellations.

"So many," orenThen said, after some time.

"Keep watching," Gau said.

OrenThen waited until he was sure no more ships were coming before he turned again to look at Gau, who was still looking into the sky.

"There are four hundred and twelve ships in your sky," Gau said. "One ship from every member race of the Conclave. This is the fleet with which we will visit every world that was colonized, without authorization, after the Agreement." Gau turned again and looked for his lieutenant, whom he could barely see in the gloom. Gau gave his lieutenant a second nod. The soldier spoke in his communicator again.

From each ship in the sky, a beam of coherent light stabbed into the colony on the riverbank, blanketing the colony in white. OrenThen let out an agonized, bursting cry.

"Spotlights, Chan," Gau said. "Only spotlights."

It took a few moments before orenThen could respond. "Spotlights," he said, finally. "But only for the moment, correct?"

"At my order, every ship in the fleet will refocus its beam," Gau said. "Your colony will be destroyed, and every member race of the Conclave will have a hand in it. This is how it has to be done. Security for all, responsibility from all. And no race can say it did not agree to the cost."

"I wish I'd killed you when I first saw you here," orenThen said. "Us standing here talking about sunsets when you had this waiting for me. You and your damned Conclave."

Gau spread his arms, opening himself. "Kill me, Chan. It won't save this colony. It won't stop the Conclave, either. Nothing you can do will stop the Conclave from taking this planet, or the next, or the next. The Conclave is four hundred peoples. Every race who fights against it fights alone. The Whaid. The Rraey. The Fran. The Humans. All of the others who have started colonies since the Agreement. If nothing else, it's a matter of numbers. We have more. One race against one other race is one thing. One race against four hundred is quite another. All it will take is time."

OrenThen turned away from Gau and toward his colony, bathed in light. "I'll tell you something," orenThen said to Gau. "You might find it ironic. When I was chosen to lead this colony, I warned the ataFuey that you would come for it. You and the entire Conclave. He told me that the Conclave would never form and that you were a fool for trying, and that I had been a fool for ever listening to you. There were too many races ever to agree to anything, much less a grand alliance. And that the enemies of the Conclave were working too hard to fail. He said the Humans would stop you if no one else did. He thought highly of their ability to set everyone against each other without getting involved themselves."

"He wasn't far wrong," Gau said. "But the Humans over-reached. They always do. The opposition they created to counter the Conclave fell apart. Most of *those* races are now more concerned about the Humans than they are about us. By the time the Conclave gets to the Humans, there may not be many of them left."

"You could have gone after the Humans first," orenThen said.

"In time," Gau said.

"Let me put it another way," orenThen said. "You didn't have to come *here* first."

"*You* were here," Gau said. "You have a history with the Conclave. You have a history with me. Anywhere else and there would be no question that this would begin with destruction. Here you and I have a chance for something else. Something that will matter beyond this moment and this colony."

"You've put a lot on me," orenThen said. "And on my people."

"I have," Gau said. "I'm sorry, old friend. I couldn't see

any other way. I saw a chance to show people that the Conclave wants peace, and I had to take it. It's a lot to ask of you. But I *am* asking you, Chan. Help me. Help me save your people, not destroy them. Help me build peace in our part of space. I beg this of you."

"You beg me?" orenThen said, his voice rising. He advanced on Gau. "You have *four hundred and twelve* battleships pointing their weapons at my colony and you beg me to help you build *peace*? Fah. Your words mean nothing, *old friend*. You come here, peddling that friendship, and in return for it ask me to exchange my colony, my loyalty, my identity. Everything I have. At the end of a gun. To help you provide the *illusion* of peace. The *illusion* that what you do here is something other than simple, raw conquest. You dangle the lives of my colonists in front of me, and tell me to choose between making them traitors or killing them all. And then you suggest to me that you're *compassionate*. You can go to hell, General." OrenThen turned and stalked away, putting distance between himself and Gau.

"That's your decision, then," Gau said, some time later.

"No," orenThen said, still facing away from the general. "It's not a decision I can make on my own. I need time to talk to my people, to let them know what their choices are."

"How much time do you need?" Gau said.

"The nights here are long," orenThen said. "Give me this one."

"It's yours," Gau said. OrenThen nodded and began to walk away.

"Chan," Gau began, walking toward the Whaid. Oren-Then stopped and held up one of his massive paws to silence the general. Then he turned and held out his paws to Gau, who took them.

"I remember meeting you, you know," orenThen said. "I was there when the old ataFuey received the invitation to meet with you and every other race who would come to that damned cold rock of a moon you so grandly called neutral ground. I remember you standing at that podium, saying welcome in all the languages you could croak, and for the first time sharing your idea of the Conclave with us. And I remember turning to the ataFuey, and telling him that without a doubt, you were absolutely and totally madhouse insane."

Gau laughed.

"And then afterward you met with us, as you met with every embassy there who would hear you," orenThen said. "And I remember you trying to convince us that the Conclave was something we wanted to be a part of. I remember you winning me over."

"Because I wasn't truly madhouse insane," Gau said.

"Oh, no, General. You were," orenThen said. "Entirely and completely. But you were also *right*. And I remember thinking to myself, what if this mad general actually pulls it off? I tried to imagine it—our part of space, at peace. And I *couldn't*. It was like a white wall of stone in front of me, keeping me from seeing it. And that's when I knew *I* would fight for the Conclave. I couldn't see the peace it would bring. I couldn't even imagine it. All I knew was that I wanted it. And I knew that if anyone could bring it into being, it would be this mad general. I believed it." OrenThen let go of the general's hands. "It's so long ago now," he said.

"My old friend," Gau said.

"Old friend," orenThen agreed. "Old indeed. And now I must go. I'm glad to have seen you again, Tarsem. I truly am. These are not the circumstances I would have chosen, of course."

"Of course," Gau said.

"But isn't that the way of things. Life surprises." Oren-Then turned again to go.

"How will I know when you've reached a decision?" Gau asked.

"You'll know," orenThen said, not looking back.

"How?" Gau asked.

"You'll hear it," orenThen said, and turned his head back to the general. "That much, I can promise." Then he turned back and walked to his transport, and with his escort drove away.

Gau's lieutenant approached him. "What did he mean when he said you'll hear his answer, General?" he asked.

"They chant," Gau said, and pointed toward the colony, still under spotlight. "Their highest art form is a ritualized chant. It's how they celebrate, and mourn, and pray. Chan was letting me know that when he's done talking with his colonists, they would chant their answer to me."

"Are we going to hear it from here?" the lieutenant asked.

Gau smiled. "You wouldn't be asking that if you'd ever heard a Whaidi chant, Lieutenant."

Gau waited the long night, listening, his vigil occasionally interrupted by the lieutenant or one of the other soldiers offering him a hot drink to keep him alert. It wasn't until the colony's sun rose out of the eastern sky that Gau heard what he was listening for.

"What is that?" the lieutenant asked.

"Quiet," Gau said, and waved his annoyance. The lieutenant backed off. "They've begun their chanting," Gau said a moment later. "Right now they're chanting a welcome to the morning."

"What does it mean?" the lieutenant asked.

"It means they're welcoming the morning," Gau said. "It's *ritual*, Lieutenant. They do it every day."

The morning prayer rose and fell in volume and intensity, continuing on for what seemed to the general a maddeningly long time. And then it came to a ragged, hesitant ending; Gau, who had been pacing through the latter parts of the morning prayer, stopped stock-still.

From the colony came a new chant, in a new rhythm, growing progressively louder. Gau listened to it for several long moments and then slumped, as if suddenly tired.

The lieutenant was at his side almost instantly. Gau waved him off. "I'm fine," he said. "I'm fine."

"What are they chanting now, General?" the lieutenant asked.

"Their anthem," Gau said. "Their national anthem." He stood up. "They're saying that they won't leave. They're saying they would rather die as Whaidi than live under the Conclave. Every man, woman and child in that colony."

"They're crazy," the lieutenant said.

"They're patriots, Lieutenant," Gau said, turning to the officer. "And they've chosen what they believe in. Don't be disrespectful of that choice."

"Sorry, General," the lieutenant said. "I just don't understand the choice."

"I do," Gau said. "I just hoped it would be different. Bring me a communicator." The lieutenant hustled off. Gau turned his attention to the colony, listening to its members chanting their defiance.

"You always were stubborn, old friend," Gau said.

The lieutenant returned with a communicator. Gau took it, keyed in his encrypted code and opened it to a common channel. "This is General Tarsem Gau," he said. "All ships recalibrate beam weapons and prepare to fire on my mark." The spotlights, still visible in the morning light, disappeared as the ships' weapons crews recalibrated their beams.

The chanting stopped.

Gau nearly dropped his communicator. He stood, mouth agape, staring at the colony. He walked slowly toward the edge of the bluff, whispering something softly. The lieutenant, standing nearby, strained to hear.

General Tarsem Gau was praying.

The moment held, suspended in the air. And then the colonists took up their anthem once more.

General Gau stood on the edge of the bluff overlooking a river, now silent, eyes closed. He listened to the anthem for what seemed like forever.

He raised his communicator.

"Fire," he said.

NINE Jane had gotten out of the medical bay and was waiting for me on the porch of our bungalow, eyes up at the stars.

"Looking for something?" I asked.

"Patterns," Jane said. "All the time we've been here, no one's made any constellations. I thought I'd try."

"How's it going?" I asked.

"Terrible," she said, looking at me. "It took me forever to see the constellations on Huckleberry, and they were already there. Making up new ones is even more trouble. I just see stars."

"Just focus on the bright ones," I said.

"That's a problem," Jane said. "My eyes are better than yours now. Better than everyone else's. They're *all* bright. That's probably why I never saw constellations until I came to Huckleberry. Too much information. You need human eyes to see constellations. Just another piece of my humanity taken away." She looked up again.

"How are you feeling?" I asked, watching her.

"I'm fine," Jane said. She raised up the hem of her shirt; the slash in her side was livid even in the dim light, but far less worrisome than it had been before. "Dr. Tsao patched it up, but it was healing even before she got to it. She wanted to take a blood sample to check for infection but I told her not to bother. It's all SmartBlood by now, anyway. I didn't tell her that." She dropped her hem.

"No green skin, though," I said.

"No," Jane said. "No cat's eyes, either. Or BrainPal. Which is not to say that I don't have increased capabilities. They're just not obvious, for which I'm grateful. Where have you been?"

"Watching the director's cut of the Whaidi colony annihilation," I said. Jane looked at me quizzically; I recounted what I'd just been watching.

"Do you believe it?" Jane asked me.

"Do I believe what?" I asked.

"That this General Gau was hoping not to destroy the colony," Jane said.

"I don't know," I said. "The discussion was honest enough. And if he simply wanted to destroy the colony, he could have done it without having to go through the mime show of trying to get the colony to surrender."

"Unless it was a terror tactic," Jane said. "Break the colonists' will, get them to surrender, destroy them anyway. Send the evidence to other races to demoralize them."

"Sure," I said. "That only makes sense if you're planning to subjugate the race. But that doesn't sound like how the Conclave is supposed to work. It sounds like it's a union of races, not an empire."

"I'd be careful of making assumptions based on one video," Jane said.

"I know," I said. "But it's bothering me. The video the CU gave us shows the Conclave simply destroying the Whaidi colony. We're supposed to see the Conclave as a threat. But the video I've just seen says to me it's not that simple."

"That's why it was edited out," Jane said.

"Because it's ambiguous?" I asked.

"Because it's confusing," Jane said. "The Colonial Union sent us here with specific instructions and gave us the information to support those instructions, without the information that would cause us to doubt them."

"You don't see that as a problem," I said.

"I see it as tactical," Jane said.

"But we've been working on the premise that the Conclave is an immediate and genocidal threat," I said. "This suggests it's not."

"You're back to making assumptions without much information," Jane said.

"*You* knew about the Conclave," I said. "Is a genocidal Conclave consistent with what you know?"

"No," Jane said. "But I've said before that what I know about the Conclave comes from Charles Boutin, who was actively planning treason against the Colonial Union. He's not credible."

"It still bothers me," I said. "I don't like it that all this information was kept from us."

"The Colonial Union manages information," Jane said. "It's how it keeps control. I've told you this before. It shouldn't be news now."

"It makes me wonder what else we don't know," I said. "And why."

"We can't know," Jane said. "We have the information the Colonial Union has provided us on the Conclave. We have what little I know. And we have this new portion of video. That's all we have."

I thought about it a minute. "No," I said. "We have something else."

"Can you two lie?" I asked Hickory. It and Dickory were standing in front of me in our bungalow's living room. I was sitting in my desk chair; Jane stood to my side. Zoë, whom we had woken up, was yawning on the couch.

"We have not yet lied to you," Hickory said.

"But you can clearly evade, since that's not what I asked you," I said.

"We can lie," Hickory said. "It is a benefit of consciousness."

"I wouldn't call it a benefit," I said.

"It opens up a number of intriguing possibilities in communication," Hickory said.

"I suppose that's true," I said. "None of which I'm interested in right now." I turned to Zoë. "Sweetheart, I want you to order these two to answer all my questions truthfully, without any lies or evasions."

"Why?" Zoë said. "What's going on?"

"Please do it, Zoë," I said. Zoë did as I asked.

"Thank you," I said. "You can go back to bed now, sweetie."

"I want to know what's going on," Zoë said.

"It's not something you need to worry about," I said.

"You order me to have these two tell you the truth, and you want me to believe it's *not* something I need to worry about?" Zoë said.

"Zoë," Jane said.

"Besides, if I leave there's no guarantee they won't lie to you," Zoë said, moving quickly before Jane could finish. Zoë knew she could negotiate with me; Jane was much more of a hard-ass. "They're emotionally equipped to lie to you, because they don't care about disappointing you. But they don't want to disappoint *me*."

I turned back to Hickory. "Is this true?" I asked.

"We would lie to you if we felt it was necessary," Hickory said. "We would not lie to Zoë."

"There you go," Zoë said.

"Breathe a word of this to anyone and you're spending the next year in a horse stall," I said.

"My lips are sealed," Zoë said.

"No," Jane said, and came over to Zoë. "I need you to understand that what you're hearing here you absolutely cannot share with anyone else. Not Gretchen. Not any of your other friends. Not anyone. It's not a game and it's not a fun secret. This is dead serious business, Zoë. If you're not ready to accept that, you need to leave this room right now. I'll take my chances with Hickory and Dickory lying to us, but not you. So do you understand that when we tell you not to share this with anyone, that you *cannot* share it with anyone else? Yes or no."

"Yes," Zoë said, staring up at Jane. "I understand, Jane. Not a word."

"Thank you, Zoë," Jane said, and then bent down and kissed the top of Zoë's head. "Go ahead," she said, to me.

"Hickory, you remember when we had the conversation where I told the two of you that I wanted you to hand over your consciousness implants," I said.

"Yes," said Hickory.

"We talked about the Conclave then," I said. "And you said that you didn't believe the Conclave was a threat to this colony."

"I said that we believed the threat to be negligible," Hickory said.

"Why do you believe that?" I asked.

"The Conclave prefers that colonies are evacuated rather than destroyed," Hickory said.

"How do you know this?" I said.

"From our own information on the Conclave, provided to us by our government," Hickory said.

"Why didn't you share this information with us before?" I asked.

"We were told not to," Hickory said.

"By whom?" I asked.

"By our government," Hickory said.

"Why would they tell you not to share this?" I asked.

"We have a standing order from our government not to share information with you on matters about which you are not substantially informed," Hickory said. "It is a courtesy to your government, which requires security and confidence from our own government on numerous matters. We have not lied to you, Dickory and I, but we are not allowed to volunteer information, either. You will recall before we left Huckleberry that we had asked you what you knew of the status of this part of space."

"Yes," I said.

"We were attempting to discover how much of our knowledge we were allowed to share with you," Hickory said. "We regret to say it did not appear you knew much. So we were not able to share much."

"You're sharing it now," I said.

"You're asking now," Hickory said. "And Zoë has told us not to lie."

"You've seen our video of the Conclave destroying the Whaidi colony," I said.

"Yes, when you shared it with all of your colonists," Hickory said.

"Did it match your own video?" I asked.

"No," Hickory said. "Ours was much longer."

"Why would our version be so much shorter?" I asked.

"We cannot speculate why your government does the things it does," Hickory said.

I paused at this; the construction of the sentence left a lot of room for interpretation.

Jane jumped in. "You said the Conclave prefers to evacuate colonies rather than destroy them. Are you saying this because of the video or do you have other information?"

"We have other information," Hickory said. "The video shows only the first attempt by the Conclave to remove a colony."

"How many others have there been?" Jane asked.

"We do not know," Hickory said. "We have been out of communication with our government for the better part of a Roanoke year. However, when we left, the Conclave had removed seventeen colonies."

"How many of those were destroyed?" Jane asked.

"Three," Hickory said. "The rest were evacuated. In ten cases the colonists repatriated with their races. Four chose to join the Conclave."

"You have evidence of this," I said.

"The Conclave extensively documents each colony removal and shares it with every nonmember government," Hickory said. "We have information on all the removals up to our arrival here on Roanoke."

"Why?" Jane asked. "What relevance does this information have to the two of you?"

"Our government was well aware this colony was being founded despite the warnings of the Conclave," Hickory said. "And while we did not know for certain, we expected that the Colonial Union would attempt to hide this colony from the Conclave. When the Conclave found your colony, we were to show you this information."

"For what purpose?" Jane asked.

"To convince you to surrender the colony," Hickory said. "We could not allow it to be destroyed."

"Because of Zoë," I said.

"Yes," Hickory said.

"Wow," Zoë said.

"Quiet, sweetheart," I said. Zoë lapsed back into silence. I studied Hickory carefully. "What would happen if Jane and I chose not to surrender the colony?" I asked. "What if she and I decided the colony should be destroyed instead?"

"We would prefer not to say," Hickory said.

"Don't evade," I said. "Answer the question."

"We would kill you and Lieutenant Sagan," Hickory said. "You and any other colonist leader who would authorize the destruction of the colony."

"You would kill us?" I said.

"It would be difficult for us," Hickory allowed. "We would have to do it without our consciousness implants active, and I believe neither Dickory nor I would choose to activate them again. The emotions would be unbearable. Also, we are aware Lieutenant Sagan has been genetically altered back to Special Forces operational parameters. This would make killing her more difficult."

"How do you know that?" Jane said, surprised.

"We observe," Hickory said. "We know you try to hide it, Lieutenant. Small things reveal you. You chop vegetables far too quickly."

"What are they talking about?" Zoë asked Jane.

"Later, Zoë," Jane said, and turned her attention back to Hickory. "What about now?" Jane asked. "Would you still kill me and John?"

"If you choose not to surrender the colony, yes," Hickory said.

"Don't you *dare*," Zoë said. She stood up, furious. "Under no circumstances will you do that."

Hickory and Dickory trembled with emotional overload, attempting to process Zoë's anger. "This one thing we must refuse you," Hickory eventually said to Zoë. "You are too important. To us. To all Obin."

Zoë was incandescent with rage. "I've already lost one parent because of the *Obin*," Zoë said.

"Everybody calm down," I said. "No one is killing anyone. All right? This is a nonissue. Zoë, Hickory and Dickory aren't going to kill us because we're not going to let the colony be destroyed. Simple as that. And there is no way I would let anything happen to *you*, Zoë. Hickory and Dickory and I *all* agree that you are too important for that."

Zoë took a sharp intake of breath and started sobbing. Jane reeled her in and sat her back down. I turned my attention to the two Obin.

"I want to make this clear to the two of you," I said. "In all circumstances, protect Zoë."

"We will," Hickory said. "Always."

"Good," I said. "Do *try* not to kill me in the process. Or Jane."

"We will try," Hickory said.

"Good," I said. "Settled. Let's move on." I had to stop a minute to recollect my thoughts; being informed I was an assassination target and Zoë's subsequent and entirely justified meltdown had well and truly rattled my cage. "You said there were seventeen colony removals that you know about," I said.

"Yes," Hickory said.

"Fourteen of them had the colonists survive, and four of those joined the Conclave," I said. "You mean those colonists joined, or the whole race joined?"

"The colonists joined," Hickory said.

"So none of the races whose colonies have been removed have joined the Conclave," I said.

"No," Hickory said. "This has been a matter of some concern within the Conclave itself. It was assumed that at least some of these races would then accept the invitation to join the Conclave. The removals seem to have hardened resolve otherwise."

"Races are not forced to join the Conclave," Jane said from the couch.

"No," Hickory said. "They are simply not allowed to expand further."

"I don't see how they could enforce that," I said. "It's a big universe."

"It is," Hickory said. "But no race has been willing to forgo administration of their colonies. There's always a way to discover the colonies."

"Except this one," I said. "That's why they've had us hide. It's more important for humans to survive in the universe than it is to control them."

"Perhaps," Hickory said.

"I want to see those files you have, Hickory," Jane said. "And the extended version of our video," she said to me.

"We will need to go to the technology lab to transfer them," Hickory said.

"No time like the present," I said. Jane and I kissed Zoë good night, and then we headed out the door to the Black Box, Hickory and Dickory taking the lead.

"Why did you say that in there?" Jane asked, as we walked.

"Say what?" I said.

"That we wouldn't allow the colony to be destroyed," Jane said.

"For one thing, our daughter was on the verge of a nervous breakdown thinking about Hickory and Dickory running us through with knives," I said. "And for another thing, if the options are surrendering and turning every man, woman and child in the colony into ash, I know what I'm going to do."

"You're making assumptions on limited information again," Jane said. "I need to look at those tapes before we make any sort of decision about anything. Until then, every option is on the table."

"I can already tell we're going to go round and round on this one," I said, and looked up at the stars. Jane looked up with me. "I wonder which one of those has Huckleberry around it," I said. "I think maybe we all should have stayed there. Then this would be someone else's problem. At least for a while."

"John," Jane said. I turned. She had stopped several steps behind me now and was still looking up.

"What?" I said. I looked up again. "Made a constellation?"

"There's a star up there that wasn't there before," Jane said, and pointed. "That one."

I squinted, and then realized it didn't matter whether I squinted or not, since I didn't know which stars were supposed to be there and which ones weren't. And then I saw it. Bright. And moving.

"Oh God," I said.

Jane shrieked and fell to the ground, clutching her head. I sprinted over to her. She was convulsing now. I tried to get hold of her and her arm whipped out, her hand smacking palm first onto the side of my head, slapping me hard into the ground. I saw a white flash and spent the next few indeterminate moments immobile, trying not to vomit.

Hickory and Dickory hauled me up from the dirt, one at each arm. I looked around groggily for Jane. She was no longer on the ground; instead she was stalking furiously, muttering like a mad woman. She stopped, arched her back and screamed like a banshee. I hollered myself, in total surprise.

Eventually she stalked over to me. "You're going to have to meet them without me, because right now I will fucking kill every last one of them," she said.

"What are you talking about?" I said.

"The fucking Colonial Union," Jane said, and stabbed

a finger skyward. "That's them, and they're coming down now. Here."

"How do you know?" I said.

Jane looked away and laughed an eerie little laugh that I'd never heard from her before and sincerely hoped I never would again. "Yes. Well. Remember when we were talking earlier about my new abilities, and I said I didn't have a BrainPal?"

"Yes," I said.

"Yeah," Jane said. "Turns out, I was wrong."

"I have to tell you, I thought you'd be happy to see me," General Rybicki said. "Everyone else seems to be." He waved out my window to the street, which was filled with the early morning image of Roanokers going out of their minds with joy that their isolation was coming to an end. "Where's Sagan?"

"You need to tell me what the fuck is going on, General," I said.

Rybicki looked back toward me. "Excuse me?" he said. "I'm not your commanding officer anymore, Perry, but I'm still your superior. A little more respect would be in order."

"Fuck that," I said. "And fuck you too. There hasn't been a thing about this colony you've been straight about since you recruited us."

"I've been as honest with you as I could," Rybicki said.

"As honest as you could," I said, and there was no mistaking the incredulousness in my voice.

"Let me rephrase," Rybicki said. "I've been as honest with you as I've been allowed to be."

"You lied to me and Jane and an entire colony's worth of people," I said. "You've shunted us to the ass end of the universe and threatened us with annihilation from a group none of us even knew existed. You took colonists trained on modern equipment and forced them to colonize with ancient machines they barely knew how to use. If some of our colonists hadn't happened to have been Mennonites, the only thing you would have found here would have been bones. And because you didn't survey this planet well enough to know it has its own goddamned intelligent species, seven of my colonists have died in the last three days. So with all due *respect*, General, you can kiss my ass. Jane's not here because if she was, you'd probably already be dead. I'm not feeling any more charitable to you myself."

"Fair enough," Rybicki said, grimly.

"Now," I said. "Answers."

"Since you mentioned annihilation, you know about the Conclave," Rybicki said. "How much do you know?"

"I know what information you sent us," I said, neglecting to mention I knew anything else.

"Then you know that it is actively seeking out new colonies and getting rid of them," Rybicki said. "As you might expect, this is not going over well with the races who have had their colonies expunged. The Colonial Union has taken the lead in resisting the Conclave, and this colony has played a major role in that."

"How?" I said.

"By staying hidden," Rybicki said. "Christ, Perry, you've been here for almost a *year*. The Conclave has been going nuts looking for you. And every day it hasn't found you, the less terrifying it looks. The more it looks like what it is: the universe's biggest pyramid scheme. It's a system where a few strong races are leveraging the gullibility of a bunch of weaker races to snap up every habitable planet in sight. We've been using this colony as a lever to pry off some of those sucker races. We're destabilizing the Conclave before it can reach critical mass and crush us and everyone else with it."

"And this required deceiving everyone, including the crew of the *Magellan*," I said.

"Unfortunately, yes," Rybicki said. "Look. The number of people who knew about this had to be kept to an absolute bare minimum. The Secretary of Colonization. Me. General Szilard of the Special Forces and a few of his handpicked soldiers. I supervised the load out and engineered some of the colonial selection. It's not an *accident* you have Mennonites here, Perry. And it's not an accident you had enough ancient machinery to get you through. It's regrettable that we couldn't tell you, and I'm sorry that we couldn't see another way to do this. But I'm not going to apologize for it, because it *worked*."

"And how is this playing back home?" I said. "How do the home planets of our people feel about you playing with the lives of their friends and families?"

"They don't know," Rybicki said. "The existence of the Conclave is a state secret, Perry. We haven't told the individual colonies about it. It's not something they need to worry about yet."

"You don't think a federation of a few hundred other races in this part of space is something most people might want to know about," I said.

"I'm sure they'd want to know about it," Rybicki said. "And between you and me, if I had my way, they probably would know about it already. But it's not up to me, or you or any of us."

"So everyone still thinks we're lost," I said.

"They do," Rybicki said. "The second lost colony of Roanoke. You're famous."

"But you've just given the game away," I said. "You're *here*. When you go back, people are going to know we're here. And *my* people know about the Conclave."

"How do they know?" Rybicki asked.

"Because we *told* them," I said, disbelieving. "Are you serious? You expect me to tell people they can't use any technology more advanced than a mechanical combine and not give them a reason? I would have been the first death on the planet. So they know. And because *they* know, everyone they know back in the Colonial Union will know, too. Unless you plan to keep us stranded. In which case those same people who are jumping for joy outside that window will string you up by your thumbs."

"No, you're not being put back in the hole," Rybicki said. "On the other hand, you're not quite out of the hole yet, either. We're here to do two things. The first is to pick up the crew of the *Magellan*."

"For which they will no doubt be eternally grateful, although I expect Captain Zane wants his ship back," I said.

"The second thing is to let you know that all the equipment you haven't been using, you can now," Rybicki said. "Say good-bye to the second millennium. Welcome to modern times. You can't send messages back to the Colonial Union yet, though. There are still a few details to develop."

"Using modern equipment will give us away," I said.

"That's right," Rybicki said.

"You're giving me whiplash," I said. "We've spent a year hiding so you can weaken the Conclave, and now you want us to give ourselves away. Maybe I'm confused, but I'm not sure how getting ourselves slaughtered by the Conclave helps the Colonial Union."

"You're presuming you're going to get slaughtered," Rybicki said.

"Is there another option?" I asked. "If we ask nicely, will the Conclave just let us pack up and go?"

"That's not what I'm saying," Rybicki said. "I'm saying that the Colonial Union has kept you hidden because we needed to keep you hidden. Now we need to let the Conclave know where you are. We have something planned. And once we spring our little surprise, then there'll be no point keeping either you or the Conclave a secret from the colonies. Because the Conclave will have collapsed, and you will have been the key."

"You need to tell me *how*," I said.

"Fine," Rybicki said, and did.

"How are you?" I asked Jane, in the Black Box.

"I don't want to knife people anymore, if that's what you're asking," Jane said, and tapped her forehead, signifying the BrainPal nestled behind it. "I'm still not happy about this."

"How could you not know it was there?" I asked.

"BrainPals are remotely activated," Jane said. "I couldn't have turned it on myself. Rybicki's ship sent out a search signal; the signal woke up the BrainPal. Now it's on. Listen, I've gone through the files Hickory gave me."

"All of them?" I asked.

"Yes," Jane said. "I've been completely made over and have the BrainPal. I can go back to Special Forces processing speed."

"And?" I asked.

"They check out," Jane said. "Hickory has video and documentation from Conclave sources, which is suspect. But he has corroborating material for each case, from Obin sources, from the races whose colonies were removed and from the Colonial Union, too."

"They could all be faked," I said. "It could be a monumental hoax."

"No," Jane said. "The Colonial Union files have a verification hash in the metatext. I ran them through the BrainPal. They're genuine."

"Certainly gives you an appreciation for ol' Hickory, doesn't it," I said.

"It does," Jane said. "He wasn't lying when he said the Obin wouldn't send just anyone to be with Zoë. Although from what I can see from these files, it's Dickory who is the superior of the two."

"Jesus," I said. "Just when you think you know a guy. Or gal. Or creature of indeterminate gender, which is what it is."

"It's not indeterminate," Jane said. "It's both."

"What about this General Gau," I said. "Do your files have anything on him?"

"Some," Jane said. "Just the basics. He's Vrenn, and what he says in the extended tape of ours appears to be correct; after the battle with the Kies he began agitating to create the Conclave. It didn't go over at first. He was thrown into prison for political agitation. But then the Vrenn ruler met an unfortunate end and the general was released by the next regime."

I raised an eyebrow. "Assassination?" I asked.

"No," Jane said. "Chronic sleep disorder. Fell asleep while eating and fell face forward on his dinner knife. Penetrated the brain. Died instantly. The general probably could have ruled Vrennu but decided to attempt the Conclave instead. He still doesn't rule Vrennu. It wasn't even one of the Conclave's founding members."

"When I was talking to Rybicki, he said that the Conclave was a pyramid scheme," I said. "Some of the races at the top were getting the benefits and those at the bottom were getting pissed on."

"Maybe," Jane said. "From what I saw in the files the first colony worlds the Conclave opened up were populated by relatively few races. But whether that was indicative of some races getting an advantage, or of matching the races to the planet, is not something I could tell you.

Even if it is the former, it's not any different than what's happening here. This colony is entirely settled by the oldest human colonies, the ones that existed before the Colonial Union. Ethnically and economically they're nothing like the rest of the colonies."

"Do you think the Conclave is a threat to us?" I asked Jane.

"Of course I do," Jane said. "These files make it clear that the Conclave will destroy a colony that doesn't surrender. Their mode of operation is always the same: Fill the sky with starships and have every single one fire on the colony. Major cities wouldn't survive that, much less a colony. Roanoke would be vaporized instantly."

"But do you think it's likely?" I asked.

"I don't know," Jane said. "I have better data than I did before, but the data are still incomplete. We're missing the better part of a year of information, and I don't think we're going to get any more. Not from the Colonial Union, anyway. I can tell you right now I'm not cleared to see the Colonial Union files that Hickory gave me. And no matter what, I'm not inclined to surrender the colony without a fight. Did you tell Rybicki what we know?"

"No," I said. "And I don't think we should tell him what we know, either. At least not yet."

"You don't trust him," Jane said.

"Let's just say I have concerns," I said. "Rybicki didn't go out of his way to offer up anything, either. I asked him if he thought the Conclave would let us just walk away from this planet if we wanted to, and he suggested that they wouldn't."

"He lied to you," Jane said.

"He chose to respond differently than total honesty would dictate," I said. "I'm not sure that's exactly a lie."

"You don't see that as a problem," Jane said.

"I see it as tactical," I said. Jane smiled at the reversal of our earlier conversation. "But it also suggests to me that we may not want to swallow every line he gives us. We've been maneuvered before. I don't doubt we're being maneuvered again."

"You sound like Trujillo," Jane said.

"I wish I *did* sound like Trujillo," I said. "He started off thinking all this was about a political scuffle he was having with the Secretary of Colonization. At this point, that seems adorably quaint. Our situation is like a puzzle box, Jane. Every time I think I know what's going on, suddenly there's another layer of complications. I just want to get this damn thing solved."

"We don't have enough information to solve it," Jane said. "All of Hickory's information checks out, but it's old and we don't know whether the Conclave policies have changed, or whether they're solidifying their power or falling apart. The Colonial Union hasn't been forthcoming with us, but I can't tell if that was malicious or if it was choosing what information to provide us so we could do our job without distraction. Both the Conclave and the Colonial Union have an agenda. But neither agenda is clear from any of the data we have, and we're stuck in the middle."

"There's a word for that," I said. "*Pawn.*"

"Whose pawn, is the question," Jane said.

"I think I know," I said. "Let me tell you the latest wrinkle."

"I can think of about a dozen different ways that could go wrong," Jane said, after I finished.

"Same here," I said. "And I'd be willing to bet they're not the same dozen."

TEN

A week after arriving in the Roanoke sky, the CUS *Sacajawea* headed for Phoenix, carrying with it 190 of the former crew of the *Magellan*. Fourteen crew members stayed behind; two had married colonists in the interim, another one was pregnant and not wanting to face her husband, one suspected there was a warrant waiting for him if he returned to Phoenix, and the other ten simply wanted to stay. Another two crew members also stayed behind; they had died, one through a heart attack and another through a drunken misadventure with farm machinery. Captain Zane had said his good-byes to all his living remaining crew, promised he'd find a way to get them their back pay, and then lit out. He was a good man, but I didn't blame him for wanting to be back in CU space.

When the *Sacajawea* returned to Phoenix, the *Magellan* crew members were not allowed to go home. Roanoke had been a largely unexplored colony world; its flora, fauna and diseases were unknown and potentially lethal to the unexposed. The entire crew was to be quarantined in a wing of the CDF medical facilities at Phoenix Station for a standard month. Needless to say the *Magellan* crew came close to rioting at the news. A compromise was reached: The *Magellan* crew members would remain in quarantine, but each would be allowed to contact a small number of loved ones on the condition that loved ones kept quiet about the crew's return until the CU officially released the news that the lost colony of Roanoke had been found. Everyone, crew members and family, happily agreed to the terms.

Needless to say, word of the *Magellan*'s crew's return leaked instantly. News media and colonial governments who tried to learn more were met with official denials from the CU government and unofficial warnings that publishing the news would lead to impressively negative consequences; the story officially remained buried. But word spread among the families of the *Magellan* crew, and from them to friends and colleagues, and from there to the crews of other civilian and military spaceships. The story was quietly confirmed by members of the *Sacajawea* crew, who, despite having landed on Roanoke and all having been exposed to members of the *Magellan* crew, were not under quarantine themselves.

The Colonial Union does not have many allies in known space, but it has a few; soon enough the crews of allied ships heard of the return of the *Magellan* crew as well. These crews manned their ships and traveled to other ports, some of which were not at all friendly to the Colonial Union, and some of which belonged to members of the Conclave. It was there that some of these crew members transmuted their knowledge of the return of the *Magellan* crew into ready cash. It was no secret that the Conclave was looking for the lost colony of Roanoke; it was likewise no secret that the Conclave was happy to pay for reliable information.

Some of those who volunteered information found themselves encouraged by the Conclave, in the form of genuinely unspeakable amounts of wealth, to discover just where in the universe the *Magellan* crew had been all this time. This information would be difficult to come by, which is why the reward was so unimaginably high. But as it happened, shortly after the *Sacajawea* returned to Phoenix Station, its assistant navigator was fired for being intoxicated at his post. The officer now found himself on a blacklist; he would never again travel the stars. A fear of destitution plus a desire for petty revenge caused this former navigator to let it be known that he was in possession of information he had heard others would be interested in, and would be willing to share it for a sum he felt would make up for the wrongs he had suffered at the hands of the Colonial Union's civilian space fleet. He got the sum; he handed over coordinates for the Roanoke colony.

Thus it was, just three days into Roanoke colony's second year, a single ship appeared in the sky above us. It was the *Gentle Star*, bearing General Gau, who sent his compliments to me as the colony leader and bade me to meet him to discuss the future of my world. It was the third of Magellan. According to the intelligence estimates of the Colonial Defense Forces, begun before the "leak" was set into motion, General Gau was right on time.

"You have lovely sunsets here," General Gau said, through a translator device slung on a lanyard. The sun had set some minutes before.

"I've heard this line before," I said.

I had come alone, leaving Jane to manage the anxiety-filled colonists at Croatoan. General Gau's shuttle had landed a klick from the village, across the stream. There were no homesteads here yet. At the shuttle, a squad of soldiers eyed me as I walked past. Their demeanor suggested they did not consider me much of a threat to the general. They were correct. I had no intention of trying to harm him. I wanted to see how much of him I recognized from the versions of him I had seen on video.

Gau motioned gracefully at my response. "My apologies," he said. "I don't mean it to be insincere. Your sunsets actually are lovely."

"Thank you," I said. "I can't take credit for them; I didn't make this world. But I appreciate the compliment."

"You're welcome," Gau said. "And I am pleased to hear that your government made information about our colony removals available to you. There was some concern that it would not."

"Really," I said.

"Oh yes," Gau said. "We know how tightly the Colonial Union controls the flow of information. We worried that we would arrive here, you would know nothing of us—or know something incomplete—and that lack of information would cause you to do something irrational."

"Like not surrender the colony," I said.

"Yes," Gau said. "Surrendering the colony would be the best course, in our opinion," Gau said. "Have you ever been in the military, Administrator Perry?"

"I have," I said. "Colonial Defense Forces."

Gau looked me over. "You're not green," he said.

"Not anymore," I said.

"I assume that you commanded troops," Gau said.

"I did," I said.

"Then you know that it is no shame to surrender when your forces are outnumbered, outgunned and you face an honorable adversary," Gau said. "One who respects your command of your people and who would treat you as he would expect you to treat his own troops, if the situation were reversed."

"I regret to say that in my experience in the CDF, the number of opponents we faced who would have taken our surrender was rather small," I said.

"Yes, well," Gau said. "An artifact of your own policies, Administrator Perry. Or the policies of the CDF, which you were obliged to follow. You humans are not especially good at taking the surrender of other species."

"I'll be willing to make an exception for you," I said.

"Thank you, Administrator Perry," Gau said. Even through his translator I could sense his dry amusement. "I don't believe it will be necessary."

"I hope you'll change your mind," I said.

"I was hoping *you* might surrender to *me*," Gau said. "If you have seen the information on how the Conclave has handled our previous removals, then you know that when colonies surrender to us, we honor their sacrifice. No harm will come to any of your people."

"I've seen how you've handled these before—the ones where you've not blown up the colony," I said. "But I've heard *we* are a special case. You've been deceived by the Colonial Union as to where we would be. We've made the Conclave look foolish."

"Yes, the disappearing colony," Gau said. "We were waiting for you, you know. We knew when your ship was supposed to skip. You were going to be welcomed by several ships, including mine. Your people wouldn't have even made it off the ship."

"You were planning to destroy the *Magellan*," I said.

"No," Gau said. "Not unless it attempted to attack or begin colonizing. Otherwise, we would have simply escorted the ship to skip distance to return to Phoenix. But you deceived us, as you say, and it's taken us this long to find you. You may say it made the Conclave look foolish. We believe it made the Colonial Union look desperate. And we *did* find you."

"It only took a year," I said.

"And it might have taken another after this," Gau said. "Or we might have found you tomorrow. It was only an issue of *when* we would find you, Administrator Perry. Not if. And I would ask you to consider that. Your government risked your life, and the life of every member of your colony, to make a shadow play of defiance against us. This was a futile colonization. Sooner or later we would have found you. We *have* found you. And here we are."

"You seem irritated, General," I said.

The general performed something with his mouth I assumed was a smile. "I *am* irritated," he admitted. "I've wasted time and resources better spent building the Conclave looking for your colony. And fending off political feints by members of the Conclave who have taken your government's insolence personally. There is a substantial group of Conclave members who want to punish your government by attacking humanity at its heart—by attacking Phoenix directly."

I felt simultaneous washes of anxiety and relief come over me. When Gau said "attacking humanity at its heart," I assumed he meant Earth; his mention of Phoenix reminded me that the only people who thought of Earth as the heart of humanity were those who were born there. As far as the rest of the universe was concerned, Phoenix was humanity's home planet. "If your Conclave is as strong as you suggest, then you could attack Phoenix," I said.

"We could," Gau said. "And we could destroy it. We could wipe out every other human colony as well, and if I may speak frankly to you, there are not very many races out there, in the Conclave or out of it, who would complain much about it. But I'll tell you what I've told those in the Conclave who want to make you extinct: The Conclave is not an engine of conquest."

"So you say," I said.

"I do say," Gau said. "This has been the hardest thing to make people understand, both in the Conclave and out of it. Empires of conquest don't last, Administrator Perry. They hollow out from within, from the greed of rulers and the endless appetite for war. The Conclave is not an empire, and I don't want to make humanity extinct, Administrator Perry. I want it to become *part* of the Conclave. Barring that, I'll leave it to its own devices, on the worlds it had before the Conclave, and only those. But I'd rather have you as part of us. Humanity is strong and incredibly resourceful. It's become immensely successful in a short period of time. There are races who have been among the stars for thousands of your years who have not accomplished as much or colonized as successfully."

"I've wondered about that," I said. "So many other races have been around and colonizing for so long, and yet *we* had to go to the stars to find any of *you*."

"I have an answer for that," Gau said. "But I guarantee you won't like it."

"Tell me anyway," I said.

"We invested in fighting more than we did in exploring," Gau said.

"That's a pretty simplistic answer, General," I said.

"Look at our civilizations," Gau said. "We're all the same size because we limit each other through war. We're all at the same level of technology, because we bargain, trade and steal from each other. We all inhabit the same area of space because that is where we began, and we choose to control our colonies rather than let them develop without us. We fight over the same planets and only occasionally explore to find new ones, which we all then squabble over like carrion animals fighting over a carcass. Our civilizations are at an equilibrium, Administrator Perry. An artificial equilibrium that is sliding all of us toward entropy. This was happening before humans arrived in this part of space. Your arrival punctured that equilibrium for a while. But now you've settled in the same pattern of stealing and squabbling as the rest of us."

"I don't know about that," I said.

"Indeed," Gau said. "Let me ask you, Administrator Perry, how many of humanity's planets were freshly discovered? And how many were simply taken from other races? How many planets have humans lost to other races?"

I thought back to the day we arrived above the other planet, the fake Roanoke, and remembered the questions of journalists, asking who we took the planet from. It was assumed it was taken; it didn't occur to them to ask if it was newly discovered. "This planet is new," I said.

"And the reason for that is that your government was trying to *hide* you," Gau said. "Even a culture as vital as your own now explores primarily out of desperation. You're trapped in the same stagnant patterns as the rest of us. Your civilization will slowly run down like the rest of ours would."

"And you think the Conclave will change this," I said.

"In any system, there is a factor that limits growth," Gau said. "Our civilizations operate as a system, and our limiting factor is war. Remove that factor and the system thrives. We can focus on cooperation. We can explore rather than fight. If there had been a Conclave, perhaps we *would* have met you before you came out and met us. Perhaps we'll explore now and find new races."

"And do what with them?" I asked. "There's an intelligent race on this planet. Besides mine, I mean. We met them in a rather unfortunate way, and some of us ended up dead. It took some doing on my part to convince our colonists not to kill every one of them we could find. What will *you* do, General, when you meet a new race on a planet you want for the Conclave?"

"I don't know," General Gau said.

"Excuse me?" I said.

"Well, I don't," Gau said. "It hasn't happened yet. We've been busy consolidating our positions with the races we know about and the worlds that have already been explored. We haven't had time to explore. It hasn't come up."

"I'm sorry," I said. "That wasn't an answer I was expecting."

"We're at a very sensitive moment, Administrator Perry, concerning the future of your colonists," Gau said. "I won't unnecessarily complicate things by lying. Especially not about something as trivial to our current situation as a hypothetical."

"At the very least, General Gau, I'd like to believe that," I said.

"That's a start, then," Gau said. He looked me up and down. "You said that you were in your Colonial Defense Forces," he said. "From what I know about humans, that means you're not originally from the Colonial Union. You're from Earth. Is that right?"

"That's right," I said.

"Humans are really very interesting," Gau said. "You're the only race who has chosen to change your home world. Voluntarily, that is. You're not the only ones to recruit your military from only one world, but you are the only ones to do it from a world that is not your primary world. I'm afraid we've never quite understood the relationship between Earth and Phoenix, and with the rest of the colonies. It doesn't make much sense to the rest of us. Perhaps one day I can get you to explain it to me."

"Perhaps," I said, carefully.

Gau took the tone for what he thought it was. "But not today," he said.

"I'm afraid not," I said.

"A pity," Gau said. "This has been an interesting conversation. We've done thirty-six removals. This is the last one. And in all but this and the first, the leaders of the colonies have not had much to say."

"It's difficult to have a casual conversation with someone who is ready to vaporize you if you don't give in to his demands," I said.

"This is true enough," Gau said. "But leadership is at least a little about character. So many of these colony leaders seemed to lack that. It makes me wonder if these colonies were begun at all seriously, or simply to see if we meant to enforce our ban on colonies. Although there was the one who tried to assassinate me."

"Clearly not successful," I said.

"No, not at all," Gau said, and motioned toward his soldiers, who were attentive but kept a respectful distance. "One of my soldiers shot her before she could stab me. There's a reason I have these meetings in the open."

"Not just for the sunsets, then," I said.

"Sadly, no," Gau said. "And as you might imagine, killing the colony leader made dealing with her second-in-command a tense affair. But this was a colony we eventually evacuated. Aside from the colony leader, there was no bloodshed."

"But you haven't turned away from bloodshed," I said. "If I refuse to evacuate this colony, you won't hesitate to destroy it."

"No," Gau said.

"And from what I understand, none of the races whose colonies you've removed—violently or otherwise—have since joined the Conclave," I said.

"That's true," Gau said.

"You're not exactly winning hearts and minds," I said.

"I'm not familiar with this term of yours," Gau said. "But I understand it well enough. No, these races haven't become part of the Conclave. But it's unrealistic to assume they would. We've just removed their colonies, and they were unable to stop us from doing so. You don't humiliate someone like that and expect them to come around to your way of thinking."

"They could become a threat if they joined together," I said.

"I'm aware your Colonial Union is trying to make that happen," Gau said. "There's not much that happens now that we're not aware of, Administrator Perry, including that. But the Colonial Union has tried this before; it helped create a 'Counter-Conclave' while we were still forming. It didn't work then. We're not convinced it will work now."

"You could be wrong," I said.

"I could be," Gau said. "We will see. In the meantime, however, I must come to it. Administrator Perry, I am asking you to surrender your colony to me. If you will, we will help your colonists safely return to their home worlds. Or you may choose to become part of the Conclave, independent of your government. Or you may refuse and be destroyed."

"Let me make you a counteroffer," I said. "Leave this colony alone. Send a drone to your fleet, which I know is at skip distance and ready to arrive. Tell it to stay where it is. Gather up your soldiers over there, return to your ship, and go. Pretend you never found us. Just let us be."

"It's too late for that," General Gau said.

"I figured it would be," I said. "But I want you to remember the offer was there."

Gau looked at me quietly for a long moment. "I suspect

I know what you are going to say to my offer, Administrator Perry," he said. "Before you say it, let me beg you to reconsider. Remember that you have options here, true options. I know the Colonial Union has given you orders, but remember that you can be led by your own conscience. The Colonial Union is humanity's government, but there is more to humanity than the Colonial Union. And you don't seem to be a man who is pushed into things, by me, by the Colonial Union or by anyone else."

"If you think I'm tough, you should meet my wife," I said.

"I would like that," Gau said. "I think I would like that very much."

"I would like to say that you are right," I said. "I would like to say that I can't be pushed into things. But I suspect that I can be. Or perhaps I can have things pushed into me that I can't resist. This is one of those times. Right now, General, I have no options, except one option that I shouldn't be offering you. And that is to ask you to leave now, before you call your fleet, and let Roanoke stay lost. Please consider it."

"I can't," Gau said. "I'm sorry."

"I can't surrender this colony," I said. "Do what you will, General."

Gau looked back toward one of his soldiers and gave him a signal.

"How long will this take?" I asked.

"Not long," Gau said.

He was right. Within minutes, the first ships arrived, new stars in the sky. Less than ten minutes later, they had all arrived.

"So many," I said. There were tears in my eyes.

General Gau noticed. "I will give you time to return to your colony, Administrator Perry," he said. "And I promise it will be quick and painless. Be strong for your people."

"I'm not crying for my people, General," I said.

The General stared at me and then looked up in time to see the first of the ships in his fleet explode.

Anything is possible, given time and the will.

The Colonial Union certainly had the will to destroy the Conclave's fleet. The existence of the fleet was an intolerable threat; the Colonial Union decided to destroy it as soon as it learned of its existence. There was no hope that the Colonial Union could destroy the fleet in a toe-to-toe battle; with 412 battleship equivalents, it was larger than the entire CDF battle fleet. The Conclave fleet was assembled in whole only when removing the colonies, so there was the possibility of attacking each ship individually. But that would have been equally futile; each ship could be replaced in the fleet by its government, and it meant the Colonial Union would be picking a fight with each of the more than four hundred races in the Conclave, many of whom posed no real threat to the CU.

But the Colonial Union wanted to do more than destroy the Conclave's fleet. It wanted to humiliate and destabilize the Conclave; to strike at the heart of its mission and its credibility. The Conclave's credibility came from its size and its ability to enforce its ban on colonization. The Colonial Union needed to hit at the Conclave in a way that would neutralize its size advantage and make a mockery of its ban. It had to strike at the Conclave at precisely the moment it was showing its strength: When it was attempting to remove a colony. One of *our* colonies.

Only the Colonial Union had no new colonies under threat from the Conclave. The most recent new colony, Everest, slipped in mere weeks before the Conclave's ban. It was not under threat. Another colony would need to be founded.

Enter Manfred Trujillo and his crusade to colonize. The Department of Colonization had ignored him for years, and not simply because the Secretary of Colonization hated his guts. It had long been understood that the best way to keep a planet was to grow so many people on it that it was impossible to kill all of them efficiently. Colonial populations were needed to make more colonists, not more colonies. *Those* could be founded with surplus population from Earth. Barring the appearance of the Conclave, Trujillo could have campaigned to colonize until he was put into the ground and he wouldn't have gotten anywhere.

But now Trujillo's campaign became useful. The Colonial Union had kept the fact of the Conclave from the colonies themselves, as it had so many other things. Sooner or later, however, the colonies would need to be made aware of its existence; the Conclave was simply too big to ignore. The Colonial Union wanted to establish the Conclave as the enemy, in no uncertain terms. It also wanted the colonies to be invested in the struggle against the Conclave.

Because the Colonial Defense Forces were comprised of recruits from Earth—and because the Colonial Union encouraged the colonies to focus primarily on their local politics and issues rather than CU-wide concerns—colonists rarely thought of anything that didn't involve their own planet. But by stocking Roanoke with colonists from the ten most-populated human planets, Roanoke would become the direct concern of more than half the population of the Colonial Union, as would its struggle against the Conclave. In all, a neat potential solution to a raft of issues.

Trujillo was informed that his initiative was being approved; then it was taken away from him. *That* was because Secretary Bell hated his guts. But it also served to remove him from the command loop. Trujillo was too smart not to have picked up the pieces if they were laid out in a way he could follow. It also helped create a political subtext that pitted the founding colonies against each other for a leadership position; this drew attention away from what the CU was really planning for the colony.

Add in two colony leaders dropped in at the last moment, and no one in Roanoke's command structure would have the context to muck up the Colonial Union's plan: to create the time and the opportunity to destroy the Conclave's fleet. Time created by hiding Roanoke.

Time was critical. When the Colonial Union concocted its plan, it was too early to implement it. Even if the Colonial Union could have moved against the Conclave, other races whose colonies were threatened by the Conclave would not follow in the CU's footsteps. The Colonial Union needed time to create a constituency of allies. The best way to do that, it was decided, would be to have them lose their colonies *first*. These races, with their amputated colonies, would see the hidden colony Roanoke as evidence that even the mighty Conclave could be confounded, raising the Colonial Union's status among them and cultivating potential allies for when the moment was right.

Roanoke was a symbol, too, for some of the more dissatisfied members of the Conclave, who saw the burden of its grand designs fall on them without the immediate benefits they had hoped to gain. If the humans could defy the Conclave and get away with it, what value was there in being in the Conclave at all? Every day Roanoke stayed hidden was a day these lesser Conclave members would stew in their own dissatisfaction with the organization they'd surrendered their sovereignty to.

Primarily, however, the Colonial Union needed time

for another reason entirely. It needed time to identify each of the 412 ships that comprised the Conclave's fleet. It needed time to discover where these ships would be when the fleet was not in action. It needed time to position a Gameran Special Forces soldier, just like Lieutenant Stross, in the general area of each of these ships. Like Stross, each of these Special Forces members were adapted to the rigors of space. Like Stross, each of them was covered in embedded nano-camouflage that would allow them to approach and even secure themselves on these ships, unseen, for days or possibly weeks. Unlike Stross, each of these Special Forces soldiers wielded a small but powerful bomb, in which perhaps a dozen grams of fine-grained antimatter were suspended in vacuum.

When the *Sacajawea* returned with the crew of the *Magellan*, the Gamerans prepared themselves for their task. They silently and invisibly hid themselves in the hulls of their target spacecraft and went with them as they assembled at the agreed-upon rendezvous point, and readied themselves for yet another awe-inspiring mass entrance above a world filled with cowering colonists. When the skip drone from the *Gentle Star* popped into space, the Gamerans oh-so-*gently* placed their bombs on the hulls of their respective starships and then just floated off the ship hulls before the ships made their skip. They didn't want to be around when those bombs went off.

They didn't need to be. The bombs were remotely triggered by Lieutenant Stross, who, stationed a safe distance away, polled the bombs to make sure they were all accounted for and active, and detonated them in a sequence determined by him to have the greatest aesthetic impact. Stross was a quirky fellow.

The bombs, when triggered, fired the antimatter like a shotgun blast onto the hulls of their spaceships, spreading the antimatter across a wide surface area to ensure the most efficient annihilation of matter and antimatter. It worked beautifully, and terribly.

Much of this I learned much later, under different circumstances. But even in my time with General Gau, I knew this much: Roanoke was never a colony in the traditional sense of the term. Its purpose never was to give humans another home, or to extend our reach in the universe. It existed as a symbol of defiance, as a creator of time, and as a honey trap to lure a being who dreamed of changing the universe, and to destroy that dream while he watched.

As I said, anything is possible, given the time and the will. We had the time. We had the will.

General Gau stared as his fleet blew itself apart silently but brilliantly. Behind us his soldiers squalled horribly, confused and terrified by what they were seeing.

"You knew," Gau said, in a whisper. He did not stop looking at the sky.

"I knew," I said. "And I tried to warn you, General. I asked you not to call your fleet."

"You did," Gau said. "I can't imagine why your masters let you."

"They didn't," I said.

Gau turned to me then, wearing a face whose map I could not read, but which I sensed expressed profound horror, and yet, even now, curiosity. "*You* warned me," Gau said. "On your own initiative."

"I did," I said.

"Why would you do that?" Gau asked.

"I'm not entirely sure," I admitted. "Why did *you* decide to try to remove colonists instead of killing them?"

"It's the moral thing to do," Gau said.

"Maybe that's why I did it," I said, looking up to where

the explosions continued their brilliance. "Or maybe I just didn't want the blood of all those people on my hands."

"It wasn't your decision," Gau said. "I have to believe that."

"It wasn't," I said. "But that doesn't matter."

Eventually the explosions stopped.

"Your own ship was spared, General Gau," I said.

"Spared," he repeated. "Why?"

"Because that was the plan," I said. "Your ship, and yours alone. You have safe passage from Roanoke to skip distance, back to your own territory, but you must leave now. This guarantee of safe passage expires in an hour unless you are on your way. I'm sorry, but I don't know what your equivalent measure of time is. Suffice to say you should hurry, General."

Gau turned and bellowed at one of his soldiers, and then bellowed again when it became clear they weren't paying attention. One came over; he covered his translator and spoke something to him in their own language. The soldier sprinted back to the others, yelling as he went.

He turned back to me. "This will make things difficult," he said.

"With all due respect, General," I said, "I think that was the intent."

"No," Gau said. "You don't understand. I told you there are those in the Conclave who want to eradicate humanity. To annihilate all of you as you've just annihilated my fleet. It will be harder now to hold them back. They are part of the Conclave. But they still have their own ships and their own governments. I don't know what will happen now. I don't know if I can control them after this. I don't know if they will listen to me anymore."

A squad of soldiers approached the general to retrieve

him, two of them training their weapons on me. The general barked something; the weapons came down. Gau took a step toward me. I fought the urge to take a step back and held my ground.

"Look to your colony, Administrator Perry," Gau said. "It is no longer hidden. From this moment forward, it will be infamous. People will want revenge for what has happened here. All of the Colonial Union will be a target. But *this* is where it happened."

"Will you take your revenge, General?" I asked.

"No," Gau said. "No Conclave ships or troops under my command will return here. This is my word to you. To *you*, Administrator Perry. You tried to warn me. I owe you this courtesy. But I can only control my own ships and my own troops." He motioned to his squad. "Right now, these are the troops I control. And I have only one ship under my command. I hope you understand what I am saying to you."

"I do," I said.

"Then fare you well, Administrator Perry," Gau said. "Look to your colony. Keep it safe. I hope for your sake that it will not be as difficult as I expect it will be." Gau turned and paced double-time to his shuttle to make his departure. I watched him go.

"*The plan is simple,*" General Rybicki had told me. "*We destroy his fleet, all of it, except for his ship. He returns to the Conclave and struggles to keep control of it all as it flies apart. That's why we keep him alive, you know. Even after this, some will still be loyal to him. The civil war the Conclave members will have with themselves in the aftermath will destroy the Conclave. The civil war will weaken the capabilities of the Conclave far more effectively than if General Gau died and the Conclave disbanded. In a year, the Conclave will smash itself to bits, and the Colonial Union will be in a position to pick up most of the big pieces."*

I watched Gau's shuttle launch, streaking up into the night.

I hoped General Rybicki was right.

I didn't think he would be.

ELEVEN Data from the defense satellite the Colonial Union parked above Roanoke would tell us that the missile cluster that attacked the colony popped into existence on the gasping edge of the planet's atmosphere and deployed its payload of five rockets almost instantly, blasting the weapons from a cold start into the ever-thickening atmosphere.

The heat shields on two of the rockets failed during the weapons' entry, collapsing against the white-hot bow wave of the atmosphere. They exploded violently, but not nearly as violently as they would have if their payloads had been armed. Failures at their task, they burned away harmlessly in the upper atmosphere.

The defense satellite tracked the three other rockets and beamed an attack warning to the colony. The message took over every one of the newly reactivated PDAs in the colony and broadcast the warning that an attack was imminent. Colonists dropped their dinner plates, grabbed their children and headed toward the community shelters in the village or family shelters out on the farms. Out among the

Mennonite farms, recently installed sirens wailed on the edges of properties.

Closer to town, Jane remotely activated the colony's defense array, hastily installed once Roanoke was allowed to use modern machinery. *Defense array* was a grand term for what the defenses were; in this case a series of linked, automated land defenses and two beam turrets at opposite ends of Croatoan village. The beam turrets could theoretically destroy the rockets blasting their way toward us, provided we had the energy to power them fully. We didn't; our energy grid was powered by solar power. It was sufficient for the colony's day-to-day energy consumption but woefully inadequate for the intense power the beam weapons required. Each of the turret's internal power cells could provide five seconds of full use or fifteen seconds of low power use. The low power level might not destroy a missile entirely, but it could fry its navigation core, knocking the thing off-course.

Jane powered down the land guns. We wouldn't be needing those. She then made a direct connection to the defense satellite and dumped data into her BrainPal at full speed, the better to understand what she would need to do with the beam turrets.

While Jane powered up our defenses the defense satellite determined which of the rockets represented the most immediate threat to the colony and blasted it with its own energy beam. The satellite scored a direct hit and punched a hole into the missile; its sudden lack of aerodynamics tore the thing apart. The satellite retargeted and hit the second of the three remaining rockets, hitting its engine. The missile veered crazily into the sky, the navigation systems unable to compensate for the damage. The missile eventually came down somewhere, so far away from us that we gave it no further thought.

The defense satellite, its own power cells depleted, was unable to do anything about the final missile; it forwarded speed and trajectory data to Jane, who passed the data immediately to the beam turrets. They came online and started tracking.

Beam weapons are focused and coherent but lose energy with distance; Jane maximized the effectiveness of her turrets by allowing the missile to close distance before firing. Jane chose to fire full-throttle at the missile, opening up with both turrets. It was the right decision, because the missile proved incredibly tough. Even with both turrets firing Jane managed only to kill the missile's brain, knocking out its weapons, engines and navigation. The missile died just above the colony, but its inertia propelled it forward and down at incredible speed.

The dead missile hit the ground a klick outside the village, gouging an unholy gash into fallow fields and spraying propellant into the air, where it ignited. The shock wave from the explosion was a fraction of what it would have been if the missile's payload had been armed, but was still enough to knock me on my ass a kilometer away and take away my hearing for the better part of an hour. Shards of the missile flew violently in every direction, their momentum increased by the energy of the propellant explosion. Parts of the missile tore through the forest, tearing up Roanoke trees and spraying flames into the foliage. Other parts punctured structures in nearby homesteads, collapsing houses and barns and turning livestock into bloody patches streaked across the ground.

One portion of the missile's engine casing flung high in the air, arced down and plummeted toward a plot of earth, below which was the recently constructed shelter of the Gugino family. The casing's impact instantly collapsed the dirt above the shelter, driving it and the casing into the shelter proper. Inside was the entire Gugino family: Bruno and Natalie Gugino, their six-year-old twins Maria and Katherina, and their seventeen-year-old son Enzo. Who had recently begun courting Zoë once more, to some greater success than he had had before.

None of them would be coming out of that shelter.

An entire family gone in an instant. It was unspeakable.

It could have been so much worse.

I spent the hour after the attack collecting reports around the colony on the extent of the damage, and then headed to the Gugino homestead with Savitri. I found Zoë on the Guginos' porch, sitting listlessly amid the broken glass of the home's blown-out windows. Hickory stood beside her; Dickory was with Jane at the remains of the shelter. They were the only two at the shelter; a small group of men stood some distance away, awaiting Jane's orders.

I went to Zoë and gave her a fierce hug; she accepted it, but didn't return it. "Oh, sweetheart," I said. "I'm so sorry."

"I'm all right, Dad," she said, in a tone that made her words a lie.

"I know," I said, letting her go. "I'm still sorry. This is a hard thing. I'm not sure this is the best place for you to be right now."

"I don't want to leave," Zoë said.

"You don't have to," I said. "I just don't know if this is good for you to be seeing."

"I needed to be here," Zoë said. "I needed to see this for myself."

"All right," I said.

"I was supposed to be here tonight," Zoë said, and motioned back toward the house. "Enzo had invited me to dinner. I told him I would come, but then I lost track of time with Gretchen. I was going to call him to apologize when the warning came up. I was *supposed* to be here."

"Honey, you can't blame yourself for that," I said.

"I don't blame myself for it," Zoë said. "I'm *glad* I wasn't here. *That's* what I feel bad about."

I laughed a shaky laugh in spite of myself and gave Zoë another hug. "Oh God, Zoë," I said. "*I'm* glad you weren't here tonight, too. And I *don't* feel bad about that. I'm sorry for what happened to Enzo and his family. But I'm glad you were safe with us. Don't feel bad about being alive, sweetie." I kissed the top of her head.

"Thanks, Dad," Zoë said. She didn't seem entirely convinced.

"I'm going to have Savitri stay with you while I go talk to your mom, okay?" I said.

Zoë gave a small laugh. "What, you don't think Hickory is comforting enough?" she said.

"I'm sure he is," I said. "But I'm going to borrow him for a few minutes. All right?"

"Sure, Dad," Zoë said. Savitri went and sat on the steps with Zoë, drawing her into a hug. I motioned Hickory over to me. He matched my stride as we walked.

"You have your emotion implant on right now?" I asked.

"No," Hickory said. "Zoë's grief became too much."

"Turn it on, please," I said. "I find it easier to converse with you when it's on."

"As you wish," Hickory said, switched on its implant and then collapsed in a heap.

"What the hell?" I said, stopping.

"I'm sorry," Hickory said, righting itself. "I told you that Zoë's emotions were incredibly intense. I'm still working through them. These were new emotions we haven't had with her before. New emotions are harder to process."

"Are you all right?" I asked.

"I am fine," Hickory said, standing. "I apologize."

"Forget it," I said. "Listen, have you been in contact with the other Obin yet?"

"We have," Hickory said. "Indirectly, through your satellite data feed. We have only reestablished contact and provided a digest of the events of last year. We have not offered a complete report."

"Why not?" I asked. We started walking again.

"Your data feed is not secure," Hickory said.

"You want to report things to your superiors without having the Colonial Union listening in," I said.

"Yes," Hickory said.

"What things?" I asked.

"Observations," Hickory said. "And suggestions."

"Some time ago you said to me that the Obin would be willing to help us if we needed help," I said. "Does that offer still stand?"

"It does, so far as I know," Hickory said. "Are you asking for our help, Major Perry?"

"Not yet," I said. "I just need to know what my options are."

Jane looked up at me as we came over. "I don't want Zoë over here," she said to me.

"It's that bad," I said.

"Worse," Jane said. "If you want my suggestion, it's to drag out this engine casing, fill this shelter all the way up with dirt and then put up a headstone. Trying to find enough to bury elsewhere is going to be an exercise in futility."

"Christ," I said. I nodded to the engine casing. "Do we know anything about this?"

Jane motioned toward Dickory, who was standing nearby. "Dickory says the markings say it's Nouri," she said.

"I don't know them," I said.

"The Colonial Union's had almost no contact with them," Jane said. "But it's probably not *from* them. They have a single planet and they don't colonize. There's no reason for them to attack us."

"Are they part of the Conclave?" I asked.

"No," Dickory said, coming closer. "But they sell weapons to some of the Conclave members."

"So this could be a Conclave attack," I said.

"It's possible," Dickory said.

"General Gau said that he wouldn't attack us," Jane said.

"He also said he didn't think he could stop others from attacking," I said.

"I don't think this *is* an attack," Jane said.

I motioned to the wreckage on the engine casing, which was still giving off heat. "This looks like an attack," I said.

"If it was an attack we'd all be dead," Jane said. "This was small and too stupidly done to be a genuine attack on the colony. Whoever did this dropped the missiles directly above our colony, where our defense satellite could pick them off and send us information to kill the ones it couldn't. Stupid for attacking the colony. Not so stupid for testing our defenses."

"So if they actually managed to destroy the colony that would just have been a bonus," I said.

"Right," Jane said. "Now whoever it is that has done this knows what sort of defenses we use and what our capabilities are. And we know nothing about *them*, other than they're not stupid enough to mount an attack without knowing how we defend ourselves."

"It also means the next attack won't just be five missiles," I said.

"Probably not," Jane said.

I studied the wreckage. "We're sitting ducks," I said. "We nearly didn't knock *this* down, and some of our people are still dead. We need better defenses, now. The Colonial Union put a target on our chests, now it needs to help us to keep people from hitting it."

"I doubt a strongly worded letter is going to make a difference," Jane said.

"No," I agreed. "The *San Joaquin* is due here in a couple of days to drop supplies. One of us should be on it when it heads back to Phoenix Station. We'll be a lot harder to ignore if we're standing in someone's doorway."

"You have more faith than I do," Jane said.

"If we don't get traction there, we may have other options," I said, looking at Hickory. I started to say more but noticed Savitri and Zoë coming toward us. I broke off toward them, mindful of Jane's wish not to let Zoë get too close.

Savitri had out her PDA. "You've got some mail," she said.

"Jesus, Savitri," I said. "Now is really not the time. Forward it on to Jann." Since Roanoke had been officially rediscovered, Jane and I had been contacted by every possible media outlet known to man, begging, cajoling or demanding interviews. Five hundred such requests came in with the first official skip drone data packet Roanoke received. Neither Jane nor I had the time or inclination to deal with them, but we knew someone who had both, which is how Jann Kranjic officially became Roanoke's press secretary.

"I wouldn't bother you with a media request," Savitri said. "It's from the Department of Colonization. It's marked 'confidential' and 'extremely urgent.'"

"What is it about?" I asked.

"I don't know," Savitri said. "It won't let me open it."

She handed the PDA over to me to show me that her access was blocked. I signed her out of the PDA and signed me in. A year's worth of going without a PDA made me realize both how much I relied on the thing before, and how little I wanted to rely on it now. I still didn't carry one with me, relying on Savitri to keep me in the loop.

The PDA accepted my biometrics and password and opened the letter.

"Fucking wonderful," I said, a minute later.

"Is everything all right?" Savitri said.

"Of course not," I said. "I need you to tell Jane to finish up here as soon as she can and meet me at the administration building the minute she's done. Then I want you to find Manfred Trujillo and Jann Kranjic and tell them to meet me there as well."

"All right," Savitri said. "What's happening? Can you tell me?"

I handed her back her PDA; she took it. "I've been relieved as colony leader," I said. "And I've been summoned to Phoenix Station."

"Well, you've only been temporarily relieved of your job, so that's a positive," Manfred Trujillo said, passing the PDA and its letter over to Jann Kranjic. The two of them, Jane, Savitri and Beata, who had accompanied Kranjic, were all jammed into my office, challenging its capacity to hold us all at once. "The fact it's temporary means that they haven't already decided to lynch you. They'll want to talk to you first before they make that decision."

"Looks like you might get my job after all, Manfred," I said, from behind my desk.

Trujillo glanced over at Jane, who was standing at the edge of the desk. "I think I would need to go through her first, and I'm not sure that's going to happen."

"I'm not going to stay in this job without John," Jane said.

"You're more than capable of doing the job," Trujillo said. "And no one would oppose you."

"I'm not questioning my competence," Jane said. "I just won't keep the job."

Trujillo nodded. "In any event, it's not clear they intend to remove you permanently," he said, pointing at the PDA, which was now in Beata's hands. "You're being hauled up in front of an inquiry. Speaking as a former legislator, I can tell you that the point of an inquiry is usually to cover someone's ass, not to actually inquire about something. And also speaking as a former legislator, I can tell you that the Department of Colonization has a lot of things to cover its ass about."

"But they still wouldn't recall you unless you did something they could point to," Kranjic said.

"Nice, Jann," Beata said. "We can always count on you for support."

"I'm not saying he *did* anything wrong, Beata," Kranjic snapped. Kranjic had rehired Beata as his assistant after he was made the colony's press secretary, but it was clear their personal relationship had not vastly improved post-divorce. "I'm saying he did something that they can use as an excuse to pin something *on* him, to get him in front of an inquiry."

"And you did, didn't you?" Trujillo asked me. "When you were with General Gau, you offered him a way out. You told him not to call his fleet. You weren't supposed to do that."

"No, I wasn't," I said.

"I find it a little confusing myself," Trujillo said.

"I needed to be able to say I made the offer," I said. "For my own conscience."

"The moral issues aside," Trujillo said, "if someone

wanted to get fussy about it, they could accuse you of treason. The Colonial Union's plan required getting the Conclave fleet here. You intentionally put their strategy at risk."

I turned to Kranjic. "You're talking to other journalists," I said. "Are you hearing anything about this?"

"About you being floated as a traitor? No," Kranjic said. "There are still a lot of journalists who want to talk to either you or Jane, but it's all about the night the Conclave fleet went down or how we've survived here. I've turned a lot of these journalists over to Manfred and the other council members. Maybe they've heard something along that line."

I turned to Trujillo. "Well?" I asked.

"Nothing like that on this end, either," Trujillo said. "But you know as well as anyone that most of what the Colonial Union is planning or thinking isn't ever discussed outside of its own halls."

"So they're going to pin you as a traitor because you weren't hopping up and down to kill a couple hundred thousand intelligent beings," Savitri said. "I'm suddenly reminded why I loathe the Colonial Union power structure."

"It might not just be that," Jane said. "John may be being made a scapegoat, but if that's true then it begs the question of what he's being made a scapegoat *for*. Alternately, if his behavior with Gau is being examined, the Colonial Union is looking at how his behavior affected events."

"You think something didn't go according to plan," I said to Jane.

"I think you don't look for scapegoats when your plans go off without a hitch," Jane said. "If the Conclave is behind tonight's attack, it suggests that it's gotten itself reorganized more quickly than the CU expected."

I looked back over to Kranjic, who picked up the meaning of my glance. "There's nothing in the media reports I've seen about the Conclave, positive or negative," he said.

"That doesn't make any sense," I said. General Rybicki had told me that part of the plan was to introduce the Conclave to the colonies in its great moment of defeat. Now they had the moment of defeat; it should be all over the media. "There's nothing about the Conclave at all?"

"Nothing by name," Kranjic said. "The media reports I've seen mention that the Colonial Union discovered the colony had been threatened by a number of alien races, which made the CU pull its deception. They also mention the battle here. But none of it has the Conclave described as *the Conclave*."

"But we know about the Conclave," Savitri said. "Everyone here knows about the Conclave. When our people send letters or video back to family and friends, they're going to talk about it. It's not going to remain a secret for long. Especially after tonight."

"There are lots of ways for the CU to spin that if they want to," Beata said, to Savitri. "We don't know who attacked us tonight. It could be any number of races, and there's nothing in the attack to suggest an alliance of races. If the Colonial Union wants to minimize the idea of the Conclave, it could just tell the media it intentionally fed us bad information for our own protection. We'd be more willing to look after our own safety if we thought the entire universe was out to get us."

Savitri pointed to me. "And his encounter with General Gau was just some sort of delusion?" she asked.

"He's being recalled," Beata said. "It's entirely possible his inquiry is going to be him being told to revise his memory of the incident."

"I didn't realize you were this conspiracy-obsessed," Savitri said to Beata.

"Welcome to me," Beata said.

"It's possible journalists and others *do* know about the Conclave," Kranjic said. "It's just not making it through the official media channels. And if the CU is actively discouraging journalists from talking about it, then they're not likely to discuss it with us—"

"—because all our communication comes via skip drone," Jane finished. "Which means it's monitored by the Colonial Union."

"Right," Kranjic said.

I remembered Hickory's concern about the CU listening in to its communication with other Obin. Apparently it wasn't the only one suspicious of the CU. "Don't you guys have code or something?" I asked Kranjic. "Some way to let other journalists know something even if you're being monitored?"

"You want me to write 'The hawk flies at midnight'?" Kranjic asked. "No, we don't have a code, and even if we did, no one would risk it. You don't think the CU looks for semantic idiosyncrasies and steganographic patterns?" He pointed to Jane. "Rumor had it she did intelligence for the CDF at one time. Ask her about it."

"So not only do we not know what the CU knows, we *can't* know what the CU knows," Savitri said. "We might as well still be lost."

"No," I said. "We can know. We just can't know from *here.*"

"Ah," Trujillo said. "Your trip to Phoenix Station. You think you can find out more there."

"Yes," I said.

"You'll be busy with your inquiry," Trujillo said. "You're not going to have a lot of time to catch up on gossip."

"You still know people in the Colonial Union government," I said to Trujillo.

"Unless there's been a coup, yes," Trujillio said. "It's only been a year. I can get you in contact with a few people."

"I'd rather you came with me," I said. "As you said, I'm going to be busy with an inquiry. And your people will talk to you more candidly than they will talk to me. Especially considering what you thought of me the last time any of them talked to you." I looked over to Kranjic. "You, too, Jann. You still know people in the media."

Beata snorted. "He knows talking heads," she said. "Let me come. I know the producers and the editors—the people who feed people like him their lines."

"Both of you come," I said, before Kranjic could get off a shot at Beata. "We need to find out as much as we can from as many different sources as we can. Manfred in the government. You two with your media contacts. Jane with Special Forces."

"No," Jane said. "I'm staying here."

I stopped, more than a little surprised at this. "Special Forces carried out the attack on the Conclave fleet," I said. "They probably know more than anyone about what the aftereffects are. I need you to find out, Jane."

"No," Jane said.

"John," Savitri said, "we've been attacked. Someone actually has to run the colony while you're away. Jane needs to be here."

There was more to it than that, but Jane's stare was flat and expressionless. Whatever it was that was going on, I wasn't going to find out about it right then. And Savitri was right in any event. "Fine," I said. "I still have a few people I can talk to as well. Unless they're planning to hold me in a cell."

"You don't think anyone will question why the three of us will be coming along with you," Trujillo said.

"I don't think so," I said. "We've been attacked. I'm going to be engaged in my inquiry. Manfred, you're going to have to stand in people's doorways and try to get the CU to increase our defenses, and fast. Beata will present herself as our cultural minister; in addition to talking to her contacts she's going to try to get permissions for entertainment and educational programming. We have the capability for that now. And as press secretary, Jann's going to be busy shopping around the story of Roanoke's first year. You all have your own reasons for going. Makes sense?"

"Makes sense," Trujillo agreed. Kranjic and Beata nodded as well.

"Good," I said. "Our ship is due here in two days, then." I stood up to end the meeting. I reached over to Jane to catch her before she left, but she was the first one out the door.

"Where's Zoë?" I asked Jane, when I came back home.

"She's over at Trujillo's," Jane said. She was sitting in her chair on the porch, petting Babar. "She and Gretchen and all of their friends are mourning Enzo. She'll probably stay the night there."

"How was she doing?" I asked.

"Someone she loved died," Jane said. "It's hard for anyone. She's lost loved ones before. But this was the first time it was one of her contemporaries. One of her friends."

"And a first love at that," I said. "That complicates matters."

"It does," Jane said. "Everything's complicated now."

"Speaking of which, I wanted to ask you what that

was about back there," I said. "You turning down going to Phoenix Station."

"Savitri said it," Jane said. "It's bad enough the colony is losing you to an inquiry, and that you're taking Trujillo with you. Someone needs to be here."

"But that's not all of it," I said. "I know you well enough to know when you're holding something back."

"I don't want to be responsible for compromising the safety of the colony," Jane said.

"How would you do that?" I said.

"For one thing, the next time I see General Szilard, I'm going to break the bastard's neck," Jane said. "They're not likely to keep me on after that. Then there would be no leadership for this colony at all."

"You were always the practical one," I said.

"It's who I am," Jane agreed. "Something I got from Kathy, perhaps."

"Perhaps," I said. It was rare that Jane would talk directly about Kathy; it's hard to talk to your husband about his first wife, especially when you are made from that wife's DNA. When Jane brought up Kathy, it was an indication that other things were on her mind. I kept quiet until she was ready to tell me what was going on in her head.

"I dream about her sometimes," Jane finally said. "About Kathy."

"What do you dream about her?" I asked.

"That she and I talk," Jane said. "And she tells me how you were when you were with her, and I tell her how you are with me. And we talk about our families and our lives and about each other. And when I wake up I don't remember anything specific about what we've talked about. Just that we've talked."

"That must be frustrating," I said.

"It's not," Jane said. "Not really. I like that we just

talk. I like feeling that connection with her. She's part of who I am. Mother and sister and self. All of it. I like that she visits me. I know it's just a dream. It's still nice."

"I bet it is," I said, remembering Kathy, who Jane was so much like, even as much as she was her own person.

"I'd like to visit her one day," Jane said.

"I'm not sure how we'd do that," I said. "She's been gone a long time."

"No," Jane said. "I mean I'd like to visit where she is now. Where she's buried."

"I'm not sure how we'd do that, either," I said. "Once we leave Earth, we're not allowed to go back."

"I never left Earth," Jane said, looking down at Babar, who thumped a lazy, happy beat with his tail. "Only my DNA did."

"I don't think the Colonial Union will make the distinction," I said, smiling at one of Jane's rare jokes.

"I know they won't," Jane said, a trace of bitterness in her voice. "Earth is too valuable as a factory to risk it being infected by the rest of the universe." She looked over at me. "Don't you ever want to go back? You spent most of your life there."

"I did," I said. "But I left because there was nothing keeping me there. My wife was dead and our kid grew up. It wasn't too hard to say good-bye. And now what I care about is here. This is my world now."

"Is it?" Jane said. She looked up at the stars. "I remember standing in the road back on Huckleberry, wondering if I could make another world my home. Make *this* world my home."

"Can you?" I asked.

"Not yet," Jane said. "Everything about this world *shifts*. Every reason we've thought we had for being here has turned out to be a half-truth. I care about Roanoke. I care about the people here. I will fight for them and I'll

defend Roanoke the best that I can, when it comes to
that. But this isn't my world. I don't *trust* it. Do you?"

"I don't know," I said. "I know that I'm worried this
inquiry will take it away from me, though."

"Do you think anyone here cares anymore about who
the Colonial Union thinks should run this colony?" Jane
asked.

"Possibly not," I said. "But it would still hurt."

"Hmmm," Jane said, and thought about that for a while.
"I still want to see Kathy one day," she eventually said.

"I'll see what I can do," I said.

"Don't say that unless you mean it," Jane said.

"I mean it," I said, and was somewhat surprised that,
in fact, I did. "I would like you to meet her. I wish you
could have met her before."

"So do I," Jane said.

"It's settled, then," I said. "Now all we have to do is
find a way to get back to Earth without getting our ship
shot out from under us by the CU. I'll have to work on
that."

"Do that," Jane said. "But later." She stood and held
out her hand to me. I took it. We went inside.

TWELVE

"Our apologies, Administrator Perry, for the late start," said Justine Butcher, Assistant Deputy Secretary for Colonial Jurisprudence for the Department of Colonization. "As you may be aware, things have been quite hectic around here recently."

I was aware. When Trujillo, Kranjic, Beata and I disembarked the shuttle from our transport ship to Phoenix Station, the general station buzz appeared to have trebled; none of us had ever recalled seeing the station as jam-packed with CDF soldiers and CU functionaries as it appeared to be now. Whatever was going on, it was big. All of us glanced at each other significantly, because whatever it was, it almost certainly involved us and Roanoke in some way. We fanned out from each other wordlessly, off to our own individual tasks.

"Of course," I said. "Anything in particular causing the rush?"

"It's a number of things, happening at once," Butcher said. "None of which you need to concern yourself with at the moment."

Butcher nodded, and signified the two other people seated at the table, before which I stood. "This inquiry has been impaneled in order to question you about your conversation with General Tarsem Gau of the Conclave," Butcher said. "This is a formal inquiry, which means that you are required to answer any and all questions truthfully, directly and completely as possible. However, this is not a trial. You have not been charged with any crime. If at a future point you are charged with a crime, you will be tried through the Department of Colonization's Court of Colonial Affairs. Do you understand?"

"I do," I said. The DoC's Colonial Affairs Courts were judge-only affairs, designed to let colony heads and their appointed judges make quick decisions so the colonists could get on with colonizing. A CA Court ruling had the force of law, although limited to that specific case only. A CA Court judge or colony head acting as judge could not circumvent Department of Colonization regulations and bylaws, but as the DoC recognized the wide range of colonial situations were not uniform in their regulatory needs, those regulations and bylaws were surprisingly few. Colonial Affairs Courts were also organizationally flat; there was no appealing a Colonial Affairs Court ruling. Essentially a CA Court judge could do whatever he or she wanted. It was not an optimal legal situation for a defendant.

"Fine," Butcher said, and looked at her PDA. "Then let's begin. When you were conversing with General Gau, you offered first to take his surrender, and then offered to allow him to leave Roanoke space without injury to himself or to his fleet." She looked up at me over the PDA. "This is correct, Administrator?"

"That's right," I said.

"General Rybicki, whom we have already called"—this

was news to me, and I was suddenly sure that Rybicki was now less than entirely pleased he ever suggested me for the colonial administrator position—"testified to us that your orders were to engage Gau in nonessential discussions only, until the fleet was destroyed, at which point you were to inform him that only his ship had survived the attack."

"Yes," I said.

"Very well," Butcher said. "Then you may begin by explaining what you were thinking when you offered to accept Gau's surrender, and then offered to let his fleet go unharmed."

"I suppose I was hoping to avoid bloodshed," I said.

"It's not your place to make that call," said Colonel Bryan Berkeley, who represented the Colonial Defense Forces at the inquiry.

"I disagree," I said. "My colony was potentially under attack. I am the colony leader. My job is to keep my colony safe."

"The attack wiped out the Conclave fleet," Berkeley said. "Your colony was never in danger."

"The attack could have failed," I said. "No offense to the CDF or to the Special Forces, Colonel, but not every attack they plan succeeds. I was at Coral, where the CDF's plans failed miserably and a hundred thousand of our people died."

"Are you saying you expected us to fail?" Berkeley asked.

"I'm saying I have an appreciation for the fact that plans are plans," I said. "And that I had an obligation to my colony."

"Did you *expect* that General Gau would surrender to you?" asked the third questioner. I took a moment to take him in: General Laurence Szilard, head of the CDF Special Forces.

His presence on the panel made me extremely nervous.

There was absolutely no reason why he of all people should be on it. He was several layers of bureaucracy more advanced than either Butcher or Berkeley; having him sitting placidly on the panel—and not even being the panel chairman—was like having your kid's day care supervisor be Dean of the College at Harvard University. It didn't make any sort of sense. If he decided that I needed to be squashed for messing up a mission the Special Forces supervised, it really wouldn't matter what either of the other two panelists thought about anything; I'd be dead meat on a stick. The knowledge made me queasy.

That said, I was also deeply curious about the man. Here was the general whose neck my wife wished to wring because he altered her back into a Special Forces soldier without her permission and also, I suspected, without much remorse. Some part of me wondered if I shouldn't attempt to wring his neck out of a sense of chivalry for my wife. Considering that as a Special Forces soldier he would probably have kicked my ass even when I was a genetically enhanced soldier, I doubted I could do much against him now that I was once again a mere mortal. Jane probably wouldn't appreciate me getting my own neck wrung.

Szilard waited for my answer, his expression placid.

"I had no reason to suspect he would surrender, no," I said.

"But you asked him to anyway," Szilard said. "Ostensibly to allow your colony to survive. I find it interesting that you asked for his surrender rather than begging for him to spare your colony. If you were simply looking to him to spare the colony and the lives of the colonists, wouldn't that have been the more prudent course? The information the Colonial Union provided you about the general gave you no reason to believe surrender would be something he'd entertain."

Careful, some part of my brain whispered. The way Szilard had phrased his comment seemed to suggest that he thought I might have had information from other sources. Which I had, but it seemed impossible that he would know that. If he did and I lied, I would be deeply into a world of shit. Decisions, decisions.

"I knew of our planned attack," I said. "Perhaps that made me overconfident."

"So you admit that what you said to General Gau could have indicated to him that our attack was imminent," Berkeley said.

"I doubt that he saw anything more in it than the bravado of a colony leader, trying to save his own people," I said.

"Nevertheless, you can see how, from the perspective of the Colonial Union, your actions could have jeopardized the mission and the safety not only of your colony but of the Colonial Union," Butcher said.

"My actions could be interpreted any number of ways," I said. "I can't give credence to any other interpretation aside from my own. My interpretation is that I was doing what I thought was necessary to protect my colony and my colonists."

"In your conversation with General Gau you admit that you shouldn't have made him the offer to withdraw his fleet," Berkeley said. "You knew that what you were offering the general was contrary to our wishes, which implies rather strongly that we had made our wishes known to you. If the general had had the presence of mind to follow your line of reasoning, the attack would have been obvious."

I paused. This was getting ridiculous. It wasn't to say that I wasn't expecting a railroading in this inquiry, just that I had expected it to be a little more subtle than this. But I suppose Butcher had noted that things were hectic and rushed recently; I don't know why my inquiry would be any different. "I don't know what to say to that line of reasoning," I said. "I did what I thought was the right thing for me to do."

Butcher and Berkeley gave each other a quick side-long glance. They had gotten what they wanted out of the inquiry; as far as they were concerned the inquiry was over. I focused on my shoes.

"What do you think of General Gau?"

I looked up, entirely surprised. General Szilard sat there, once again blandly awaiting my answer. Butcher and Berkeley also looked surprised; whatever Szilard was doing, it was apparently off the script.

"I'm not sure I understand the question," I said.

"Sure you do," Szilard said. "You spent a reasonable amount of time with General Gau, and I'm sure you have had time to reflect and speculate on the nature of the general, both before and after the destruction of the Conclave fleet. Given your knowledge of him, what do you think of him?"

Oh, fuck, I thought. There was no doubt in my mind that Szilard knew I knew more about General Gau and the Conclave than the information the Colonial Union gave me. How he knew that was a matter I could table for now. The question was how to answer the question.

You're already screwed, I thought. Butcher and Berkeley were already clearly planning to punt me to Colonial Affairs Court, where my trial on whatever charge (I was assuming incompetence, although dereliction of duty was not out of the question, and for that matter, neither was treason) would be short and not especially sweet. I had been working under the assumption that Szilard's presence was his way of making sure he got a result he wanted—he couldn't have been pleased at the idea of me potentially messing with his mission—but now I wasn't at all sure.

Suddenly I hadn't the first damn clue what Szilard really wanted from this inquiry. Only that no matter what I said here, I was already done for.

Well, it was an official inquiry. That meant it was going into the Colonial Union archives. So what the hell.

"I think he's an honorable man," I said.

"Excuse me?" Berkeley said.

"I said, I think he's an honorable man," I repeated. "He didn't simply attempt to destroy Roanoke, for one thing. He offered to spare my colonists or allow them to join the Conclave. None of the information the Colonial Union gave me indicated that these were options. The information I got—that all the colonists at Roanoke got, through me—was that Gau and the Conclave were simply wiping out the colonies that they discovered. It's why we kept our heads down for an entire year."

"Simply saying to you that he was going to allow your colonists to surrender doesn't mean that he would do any such thing," Berkeley said. "Surely as a former CDF commander you understand the value of disinformation, and providing such to your enemy."

"I don't think Roanoke colony would have qualified as an enemy," I said. "There are fewer than three thousand of us against four hundred twelve capital ships. There were no defenses we could bring to bear, no possible military advantage in securing our surrender simply to destroy us. That would have been profoundly cruel."

"You're not aware of the psychological value of cruelty in warfare?" Berkeley said.

"I'm aware of it," I said. "I wasn't aware from the information the Colonial Union gave me that it was part of the general's personal psychological profile or of his military tactics."

"There's much you don't know of the general," Butcher said.

"I agree," I said. "Which is why I chose to go with my own intuition of his character. But I seem to recall that the general noted that he had overseen three dozen of these colony removals before he got to Roanoke. If you have information about those incidents and how the general acted toward those colonies, that would be instructive regarding his honor and his position on cruelty. Do you have that information?"

"We have it," Butcher said. "We are not at liberty to provide it to you, as you've been temporarily removed from your administrative position."

"I understand," I said. "Did you have any of this information *before* I was stripped of my administrative status?"

"Are you implying that the Colonial Union withheld information from you?" Berkeley asked.

"I'm not implying a thing," I said. "I was asking a question. And my point was that in the absence of information provided to me by the Colonial Union, I have only my own judgment to guide me, to complement the information I have." I looked directly at Szilard. "In my judgment, from what *I* know of the man, General Gau is honorable."

Szilard considered this. "What would you have done, Administrator Perry, if Gau had appeared in your sky before the Colonial Union had its attack plan finalized?"

"Are you asking if I would have surrendered the colony?" I asked.

"I'm asking what you would have done," Szilard said.

"I would have taken advantage of Gau's offer," I said. "I would have let him take the Roanoke colonists back to the Colonial Union."

"So you *would* have surrendered the colony," Butcher said.

"No," I said. "I would have stayed behind to defend Roanoke. I suspect my wife would stay with me. Anyone else who wished to stay could stay." *With the exception of Zoë*, I thought, although I didn't like the scene of Zoë being dragged, kicking and screaming, to a transport by Hickory and Dickory.

"That's a distinction without a difference," Berkeley said. "There's no colony without colonists."

"I agree," I said. "But one colonist is enough for the colony to stand, and one colonist is enough to die for the Colonial Union. My responsibility is to my colony *and* to my colonists. I would refuse to surrender the colony of Roanoke. I would also do everything in my power to keep the colonists alive. From a practical point of view, twenty-five hundred colonists are no more able to stand up to an entire fleet of warships than a single colonist would be. My death would be sufficient to make the point the CU would wish for me to make. If you think I would force every *other* Roanoke colonist to die to satisfy some arcane accounting of what defines the destruction of a colony, Colonel Berkeley, then you're a goddamned fool."

Berkeley looked as if he were ready to come over the table at me. Szilard sat there with the same damned inscrutable look he'd had through the entire inquiry.

"Well," Butcher said, trying to get the inquiry back under control. "I think we've gotten everything we need from you, Administrator Perry. You are free to go and to await the resolution of our inquiry. You will not be allowed to leave Phoenix Station prior to the resolution. Do you understand?"

"I understand," I said. "Do I need to find some sort of lodging?"

"I don't expect it will take that long," Butcher said.

"Understand that everything I've heard is off the record," Trujillo said.

"At this point, I don't know that I would trust information that is *on* the record," I said.

Trujillo nodded. "Amen to that," he said.

"What have you heard?" I said.

"It's bad," he said. "And it's getting worse."

Trujillo, Kranjic, Beata and I sat in my favorite commissary at Phoenix, the one with the truly spectacular burgers. We had all ordered one; the burgers cooled, neglected, as we talked in as secluded a corner as we could find.

"Define *bad*," I said.

"There was a missile attack on Phoenix the other night," Trujillo said.

"That's not bad, that's stupid," I said. "Phoenix has the most advanced planetary defense grid of any of the human planets. You couldn't get a missile larger than a marble past it."

"Right," Trujillo said. "And everyone knows it. There hasn't been an attack of *any* size against Phoenix in over a hundred years. The attack wasn't meant to be successful. It was meant to send a message that no human planet should be considered safe from retaliation. That's a pretty big statement."

I thought about this while I took a bite of my burger. "Presumably Phoenix wasn't the only planet to get a missile attack," I said.

"No," Trujillo said. "My people tell me that all the colonies have been attacked."

I nearly choked. "All of them," I repeated.

"*All* of them," Trujillo said. "The established colonies were never in any danger; their planetary defense grids picked off the attacks. Some of the smaller colonies saw some damage. Sedona colony had an entire settlement wiped off the map. Ten thousand people dead."

"You're sure about that," I said.

"Secondhand," Trujillo said. "But from a source I trust, who spoke to the Sedonan representative. I trust my source as much as I trust anyone."

I turned to Kranjic and Beata. "This fits in with what you've heard?"

"It does," Kranjic said. "Manfred and I have different sources, but what I'm hearing is the same." Beata nodded as well.

"But none of this is on the news feeds," I said, glancing down at my PDA, which lay on the table. I had it open and active, awaiting the determination of the inquiry.

"No," Trujillo said. "The Colonial Union has slapped a blanket prohibition on information about the attacks. They're using the State Secrecy Act. You'll remember that one."

"Yeah." I winced at the memory of the werewolves and Gutierrez. "Didn't do me a whole lot of good. I doubt it'll do the CU much better."

"The attacks explain the chaos we're seeing here," Trujillo said. "I don't have any sources from the CDF—they're clammed up tight—but I know that every single colony representative is screaming their head off for direct CDF protection. Ships are being recalled and reassigned, but there's not enough for every colony. From what I hear, the CDF is doing triage—deciding which colonies it can protect and which colonies it can afford to lose."

"Where does Roanoke fit into that triage?" I asked.

Trujillo shrugged. "When it comes down to it, everyone wants defense priority," he said. "I sounded out the legislators I know about increasing Roanoke's defenses. They all said they'd be happy to—once their own planets were taken care of."

"No one's talking about Roanoke anymore," Beata said. "Everyone is focused on what's happening at their own homes. They can't report it, but they're sure as hell following it."

We focused on our burgers after that, lost in our own thoughts. I was preoccupied enough that I didn't notice someone standing behind me until Trujillo looked up and stopped chewing. "Perry," he said, and glanced meaningfully over my shoulder. I turned to see General Szilard.

"I like the burgers here, too," he said. "I'd join you, but given your wife's experience, I doubt you'd be willing to eat at the same table as me."

"Now that you mention it, General," I said, "you'd be entirely correct about that."

"Then walk with me please, Administrator Perry," Szilard said. "We have a lot to discuss, and time is short."

"All right," I said. I picked up my tray, giving a glance over at my lunch mates. Their expressions were carefully blank. I dropped the contents of my tray into the nearest receptacle and faced the general. "Where to?" I asked.

"Come on," Szilard said. "Let's go for a ride."

"There," Szilard said. His personal shuttle hung in space, with Phoenix visible to port and Phoenix Station off to starboard. He motioned to indicate both. "Nice view, isn't it?"

"Very nice," I said, wondering why the hell Szilard had taken me here. Some paranoid part of me wondered if he were planning to pop the shuttle's access hatch and toss me into space, but he didn't have a space suit, so this seemed somewhat unlikely. Then again, he was Special Forces. Maybe he didn't need a space suit.

"I'm not planning to kill you," Szilard said.

I smiled in spite of myself. "Apparently you can read minds," I said.

"Not yours," Szilard said. "But I can guess what you're

thinking well enough. Relax. I'm not going to kill you, if for no other reason because then Sagan would track me down and kill *me*."

"You're already on her shit list," I said.

"Of that I have no doubt," Szilard said. "But it was necessary, and I don't plan to apologize for it."

"General," I said, "why are we here?"

"We're here because I like the view, and because I want to speak frankly to you, and because this shuttle is the one place I'm entirely sure where anything I say to you is not going to be overheard by anyone else in any way." The general reached over to the control dash of the shuttle and pressed a button; the view of Phoenix and Phoenix Station disappeared and was replaced with a depthless black.

"Nanomesh," I said.

"Indeed," Szilard said. "No signals in, no signals out. You should know that being cut off is unspeakably claustrophobic for Special Forces; we're so used to being in constant contact with each other through our BrainPals that dropping the signal is like losing any three of our senses."

"I knew that," I said. Jane had recounted to me the mission in which she and other Special Forces hunted Charles Boutin; Boutin had devised a way to cut off the BrainPal signal of the Special Forces, killing most of them and driving some of those who survived completely insane.

Szilard nodded. "Then you'll understand how difficult something like this is, even for me. Honestly I have no idea how Sagan was able to leave it behind when she married you."

"There are other ways to connect with someone," I said.

"If you say so," Szilard said. "The fact I'm willing to do this should also communicate to you the seriousness of what I'm going to say to you."

"All right," I said. "I'm ready."

"Roanoke is in serious trouble," Szilard said. "We all are. The Colonial Union had anticipated that destroying the Conclave fleet would throw the Conclave into a civil war. That much was correct. Right now the Conclave is tearing itself apart. The races loyal to General Gau are squaring off against another faction who has found a leader in a member of the Arris race named Nerbros Eser. As it stands there's only one thing that has kept these two factions of the Conclave from destroying each other entirely."

"What's that?" I said.

"The thing the Colonial Union *didn't* anticipate," Szilard said. "And that is that every single member race of the Conclave is now bent on destroying the Colonial Union. Not just containing the Colonial Union, as General Gau was content to do. They want to eradicate it completely."

"Because we wiped out the fleet," I said.

"That's the proximate cause," Szilard said. "The Colonial Union forgot that in attacking the fleet we weren't only striking at the Conclave but at every member of the Conclave. The ships in the fleet were often the flagships for their races. We didn't just destroy a fleet, we destroyed racial symbols. We kicked every single member race of the Conclave hard and square in the balls, Perry. They're not going to forgive that. But beyond that we're trying to use the destruction of the Conclave fleet as a rallying point for other unaffiliated races. We're trying to get them to become our allies. And the Conclave members have decided that the best way to keep those races unaffiliated is to make an example out of the Colonial Union. All of it."

"You don't sound surprised," I said.

"I'm not," Szilard said. "When destroying the Conclave fleet was first considered, I had the Special Forces intelligence corps model out the consequences of that act. This was always the most likely result."

"Why didn't they listen?" I asked.

"Because the CDF models told the Colonial Union what it wanted to hear," Szilard said. "And because at the end of the day the Colonial Union is going to place more weight on the intelligence generated by real humans than the intelligence created by the Frankenstein monsters it creates to do its dirty work."

"Like destroy the Conclave fleet," I said, recalling Lieutenant Stross.

"Yes," Szilard said.

"If you believed this was going to be the result, you should have refused to do it," I said. "You shouldn't have let your soldiers destroy the fleet."

Szilard shook his head. "It's not that simple. If I were to have refused, I would have been replaced as the commander of Special Forces. Special Forces are no less ambitious and venal than any other sort of human being, Perry. I can think of three generals under me who would have been happy to take my job for the simple cost of following foolish orders."

"But you followed foolish orders," I said.

"I did," Szilard said. "But I did so under my own terms. Part of which was helping to install you and Sagan as colony leaders at Roanoke."

"*You* installed me," I said. This was news to me.

"Well, actually, I installed Sagan," Szilard said. "You were merely part of the package deal. It was acceptable because you seemed unlikely to fuck things up."

"Nice to be valued," I said.

"You did make it easier to suggest Sagan," Szilard said. "I knew you had a history with General Rybicki. In all, you came in handy. But in point of fact neither you nor Sagan was the key to the equation. It was your daughter,

Administrator Perry, who really matters here. Your daughter was the reason I chose the two of you to lead Roanoke."

I tried to puzzle this one out. "Because of the Obin?" I asked.

"Because of the Obin," Szilard agreed. "Because of the fact the Obin consider her something only a little short of a living god, thanks to their devotion to her true father, and the debatably beneficial boon of consciousness that he gave them."

"I'm afraid that I don't understand how the Obin matter here," I said, although that was a lie. I knew precisely, but I wanted to hear it from Szilard.

He obliged. "Because Roanoke is doomed without them," he said. "Roanoke has served its primary purpose of being a trap for the Conclave fleet. Now the entire Colonial Union is under attack and the CU will have to decide how best to portion out its defensive resources."

"We're already aware Roanoke doesn't rate much of a defense," I said. "I and my staff have had our face rubbed in that fact today."

"Oh, no," Szilard said. "It's worse than that."

"How can it be worse?" I asked.

"This way: Roanoke is more valuable to the Colonial Union dead than alive," Szilard said. "You have to understand, Perry. The Colonial Union is about to fight for its life against most of the races we know of. Its nice little system of farming decrepit Earthlings for soldiers isn't going to get the job done anymore. It's going to need to raise troops from the worlds of the Colonial Union, and fast. This is where Roanoke comes in. Alive, Roanoke is just another colony. Dead, it's a symbol for the ten worlds who gave it colonists, and to all the rest of the worlds in the Colonial Union. When Roanoke dies, the citizens of the Colonial Union are going to demand that they be allowed to fight. And the Colonial Union will let them."

"You know this for sure," I said. "This has been discussed."

"Of course it hasn't," Szilard said. "It never will be. But it's what will happen. The Colonial Union knows that Roanoke is a symbol for the Conclave races as well, the site of their first defeat. It's inevitable that defeat will be revenged. The Colonial Union also knows that by not defending Roanoke, that revenge will happen sooner than later. And sooner will work better for what the Colonial Union needs."

"I don't understand," I said. "You're saying that in order to fight the Conclave, the Colonial Union needs its citizens to become soldiers. And to motivate them into volunteering, Roanoke needs to be destroyed. But you're telling me that the reason you chose Jane and me to lead Roanoke was because the Obin revere my daughter and would not allow the colony to be destroyed."

"It's not quite that simple," Szilard said. "The Obin would not allow your daughter to die, that much is true. They may or may not defend your colony. But the Obin offered you another advantage: knowledge."

"You've lost me again," I said.

"Stop playing the fool, Perry," Szilard said. "It's insulting. I know you know more about General Gau and the Conclave than you let on in that sham of an inquiry today. I know it because it was the Special Forces who prepared the dossier on General Gau and the Conclave for you, the one that rather sloppily left a tremendous amount of metadata in its files for you to find. I also know that your daughter's Obin bodyguards knew rather more about the Conclave than we could tell you in our dossier. That's how you knew you could trust General Gau at his word. And that's why you tried to convince him not to call his fleet. You knew it would be destroyed and you knew he would be compromised."

"You couldn't have known I'd look for that metadata," I said. "You were risking a lot on my curiosity."

"Not really," Szilard said. "Remember, *you* were largely incidental to the selection process. I left that information for Sagan to find. She was an intelligence officer for years. She would have looked for metadata in the files as a matter of course. The fact you found the information first is trivial. It would have been found. It does me no good to leave things to chance."

"But none of that information does me any good *now*," I said. "None of this changes the fact that Roanoke is in the crosshairs, and there's not a thing *I* can do about it. You were at the inquiry. I'll be lucky if they let me tell Jane what prison I'll be rotting in."

Szilard waved this off. "The inquiry determined that you acted responsibly and within your duties," he said. "You're free to return to Roanoke as soon as you and I are done here."

"I take it back," I said. "You *weren't* at the same inquiry I was at."

"It is true that both Butcher and Berkeley are entirely convinced you're absolutely incompetent," Szilard said. "Both of them initially voted to move you to the Colonial Affairs Court, where you would have been convicted and sentenced in about five minutes. However, I managed to convince them to switch their vote."

"How did you do that?" I asked.

"Let's just say that it never pays to have things you don't want other people to know," Szilard said.

"You're blackmailing them," I said.

"I made them aware that every action has a consequence," Szilard said. "And in the fullness of their consideration they preferred the consequences of allowing you to return to Roanoke as opposed to the consequences of keeping you here. Ultimately it was all the same to them. They think you're going to die if you go back to Roanoke."

"I don't know that I blame them," I said.

"You could very well die," Szilard said. "But as I said, you have certain advantages. One of them is your relationship to the Obin. Another is your wife. Between them you might manage to help Roanoke survive, and you with it."

"But we're back to the problem," I said. "The way you tell it, the Colonial Union needs Roanoke to die. By helping me to save Roanoke, you're working against the Colonial Union, General. You're a traitor."

"That's my problem, not yours," Szilard said. "I'm not worried about being branded a traitor. I'm worried about what happens if Roanoke falls."

"If Roanoke falls, the Colonial Union gets its soldiers," I said.

"And then it will go to war with most of the races in this part of space," Szilard said. "And it will *lose*. And in losing, humanity will be wiped out. All of it, from Roanoke all the way up. Even Earth will die, Perry. It will be wiped out and the billions there will have no idea why they're dying. Nothing will be saved. Humanity is on the brink of genocide. And it's a genocide we will have inflicted on ourselves. Unless you can stop it. Unless you can save Roanoke."

"I don't know if I can do that," I said. "Just before I came here, Roanoke was attacked. Just five missiles, but it took everything we had to keep them from wiping us out. If a whole group of Conclave races wants to grind us into dirt I don't know how we can stop them."

"You need to find a way," Szilard said.

"You're a general," I said. "You do it."

"I *am* doing it," Szilard said. "By giving the responsibility to you. I can't do any more than that without losing my place in the Colonial Union hierarchy. And then I *would* be powerless. I've been doing what I can since this insane plan to attack the Conclave was formed. I used you as long as I could without letting you know, but we're beyond that now. Now you know. It's your job to save humanity, Perry."

"No pressure there," I said.

"You did it for years," Szilard said. "Don't you remember what they told you the job of Colonial Defense Forces was? 'To keep a place for humanity among the stars.' You did it then. You need to do it now."

"Then it was me and every other member of the CDF," I said. "The responsibility is a little more focused now."

"Then let me help," Szilard said. "Again, and for the last time. My intelligence corps has told me that General Gau is going to be assassinated by a member of his own circle of advisers. Someone he trusts; indeed, someone he loves. This assassination will happen within the month. We have no other information. We have no way of informing General Gau of the assassination attempt, and even if we had a way, there's no way we could inform him, and no chance he would accept the information as genuine even if we could. If Gau dies, then all the Conclave will reform around Nerbros Eser, who plans to destroy the Colonial Union. If Nerbros Eser takes power, it's all over. The Colonial Union will fall. Humanity dies."

"What am I supposed to do with this information?" I asked.

"Find a way to use it," Szilard said. "And find it fast. And then be ready for everything that happens afterward. And one other thing, Perry. Tell Sagan that while I don't apologize for enhancing her abilities, I do regret the necessity. Let her also know that I suspect she has not yet explored the full range of her capabilities. Tell her that her BrainPal offers the complete range of command functions. Use those words, please."

"What does 'complete range of command functions' mean here?" I asked.

"Sagan can explain it to you if she likes," Szilard said. He reached over to the dash, pressed a button. Phoenix and Phoenix Station reappeared in the windows.

"Now," Szilard said. "Time to get you back to Roanoke, Administrator Perry. You've been gone too long, and you have much to do. Time to get to it, I'd say."

THIRTEEN   Save for Roanoke itself, the colony of Everest was the youngest human colony, settled just before the Conclave gave its warning to other races not to colonize any longer. Like Roanoke, Everest defenses were modest: a pair of defense satellites and six beam turrets, three each for the two settlements, and one CDF cruiser on rotation. When Everest was hit, it was the *Des Moines* stationed over the settlements. A good ship and a good crew, but the *Des Moines* was not enough to counter the six Arrisian ships that skipped with daring precision into Everest space, firing missiles at the *Des Moines* and the defense satellites as they arrived. The *Des Moines* sheared down its length and began the long fall toward the Everest surface; the defense satellites were rendered into so much floating junk.

The planet's defenses collapsed, the Arrisian ships took their time searing the Everest settlements from orbit, finally dispatching a company to clean up the straggling colonists who remained. In the end 5,800 Everest colonists were dead. The Arrisians left behind no colonists or garrison and made no claim to the planet. They simply eradicated the human presence there.

Erie was no Everest—it was one of the oldest and most heavily populated of the human worlds, with a planetary defense grid and permanent CDF presence that would make it impossible for all but the most insanely ambitious races to make a play for. But even planetary defense grids can't track every single chunk of ice or rock that falls into the gravity well. Several dozen such apparent chunks fell into Erie's atmosphere, over the Erie city of New Cork. As they fell, the heat generated by the friction of the atmosphere was channeled and focused, powering the compact chemical lasers hidden within the rock.

Several of the beams struck strategic manufacturing concerns in New Cork, related to CDF weapons systems. Several more appeared to strike randomly, slashing through homes, schools and markets, killing hundreds. Their beams spent, the lasers burned up in the atmosphere, leaving no clue who had sent them or why.

This happened as Trujillo, Beata, Kranjic and I made our way back to Roanoke. We were unaware of it at the time, of course. We were unaware of the specific attacks that were going on around the Colonial Union, because the news was kept from us, and because we were focused on our own survival.

"You've offered us the protection of the Obin," I said to Hickory within hours of my return to Roanoke. "We'd like to take advantage of that offer."

"There are complications," Hickory said.

I glanced over at Jane, and then back to Hickory. "Well, of course there are," I said. "It wouldn't be *fun* without complications."

"I sense sarcasm," Hickory said, with utterly no sense of humor whatsoever.

"I apologize, Hickory," I said. "I'm having a bad week and it's not getting any better. Please tell what these complications might be."

"After you left, a skip drone arrived from Obinur, and we were finally able to communicate with our government. We have been told that once the *Magellan* disappeared, the Colonial Union formally requested that the Obin not interfere with the Roanoke colony, openly or covertly."

"Roanoke was specified," Jane said.

"Yes," said Hickory.

"Why?" I asked.

"The Colonial Union did not explain," Hickory said. "We now assume it was because an Obin attempt to locate the planet could have disrupted the Colonial Union's attack on the Conclave fleet. Our government agreed not to interfere but noted that should any harm come to Zoë, we would be greatly displeased. The Colonial Union assured our government that Zoë was reasonably safe. As she was."

"The Colonial Union's attack on the Conclave fleet is over," I said.

"The agreement did not specify when it would be acceptable to interfere," Hickory said, again with no trace of humor. "We are still bound to it."

"So you can do nothing for us," Jane said.

"We are charged with protecting Zoë," Hickory said. "But we have been made to understand that the definition of *protection* extends only so far."

"And if Zoë orders you to protect the colony?" I asked.

"Zoë may order Dickory and me as she wishes," Hickory said. "But it is doubtful that even her intercession would be enough."

I got up from my desk and stalked over to the window to look up at the night sky. "Do the Obin know the Colonial Union is under attack?" I asked.

"We do," Hickory said. "There have been numerous attacks since the destruction of the Conclave fleet."

"Then you know that the Colonial Union will have to make choices as to which colonies it needs to defend and which it will sacrifice. And that Roanoke is more likely to be in that second category."

"We know this," Hickory said.

"But you'll still do nothing to help us," I said.

"Not so long as Roanoke remains part of the Colonial Union," Hickory said.

Jane was on this before I could open my mouth. "Explain that," she said.

"An independent Roanoke would require a new response from us," Hickory said. "If Roanoke declares itself independent of the Colonial Union, the Obin would feel obliged to offer support and aid on an interim basis until the Colonial Union reacquired the planet or agreed to its secession."

"But you would risk alienating the Colonial Union," Jane said.

"The Colonial Union has a number of other priorities at the moment," Hickory said. "We do not feel the repercussions of aiding an independent Roanoke will be significant in the long run."

"So you *will* help us," I said. "You just want us to declare ourselves independent of the Colonial Union first."

"We neither advise you to secede nor to stay," Hickory said. "We merely note that if you should secede, we will help defend you."

I turned to Jane. "What do you think?"

"I doubt the people of this colony are ready for us to declare their independence," Jane said.

"If the alternative is death?" I said.

"Some of them probably would prefer death to being a traitor," Jane said. "Or to being permanently cut off from the rest of humanity."

"Let's ask them," I said.

The attack on Wabash colony was not much of an attack at all; a few missiles to destroy the colony's administrative offices and landmarks, and a small invading force of a few hundred Bhav soldiers to shoot up the place. But then Wabash wasn't the target. The targets were the three CDF cruisers that skipped in to defend the colony. The skip drone that had alerted the CDF to the attack indicated one Bhav cruiser and three smaller gunboats, all of which could be easily handled by three cruisers. What the skip drone could not indicate is that shortly after it skipped away from Wabash space, six additional Bhav cruisers skipped in, destroyed the satellite that launched the skip drones, and readied themselves for an ambush.

The CDF cruisers entered Wabash space cautiously—by this time it was clear that the Colonial Union was under a general attack, and the CDF ship commanders were neither stupid nor rash. But the odds were against them from the moment they arrived in Wabash space. The CDF cruisers *Augusta, Savannah* and *Portland* took down three of the Bhav cruisers and all of the smaller gunships before they were overwhelmed and destroyed, scattering metal, air and crew into the space above the planet. It was three fewer cruisers the CDF had to defend the Colonial Union. It was also a signal that every new incident would have to be met with overwhelming force, constricting the number of colonies the CDF could defend at one time. Priorities already shifted to the new realities of war shifted once again, and not in the CU's favor, nor in Roanoke's.

"You're out of your mind," said Marie Black. "We're under attack from this Conclave, it wants to kill us all dead, and your solution to the problem is to go it alone, with no help from the rest of the human race? That's just insane."

The looks up and down the Council table told me that Jane and I were all alone on this one, just like Jane suspected we would be. Even Manfred Trujillo, who knew the situation better than anyone, was taken aback by the suggestion we declare our independence. This was the original tough crowd.

"We wouldn't be alone," I said. "The Obin will help us if we're independent."

"*That* makes me feel safer," Black said, mockingly. "Aliens are planning to murder us all, but don't worry, we've got these *pet* aliens to keep us safe. That is, until they decide they're better off siding with the other aliens."

"That's not a very accurate assessment of the Obin," I said.

"But the Obin's primary concern isn't *our* colony," said Lee Chen. "It's *your* daughter. God forbid something happens to your daughter, because then where will *we* be? The Obin will have no more reason to help us. We'd be isolated from the rest of the Colonial Union."

"We're *already* isolated from the rest of the Colonial Union," I said. "Planets are under attack all over the union. The CDF is already scrambling to respond. We're not a priority. We won't be a priority. We've served our purpose."

"We have only your word for that," Chen said. "We're getting news reports, now that we've got access to our PDAs. There's nothing in the news about anything of this."

"You have my word for it as well," Trujillo said. "I'm not ready to sign on to independence, either, but Perry's not lying. The Colonial Union has its priorities right now, and we're definitely not one of them."

"I'm not trying to say that either of you are not as good as your word," Chen said. "But think of what you're asking us to do here. You're asking us to risk everything— *everything*—on your word."

"Even if we were to agree to this, what then?" asked Lol Gerber, who had replaced Hiram Yoder on the council. "We'd be isolated. If the Colonial Union survives, we'd have to settle with them for raising rebellion. If the Colonial Union were to fall, then we'd be all that is left of the human race, and reliant on the grace of another people for our survival. How long could we expect them to shelter us, if the whole host of the intelligent races want us dead? How could we in good conscience ask the Obin to put their own survival at stake for ours? The Colonial Union is humanity. We belong *in* it, for better or worse."

"It's not all of humanity," I said. "There's Earth."

"Which is kept in a corner by the Colonial Union," Black said. "It's not going to be any help to us now."

I sighed. "I can see where this is going to go," I said. "I asked the Council for its vote, and Jane and I will abide by it. But I beg you, think about it. Don't let your prejudice of the Obin," I glanced at Marie Black, "or a feeling of patriotism blind you to the fact that we are now in a war, and *we* are at the front line—and we have no support from home. We *are* on our own. We need to consider what we have to do to survive, because no one else is looking out for us."

"You've never been this bleak before, Perry," said Marta Piro.

"I don't think things have been this bleak before," I said. "All right then. Let's vote."

I voted to secede. Jane abstained; it was our tradition to only cast one vote between us. Every other member of the Council voted to stay in the Colonial Union.

Technically speaking, mine was the only vote that counted. Of course, technically speaking, by voting to leave the Colonial Union, I had just voted for treason. So maybe everyone else was doing me a favor.

"We're a colony," I said. "Still." Smiles broke out across the table.

"Now what do we do?" Marie Black asked.

"I'm thinking," I said. "Believe me, I'm thinking."

Bonita was a planet that lived up to its name, a lovely place with abundant wildlife with just the right genetic components for human consumption. Bonita had been settled fifteen years earlier; still a young colony, but established enough to have its own personality. Bonita was attacked by the Dtrutz, a species of more ambition than brains. This is one encounter that went decisively for the Colonial Union; the trio of CDF cruisers over Bonita made short work of the Dtrutz invading force, picking off their poorly designed ships first during the initial attack and then in a more leisurely fashion as the Dtrutz ships attempted to reach skip distance before the CDF rail gun projectiles reached the Dtrutz ships. The Dtrutz were not at all successful in this endeavor.

What made the Dtrutz attack notable was not its complete incompetence but the fact that the Dtrutz were not a Conclave species; like the Colonial Union, they were unaffiliated. The Dtrutz were under the same ban on colonization as the Colonial Union. They attacked anyway. They knew—as did an increasing number of races—that the Colonial Union was locked in a wide struggle with elements of the Conclave, and that meant the possibility of peeling away some of the lesser human colonies while the CDF was otherwise occupied. The Colonial Union was wounded and shedding blood in the water, and the lesser fish were coming up from the depths to get a taste.

"We've come for your daughter," Hickory said to me.

"I beg your pardon," I said. Despite everything, I couldn't resist the urge to crack a grin.

"Our government has determined that it is inevitable that Roanoke will be attacked and destroyed," Hickory said.

"Swell," I said.

"Dickory and I both regret this eventuality," Hickory said, leaning forward slightly for emphasis. "And our inability to assist you in preventing this."

"Well, thanks," I said, hoping it didn't sound too insincere.

Apparently, it did not. "We are not allowed to interfere or offer aid, but we have decided that it is acceptable to remove Zoë from danger," Hickory continued. "We've requested a transport ship for her and for us; it is on its way. We wanted to let you know of these plans because she is your daughter, and because we have also secured permission to transport you and Lieutenant Sagan if you wish."

"So the three of us can escape from this mess," I said. Hickory nodded. "What about everyone else?"

"We have no permission to accommodate others," Hickory said.

"But does no permission mean you *can't* accommodate others?" I asked. "If Zoë wants to take her best friend Gretchen, are you going to tell her no? And do you think Zoë is going to leave if Jane and I stay?"

"Do you plan to stay?" Hickory asked.

"Of course we do," I said.

"You will die," Hickory said.

"We might," I said, "although I'm working to avoid that right now. But regardless, Roanoke is where we belong. We're not leaving, and I suspect you'll have a difficult time convincing Zoë to leave without us, or without her friends."

"She would leave if you told her to," Hickory said.

I smiled, reached on my desk to key my PDA, and sent a message to Zoë to meet me immediately in my office. She arrived a few minutes later.

"Hickory and Dickory want you to leave Roanoke," I said.

"Are you and Mom coming?" Zoë asked.

"No," I said.

"Then the hell with that," Zoë said, looking directly at Hickory as she said so.

I held my hands open in supplication to Hickory. "Told you," I said.

"You didn't tell her to come away," Hickory said.

"Go away, Zoë," I said.

"Screw you, ninety-year-old dad," Zoë said, smiling and yet deadly serious at the same time. Then she turned back to the Obin. "And screw the both of you, too. And while we're at it, screw being whatever it is that I am to the Obin. If you want to protect me, protect the people I care about. Protect this colony."

"We cannot," Hickory said. "We've been forbidden to do so."

"Then you have a problem," Zoë said. Her smile was gone, and her eyes were glistening. "Because I'm not going *anywhere*. And there's nothing either you or anyone can do to change that." Zoë stormed out.

"That went pretty much exactly as I expected," I said.

"You didn't do all you could do to convince her," Hickory said.

I squinted at Hickory. "You're suggesting I was insincere."

"Yes," Hickory said. Its expression was even more unreadable than usual, but I can't imagine that saying something like that was easy for it; the emotional response would probably cause it to shut down its interface soon.

"You're right," I said. "I *was* insincere."

"But *why*?" Hickory asked, and I was surprised by the plaintiveness in its voice. It was shaking now. "You have killed your own child, and the child of Charles Boutin."

"She's not dead yet," I said. "And neither are we. Neither is this colony."

"You know we cannot allow Zoë to come to harm," Dickory said, breaking his silent act. I was reminded that he was in actuality the superior of the two Obin.

"Are you going to go back to the plan of killing me and Jane to protect Zoë?" I asked.

"It is to be hoped not," Dickory said.

"What a delightfully ambiguous answer," I said.

"It's not ambiguous," Hickory said. "You know what our position is. What it must be."

"And I'd ask you to remember what *my* position is," I said. "I've told you that in every circumstance you should protect Zoë. That position has not changed."

"But you have made it substantially more difficult," Hickory said. "You may have made it impossible."

"I don't think so," I said. "Let me make a proposal to the two of you. You have a ship arriving soon. I'm going to promise you that Zoë will leave with you on that ship. But you have to promise me that you take her where I am going to ask her to go."

"Where is that?" Hickory said.

"I'm not going to tell you yet," I said.

"That will make it difficult for us to agree," Hickory said.

"That's the breaks," I said. "But I guarantee you where you're taking her will be more safe than here. Now. Agree, and I'll make sure she goes with you. Don't, you'll have to find a way to protect her here, or kill me and Jane trying to drag her away. These are your choices."

Hickory and Dickory leaned in and conversed for several minutes, longer than I had ever seen them converse before.

"We accept your condition," Hickory said.

"Good," I said. "Now all I have to do is get Zoë to agree. Not to mention Jane."

"Will you tell us now where we will be taking Zoë?" Hickory asked.

"To deliver a message," I said.

The *Kristina Marie* had just docked at Khartoum Station when its engine compartment shattered, vaporizing the back quarter of the trading ship and driving the front three-quarters of the ship directly into Khartoum Station. The station's hull buckled and snapped; air and personnel burst from the fracture lines. Across the impact zone airtight bulkheads sprang into place, only to be torn from their moorings and sockets by the encroaching inertial mass of the *Kristina Marie*, itself bleeding atmosphere and crew from the collision. When the ship came to rest, the explosion and collision had crippled Khartoum Station, and killed 566 people on the station and all but six members of the *Kristina Marie*'s crew, two of whom died shortly thereafter of their injuries.

The explosion of the *Kristina Marie* did more than destroy the ship and much of Khartoum Station; it coincided with the harvest of Khartoum's hogfruit, a native delicacy that was one of Khartoum's major exports. Hogfruit spoiled quickly after ripening (it got its name from the fact Khartoum's settlers fed the overripe fruit to their pigs, who were the only ones who would eat them at that point), so Khartoum had invested heavily to be able to harvest and ship for export its hogfruit crop within days of ripening, via Khartoum Station. The *Kristina Marie* was only one of a hundred Colonial Union trade ships above Khartoum, awaiting its share of the fruit.

With Khartoum Station down, the streamlined distribution system for the hogfruit ground into disarray. Ships dispatched shuttles to Khartoum itself to try to pack in as many crates of the fruit as possible, but this led to confusion on the ground in terms of which hogfruit producers had priority in shipping their product, and which trade ships had priority in receiving them. Fruit had to be unpacked from storage containers and repacked into shuttles; there were not nearly enough cargo men for the job. The vast majority of hogfruit rotted in its containers, delivering a major shock to the Khartoum economy, which would be compounded in the long term by the need to rebuild Khartoum Station—the economic lifeline for other exports as well—and bolster the defenses of Khartoum from further attack.

Before the *Kristina Marie* docked at Khartoum Station, it transmitted its identification, cargo manifest and recent itinerary as part of the standard security "handshake." The records showed that two stops previous, the *Kristina Marie* had traded at Quii, the homeworld of the Qui, one of the Colonial Union's few allies. It had docked next to a ship of Ylan registry, the Ylan being members of the Conclave. Forensic analysis of the explosion left no doubt that it was intentionally triggered and not an accidental breach of the engine core. From Phoenix came the order that no trade ship that had visited a nonhuman world in the last year was to approach a space station without a thorough scan and inspection. Hundreds of trade ships floated in space, their cargo unpacked and crews quarantined in the original Venetian sense of the word, awaiting the eradication of a different sort of plague.

The *Kristina Marie* had been sabotaged and sent on its way, to the place where its destruction could have the most impact, not just in deaths but in paralyzing the economy of the Colonial Union. It worked brilliantly.

The Roanoke Council didn't react well to the news that I had sent Zoë to deliver a message to General Gau.

"We need to discuss your treason problem," Manfred Trujillo said to me.

"I don't have a problem with treason," I said. "I can stop anytime." I looked around the table at the rest of the Council members. The little joke didn't go over well.

"Goddamn it, Perry," Lee Chen said, angrier than I'd ever seen him. "The Conclave is planning to kill us, and you're passing notes to its leader?"

"And you've used your daughter to do it," Marie Black said, disgust creeping into her voice. "You've sent your only child to our enemy."

I glanced over at Jane and Savitri, both of whom nodded to me. We knew this was going to come up; we had discussed how best to handle it when it did.

"No, I didn't," I said. "We have enemies and lots of them, but General Gau isn't one of them." I told them of my conversation with General Szilard of the Special Forces, and his warning of the assassination attempt on Gau. "Gau has promised us that he wouldn't attack Roanoke," I said. "If he dies, there's nothing between us and whoever wants to kill us."

"There's nothing between us and them *now*," Lee Chen said. "Or did you miss the attack on us a couple of weeks back?"

"I didn't miss it," I said. "And I suspect it would have been much worse if Gau didn't have at least some control over the Conclave. If he knows about this assassination attempt he can use it to get back control of the rest of the Conclave. And then we'll be safe. Or at least safer. I decided it was worth it to take the risk to let him know."

"You didn't put it up for a vote," said Marta Piro.

"I didn't have to," I said. "I am still colony leader. Jane and I decided that this was the best thing to do. And it's not like you would have said 'yes,' anyway."

"But it's *treason*," Trujillo repeated. "For real this time, John. This is more than coyly asking the general not to bring his fleet here. You're interfering with the internal politics of the Conclave. There's no way the Colonial Union is going to let you do this, especially when they've already hauled you up in front of an inquiry."

"I'll take responsibility for my actions," I said.

"Yes, well, unfortunately, we will all have to take

responsibility for them, *too*," Marie Black said. "Unless you think the Colonial Union is going to assume you've been doing this all on your own."

I eyed Marie Black. "Just out of curiosity, Marie, what do you think the CU is going to *do*? Send CDF troops here to arrest me and Jane? Personally I think that would be *fine*. Then at least there'd be a military presence here if we're attacked. The only other option would be that they hang us out to dry, and you know what? That's what's happening *already*."

I looked around the table. "I think we need to reemphasize again a salient fact that keeps getting overlooked, here: We are completely, entirely and utterly *on our own*. Our value to the Colonial Union now is in our demise, to rally the other colonies to join in the fight with their own citizens and treasuries. I don't mind being a symbol for the rest of the Colonial Union, but I don't want to have to die for the privilege. I don't want any of *you* to have to die for the privilege, either."

Trujillo looked over to Jane. "You agree with all of this," he said to her.

"John got his information from my former commanding officer," Jane said. "I have issues to settle with him on a personal level. I don't doubt the information is good."

"But does he have an agenda?" Trujillo asked.

"Of course he has an agenda," Jane said. "He wants to keep the rest of the universe from stomping on us like we're fucking bugs. I thought he made that pretty clear."

That put a pause to Trujillo. "I mean does he have an agenda we don't see," he said, finally.

"I doubt it," Jane said. "Special Forces are pretty straightforward. We're sneaky when it's necessary, but when it comes to it, we come at you straight on."

"Which makes him the first," I said. "The Colonial Union hasn't dealt with us honestly in any of this."

"They didn't have a choice," Lee Chen said.

"Don't give me that," I said. "We're too far along in this to swallow that one whole anymore. Yes, the CU was playing a deep game with the Conclave, and it didn't bother to tell us pawns what the game was. But now the CU is playing a new game and it's dependent on us being taken off the board."

"We don't know that for sure," Marta Piro said.

"We know we have no defenses," Trujillo said. "And we know where we stand in the line to get more. Regardless of the reasons, John's right. We're up against it."

"I still want to know how you can live with sending your daughter to negotiate with this General Gau," Marie Black said.

"It made sense," Jane said.

"I don't see how," Black said.

"Zoë is traveling with the Obin," Jane said. "The Obin are not actively hostile with the Conclave. General Gau will receive the Obin, where he could not receive a Colonial ship."

"Even if we could somehow *get* a Colonial ship, which we can't," I said.

"Neither John nor I can leave the colony without our absence being noted by both the Colonial Union and our own settlers," Jane said. "Zoë, on the other hand, has a special relationship with the Obin. Her leaving the planet at the Obin's insistence was something the Colonial Union would expect."

"There's another advantage, too," I said. Heads swiveled to me. "Even if I or Jane could have made the trip, there'd be no reason for Gau to accept our information as genuine or in earnest. The leaders of colonies have sacrificed themselves before. But with Zoë, we're giving Gau more than information."

"You're giving him a hostage," Trujillo said.

"Yes," I said.

"You're playing a risky game," Trujillo said.

"*This* isn't a game," I said. "We had to make sure we were heard. And it's a calculated risk. The Obin are with Zoë, and I don't think they'll stand idly by if Gau does anything stupid."

"You're still risking her life," Black said. "You're risking her life and she's only a child."

"If she stayed here, she would have died like the rest of us," Jane said. "By going, she'll live, and she gives us a chance to survive. We did the right thing."

Marie Black opened her mouth to respond. "You need to think *very* hard about the next thing you say concerning my daughter," Jane said. Black closed her mouth with an audible *clack*.

"You've set this course of action without us," Lol Gerber said. "But you're telling us now. I'd like to know the reason why."

"We sent Zoë because we thought it was necessary," I said. "That was our decision to make, and we made it. But Marie is right: *You* are going to have to live with consequences of our actions. We had to tell you. If Marie's any indication, some of you have lost confidence in us. Right now you need leaders you feel you can trust. We've told you what we've done and why. One of the consequences of our actions is that now you need to vote on whether you want us to lead the colony any further."

"The Colonial Union won't accept anyone new," Marta Piro said.

"I think that depends on what you tell them," I said.

"If you tell them we've been consorting with the enemy, I'm guessing they'd approve the change."

"So you're also asking us whether or not to turn you in to the Colonial Union," Trujillo said.

"We're asking you to do what you think is necessary," I said. "Just as we have done." I stood up; Jane followed. We walked outside of our office and into the Roanoke sunlight.

"How long do you think it will take?" I asked Jane.

"Not long," Jane said. "I expect Marie Black will make sure of that."

"I want to thank you for not killing her," I said. "It would have made the vote of confidence problematic."

"I *did* want to kill her, but not because she was wrong," Jane said. "She's right. We're risking Zoë's life. And she's a child."

I walked over to my wife. "She's almost as old as you are," I said, rubbing her arm.

Jane pulled away. "It's not the same and you know it," she said.

"No, it's not," I said. "But Zoë's old enough to understand what she's doing. She's lost people she's cared for, just like you have. Just like I have. And she knows that she stands to lose a lot more. She chose to go. We gave her a choice."

"We gave her a *false* choice," Jane said. "We stood in front of her and gave her the choice of risking her own life or risking the lives of everyone she knows, including ours. You can't tell me that was a fair set of choices to give her."

"It's not," I said. "But those were the choices we had to give her."

"I hate this fucking universe," Jane said, looking away. "I hate the Colonial Union. I hate the Conclave. I hate this colony. I hate all of it."

"How do you feel about me?" I asked.

"Now is not a good time to ask," Jane said. We sat and waited.

A half hour later Savitri walked out of the administration office. Her eyes were red. "Well, there's good news and bad news," she said. "The good news is that you have ten days before they tell the CU that you've been talking to General Gau. You have Trujillo to thank for that."

"That's something," I said.

"Yeah," Savitri said. "The bad news is that you're out. Both of you. Unanimous vote. I'm just the secretary. I couldn't vote. Sorry."

"Who has the job now?" Jane asked.

"Trujillo," Savitri said. "Of course. Bastard started angling for the job before you two closed the door."

"He's really not that bad," I said.

"I know," Savitri said, and wiped her eyes. "I'm just trying to make you feel like I'll miss you."

I smiled. "Well, I appreciate that." I gave her a hug. She hugged me back fiercely, and then stepped back.

"What now?" Savitri asked.

"We have ten days," I said. "Now we wait."

The ship knew the Roanoke defenses, or lack thereof, which is why it appeared in the sky on the other side of the planet, where the colony's single defense satellite couldn't see it. The ship let itself down gently into the atmosphere to avoid the heat and drama of reentry, and slowly crossed the longitudes of the globe, heading toward the colony. Before the ship crossed the defense satellite's perceptual horizon, and the heat of its engines would be sensed by it, the ship cut them out, and began a long gravity-assisted glide toward the colony, its small mass supported by immense but whisper-thin electrically generated wings. The ship fell, silently, toward its target, us.

We saw it just as it finished its long glide and discarded its wings, switching over to maneuvering jets and flotation fields. The sudden plumes of heat and energy were caught by the satellite, which immediately sent a warning—too late, as it turned out, because by the time it had signaled, the ship had already maneuvered to land. The satellite sped telemetry to our beam turrets and warmed up its own beam defenses, which were now fully recharged.

Jane, who was still in charge of colony defense, signaled for the satellite to stand down. The ship was now within colony borders, if not within the walls of Croatoan; if the satellite fired, the colony itself would be damaged. Jane likewise took the beam turrets offline; they too would end up causing more damage to the colony than the ship would.

The ship landed; Jane and Trujillo and I walked out to meet it. As we walked a bay on the ship slid open. A passenger shot out from the bay, yelling and running at Jane, who prepared herself for the impact. Badly, as it turned out, because she and Zoë both tumbled to the ground. I went over to laugh at them; Jane grabbed an ankle and pulled me down to the pile. Trujillo stood at a prudent distance, so as not to get caught up in the mess.

"It took you long enough," I said to Zoë, after I finally detangled myself. "Another day and a half, and your mom and I would be headed to Phoenix on a treason charge."

"I haven't the slightest idea what you're talking about," Zoë said. "I'm just glad to see you." She grabbed me in another hug.

"Zoë," Jane said. "You saw General Gau."

"Saw him?" Zoë said. "We were there for the assassination attempt."

"You *what*?" Jane and I said simultaneously.

Zoë held up her hands, placatingly. "Survived it," she said. "As you can see."

I looked over to Jane. "I think I just wet myself," I said.

"I'm fine," Zoë said. "It wasn't that bad, really."

"You know, even for a teenager, you might be a bit blasé about this," I said. Zoë grinned. I hugged her again, even more tightly.

"And the general?" Jane said.

"Survived it too," Zoë said. "And not *just* survived it. Came out of it furious. He's using the attempt to call people on the carpet. To demand their loyalty to him."

"To him?" I said. "That doesn't sound like him. He said to me that the Conclave wasn't an empire. If he's demanding loyalty, it sounds like he's making himself an emperor."

"Some of his closest advisers *did* just try to murder him," Zoë said. "He could use some personal loyalty right now."

"I can't argue that," I said.

"But it's not over," Zoë said. "That's why I came back. There's still a group of planets holding out. They're led by someone named Eser. Nerbros Eser. They've been the ones attacking the Colonial Union, he said."

"Right," I said, remembering what General Szilard had said about Eser.

"General Gau gave me a message for you," Zoë said. "He says that Eser is coming here. Soon. Eser wants to take Roanoke because the general couldn't. Taking Roanoke gives him leverage, the general said. A way to show he's more able to lead the Conclave."

"Of course," I said. "Everyone else is using Roanoke as a pawn. Why not this asshole?"

"If this Eser is attacking the Colonial Union at large,

then he's not going to have any trouble finishing us off," Trujillo said. He was still keeping his distance from the pile.

"The general said that his information says that Eser doesn't plan to hit us from space," Zoë said. "He wants to land here, to take Roanoke with troops. The general said he would use just enough to take the colony. Sort of the opposite of what the general did with his fleet. To make a point. There's more in the files the general gave me."

"So it will be a small attack force," I said. Zoë nodded.

"Unless he's coming with just himself and a couple of friends, we're still going to have a problem," Trujillo said, and nodded toward me and Jane. "You two are the only ones with any real military training. Even with our ground defenses, we won't last long against real soldiers."

Jane was about to respond, but Zoë beat her to it. "I've thought of that," she said.

Trujillo appeared to stifle a grin. "*You* have," he said.

Zoë turned serious. "Mr. Trujillo, your daughter is my best friend in the world," she said. "I don't want her to die. I don't want *you* to die. I'm in a position to help. Please don't condescend to me."

Trujillo straightened up. "I apologize, Zoë," he said. "I meant no disrespect. It's just I wasn't expecting you to have a plan."

"And neither was I," I said.

"You remember a long time ago I complained that being an object of worship for an entire race of people wasn't even good enough to get me out of homework," Zoë said.

"Vaguely," I said.

"Well, while I was away I decided to find out what it *was* actually good for," Zoë said.

"I still don't get it," I said.

Zoë took my hand, and then reached out to Jane for hers. "Come on," she said. "Hickory and Dickory are still inside the ship. They're keeping an eye on something for me. I want to show it to you."

"What is it?" Jane asked.

"It's a surprise," Zoë said. "But I think you're going to like it."

FOURTEEN

Jane woke me up by pushing me out of bed.

"What the hell?" I said, groggily, from the floor.

"The satellite feed just went down," she said. Jane was up, grabbed a pair of high-powered binoculars from the dresser, and went outside. I woke up quick and followed her.

"What do you see?" I said.

"The satellite's gone," she said. "There's a ship not too far from where the satellite should be."

"This Eser is not one for subtlety," I said.

"He doesn't think he has to be," Jane said. "It wouldn't suit his purposes anyway."

"Are we ready for this?" I said.

"It doesn't matter if we're ready," Jane said, and dropped her binoculars to look at me. "It's time."

To be fair, after Zoë returned, we let the Department of Colonization know that we believed we were under imminent threat of attack and that our defenses against such an attack were almost nil. We begged for more support. What we got was a visit from General Rybicki.

"You two must have swallowed a handful of pills," Rybicki said, without preamble, when he walked into the administrator's office. "I'm beginning to be sorry I suggested you for colony leaders."

"We're not the colony leaders anymore," I said, and pointed at Manfred Trujillo, who was seated behind my former desk. "He is."

This threw Rybicki off stride; he looked at Trujillo. "You have no authorization to be colony leader."

"The colonists would disagree with you," Trujillo said.

"The colonists don't get a vote," Rybicki said.

"They'd disagree with you on that, too," Trujillo said.

"Then *they've* swallowed stupid pills along with you three," Rybicki said, and turned back to me and Jane. "What the hell is going on here?"

"I thought our message to the Department of Colonization was pretty clear," I said. "We have reason to believe we're about to be attacked, and those who are going to attack us are planning to wipe us out. We need defenses or we're going to die."

"You sent the message *in the clear*," Rybicki said. "Anyone could have picked it up."

"It was encrypted," I said. "Military encryption."

"It was encrypted with a protocol that's compromised," Rybicki said. "It's been compromised for years." He looked up at Jane. "*You* of all people should have known that, Sagan. You're responsible for this colony's safety. You know which encryption to use."

Jane said nothing.

"So you're saying that now anyone who cares to hear knows we're vulnerable," I said.

"I'm saying that you might as well have taped bacon to your head and walked into a tiger pit," Rybicki said.

"Then all the more reason for the Colonial Union to defend us," Trujillo said.

Rybicki glanced back over to Trujillo. "I'm not talking anymore with him around," he said. "It doesn't matter what sort of cozy agreement you have going here, the fact of the matter is you two are on the hook for the colony, not him. It's time to get serious, and what we need to talk about is classified. *He* doesn't rate."

"He's still colony leader," I said.

"I don't care if you've crowned him King of Siam," Rybicki said. "He needs to go."

"Your call, Manfred," I said.

"I'll go," Trujillo said, standing up. "But you need to know this, General Rybicki. We know here how the Colonial Union has used us, played with our destiny and toyed with the lives of all of us. Our lives, the lives of our families and the lives of our children. If the Colonial Union doesn't defend us now, we'll know who really killed us. Not some other species and not the Conclave. The Colonial Union. Pure and simple."

"That's a nice speech, Trujillo," Rybicki said. "It doesn't make it true."

"General, at the moment, I wouldn't place you as an authority on truth," Trujillo said. He nodded to me and Jane and left before the general could retort.

"We're going to tell him everything you say to us," I said, after Trujillo left.

"Then you'll be treasonous as well as incompetent," Rybicki said, sitting at the desk. "I don't know what you two think you're doing, but whatever it is, it's insane. You," he looked up at Jane, "I *know* you know that encryption protocol had been compromised. You had to know that you were broadcasting your vulnerability. I can't even begin to fathom why you did it."

"I have my reasons," Jane said.

"Fine," Rybicki said. "Tell me."

"No," Jane said.

"Excuse me?" the general asked.

"I said no," Jane said. "I don't trust you."

"Oh, that's *rich*," Rybicki said. "You've just painted a big fat target on your colony and *I* can't be trusted."

"There are a lot of things the Colonial Union did with Roanoke they didn't bother to tell us about," I said. "Turnabout is fair play."

"Christ," Rybicki said. "We're not in a goddamn *schoolyard*. You're gambling with the lives of these colonists."

"And this is different from what the CU did how?" I asked.

"Because you don't have the authority," Rybicki said. "You don't have the right."

"The Colonial Union has the *right* to gamble with the lives of these colonists?" I asked. "It has the right to place them in the path of an enemy military who means to destroy them? These aren't soldiers, General. They're civilians. Some of our people are religious pacifists. *You* made sure of that. The Colonial Union may have had the *authority* to put these people in harm's way. But it sure as hell didn't have the *right*."

"Have you ever heard of Coventry?" Rybicki said.

"The English city?" I asked.

Rybicki nodded. "In the Second World War, the British learned through intelligence that their enemies were going to bomb the town. They knew when it was going to happen. But if they evacuated the town they'd reveal that they knew the enemies' secret code, and they would lose their ability to listen in on the enemies' plans. For the good of all of Britain they let the bombing happen."

"You're saying Roanoke is the Colonial Union's Coventry," Jane said.

"I'm saying that we have an implacable enemy who wants us all dead," Rybicki said. "And that we have to look at what's best for humanity. *All* of humanity."

"This assumes that what the Colonial Union does is what's best for all of humanity," I said.

"Not to put too fine a point on it, but what it does is better than what anyone else has planned for humanity," Rybicki said.

"But *you* don't think that what the Colonial Union is doing is what's best for all humanity," Jane said.

"I didn't say that," Rybicki said.

"You're thinking it," Jane said.

"You have no idea what I'm thinking," Rybicki said.

"I know precisely what you're thinking," Jane said. "I know you're here to tell us that the Colonial Union doesn't have ships or soldiers to defend us. I know you know that there are ships and soldiers for our defense but that they've been assigned to roles you find redundant or nonessential. I know you're supposed to deliver a convincing lie to us about that. That's why you're here personally, to give the lie a personal touch. And I know it disgusts you that you're being made to do this, but that it disgusts you even more that you've allowed yourself to do it."

Rybicki stared at Jane, mouth open. So did I.

"I know you think the Colonial Union is acting stupidly in sacrificing Roanoke to the Conclave. I know you know that there are already plans to use our loss for recruiting among the colonies. I know you think that recruiting from the colonies makes them more vulnerable to attack, not less, because now the Conclave will have a reason to target civilian populations in order to cut down the number of potential soldiers. I know you see this as an endgame for the Colonial Union. I know you think the Colonial Union will lose. I know you fear for me and John, for this colony, and for yourself, and for all of humanity. I know you think there's no way out."

Rybicki sat in silence for a long moment. "You seem to know a lot," he said, finally.

"I know enough," Jane said. "But now we need to hear all of this from you."

Rybicki looked over to me, and back to Jane. He sagged and shifted uncomfortably. "What can I tell you that you don't seem to know already?" he said. "The Colonial Union has nothing for you. I argued for them to give you something, *anything*"—he looked over to Jane to see if she would acknowledge the truth of this, but she only stared impassively—"but they've made the decision to hold the line at the more developed colonies. I was told it was a more strategic use of our military strength. I don't agree, but it's not an indefensible argument to make. Roanoke isn't the only newer colony left exposed."

"We're just the one that's known to be targeted," I said.

"I'm supposed to give you a reasonable story for the lack of defenses," Rybicki said. "The one I settled on was that your sending your plea for help with compromised encryption put our ships and soldiers at risk. This has the advantage of possibly being true"—he looked sharply at Jane when he said this—"but it's primarily a cover story. I didn't come just to give it a convincing touch. I came because I felt I owed it to you to say it to your faces."

"I don't know how to feel about the fact you're more comfortable lying to us up close than far away," I said.

Rybicki smiled a bitter smile. "In retrospect, it appears not to have been one of my best decisions." He turned back to Jane. "I still want to know how you knew all this."

"I have my sources," Jane said. "And you've told us what we need to know. The Colonial Union has cut us loose."

"It wasn't my decision," Rybicki said. "I don't think it's right."

"I know," Jane said. "But that doesn't really matter at this point."

Rybicki looked to me for a more sympathetic view. He didn't get one.

"What do you plan to do now?" he asked.

"We can't tell you," Jane said.

"Because you don't trust me," Rybicki said.

"Because the same source that lets me know what you're thinking will let someone else know what we're planning," Jane said. "We can't afford that."

"But you're planning *something*," Rybicki said. "You used a cracked encryption to send us a message. You wanted it to be read. You're trying to draw *someone* here."

"It's time for you to go, General," Jane said.

Rybicki blinked, unused to being dismissed. He got up and went to the door, turning back to us as he got to it. "Whatever you two are doing, I hope it works," he said. "I don't know how it will all turn out if you manage to save this colony. But it's got to be better than how it turns out if you don't." He left.

I turned to Jane. "You need to tell me how you did that," I said. "How you got that information. You didn't share that with me before."

"I didn't have it before," she said, and tapped her temple. "You told me that General Szilard said that he gave me the full range of command functions. One of those command functions, in the Special Forces at least, is the ability to read minds."

"Excuse me?" I said.

"Think about it," Jane said. "When you have a Brain-Pal, it learns to read your thoughts. That's how it works. Using it to read *other* people's thoughts is just a software issue. Generals in the Special Forces have access to their soldiers' thoughts, although Szilard told me most of the time it's not very useful, since people are thinking about pointless things. This time, it came in handy."

"So anyone who has a BrainPal can have their thoughts read," I said.

Jane nodded. "And now you know why I couldn't come to Phoenix Station with you. I didn't want to give anything away."

I motioned toward the door Rybicki had just stepped out of. "You just gave it away to him," I said.

"No," Jane said. "He doesn't know I've been enhanced. He's just wondering who on his staff leaked, and how it got to me."

"You're still reading his mind," I said.

"Haven't stopped since he landed," Jane said. "Won't stop until he's gone."

"What's he thinking now?" I asked.

"He's still thinking about how I knew that information," Jane said. "And he's thinking about us. He's hoping we succeed. That part wasn't a lie."

"Does he think we will?" I asked.

"Of course not," Jane said.

The beam turrets focused on the incoming missiles and fired, but there were too many missles to focus on; the turrets went up in an excessive blast that flung debris across the fields in which they were located, some distance from Croatoan.

"I'm getting a message," Jane said, to me and Trujillo.

"It's an order to stop fighting and to prepare for a landing." She paused. "I'm being told that any further resistance will result in a complete carpet-bombing of the colony. I'm being asked to acknowledge the message. Failure to reply within about a minute will be taken as defiance and bombing will proceed."

"What do you think?" I asked Jane.

"We're as ready as we're going to be for this," Jane said.

"Manfred?" I said.

"We're ready," he said. "And I hope to God this works."

"Kranjic? Beata?" I turned back to where Jann Kranjic and Beata stood, the two of them fully decked out in reporter gear. Beata nodded; Kranjic gave a thumbs-up.

"Tell them that we acknowledge their message and that we are ceasing fire," I said, to Jane. "Tell them we look forward to their arrival to discuss terms of surrender."

"Done," Jane said, a moment later. I turned to Savitri, who was standing next to Beata. "You're on," I said.

"Great," Savitri said, in an entirely unconvincing tone of voice.

"You'll be fine," I said.

"I feel like I'm going to throw up," she said.

"I'm afraid I left the bucket back at the office," I said.

"I'll just throw up on your boots," Savitri said.

"Seriously," I said. "Are you ready to do this, Savitri?" She nodded. "I'm ready," she said. "Let's do it."

We all went to our positions.

Some time later a light in the sky resolved itself into two troop transports. The transports hovered over Croatoan for some small amount of time before landing a klick away in an unsown field. The field had originally been sown; we had plowed under the early seedlings. We'd planned on troop transports and we hoped to convince them to land in a particular spot by making it more appealing than other places. It worked. In the back of my head I imagined Jane smiling grimly. Jane would have been cautious about landing in the one agricultural field that didn't have plants sticking out of it, but that's one of the reasons we did it. I would have been cautious, too, when I was leading troops. Basic military competence was going to matter here, and this was our first clue as to what sort of fight we had on our hands.

I took my binoculars and peered through. The transports had opened and soldiers were piling out of the bays. They were compact, mottled and thickly skinned; Arrisian, all of them, like their leader. This was another way this invasion force differed from General Gau's fleet. Gau spread the responsibility for his incursions among the entire Conclave; Eser was saving the glory of this attack for his own people.

The soldiers formed into platoons; three platoons, thirty or thirty-five soldiers each. About a hundred overall. Eser was definitely feeling cocky. But then, the one hundred soldiers on the ground were an illusion; no doubt Eser had a few hundred more back on his ship, not to mention that the ship itself was capable of blasting the colony from orbit. On the ground or above, Eser had more than enough firepower to kill us all several times over. Most of the Arrisian soldiers slung the standard Arrisian automatic rifle, a slug-thrower known for its velocity, accuracy and high rate of fire. Two soldiers in each platoon carried shoulder-mounted missile launchers; given the incursion, this looked like they were going to be for show more than anything else. No beam weapons or flamethrowers as far as I could see.

Now came Eser, flanked by an honor guard. Eser was dressed in Arrisian military gear, a bit of show because he'd never served, but I suppose if you're going to try to show up a general in a military mission, you'd best dress for the part. Eser's limbs were thicker and the fiber tufts around his eyestalks were darker than those of his soldiers; he was older and more out of shape than those who were serving him. But inasmuch as I could figure out any emotion from his alien head, he seemed pretty pleased with himself. He stood in front of his soldiers, gesticulating; it looked like he was giving a speech. .

Asshole. He was only a klick away, motionless over flat ground. If I or Jane had the right rifle, we could have taken the top of his head clean off. Then we might be dead, because then his soldiers and his ship would flatten the colony. But it would be fun while it lasted. It was moot; we didn't have the right kind of rifle, and anyway, no matter what happened, we wanted Eser alive at the end of it. Killing him was not in the cards. Alas.

While Eser talked, his guard was actively scanning the environment, looking for threats. I hoped that Jane, in her position, was making note of that; not everyone in this little adventure was entirely incompetent. I wistfully wished I could tell her to make a note of it, but we were in radio silence; we didn't want to give away the game before it had begun.

Eser finally stopped with his talk and the whole company of soldiers began to walk across the field toward the road that linked the farm to Croatoan. A squad of soldiers took the lead, looking for threat and movement; the rest moved in formation but without much discipline. No one expected much resistance.

Nor would they find any on the road to Croatoan. The entire colony was awake and aware of the invasion, of course, but we warned them all to stay in their homes or in their shelters and not to engage while the soldiers passed into Croatoan. We wanted them to play the part of the cowed and frightened colonists they were supposed to be. For some of them, this wasn't going to be a problem;

for others it was going to take effort. The former group we wanted to be safe as possible; the latter group we wanted contained. We gave them tasks for later, if there was a later.

No doubt the forward squad were scanning the surroundings with infrared and heat sensors, looking for sneak attacks. All they would find were colonists up and at their windows, staring into the darkness as the soldiers marched by. I could see in my binoculars that at least a couple of colonists stood on their porches to see the soldiers. Mennonites. They were pacifists, but they sure as hell weren't scared of anything.

Croatoan remained as it was when we had begun: a modern-day take on the Roman legion camp, still ringed by two sets of cargo containers. Most of the colonists who had lived there had long abandoned it for homes and farms of their own, but a few people continued to live there, including me and Jane and Zoë, and several permanent buildings stood where the tents used to be. The recreation area at the center of the camp still remained, in front of a lane that passed along it and behind the administration building. In the center of the recreation area stood Savitri, alone. She would be the first human the Arrisian soldiers and Eser would see; the only one, hopefully, that they would see.

I could see Savitri from where I was. The early morning was not cold, but she was clearly shivering.

The first of the Arrisian soldiers reached the perimeter of Croatoan and called a halt to the march as they examined the surroundings to be sure they weren't walking into a trap. This took several minutes, but eventually they were satisfied that there was nothing there that could harm them. They restarted the march and the Arrisian soldiers tromped in, piling up in the recreation center, keeping a wary eye on Savitri, who stood there, silent and now shivering only a little. In a very short amount of time all the soldiers were within the cargo container-lined borders of Croatoan.

Eser came up through the ranks with his guard and stood before Savitri. He motioned for a translator device.

"I am Nerbros Eser," he said.

"I'm Savitri Guntupalli," Savitri said.

"You're the leader of this colony," Eser said.

"No," Savitri said.

Eser's eyestalks jiggled at this. "Where are this colony's leaders?" he asked.

"They're busy," Savitri said. "That's why they sent me out to talk to you."

"And who are you?" Eser said.

"I'm the secretary," Savitri said.

Eser's eyestalks extended angrily and almost banged together. "I have the power to level this entire colony, and its leader sends his *secretary* to meet me," he said. Clearly any hint of magnanimity Eser may have been planning in victory was flying right out the window.

"Well, they did give me a message for you," Savitri said.

"They *did*," Eser said.

"Yes," Savitri said. "I was told to tell you that if you and your troops were willing to get back into your ships and just go back where you came from, we'd be happy to let you live."

Eser goggled and then emitted a high *screee*, the Arrisian noise for amusement. Most of his soldiers *screed* along with him; it was like a convention of angry bees. Then he stopped his *scree* and stalked right up to Savitri, who like the star she is, didn't even flinch.

"I was planning to let most of your colonists survive," Eser said. "I was going to have this colony's leaders executed for the crimes against the Conclave, when they helped the Colonial Union ambush our fleet. But I was going to spare your colonists. You are tempting me to change my mind on that."

"So, that's a *no*, then," Savitri said, staring directly into his eyestalks.

Eser stepped back, and turned to one of his guards. "Kill her," he said. "Then let's get to work."

The guard raised his weapon, sighted in on Savitri's torso, and tapped the trigger panel on his rifle.

The rifle exploded, shearing vertically in the plane perpendicular to the rifle's firing mechanism and sending a vertical planar array of energy directly upward. The guard's eyestalks intersected that plane and were severed; he fell screaming in pain, clutching what remained of his stalks.

Eser looked again at Savitri, confused.

"You should have left when you had the chance," Savitri said.

There was a *bang* as Jane kicked open the door of the administration building, the nanomesh suit that hid her body heat covered by standard Department of Colonization police armor, same as the others of us in our little squad. In her arms was something that was *not* standard Department of Colonization issue: A flamethrower.

Jane motioned Savitri back; Savitri didn't need to be told twice. From in front of Jane came the sound of Arrisian screams as panicked soldiers tried to shoot her, only to have their rifles shear and erupt violently in their arms. Jane walked right up to the soldiers, who had begun to wheel back in fear, and poured fire into their midst.

"What is this?" I asked Zoë, when she directed us into the shuttle to look at whatever it was she wanted us to look at. Whatever it was, it was the size of a baby elephant.

Hickory and Dickory stood next to it; Jane went to it and started to examine the control panel on one side.

"It's my present to the colony," Zoë said. "It's a sapper field."

"Zapper field," I said.

"No, *sapper*," Zoë said. "With a *ssss*."

"What does it do?" I asked.

Zoë turned to Hickory. "Tell him," she said.

"The sapper field channels kinetic energy," Hickory said. "Redirects the energy upward or any other direction the user chooses and uses the redirected energy to feed the field itself. The user can define at what level the energy is redirected, over a range of parameters."

"You need to explain this to me like I'm an idiot," I said. "Because clearly I am."

"It stops bullets," Jane said, still looking at the panel.

"Come again?" I said.

"This thing generates a field that will suck the energy out of any object that goes faster than a certain speed," Jane said. She looked at Hickory. "That's right, isn't it."

"Velocity is one of the parameters a user may define," Hickory said. "Other parameters can include energy output over a specified time or temperature."

"So we program it to stop bullets or grenades, and it will do it," I said.

"Yes," Hickory said. "Although it works better with physical objects than with energetic ones."

"Works better with bullets than with beams," I said.

"Yes," Hickory said.

"When we define the power levels, anything under that power level retains its energy," Jane said. "We could tune it to stop a bullet but let an arrow fly."

"If the energy of the arrow is below the threshold you define, yes," Hickory said.

"This has possibilities," I said.

"I told you you would like it," Zoë said.

"This is the best present you ever got me, sweetheart," I said. Zoë grinned.

"You should know that this field is of very limited duration," Hickory said. "The power source here is small and will only last a few minutes, depending on the size of the field you generate."

"If we use it to cover Croatoan, how long would it last?" I asked.

"About seven minutes," Jane said. She had figured out the control panel.

"Real possibilities," I said. I turned back to Zoë. "So how did you manage to get the Obin to give us this?" I asked.

"First I reasoned, then I bargained, then I pleaded," Zoë said. "And then I threw a tantrum."

"A tantrum, you say," I said.

"Don't look at me like that," Zoë said. "The Obin are incredibly sensitive to my emotions. You know that. And the idea of every person I love and care about being killed is something I could get emotional about pretty easily. And on top of every other argument I made, it worked. So don't give me grief for it, ninety-year-old dad. While Hickory and Dickory and I were with General Gau, other Obin got this for us."

I glanced back at Hickory. "I thought you said you weren't allowed to help us, because of your treaty with the Colonial Union."

"I regret to say that Zoë has made a small error in her explanation," Hickory said. "The sapper field is not our technology. It is far too advanced for that. It is Consu."

Jane and I looked at each other. Consu technology was generally breathtakingly advanced over the technology of other species, including our own, and the Consu never parted lightly with any technology they possessed.

"The Consu gave this to you?" I asked.

"They gave it to you, in point of fact," Hickory said.

"And how did they know about us?" I asked.

"In an encounter with some of our fellow Obin, the topic came up in conversation, and the Consu were moved to spontaneously offer you this gift," Hickory said.

I remembered once, not long after I met Jane, that she and I needed to ask the Consu some questions. The cost of answering those questions was one dead Special Forces soldier and three mutilated ones. I had a hard time imagining the "conversation" that resulted in the Consu parting with a piece of technology like this one.

"So the Obin have nothing to do with this gift," I said.

"Other than transporting it here at the request of your daughter, no," Hickory said.

"We must thank the Consu at some point," I said.

"I don't believe that they expect to be thanked," Hickory said.

"Hickory, have you ever lied to me?" I asked.

"I do not believe you are aware of me or any Obin ever lying to you," Hickory said.

"No," I said. "I don't believe I am."

At the rear of the Arrisian column, soldiers scrambled in retreat, back toward the gate of the colony, where Manfred Trujillo waited, sitting at the controls of a cargo lorry we'd stripped down and tinkered with for the purposes of acceleration. The lorry had sat at the side of a close field, quiet and with Trujillo hunkered down until the soldiers had completely entered into Croatoan. Then he powered the lorry's battery packs and slowly crept it along the road, waiting for the screams that would be his signal to put the pedal to the metal.

When Trujillo saw the plumes of Jane's flamethrower, he accelerated hard toward the gate opening of Croatoan. As he passed through the gates he threw on the lorry's floodlights, stunning a trio of fleeing Arrisian soldiers into immobility. These soldiers were the first to be knocked out of their mortality by the massive hurtling truck; more than a dozen others followed as Trujillo plowed through the ranks. Trujillo turned left at the road in front of the town square, sideswiping two more Arrisian soldiers, and prepared to make another run.

As Trujillo's lorry passed through Croatoan's gates, Hickory hit the button to close the gates and then it and Dickory both unsheathed a pair of wickedly long knives and prepared to meet the Arrisian soldiers who had the misfortune to run into them. The Arrisian soldiers were out of their wits with confusion as to how a milk run of a military mission could have turned into a massacre—of *them*—but unfortunately for them both Hickory and Dickory were in full possession of their wits, were good with knives and had turned off their emotional implants so that they could slaughter with efficiency.

By this time Jane had also started in with knives, having burned through her flamethrower fuel at the expense of nearly a platoon's worth of Arrisian soldiers. Jane dispatched some of the more grievously burnt soldiers and then turned her attention to those that were still standing, or, actually, running. They ran fast but Jane, modified as she was, ran faster. Jane had researched the Arrisians, their armaments, their armor and their weaknesses. It happened that Arrisian military body armor was vulnerable at the side joins; a sufficiently thin knife could slip in and sever one of the major arteries that ran bilaterally down the Arrisian body. As I watched I saw Jane exploit that knowledge, reaching out to grab a fleeing Arrisian soldier, yanking him back, sinking her knife into his side armor and leaving him to sag away his life, and then reaching out to the next fleeing soldier, without breaking stride.

I was in awe of my wife. And I understood now why General Szilard didn't apologize for what he had done for her. Her strength and speed and pitilessness was going to save us as a colony.

Behind Jane a quartet of Arrisian soldiers had sufficiently calmed themselves to begin to think tactically once more and had begun to slink toward her, guns abandoned, knives out. This is where I, stationed on top of the inside track of the cargo containers, came in handy: I was air support. I took my compound bow, nocked an arrow and shot it into the neck of the forward-most of the soldiers; not a good thing as I was aiming for the one behind him. The solider pawed at the arrow before falling forward; the other three broke into a sprint but not before I shot another one in the foot, once more not good because I was aiming for its head. He went down with a *screee*; Jane turned at the sound, and then headed toward him to deal with him.

I looked for the other two among the buildings but didn't see them, and then heard a *clang*. I looked down to see that one of the soldiers was climbing up on the cargo container, the trash bin he had jumped on to get up to where I was clattering away on the ground. I nocked another arrow and shot at him; the arrow struck right in front of him. Clearly the bow was not meant to be my weapon. There was no time to string another arrow; the soldier was up on the cargo container and headed toward me, knife out, screaming something. I had the sinking suspicion I killed someone he really cared about. I grabbed for my own knife and as I did so, the Arrisian attacked, covering the distance between us in an astoundingly short time. I went down; my knife flew off the side of the cargo container.

I rolled with the Arrisian's attack and kicked him off me, scrambling to the side and out of his way. He was on me again instantly, stabbing me in the shoulder and meeting the police armor there. He readied to stab me again; I grabbed an eyestalk and yanked it hard. He scrambled away, squealing and grabbing at the eyestalk, backing up toward the edge. Both my knife and bow were too far away to get to. *Fuck it*, I thought, and launched myself at the Arrisian. We both flew off the side of the cargo container; as we fell I jammed my arm into his neck. We landed, me on top of him, my arm crushing his windpipe or whatever the equivalent was for him. My arm throbbed in pain; I doubted I would be using that arm productively for a while.

I rolled off the dead Arrisian and looked up; a shadow was hovering up on the cargo container. It was Kranjic; he and Beata were using their cameras to record the battle.

"You alive?" he asked.

"Apparently," I said.

"Look, could you do that again?" he said. "I missed most of it."

I flipped him the middle finger; I couldn't see his face but I suspected he was grinning. "Throw me down my knife and bow," I said. I glanced at my watch. We had another minute and a half to go before we dropped the shield. Kranjic handed down my weapons, and I stalked through the streets, trying to pick off soldiers until I ran out of arrows, and then kept out of their way until time ran out.

Thirty seconds before the shield dropped, Hickory opened the gates of the village and he and Dickory stepped away to let the survivors of the attack flood out in retreat. The couple dozen or so remaining soldiers didn't stop to wonder how the gate had opened; they got the hell out and broke toward their transports stationed a klick in the distance. The last of these soldiers cleared the gate as we dropped the field. Eser and his remaining guard were midway in this pack, the guard rudely pushing his charge along. He still had his rifle; most left their rifles behind, having seen what happened to those who had used them in the village, and assuming they were now entirely useless. I picked up one, as I followed them out; Jane picked up one of the missile launchers. Kranjic and Beata hopped down from the cargo containers and followed; Kranjic bounding ahead and disappearing in the darkness, Beata keeping time with Jane and I.

The retreating Arrisian soldiers were making two assumptions as they retreated. The first was that bullets had no currency on Roanoke. The second was that the terrain they were retreating across was the same as the terrain they had marched in on. Both of these assumptions were wrong, as the Arrisians discovered when the automatic turret defenses along the retreat path opened fire on them, cutting them down in precise bursts controlled by Jane, who electronically signed off on each target with her BrainPal before they opened fire. Jane didn't want to shoot Eser by accident. The portable turrets had been placed by the colonists after the Arrisians had been shut in Croatoan; they had pulled them out of holes they had dug and covered. Jane had mercilessly drilled the colonists who placed the turrets so they could move them and place them in the space of just a few minutes. It worked; only one turret was unusable because it was pointing in the wrong direction.

By this time those few remaining Arrisian soldiers with their rifles began to fire them out of desperation and seemed surprised when they worked. Two of them dropped to the ground and began to fire in our direction, to give their compatriots time to get to the transports. I felt a round whistle past before I heard it; I likewise dropped to the ground. Jane turned the turrets on these two Arrisians and made short work of them.

Shortly only Eser and his guard remained, save for the pilots of the two transports, both of whom had fired up their engines and were preparing to get the hell out of Dodge. Jane steadied the shoulder-mounted missile, warned us to hit the deck (I was still there) and fired her missile at the closest transport. The missile blasted past Eser and his guard, causing both to dive to the ground, and slammed into the transport's bay, bathing the interior of the shuttle in explosive flame. The second pilot decided he'd had enough and launched; he got fifty meters up before his transport was struck by not one but two missiles, launched by Hickory and Dickory, respectively. The impacts crushed the transport's engines and sent it careening downward into the woods, tearing trees from the ground with a wrenching, woody sound before crashing with a shattering roar somewhere out of sight.

Eser's guard kept his charge down and stayed low himself, firing in an attempt to take some of us with him when he went.

Jane looked down at me. "That rifle have ammunition?" she asked.

"I hope so," I said.

She dropped the shoulder rocket. "Make enough noise to keep him down," she said. "Don't actually shoot at him."

"What are you doing?" I asked.

She stripped out of her police gear, revealing the skintight, matte black nanomesh underneath. "Getting close," she said, and moved away. She quickly became next to invisible in the dark. I fired at random intervals and stayed low; the guard wasn't hitting me, but it was a matter of centimeters.

There was a surprised grunt in the distance, and then a rather louder *scree*, which stopped soon enough.

"All clear," Jane said. I popped up and headed toward her. She was standing over the body of the guard, the guard's former weapon in her hand, trained on Eser, who lay cowering on the ground.

"He's weaponless," Jane said, and handed me the translation device she apparently took off him. "Here. You get to talk to him."

I took the device and bent down. "Hi there," I said.

"You're all going to die," Eser said. "I have a ship above you right now. It has more soldiers in it. They will come down and hunt all of you. And then my ship will blast every bit of this colony to dust."

"Is that so," I said.

"Yes," said Eser.

"I see I have to be the one to break this to you, then," I said. "Your ship's not there anymore."

"You're lying," Eser said.

"Not really," I said. "The thing is, when you took out our satellite with your ship, that meant the satellite couldn't signal a skip drone we had out there. That drone was programmed to skip only if it didn't receive a signal. Where it went, there were some skip-capable missiles waiting. Those missiles popped into Roanoke space, found your ship and killed it."

"Where did the missiles come from?" Eser demanded.

"It's difficult to say," I said. "The missiles were of Nouri manufacture. And you know the Nouri. They'll sell to just about anyone."

Eser sat there and glowered. "I don't believe you," he finally said.

I turned to Jane. "He doesn't believe me," I said.

Jane flipped me something. "It's his communicator," she said.

I handed it to him. "Call your ship," I said.

Several minutes and some very angry *screees* later, Eser flung his communicator into the dirt. "Why haven't you just killed me?" he asked. "You've killed everyone else."

"You were told that if you left all of your soldiers would live," I said.

"By your *secretary*," Eser spat.

"Actually, she's not my secretary anymore," I said.

"Answer my question," Eser said.

"You're worth more to us alive than dead," I said. "We have someone who is quite interested in keeping you alive. And we were led to believe that turning you over to him in that condition would be useful to us."

"General Gau," Eser said.

"Right you are," I said. "I don't know what Gau has planned for you, but after an assassination attempt and a play to take over the Conclave, I can't imagine it will be very pleasant."

"Perhaps we—" Eser began.

"Let's not even pretend we are going to have that conversation," I said. "You don't get to go from planning to kill everyone on the planet to cutting a deal with me."

"General Gau has," Eser said.

"Very nice," I said. "The difference is that I don't believe you ever planned to spare any of my colonists, while Gau went out of his way to assure that they could be spared. It matters. Now. What's going to happen is that I'm going to hand this translation device over to my wife here, and she's going to tell you what to do. You're going to listen to her, because if you don't, she won't kill you but you'll probably wish she had. Do you understand?"

"I understand," Eser said.

"Good," I said, and stood up to hand the translation to Jane. "Jam him into that cargo hold we use for a jail."

"Way ahead of you," Jane said.

"We still have the skip drone set up to deliver a message to General Gau?" I asked.

"We do," Jane said. "I'll send it once I get Eser squared away. What do we want to tell the Colonial Union?"

"I haven't the slightest idea," I said. "I suppose when they haven't gotten any skip drones for a couple of days they'll realize something has happened. And then they'll be pissed off we're still here. I'm inclined at the moment to say 'screw them.' "

"That's not a real plan," Jane said.

"I know, but that's what I've got at the moment," I said. "In other news, holy shit. We pulled this off."

"We pulled it off because our enemy was arrogant and incompetent," Jane said.

"We pulled it off because we had *you*," I said. "You planned it. You pulled it off. You made it work. And as much as I hate to say this to you, your being a fully functional Special Forces soldier made a difference."

"I know it has," Jane said. "I'm not ready to think about that yet."

In the distance we heard someone crying.

"That sounds like Beata," Jane said. I took off toward the sound of the crying, leaving Jane to deal with Eser. I found Beata a couple hundred meters later, hunched over someone.

It was Kranjic. Two of the Arrisians' bullets had hit him, in the collarbone and in the chest. Blood had soaked out into the ground beneath him.

"You dumb son of a bitch," Beata said, holding Kranjic's hand. "You always had to chase a story."

She leaned over to kiss his forehead, and to close his eyes.

FIFTEEN

"You know you can't stay on Roanoke," General Gau said.

I smiled and looked across at him in the tiny conference room of his flagship, the *Gentle Star*. "Why on earth not?" I said.

Gau paused for a moment; the expression was new to him. "Because you survived," he said, eventually. "Because your colony survived, no doubt to the surprise and irritation of the Colonial Union. Because you gave the enemy information vital to his survival, and because you accepted information from him vital to yours. Because you allowed me to come here to retrieve Nerbros Eser. Because you're here on this ship now, talking to me."

"I'm a traitor," I said.

"I didn't say that," Gau said.

"You *wouldn't* say that," I said. "You're alive because of me."

"Fair point," Gau said. "But that's not what I meant. I meant you're not a traitor because your allegiance was to your colony. To your people. You've never betrayed them."

"Thanks," I said. "Although I don't think the Colonial Union will like that argument much."

"No," Gau said. "I don't expect they would. Which brings me back to my original point."

"What are you going to do with Eser?" I asked.

"My current plan is to put him on trial," Gau said.

"You could just throw him out of an air lock," I said.

"That would give me a great deal of personal satisfaction," Gau said. "But I don't think it would be good for the Conclave."

"But from what Zoë tells me, you've started making people give you personal loyalty oaths," I said. "It's just a short jump from that to having the right to space those who annoy you."

"All the more reason for the trial, wouldn't you say," Gau said. "I would prefer not to have had the loyalty oaths. But apparently there's only so much humility people will take out of their leaders, especially when their leaders have had their fleets blown out from under them."

"Don't blame me," I said.

"I don't," Gau said. "Whether I blame the Colonial Union is another matter entirely."

"What do you plan to do about the Colonial Union now?" I asked.

"The same thing I originally planned to do," Gau said. "Contain it."

"Not attack it," I said.

"No," Gau said. "All the Conclave's internal rebellions are tamped down. Eser isn't the only one facing a trial. But I think it's clear to the Colonial Union now that the Conclave is not easily eradicated. I'd hope they wouldn't try to break out of their box again."

"You haven't learned much about humans," I said.

"On the contrary," Gau said. "If you think I'm simply

going back to my old plan, you're a fool. I'm not planning to attack the Colonial Union, but I'm also going to make sure it doesn't get a chance to attack either me or the Conclave a second time."

"How?" I asked.

"You don't really expect me to tell you," Gau said.

"Thought I'd ask," I said. "It was worth a shot."

"Not really," Gau said.

"And what are your plans for Roanoke?" I asked.

"I've already told you that I have no plans to attack it," Gau said.

"You did," I said. "Of course, that was when you had no fleet."

"You doubt me," Gau said.

"No," I said. "I fear you."

"I wish you wouldn't," Gau said.

"I wish I wouldn't, either," I said. "Convince me."

"Roanoke is safe from any further Conclave attack," Gau said. "The Conclave recognizes it as a legitimate human colony. The last colony"—he tapped the conference room table to make the point—"but a legitimate colony nonetheless. You and I can make a treaty, if you like."

"I don't think the Colonial Union would find it binding," I said.

"Probably not," Gau said. "However, I will send an official declaration to your government, with a warning that the Conclave's ban on colonization is unbreakable beyond this. Unofficially, I'll pass the word to unaffiliated races that the Conclave would be extremely displeased if one of them made a play for the planet. They're not supposed to anyway, under the ban. But it doesn't hurt to accentuate the point."

"Thank you, General," I said.

"You're welcome," Gau said. "I'm glad not every world leader was as troublesome as you, however."

"I'm the easygoing one," I said. "It's my wife who's the real hard-ass."

"So I've gathered from Eser and the recordings of the battle," Gau said. "I hope she is not offended that I asked to speak to you alone."

"She's not," I said. "I'm the one who is supposed to be good with people. Although Zoë is disappointed she's not able to see you. You made an impression on her."

"And she on me," Gau said. "You have a remarkable family."

"I agree," I said. "I'm glad they keep me around."

"Technically, your wife and daughter could be charged for treason as well," Gau said. "They will have to leave Roanoke, too, you know."

"You keep bringing that up," I said. "I've been trying not to think about it."

"I don't think that's wise," Gau said.

"Of course it's not wise," I said. "That doesn't mean I don't want to do it."

"Where will you go?" Gau said.

"I haven't the slightest idea," I said. "We can't go anywhere in the Colonial Union unless we want to spend our lives in a family cell block. The Obin would take us in because of Zoë, but there would always be pressure on the Obin to extradite us."

"There's another option," Gau said. "I've offered to have you join the Conclave before. The offer still stands. You and your family could live among us."

"You're very kind," I said. "I don't know that I could do that. That's the problem with living among the Obin as well. I'm not ready to be cut off from the rest of humanity."

"It's not that bad," Gau said, and I caught the hint of sarcasm there.

"Maybe not for you," I said. "But I would miss my kind."

"The idea behind the Conclave is that many races would live among each other," Gau said. "Are you saying you couldn't do that?"

"I could do that," I said. "But only three humans wouldn't be enough."

"The Conclave would still be happy to admit the Colonial Union," Gau said. "Or any of the individual colony worlds. Or even just Roanoke."

"I don't think that idea will get much traction on Roanoke," I said. "Or with the Colonial Union. And as far as the individual colonies go, I think they're still officially in the dark about the Conclave."

"Yes, the Colonial Union's informational stranglehold," Gau said. "I have to tell you that I've given very serious thought to skipping satellites over the Colonial Union worlds and simply blasting down a data stream on the Conclave until the satellite is shot down. It wouldn't be efficient. But at least then the Conclave could be heard."

I thought about that for a moment. "No," I said. "A data feed wouldn't do."

"Then what would you suggest?" Gau said.

"I'm not sure yet," I said. I looked directly at Gau. "General, I may want to propose something to you."

"What is it?" Gau said.

"Something big," I said. "Something expensive."

"That's not really an answer," Gau said.

"It's going to have to do for now," I said.

"I will be happy to listen to your proposal," Gau said. "But 'something big, something expensive' is a little too vague for me to give approval."

"Fair enough," I said.

"Why can't you tell me what it is now?" Gau asked.

"I need to talk to Jane first," I said.

"Whatever it is, Administrator Perry, if it's something that involves my help, then you'll be permanently in traitorous territory," Gau said. "At least in the eyes of the Colonial Union."

"It's like you said, General," I said. "It's with whom your allegiances lie."

"I've been ordered to place you under arrest," said Manfred Trujillo.

"Really," I said. The two of us stood in front of the shuttle I was about to leave in.

"The orders came in a couple of hours ago," Trujillo said. "Along with the new communications satellite the CU just gave us. The CU's not pleased about a Conclave ship being in our sky, incidentally."

"So are you arresting me?" I asked.

"I'd love to, but it seems that you and your family can't be found," Trujillo said. "I suspect that you've already left the planet. We'll do a colony-wide search, of course. But I wouldn't really lay good odds on us finding you."

"I'm sneaky, I am," I said.

"I always said that about you," Trujillo said.

"You could get in trouble for that," I said. "The last thing this colony needs is another leader hauled up in front of an inquiry."

"As your colony leader, I can officially tell you to mind your own business," Trujillo said.

"So your ascension has been formally approved," I said.

"If it wasn't, how would I be able to arrest you?" Trujillo said.

"Good point," I said. "Congratulations. You always wanted to run the colony. Now you are."

"It's not the way I planned to get the job," Trujillo said.

"I'm sorry we got in your way, Manfred," I said.

304 | John Scalzi

"I'm not," Manfred said. "If I had been leading the colony, we would all be dead now. You, Jane and Zoë saved this colony. I'm happy to have waited in line."

"Thanks," I said.

"I want you to know it took a lot for me to say that," Trujillo said. I laughed, and looked over to where Zoë was giving a tearful good-bye to Gretchen and other friends.

"Zoë is going to miss Gretchen," I said.

"Gretchen is going to miss Zoë," Trujillo said. "I have half a mind to ask you to let Zoë stay. For Gretchen and for us." Trujillo nodded toward Hickory and Dickory, who stood off to the side, soaking up Zoë's emotional farewell to her friends. "You said you reached an agreement with the Conclave, but I still wouldn't mind having the Obin watching our back."

"Roanoke will be fine," I assured him.

"I think you're right about that," Trujillo said. "I hope so. It would be nice just to be another colony. We've been the center of attention long enough."

"I think I'll be able to draw some attention off you," I said.

"I wish you would tell me what you have planned," Trujillo said.

"As I'm no longer your colony leader, I can't officially tell you to mind your own business," I said. "But mind it anyway."

Trujillo sighed. "You understand my concern," he said. "We've been at the center of everyone else's plans, and none of the plans have worked out even remotely as they should have."

"Including yours," I reminded him.

"Including mine," Trujillo agreed. "I don't know what you're planning, but given the failure rate around here, I'm concerned that the backlash is going to get back here to Roanoke. I'm looking out for my colony. *Our* colony. Our home."

"Our colony," I agreed. "But not my home anymore."

"Even so," Trujillo said.

"You're going to have to trust me, Man," I said. "I've worked hard to keep Roanoke safe. I'm not going to stop doing that now."

Savitri stepped down from the shuttle bay and walked over to us, PDA in hand. "Everything's stowed," she said, to me. "Jane says we're ready when you are."

"You said good-bye to everyone?" I asked her.

"I have," Savitri said, and held up her wrist, which had a bracelet on it. "From Beata. Says it was her grandmother's."

"She's going to miss you," I said.

"I know," Savitri said. "I'm going to miss her. She's my friend. We're all going to miss people. That's why it's called *leaving*."

"*You* could still stay," Trujillo said to Savitri. "There's no reason you need to go with this idiot. I'll even give you a twenty percent raise."

"Oooh, a raise," Savitri said. "It's tempting. But I've been with this idiot for a long time. I like him. I like his family more, of course, but who wouldn't."

"Nice," I said.

Savitri smiled. "If nothing else he keeps me amused. I never know what's going to happen next, but I know I want to find out. Sorry."

"All right, a thirty percent raise," Trujillo said.

"Sold," Savitri said.

"What?" I said.

"I'm kidding," Savitri said. "Idiot."

"Remind me to dock your pay," I said.

"How *are* you going to pay me now, anyway?" Savitri said.

"Look," I said. "Something that needs your attention. Over there. Away from here."

"Hmmmph," Savitri said. She went over to give Trujillo a hug, then jerked a thumb at me. "If things don't work out with this guy, I may come crawling back for my old job."

"It's yours," Trujillo said.

"Excellent," Savitri said. "Because if the last year has taught me anything, it's to have a backup plan." She gave Trujillo another quick hug. "I'm going to go collect Zoë," she said to me. "As soon as you're in the shuttle, we're ready."

"Thanks, Savitri," I said. "I'll be there in a minute. See you then." She squeezed my shoulder and walked off.

"Have *you* said good-bye to everyone you want to?" Trujillo asked.

"I'm doing it now," I said.

Minutes later our shuttle was in the sky, heading toward the *Gentle Star*. Zoë was crying silently, patting Babar and missing her friends. Jane, sitting next to her, gathered her in a hug. I looked out the porthole as I left behind another world.

"How do you feel?" Jane asked me.

"Sad," I said. "I wanted this to be my world. Our world. Our home. But it wasn't. It's not."

"I'm sorry," Jane said.

"Don't be," I said. I turned and smiled at her. "I'm glad we came. I'm just sad it wasn't to stay."

I turned back to the porthole. The Roanoke sky was fading to black around me.

"This is *your* ship," General Rybicki said to me, motioning around the observation deck he'd just been led into. I had been waiting for him there.

"It is," I said. "For now. You could say we're leasing it. I think it's originally Arrisian, which is some irony for you. It also explains the low ceilings."

"So I should address you as Captain Perry?" Rybicki asked. "That's a step down from your previous rank."

"Actually, Jane's the captain. I'm her nominal superior, but she's in charge of the boat. I think that makes me a commodore. Which is a step up."

"Commodore Perry," Rybicki said. "Catchy. Not very original, I'm afraid."

"I suppose not," I said. I held up the PDA I had in my hand. "Jane called me as you were being led up here. She told me that it had been suggested to you that you might try killing me."

"Christ," Rybicki said. "I'd like to know how she knows these things."

"I hope you're not planning to go through with it," I said. "It's not that you couldn't do it. You're still CDF. You're fast and strong enough to snap my neck before anyone could stop you. But you wouldn't make it out of this room afterward. I don't want you to die."

"I appreciate that," Rybicki said, dryly. Then, "No. I'm not here to kill you. I'm here to try to understand you."

"I'm glad to hear it," I said.

"You can start by telling me why you sent for *me*," Rybicki said. "The Colonial Union has all sorts of diplomats. If the Conclave is going to start a parlay with the CU, that's who should be here talking to you. So I'm wondering why you asked for me."

"Because I felt I owed you an explanation," I said.

"For what?" Rybicki said.

I motioned. "For this," I said. "Why I'm here and not on Roanoke. Or anywhere in the Colonial Union."

"I assumed it was because you didn't want to be tried for treason," Rybicki said.

"There is that," I said. "But that's not it. How are things in the Colonial Union?"

"You're not seriously expecting me to tell you anything *here*," Rybicki said.

"I mean very generally," I said.

"They're fine," Rybicki said. "The Conclave attacks have stopped. Roanoke has been secured and we'll be landing a second wave of colonists there within a month."

"That's ahead of schedule," I said.

"We decided to move quickly there," Rybicki said. "We'll be massively fortifying its defenses as well."

"Good," I said. "A shame that couldn't have happened earlier, before we were attacked."

"Let's not pretend we don't know the whys and wherefores of that," Rybicki said.

"How did the Colonial Union take our victory, incidentally?" I asked.

"It was naturally extremely pleased," Rybicki said.

"Officially, at least," I said.

"You know the Colonial Union," Rybicki said. "The official story is the only story."

"I know," I said. "And that's the reason for all of *this*."

"I'm not following you," Rybicki said.

"Just before our battle with Eser back on Roanoke, you said something to me," I said. "You said that the Colonial Union more than anyone else was acting in the best interests of humanity."

"I remember that," Rybicki said.

"You were right," I said. "Out of every government or species or intelligent race, the Colonial Union is the one that is the best at looking out for us. For humans. But I've come to doubt that the Colonial Union is doing that job *well*. Look how the Colonial Union treated us at Roanoke. It deceived us in the purpose of the colony. It deceived us in the intent of the Conclave. It made us complicit in an act of war that could have destroyed the entire CU. And then it was willing to sacrifice us for the good of humanity. But none of the rest of humanity ever knew the whole story, did they? The Colonial Union controls communication. Controls information. Now that Roanoke survived, the Colonial Union will never tell any of it. No one outside the CU power structure even knows the Conclave exists. *Still*."

"The Colonial Union believed it was necessary to do it that way," Rybicki said.

"I know," I said. "And they've *always* believed it to be necessary to do it that way. You came from Earth, General. You remember how little we knew about out here. How little we knew about the Colonial Union. We signed up for a military we knew nothing about, whose goals we knew nothing of, because we didn't want to die old and alone back at home. We knew that somehow we'd be made young again, and that was enough. It got us here. And that's the Colonial Union way. To tell just enough to achieve a goal. Never more."

"I don't always agree with the Colonial Union's methods," Rybicki said. "You know I disgreed with the CU's plan to cut Roanoke loose. But I'm not sure I'm following you. It would have been disastrous if the Conclave had known of our plans for Roanoke. The Conclave wants to keep humanity boxed up, Perry. It still does. If we don't fight, the rest of the universe gets filled up without us. Humanity dies."

"You're confusing humanity with the Colonial Union," I said. "The Conclave wants to keep the Colonial Union boxed up, because the Colonial Union refuses to join it. But the Colonial Union is not humanity."

"It's a distinction without a difference," Rybicki said.

"True enough," I said. I pointed out the curving window of the observation deck. "You saw the other ships here as you arrived," I said.

"Yes," Rybicki said. "I didn't count them all, but I'm guessing there are four hundred and twelve."

"Close," I said. "Four hundred and thirteen, including this one. Which, incidentally, I've named the *Roanoke*."

"Wonderful," Rybicki said. "The fleet that attacks our next colony world will have an ironic tinge to it."

"The Colonial Union is still planning to colonize, then," I said.

"I'm not going to comment about that to you," Rybicki said.

"If or when the Conclave and the Colonial Union square off again, this ship won't be part of it," I said. "This is a trade ship. So are all the other ships in this fleet. Every ship in this fleet is carrying goods from the race whose ship it is. This took a lot of doing, you should know. It took a couple of months before every race signed on to this. General Gau had to twist a few arms, or whatever. It's easier to get some races to give a warship than a cargo ship filled with goodies."

"If a fleet of warships isn't going to convince the Colonial Union to join the Conclave, I doubt a fleet of trade ships is going to do it either," Rybicki said.

"I think you're right about that," I said, and raised my PDA. "Jane, you can skip now."

"What?" Rybicki said. "What the hell are you doing?"

"I told you," I said. "I'm explaining myself to you."

The *Roanoke* had been floating in space, a prudent distance from any gravity well that might interfere with her Skip Drive. Now Jane gave the order to engage the drive. We punched a hole through space-time and landed somewhere else.

From the observation deck, the difference was not great: One moment we were looking at a random field of stars, and the next, we were looking at another random field of stars. Until we began to see the patterns.

"Look," I said, pointing. "Orion. Taurus. Perseus. Cassiopeia."

"Oh my God," Rybicki said, whispering the words.

The *Roanoke* turned on its axis, and the stars faded out, replaced by the immense glowing orb of a planet, blue and green and white.

"Welcome home, General," I said.

"Earth," Rybicki said, and anything he meant to say after that was lost in his need to stare at the world he left behind.

"You were wrong, General," I said.

It took a second for Rybicki to shake himself out of his reverie. "What?" he said. "Wrong about what?"

"Coventry," I said. "I looked it up. The British knew there was an attack coming. You were right about that. But they didn't know where it would strike. The British didn't sacrifice Coventry. And the Colonial Union shouldn't have been willing to sacrifice Roanoke."

"Why are we here?" Rybicki asked.

"You said it, General," I said. "The Colonial Union will never join the Conclave. But maybe Earth might."

"You're going to take Earth into the Conclave," Rybicki said.

"No," I said. "We're going to offer it a choice. We're going to offer it gifts from each world of the Conclave. And then I'm going to offer it my gift."

"Your gift," Rybicki said.

"The truth," I said. "All of it. About the Colonial Union and about the Conclave and about what happens when we leave our homeworld and come out to the universe. The Colonial Union is free to run its worlds however it wants, General. But *this* world gets to decide for its own. Humanity and the Colonial Union aren't going to be interchangeable anymore. Not after today."

Rybicki looked at me. "You don't have the authority

to do this," he said. "To make this decision for all these people."

"I may not have the authority," I said. "But I have the right."

"You don't know what you're doing," Rybicki said.

"I think I do," I said. "I'm changing the world."

Out the window another ship popped into view. I raised my PDA; on the screen was a simple representation of Earth. Around the glowing circle dots appeared, singly, doubly, in groups and in constellations. And when they all arrived, they began broadcasting, all of them, a message of welcome, in as many human languages as could receive them, and a stream of data, unencrypted, catching up Earth on decades of history and technology. The truth, as near as I could tell it. My gift to the world that had been my home, and which I hoped would be again.

SIXTEEN I didn't recognize him at first. Partly this was because of where I was seeing him. It was odd enough that I would be on the steps of the U.S. House of Representatives; to see him there was entirely unexpected. It was also partly because he looked rather older than I remembered him being. And partly because he wasn't green.

"General Szilard," I said. "This is a surprise."

"It was intended to be," he said.

"You look different," I said.

"Yes, well," Szilard said. "Now that the Colonial Union has to deal with human governments here on Earth, one of the things we've discovered is that the politicians here don't take us very seriously if we look like we usually do."

"It's not easy being green," I said.

"Indeed not," Szilard said. "So I've made myself look older and pinker. It seems to be working."

"I assume you're not telling them that you're not old enough to rent a car," I said.

"I don't see the need to confuse them any more than

they are," Szilard said. "Do you have a minute? There are things to say."

"I'm done with my testifying for today," I said. "I have time."

Szilard looked around me in an exaggerated fashion. "Where's your mob of reporters?"

"Oh, *that*," I said. "General Gau's testifying before the Senate Intelligence Committee today. I was just talking to a House agricultural subcommittee. There was a single public access camera there and that was it. It's been months since anyone bothered to follow me around, anyway. Aliens are more interesting."

"How the mighty have fallen," Szilard said.

"I don't mind," I said. "It was nice to be on magazine covers for a while, but it gets old. Do you want to walk?"

"By all means," Szilard said. We set off in the direction of the Mall. Occasionally someone would glance my way—off magazine covers or not, I was still all-too-recognizable—but residents of D.C. were proudly jaded regarding famous politicians, which I now suppose I was, for lack of a better term.

"If you don't mind me asking, General," I said, "why are you here?"

"I'm lobbying senators today," Szilard said. "The U.S. moratorium on CDF recruiting is a problem. The U.S. always accounted for the bulk of our recruits. This was why it was never a problem when other countries forbade their citizens from signing up; their contributions were trivial. But without the U.S. we're not meeting recruitment goals, especially now that so many other countries also have recruiting moratoriums."

"I know about the moratorium," I said. "I'm asking why *you*."

"I seem to be good at speaking the politicians' language," Szilard said. "Apparently there's an advantage around here to being mildly socially retarded, and that's the Special Forces for sure."

"Do you think you'll get the moratorium lifted?" I asked.

Szilard shrugged. "It's complicated," he said. "Everything's complicated because at the end of the day the Colonial Union has kept Earth in the dark for so long. You came along and told everyone here how much they've been missing out on. They're angry. The question is whether they're ultimately angry enough to side with the Conclave instead of other humans."

"When's the vote?" I said.

"Three weeks," Szilard said.

"Should be interesting," I said.

"I understand there's a curse about living in interesting times," Szilard said.

We walked silently for a few minutes.

"What I'm saying to you now comes from me alone," Szilard said. "So we're clear on that."

"All right," I said.

"First, I want to thank you," he said. "I never thought I'd ever get to visit Earth. If you hadn't completely fucked up the Colonial Union's way of doing things, I never would have. So thanks for that."

I found it very difficult to hide my amusement. "You're welcome," I said.

"Second, I need to apologize to you."

"You need to apologize to Jane, General," I said. "She's the one you altered."

"I altered her, but I used you both," Szilard said.

"You said you did it to keep humanity alive," I said. "I'm not thrilled about being used by you or anyone else, but at least I have more sympathy for your goal."

"I wasn't entirely honest with you," Szilard said. "Yes, I worried about the Colonial Union causing the eradication of the human race. Trying to stop that was my primary goal. But I had another goal as well. A selfish goal."

"What is it?" I said.

"Special Forces are second-class citizens in the Colonial Union," Szilard said. "We always have been. We're needed but not trusted. We do the difficult work of keeping the Colonial Union alive—it was we who destroyed the Conclave fleet, but our reward is only more work, more responsibility. I wanted a way to make the Colonial Union recognize *my* people, and how important we are to the Union. And the answer was you."

"Me," I said. "You said that we were chosen because of Jane and Zoë, not me."

"I lied," Szilard said. "You all had your part to play. Jane and Zoë's were the most critical to keeping humanity alive, yes. But your part was critical to *my* goal."

"I don't see how," I said.

"Because you're the one who would get *indignant* at being used," Szilard said. "Lieutenant Sagan no doubt got angry at how she and Roanoke were manipulated for the Colonial Union's ends. But her solution is to deal directly with the immediate problem. That's how she was trained. Direct-line thinking. Your wife is many things, Perry, but subtle is not one of them. You, on the other hand. You would *stew*. You would look for a long-term solution, to punish those who used you, and to make sure that humanity wouldn't face the same threat twice."

"Bringing the Conclave here to Earth," I said. "Cutting off the Colonial Union's supply of soldiers."

"We saw it as a possibility," Szilard said. "A small one. But a real one. And as a consequence the Colonial Union would need to fall back on its ready source of military power. Us."

"There are always the colonists," I said.

"The colonists haven't fought their own wars for nearly

two centuries," Szilard said. "It would be a disaster. Sooner or later it comes down to the Special Forces."

"But you're here lobbying to end the recruiting moratorium," I said.

"The last time we had a conversation I told you the reason I let my Special Forces soldiers be used to destroy the Conclave fleet," Szilard said.

"So you could stay in control of the situation," I said.

Szilard spread his hands as if to say, *And so*.

"I'm having a hard time believing you planned for this," I said.

"I planned none of it," Szilard said. "I left open the possibility it might occur, and was ready to act on it if it did. I certainly didn't expect you to do what you ended up doing. Trade ships. That's weird thinking. I would have expected another armada."

"I'm happy to surprise you," I said.

"I'm sure you are," Szilard said. "And now let me return the favor to you. I know Lieutenant Sagan has yet to forgive me for altering her."

"She hasn't forgiven you," I agreed. "It took her a long time to get used to being human, and you took it away from her."

"Then tell her this," Szilard said. "She was a prototype. A version of Special Forces soldier designed entirely from the human genome. She is one hundred percent human, right down to the number of chromosomes. She's *better* than human, of course, but human all the same. She never stopped being human through any of this."

"She has a BrainPal in her head," I said.

"We're particularly proud of that," Szilard said. "The most recent generation of BrainPals were largely organic as it was. It took a substantial amount of tweaking to get one to generate out of the human genome. She was the first to have a wholly integrated, human BrainPal."

"Why did you test it on her?" I asked.

"Because I knew she would need it, and I knew she valued her humanity," Szilard said. "I wanted to honor both, and the technology was ready to be tested. Tell her I am sorry I wasn't able to tell her this before now. I had my reasons for not wanting the technology to be common knowledge."

I looked at Szilard closely. "You're using the same technology now, aren't you," I said.

"I am," Szilard said. "For the first time I am entirely human. As human as anyone. And in time every member of Special Forces will be the same. It matters. It matters to who we are, and for what we can become to the Colonial Union and to humanity. Let Jane know, Perry. She is the first of us. The most human of us. Let her know."

Not long after, I took Jane to meet Kathy.

My Ohio hometown was as I had left it, almost two decades before, only slightly worse for wear. We drove up the long driveway of my old house to find my son Charlie, his family and every person I was even tangentially related to waiting for us. I had seen Charlie twice since my return, when he had visited Washington, D.C., to see me. We had been able to get over the shock of me appearing decades younger than he, and he had been able to get over the shock of Jane looking so much like his own mother. For everyone else, however, it was an awkward first.

It would have kept being so if Zoë hadn't dived in and broken the ice, starting with Charlie's son Adam, who Zoë demanded call her "Aunt Zoë," even though she was younger than he was. Slowly our clan began to warm to us, and to me. I was filled in on all the gossip of the last double decade. Jane was told stories of Kathy she had never known before. Zoë was fussed on by old relatives and moony teenage boys alike. Savitri told Charlie jokes about my days as ombudsman. Hickory and Dickory tolerated being curiosities.

As the sun sank in the sky, Jane and I gave Zoë a quick kiss and slipped away, walking east on my county road to Harris Creek Cemetery, and to the simple marker that held my wife's name.

"Katherine Rebecca Perry," Jane read, kneeling.

"That's right," I said.

"You're crying," Jane said, not looking back. "I can hear it in your voice."

"I'm sorry," I said. "I just never thought I would be back here."

Jane looked back. "I didn't mean for this to hurt you," she said.

"It's all right," I said. "It's supposed to hurt. And I wanted you to meet her. I wanted to be here when you did."

"You still love her," Jane said, looking back down at the marker.

"I do," I said. "I hope you don't mind."

"I'm part of her," Jane said. "She's part of me. When you love her, you love me. I don't mind that you keep loving her. I hope you do. I hope you always do."

I reached out a hand to her; she took it. We stayed that way, silent at my wife's grave, for a very long time.

"Look at the stars," Jane said, finally.

"There's the Big Dipper," I said, pointing.

Jane nodded. "I see it."

I wrapped my arms around Jane. "I remember you said on Huckleberry that it was when you finally saw the constellations that you knew you were home."

"I remember saying that," Jane said.

"Is it still true?" I asked.

"It is," Jane said, and turned to face me. "I'm home. We're home."

I kissed my wife.

"The Milky Way," she said, looking up, after we broke our kiss.

"Yes," I said, looking up myself. "You can see it really well from here. That's one of the reasons I liked living in a little country town. In the cities the light drowns it out. But here, you can see it. Although I imagine with your eyes, you're getting quite a show."

"It's beautiful," Jane said.

"That reminds me," I said, and told her what General Szilard said about her being the first entirely human Special Forces soldier.

"Interesting," she said.

"So you're completely human after all," I said.

"I know," Jane said. "I figured it out already."

"Really," I said. "I'd like to know how."

"I'm pregnant," Jane said, and smiled.

ACKNOWLEDGMENTS

With this book we've reached the end of our journeys with John Perry and Jane Sagan. I like to think they go on. But they go on without us. It's possible I'll return one day to this universe, to explore other corners of it, and to see how it has changed through the events of this book. For the moment, however, I'm stepping back, to explore other places and people. I hope you don't mind.

I'd like to thank each of you who have taken this journey with me, whether this is your first encounter with this universe, or whether you came through all three books to arrive here. One of the great joys of writing this series has been hearing the feedback and reading the mail from those of you who have thanked me for writing these books and encouraged (and in some cases, demanded) that I get off my ass and write the next one. You sure do know how to make a writer feel good.

I have been immensely fortunate through these books to have Patrick Nielsen Hayden as my editor. Patrick's practical sense of the science fiction book industry is matched by his aspirations for the books he shepherds; I have benefited from both. And in particular, this book benefited from Patrick's patience, as I tore out entire chapters and pushed certain annoying characters none of the rest of you will ever meet down wells, all of which extended the time required to finish the book. Patrick didn't complain (much). I deeply appreciate that faith. Many thanks also to Tom Doherty, whose encouragement through this series has meant an incredible amount to me.

Other folks at Tor to whom I owe more thanks than I can express: Teresa Nielsen Hayden, Liz Gorinsky, Irene Gallo, Dot Lin and Tor's merciless marketing folks. Thanks are also in order for John Harris, who once again has done a kick-ass cover, to copy editor Justine Gardner, who makes it look like I actually know grammar and spelling, and to Nicole de las Heras for interior book design. All I did was write the book; these folks made it look good. Thanks also to Ethan Ellenberg, my invaluable agent.

Friends helped keep me sane as I wrestled this book to the ground. Among them: Nick Sagan, who shared deadline misery as we were both finishing our books, as did Justine Larbalestier. In both cases you should seek out their books to find out what you were missing. Other friends who helped me keep my head screwed on and otherwise made sure I had sufficient human contact: Scott Westerfeld, Doselle and Janine Young, Deven Desai, Anne KG Murphy and Karen Meisner. There are so many other people I'd like to single out and thank, particularly in the science fiction writing community, but really, we would be here all day if I did, so if you think I should be thanking you (and there are many of you I should thank), please do assume I'm talking about you here. I'd also make special mention of the readers of my blogs, *Whatever* and *By the Way*, for their daily encouragement to get my work done, even if it meant posting less at the blogs.

During the writing of the *The Last Colony* I was nominated for and won the John W. Campbell Award for best new writer in science fiction. I was nominated with Sarah Monette, Chris Roberson, Brandon Sanderson, K. J. Bishop and Steph Swainston, and was fortunate enough to become friends with Sarah, Chris and Brandon. The suggestion that I'm a better writer than any of these folks is a flattering lie, and I encourage you to look up their work the next time you're in a bookstore or book-buying online. You won't be disappointed.

I killed off a character named Joseph Loong in this book; the real Joseph Loong, with whom I work at AOL, I wish a long and happy life, and I thank him for letting me use his name. Lieutenant Stross in the book is an obvious tuckerization of Charles Stross, the unspeakably talented science fiction writer, and also a friend of mine. The real Stross is not as spacey as the one I put in the book. General Rybicki is named for Joe Rybicki, my longtime friend and editor. I hope he likes his character.

Yet again, many thanks to Regan Avery, who continues to be my frontline reader, and helps make my books better. She's been my frontline reader for a decade now; I consider her my lucky charm.

Finally, thanks to Kristine and Athena Scalzi, my wife and daughter, respectively, and especially to Kristine. Those people who know Kristine and me have suggested that Jane Sagan is rather obviously modeled after Kristine. There is only so far the comparison goes—as far as I know my wife has not taken out entire platoons of soldiers armed only with knives—but it is a fact that Jane's intelligence, strength and personal character are based on my wife's own intelligence, strength and personal character. To be blunt about it, my wife totally rocks.

She also is kind enough not only to put up with me but to encourage me, support me and love me. I am lucky to be with her. I dedicate this entire series to her—*Old Man's War, The Ghost Brigades* and *The Last Colony*. These are her books. I just wrote them.

JOHN SCALZI
September 20, 2006

Visit **www.panmacmillan.com** to read more about all our books and to buy them. You will also find features, author interviews and news of any author events, and you can sign up for e-newsletters so that you're always first to hear about our new releases.

www.panmacmillan.com

GIFT SELECTOR
YOUR ACCOUNT
WISH LIST
WAITING LIST

HOME   ABOUT US   IMPRINTS   TRADE/MEDIA   CONTACT US   ADVANCED SEARCH   SEARCH   GO

BOOK CATEGORIES   WHAT'S NEW   AUTHORS/ILLUSTRATORS   BESTSELLERS   READING GROUPS

Coming Soon...

Reading Groups

Competitions
Feeling Lucky?

Extracts
Sneak Previews

Interviews

Events
Meet Our Stars

Reviews
What The Critics Say

News & Awards

Editor's Choice
What We're Reading

© 2005 PAN MACMILLAN   ACCESSIBILITY   HELP   TERMS & CONDITIONS   PRIVACY POLICY   SEND PAGE TO A FRIEND